SUZANNAH ROWNTREE

A Stab in the Dark

Miss Dark's Apparitions, Vol. V

A dead thing can go with the stream,
but only a living thing can go against
it.

—G.K. Chesterton,
The Everlasting Man

Chapter I.

It was a grey, still December day, somewhere on the English Channel between Dover and Calais, when I became aware that one of my powers had deserted me.

I do not, of course, refer to that power by which I am able to summon up and observe lingering apparitions of the dead. *That* was in better working-order than ever; by it I was able to ascertain that an unfortunate old lady had, not too long ago, succumbed to a heart attack in my berth. It was for this reason, in fact, that I was not presently occupying the berth in question. Instead, I had chosen to sit limply in the restaurant fortifying myself with a strong Earl Grey.

Nor do I allude to the sea-legs I had developed during my recent long voyage from Hong Kong to London, for they were already lost. I am a very bad sailor, and the two-week sojourn with my family in the English metropolis had sufficed to re-accustom me to the feeling of solid ground beneath my feet. That I was not at present sharing a berth with the expiring matron, who alone might sympathise with my state, was due only to the unseasonable stillness of the weather. I hoped fervently that this happy state of affairs would continue until we reached France.

No—I am referring, of course, to that special faculty by

which a female of spinsterish age and occupation is able to become quite invisible. It is simple. One dons a grey gown five years out of date, pins on a simple straw hat, pulls on a pair of serviceable boots and well-darned gloves, and applies for a situation as a governess. Voilà! —one vanishes. In order to become visible again, one would absolutely need to perform the *Marseillaise* while waving a red flannel petticoat on the end of a rifle, and then I am afraid the visibility would be of a nature particularly detrimental to one's social standing.

This effect is particularly pronounced when it comes to handsome and eligible young men. Yet here I was languishing over my cup of tea somewhere on the English Channel, feeling like something the cat warmed up, when a shadow fell over me, and a solicitous voice inquired in melodious French, "Mademoiselle, you seem unwell. Will you permit me to call a steward?"

Once, six years ago as a governess in Paris, I had sat in a drawing-room for a good twenty minutes while the younger brother of my employer, the elegant Mme Chardigny, had searched in vain for a partner at bridge. I play bridge extremely well, and had made so bold as to say so, two or three times over the course of that period; at the end of which, the dashing young M. Deleuze had thrown himself down at the card table and proclaimed that since no fourth partner was to be had, a game of forfeits must suffice instead. I had fancied M. Deleuze. He was handsome, for a Frenchman, and rich, and witty; and his name was like music—Célestin. That evening he dealt me a thoughtless injury, from which I had never quite recovered.

This gentleman who now addressed me, of course, was this same Célestin Deleuze.

For a moment I could not say a single word. The six years that had passed since I last saw M. Deleuze had been very kind to him. His shoulders had broadened, he had succeeded in growing a very natty little moustache, and he had discovered a cravat of the precise rich shade of purplish-blue that best suited his pale complexion and raven-dark hair. Perhaps I have always been partial to dark-haired men! Regardless, my first impulse was to dive beneath the table, for I was not sure that my cloak of invisibility, six years ago, had been sufficient to conceal my girlish looks of longing.

Finding my voice with difficulty, I said, "Oh, it's only the sea-sickness, monsieur! Please don't worry about me!"

"Ah, but it's a gentleman's privilege to come to the aid of beauty in distress," he said, summoning a steward despite my objections. "Some crystallised ginger for the lady, my good man. That ought to set you right in a moment," he added, seating himself beside me, and slanting a very sharp gaze beneath the brim of my hat. "May I know whom I have the honour of assisting?"

I was once more at a loss for words. Was it possible that M. Deleuze did not recognise the governess, Molly Dark, at all? —and if I had been so utterly invisible to him on previous occasions, what had I now done to attract his attention? I wasn't dancing about, singing the *Marseillaise;* I wasn't even trying to rob the man of his money in one of the clever little charades I so often find myself playing.

And then the answer came to me.

I wasn't wearing a plain little straw boater, but a sweeping vista of ostrich feathers. My travelling-dress was new, modish, and the exact shade of dove-grey found inside an angel's wing. I had a lovely collar of silver-fox fur and nobody had had the chance to darn my gloves because I had purchased them just this morning in Bond Street.

In fact—I was no longer invisible.

In the course of a recent jaunt to Hong Kong, I had practiced the arts of the confidence-trickster with such success as to render myself and my sisters not merely solvent but now positively gushing with filthy lucre. It is true, no doubt, that the inheritance we had stolen *belonged* to us, by all legal measures; but I cannot say that it was not tainted, having been accumulated in the course of many years' trade in that noxious drug, opium. In any case, since the money could not be said to be the rightful property of any other person, why should it not belong to us? In that conviction, therefore, I had taken the lucre home to my family. The past two weeks had been a whirl of unaccustomed gaiety: we had attended pantomimes and modistes and solicitor's offices and house-auctions. The fortunes of the house of Dark were at last restored—the company begun by my father set back upon its right course—and the alteration in my situation had found its expression in my attire.

A cynical thought struck me. Perhaps, by *beauty in distress,* M. Deleuze really meant *money in distress.*

For a moment I wavered; but then I made up my mind to enjoy myself. Summoning to mind the false identity under which I was, at present, travelling, I put out a hand. "I am Maria von Jörger. I'm on the way to Paris to see my husband."

"Von Jörger? Why, then your husband must be—"

"Baron von Jörger," I said wistfully, "the newly appointed manager at the Paris Opera? Yes, that is he."

Not even the exquisite perfection of my grammar recalled to him the circumstances under which we had last met.

"I'm desolated," said M. Deleuze, taking my hand, and bowing until his lips nearly brushed it. "Alas, that so charming a lady should have a husband!"

I maintained a straight face. How my sisters would laugh to hear that a young man who had snubbed me as a governess was now shamelessly fawning over me! And yet—how satisfying that my masquerade should allow me to egg him on, just a little!

"Believe me, monsieur, I share your sorrow! In fact, I'm afraid that I must shortly desire my solicitor to be in communication with the Baron." I sent a shuddering glance about the restaurant, and lowered my voice. "My situation has become impossible."

Deleuze pulled a long face, but his eyes lit up as he scented scandal. "His fault, naturally?"

Célestin always *had* loved to gossip. What a stroke of luck that I had stumbled upon him like this!

"Indeed," I said, getting out my trusty handkerchief, lest my indisposition did not make me a suitably pathetic figure. "He is so dreadfully jealous! When I tell you that he had a prosthetic eye installed to spy upon me!"

"Shocking! Cruel!" Deleuze murmured, patting my hand.

He might have gone on, but at that moment the steward appeared bearing crystallised ginger. I am by no means averse to the delicacy, and my chevalier was correct: it did do something to settle my stomach. I nibbled upon it, accordingly, and told other stories of my "husband's" cruelty until M. Deleuze no doubt thought us firm friends.

"I take it that this will not be your first visit to Paris," he said at length, when that conversation—and my imagination—flagged. "Allow me to compliment you on your excellent

French!"

"Thank you," I said, omitting to inform him that my French had been perfected largely in his sister's school-room, instructing his nephews how to fold paper darts. "It has been some years, and I did not see much of the city on that occasion. If my business was not so grave…or if I had the advantage of a guide who knew the city…"

"But I would be delighted to show you Paris, my dear Baroness! I know everyone, you see!" He sent a wicked glance about the room, and then leaned forward conspiratorially. "Do you see that little ragged old man with the great moustache, like a walrus? That's Mallarmé the poet, a great friend of mine. Every Tuesday he holds a salon in the Rue de Rome. He's thought to be a great wit and considers himself the king of intellectual Paris. A king! I should as soon call him a jester. I'll take you to see him, if you like."

I bit my lip. "Hush! Hush! He'll hear you!"

"What if he does?" Deleuze asked, with a laugh. "Let him break his wits against me. In the end, he'll still be nothing but a clever pauper."

He said these words in a contemptuous manner, which suggested that I had said something terribly gauche. I felt suddenly tired of the gentleman's company, and grateful to a merciful Providence for shielding me from his attentions in the days that I was little more than a pauper myself, and not a particularly clever one, either. "Thank you for the ginger," I told him, arising from my seat. "You're too kind, but I think I ought to go to my berth. The sea is becoming restless."

"Wait," Deleuze said, taking out a card-case, and handing me a card. "Don't vanish away, my dear Baroness, like a cruel fairy. I'll see you in Paris."

I glanced down at the card, which proclaimed the name of the man before me to be *de Leuze*—two words, instead of one. I restrained the smile which arose to my lips. "Dear me! What an aristocratic name!"

"A very old Picardy family," he said, with unblushing self-satisfaction. I made a bow and went away, moving slowly to spare my stomach. As I went, I marvelled at the chance that should have brought me back into the society of one I had known so long ago. In the business which awaited me in Paris, I should doubtless find M. Deleuze a very useful tool.

But I must try not to appear too naïve. Deleuze fancied himself a man of the world—and an aristocrat, too, if the way he spelled his name was any indication! As the Baroness von Jörger, it was surely my task to seem to be as worldly, jaded, and heartless as himself—for such behaviour would be expected in the exalted circles to which I sought admission. The rich, as I had seen on more than one occasion, were inclined to consider nobody's feelings but their own.

I spent the rest of the crossing in a rather sad state in my berth, crowded as it was with memories of the dead. I shall spare you the tedious account of my sufferings; but at this point some words of explanation may be necessary, as to my errand aboard the Calais boat.

My crew and I, as I have mentioned, had recently returned from a job in Hong Kong. Since important business connected with the winding-up of my late father's estate demanded my presence in London, it was to London that we had returned; and it was in London, moreover, that we were met by our employer, Herr Haber.

Those of you who are familiar with my memoirs will recall Franz Haber as the impecunious Jewish violin-teacher whom

I had, rather unexpectedly, put in the possession of the family fortune of the late Bourbon monarchs. He had chosen to employ a small part of that fortune in funding the activities of my crew and myself, investigating and setting right injustices to which only the dead might bear witness. Since Herr Haber had benefited himself from our philanthropic thievery, he did not wish our special talents to go to waste.

On this occasion we found him inhabiting a room at the Savoy Hotel. Wealth agreed with Herr Haber as much as it did with me: he was now far from the hollow-cheeked, distraught-looking widower I had first met in a miserable Viennese tenement. His figure had filled out a little, he stood up straighter, and the ardent eyes and dark curls were more ardent and curly than ever. For some reason I glanced at Mimi Laine, our cat-burglar, wondering for a moment what impression this handsome figure had made upon *her*. Mimi had never betrayed any particular tenderness for Herr Haber, but she *was* partial to handsome young men.

"My friends, I'm so glad you have come at last," Herr Haber greeted us. Indeed, the voyage from Hong Kong to London had taken us the best part of three months, and for much of that time we had known of the new mission awaiting us in Paris. "Shall I explain the situation?"

It seemed that Herr Haber had received news from a friend of his from younger days at the Wiener Staatsoper—a musician of some genius, who had now become the musical director of the Paris Opera. In the opinion of Herr Haber's friend, some skullduggery was afoot at the great Palais Garnier. First, the leading tenor was found hanging in his dressing-room, throwing the new production of Wagner's *Tannhäuser* into disarray. Then, just a few weeks ago, one of the co-managers had suffered a nervous breakdown and gone away to the spas of Baden to recover. His resignation had followed in due course.

At this point, Miss Nijam, our charmingly crepuscular inventor, had frowned. "It's unfortunate, of course, but surely there's no need to suspect foul play."

"There is, according to my friend Gustav," said Herr Haber. "He assures me that M. Larousse—the tenor, that is—had no reason to do away with himself. The police avow themselves satisfied, but Gustav is worried. He told me that matters at the Opera have been—tense, whatever that is supposed to mean. There was trouble between the co-managers; it seems they could not agree on repertoire."

"In fact, Gustav thinks this M. Larousse was murdered to stop the Wagner production?" Mimi asked cheerfully. "What fun!"

Herr Haber sent her a rather startled look. It is true that not many people see eye to eye with Mimi on the subject of *fun*. "If Larousse was murdered in his dressing-room, it's possible that Fraulein Dark may be able to summon up some evidence of a more—er—spiritual nature," he said.

After so many months away from home, and with so many new demands upon my time—truly the rich are beset by the cares of the world! —I was not entirely sure I wished to dash away to Paris to summon up memories of horrible death. "I'm not fond of Wagner myself," said I. "A lot of sound and fury, signifying nothing, if you ask me. But who would stoop to *murder* over such a thing?"

Franz Haber laughed. "You don't know much about opera, do you?"

"But if the police have investigated—"

"The police," said Vasily smoothly, "might equally well have been paid to investigate very little, if at all." As a Romanov Grand Duke in hiding, he ought surely to know. I had never been in any country more thoroughly infested with policemen and informers than the Russian Empire.

"I want to go," Mimi said. "Of course there is something to it. Also, the Paris Opera is the birthplace of ballet, and the director of ballet there is a *master.*"

I was amused. "What's this, Mimi? Do I detect an ulterior motive?" Our burglar had begun a career at the Imperial Ballet School in Petersburg, sadly cut short when she aired her views upon the cause of Finnish national independence. It had been her ambition ever since to complete her training and become a leading light of the Continental stage.

"Then it's settled," Herr Haber said. "Fraulein Laine may join the *corps de ballet;* she'll be very useful there. I've also taken the liberty of preparing this." He proffered an envelope in thick, creamy paper to Vasily. "This is a letter of introduction to the French minister of the Beaux-Arts, recommending my good friend 'blank' as a new co-manager. I'm a famous patron of the arts these days, and I've taken recent steps to announce a scholarship for French students, so the good minister has just been fêting me around Paris. If he takes my advice, that will give us someone in management."

"Will it be safe for you in Paris, Vasily?" I inquired, with some anxiety. Vasily was now supposed to be dead, but I lived in fear of his being discovered. No girl likes to think of her lover being chased about the European capitals by agents of the Russian Emperor.

"Safe as houses, so long as I take the necessary precautions," he assured me. "I shall have to alter my appearance again, I suppose! I am exactly like that unfortunate lady in the ballad, cursed to be ugly by day and beautiful only by night. Well, I don't like it, but I will do it!"

There was evidently no use trying to get any sense out of him. I turned to Mimi with a sigh. "The two of you were in Paris not too long ago, Mimi. Is he likely to run into anyone who knows him?"

Mimi shrugged. "Likely not. We lived in Montmartre, among the rabble. None of them would be seen dead at the Paris Opera, with the ministers and the aristocrats and the state-approved artists."

"I didn't want to run into any of my Russian friends or family," Vasily explained. "It's customary for my cousins to run away to Paris whenever they want to marry their mistresses. But don't worry, I'll arrange to avoid them this time as well. I shall be very industrious and remain shut up in my office. What should I call myself? Shall I resurrect that useful Bulgarian nobleman, Baron Dragomir Smilets?"

Mimi sniffed. "No one in Europe will believe in the existence of such a creature as a 'Bulgarian nobleman.'"

There was a silence as the gentlemen, who had grown up in closer proximity to the Balkans than either Nijam or myself, considered this.

Herr Haber gave a conceding grimace. "A Viennese nobleman would be more believable. You shall be Baron von Jörger, a well-known patron of the Wiener Staatsoper. Once you are installed, you can appoint the rest of the crew to various stations around the Opera, so that your investigations should not be impeded. What do you think?"

"Schmidt?" I asked, glancing at Alphonse Schmidt, who until now had remained silent. Officially, Schmidt was

Vasily's manservant and the one upon whom we called when we required our enemies to be pulverised to rubble. Unofficially, Schmidt was more than just the golden Adonis for whom Miss Nijam nursed a secret and hopeless passion. He was the one member of our crew whose opinion counted for the most, for we all knew him to be the best and kindest of us.

He reddened somewhat to be called upon, but said, "I don't think Herr Haber's friend would go to all the trouble of calling upon him, if there wasn't really something wrong at the Opera. We should investigate, and we should make sure M. Larousse's family has been adequately provided for."

"Then it's decided," Nijam said. "Another murder to solve!" Her eyes fairly sparkled. I have seen the same look on her face when passing a sweet-shop and noticing a display of peppermint bulls-eyes.

"All right," I said, trying to be equally cheerful. "It's been ages since I was in Paris, and when I did I never had the chance to see the Opera!"

"Isn't there one thing we're overlooking?" Vasily asked suddenly. He had been perusing Herr Haber's letter of introduction with a slight frown pinched between his brows. "It's all very well for the rest of you, but if I'm about to be appointed to the management of the Paris Opera by the French Minister of Beaux-Arts, how in the world am I going to get out of it again? I don't want to run a playhouse for the rest of my life."

"You might like it," I suggested. "Imagine! The theatrics—the productions—and you running the whole show!"

Vasily shuddered. "I can't think of anything worse. If I'm to inflict such a fate upon myself, I insist upon having a way out."

"Just fake your death again, Vasya," said Mimi impatiently.

"My dear, one can only do that so many times before people catch on." Vasily stroked his short, fashionable imperial beard—feeling regretful, no doubt, that he might shortly have to bid it farewell. "Aha! I have it! A scandal! Molly-my-dear, will you marry me?"

That caught me quite unawares. I gaped at him. "I beg your pardon! I haven't yet made up my mind about that!"

"Of course I'll need to betray you with a ballerina," he explained. "Then, when it is time to wind up our little charade, you can serve me with divorce papers and weep at some journalists in that irresistible way you have. After that there should be no great difficulty in tendering my resignation—or otherwise shooting myself—whichever one does the trick."

"Oh! is *that* what you meant?" I did not know that I *liked* the idea of playing at something that was of such grave importance to me, but I had undergone far more dangerous masquerades in the course of my career. "Very well; I accept."

"Then it's settled," Herr Haber repeated. "Don't feel you must rush away from London, Fraulein Dark. It will take a little while to install the Baron at the Opera, and in the meanwhile you might remain with your family."

That made me feel considerably brighter. "I'll use the time well," I assured him, moving towards the door. "If I'm to be the Baroness von Jörger, I'll need an appropriate wardrobe. My own clothes are sadly travel-worn."

"You'll also need a wedding-ring," Vasily declared, arising from the armchair in which he had been lounging with rakish abandon. "Come along and help me pick one out before I leave."

I had taken up my umbrella from the little brass stand by the door; and now I whipped it up and prodded him with it, around the second button of his silk waistcoat. "Not on your life," I told him. "My sisters are waiting for me in the restaurant downstairs, and I certainly don't mean to bring *them* along to buy a wedding-ring with a man I'm about to divorce."

"That's nonsense," Vasily protested. "Your sisters would like nothing better in the world, and you know it." He was, of course, correct. My sisters and Vasily rather egged each other on in their misbehaviour than otherwise. But he did not press the issue, and despite my former misgivings, I went downstairs feeling a pleasurable excitement. A new game was afoot; one which promised to be full of gaiety and excitement and all the money I needed to enjoy myself. I cautioned myself not to buy more frocks in London than absolutely necessary— for in Paris, I should have the chance to visit the famous Mr Worth!

Chapter II.

The reader knows something of my voyage across the Channel. A night spent in Calais allowed me to get over the worst of my sea-sickness, and by the time my train arrived at the Gare Saint-Lazare in Paris the following day, I was feeling more myself again.

It was a cold, grey afternoon like a water-colour painting. The station was dark and gloomy despite the great panes of glass in the pitched roof high above, and the great puffing clouds of white steam that filled it. Wallowing luxuriously in my thick woollen coat with its collar of the softest fur, I glanced up and down the platform and quickly spotted the splash of violet which marked out Nijam's Alphonse. My sister Lilias had knitted him a scarf in her favourite colour. I hoped that it was a platonic scarf, because as good and kind as Schmidt was, and as little as I should ever worry about my sisters were any of them entrusted to his care, his heart was also very much not at liberty.

The object of Schmidt's hopeless affections stood beside him looking more than usually murderous. Nijam glared at her pocket-watch as though she would have preferred the train to be late, so that she could vent her mood upon it. It had, in fact, been a good three minutes early.

"Come along," she said without ceremony as I approached. "You'll need to get ready for the Opera."

Schmidt looked a little red about the face as he took my valise. All *he* said, despite the explosive feeling hanging in the air, was, "I trust you weren't too ill on the crossing. Will you be able to attend the Opera tonight?"

"I'm right as rain," I assured him, following them out into the chilly afternoon. In the carriage, Nijam launched at once into a spate of information.

"We've leased you a flat in a fashionable tenement on the Boulevard Haussmann, not too far from Vasily's. That's where we're taking you now. There's a gala performance tonight, to mark Baron von Jörger's appointment as co-manager. Mimi's already managed to secure a place with the ballet—ordinarily you only get into the corps de ballet if you've grown up at the Opera school, but they took her on as a soloist. Dumortier, the other manager, is a balletomane, so there are always ballets being staged. I don't know how much use Mimi will be to us, mind you; the ballet master is giving her special coaching, in addition to the regular rehearsals, so she's been pretty busy. I'm supposed to be Mimi's lady's maid, so I have pretty free access to the dressing-rooms and backstage area, and Schmidt is supposed to be the Baron's chargé d'affaires and general factotum."

Schmidt had opened his mouth once or twice during this lecture as though to say something, but Nijam rattled off the speech without let or hindrance. I wondered what had brought about this awkwardness. Had Schmidt at last summoned up the courage to tell Nijam that *he* was the secret admirer who had sent her the bubonic plague as a gift?

Whatever it was, both of them were evidently eager to avoid

further discussion, and I was bound to respect their wishes. "Has anyone interviewed the dead tenor's family?"

"We'll leave that to you and your social graces," Nijam said. "I've had enough of that sort of work, Schmidt's too busy keeping Vasily's suits pressed, and can you imagine the hash Mimi would make of the job?"

There was something bitter in her voice when she mentioned Schmidt's sartorial preoccupations. Casting about for an alternative topic of conversation, I nodded towards the book Nijam carried in one gloved hand. "Is that volume three of *Can You Forgive Her?*"

"I've finished; you can have it back," Nijam said, handing it over. I accepted gratefully: I had reached the end of volume two around the Gulf of Oman and had been at a standstill ever since.

"And what did you think?"

Nijam sniffed. "I don't know why Alice Vavasour ever took John Grey back. He will make her a very agreeable husband for a year or two, and then next time they have a disagreement he will go back to telling her that she is sick in the head and imagining things. It isn't as though he's really *changed.*"

I thought of my own lover, and of my tentative hopes that Vasily *had* changed, unlike John Grey. Certainly he seemed to be *trying,* and Mimi assured me that he was already greatly altered from what he had been.

I had hopes of Vasily; but sometimes I wished that I could have the comfort of peering ahead in our book to see how our story ended.

Then I happened to glance at Schmidt, who was peering studiously out the window with a deep line etched between his brows. But his neck had gone red, and it suddenly occurred to me that in doubting John Grey's capacity to change, Nijam might not have been referring to *Vasily*. But what did Schmidt have to change? Where Vasily was old in corruption, Schmidt was young, conscientious, and innocent. I did not see why Nijam should hurl those words at him like a gentleman in a French melodrama challenging another to a duel. Did she not see that it hurt him?

This, I thought, was why *I* could never love Nijam, despite my own inclinations, and the manifest charms of a face and form that might have put Cleopatra to shame. It was her personality that I found rebarbative. She had too little tenderness for the feelings of others. That Schmidt, who had always been more or less afraid of her, should manage to love her anyway was a great mystery to me.

There was no point in dwelling upon it: I could not solve this interesting puzzle alone—not without a good deal more information, with which perhaps Vasily or Mimi could provide me. In any case the carriage ride was not a long one. I might have been inclined to walk, had the day not been so cold. Who is not familiar with the charms of Paris, with its broad boulevards, its narrow alleys, and the great, luxurious neoclassical tenements, like wedges of cake, which adorn its streets?

In one respect the great metropolis was not as I recalled it: once it had been swarming with the ghastly faces and lurching gait of the revenant policemen, employed by the Quai des Orfèvres to keep down the anarchist threat. Today the only gendarmes who could be seen patrolling the boulevards or directing the traffic were ordinary living men. On the whole, I liked the city far better without the revenants, and I thought that the anarchists did, too. They certainly seemed to have calmed their sentiments; for no longer did the headlines of Europe proclaim, every second week, news of some Parisian dynamite outrage.

In another minute we arrived outside one of the tenement-buildings, which was distinguished by three or four tiers of balcony railings in cast-iron curlicues. Nijam led the way up the stairs, and Schmidt brought up the rear with my luggage. We very quickly found ourselves in an extravagantly furnished flat on the second floor, with three or four assorted Persian rugs and animal-skins beneath our feet, several sets of tasteful oils and watercolours upon the walls, and a great mirror at one end fitted with stiff jacquard draperies. Vasily was stretched out in a gilt armchair, perusing a hand-written sheet of paper which seemed to fill him with quiet amusement. On the sofa nearby, Mimi had appropriated one of the many tiny side-tables which dotted the room, and was busy with an array of brushes and pots of paint and powder.

"At last!" Vasily cried, tucking the paper back into his breast-pocket and arising with haste from his seat. His lissom movements belied the years added to his appearance by the slightly old-fashioned clothing he wore, the square-cut beard which had gone out of style ten years ago, and the grey that had been added by some art to his hair. "Molly-my-dear, you're lucky I'm not the sort of man to throw himself into the Seine, only on account of being parted from the woman he loves."

"No, you just endlessly complain," Mimi muttered.

Despite all the pleasures of London, and my family's loving embraces, I had missed Vasily myself. "If you do that I shall only fish you out again, and Nijam will make you wash your own clothes."

"What a ghastly notion. Here, wear this; it means nothing, but it will make me feel ever so much better." He took my hand and slid a wedding-ring onto the third finger—a wide golden band engraved with a pretty motif of acanthus leaves. I could not help catching my breath in delight.

"Do you like it?"

"Oh, Vasily! I could not imagine anything prettier. What exquisite taste you have!" My words caused a look of great self-satisfaction to take up residence on his face, so I added: "Should you ever feel the impulse to buy me more jewellery, I shall not complain."

"But will you give me a kiss in thanks? —Ow!" He danced away from the sofa, and I perceived that Mimi had driven the hard end of her paintbrush into his ribs. She took her duties as one of my chaperones very seriously.

Today, Mimi seemed in no better a mood than Nijam and Schmidt. "Stop fooling around, Vasya," she said, scowling. "*You* may have nothing better to do, but I have to perform tonight, and I ought to be getting ready."

"There, there, Mimi, don't growl! Tell Miss Dark about the solo you're to have, now that that Wagner production is on hold."

Mimi brightened at once. "Didn't they tell you, Dark? Since *Tannhäuser* is dead, M. Dumortier means to revive *Giselle*. M. Christophe—the ballet master here at the Opera—wants me to dance Myrtha, and he's giving me special tutoring to prepare for it!"

"Oh, Mimi, it's the chance you've always wanted!" I cried. "Is it a very large rôle?"

"Myrtha is the queen of the spirits, who seize upon young men in the forest and dance them to death," Mimi explained with ghoulish relish. "After Giselle herself she is the best rôle in the ballet! I never imagined *I* would be selected for her!"

I beheld my fierce little friend with affection. "No one else could possibly do it justice."

"That is what M. Christophe told me," Mimi said, glowing.

"Mimi's right—we ought to get on with business," Nijam broke in. The prospect of the task at hand seemed to have lightened her mood somewhat. "Vasily—the Baron, I mean—will be officially installed tonight, and after that we shall have free run of the Opera. Mimi, what have you discovered so far? Any evidence of foul play in Larousse's death?"

Mimi shrugged. "There is gossip. People say he was driven to madness by the ghosts, or that his wife had chosen to leave him, or that the Jockey Club hounded him into hanging himself because there is no ballet in *Tannhäuser*. But when I ask, no one can give any reason to believe any of it."

"The Opera is haunted?" I asked.

"Yes, by just about everyone," Mimi said promptly. "Revolutionaries from the days of the Commune and their prisoners—people who've disappeared into the cellars, never to be seen again—stage-hands who've hung themselves among the backdrops—jealous lovers who've shot themselves during a *bal masqué*."

"How exciting," I remarked, infusing my words with all the lack of enthusiasm I felt. The imprints of the dead carry with them such vivid sensations of their unfortunate ends that I do not particularly enjoy meeting with them, and the prospect of a night at the opera spent trying to avoid them did not appeal to me.

"We aren't interested in Communards and stage-hands; our only business is to find out who killed the tenor," Nijam put in. "Dark, you can leave the Opera to the rest of us; your task will mostly lie outside, investigating the Larousse family and the Opera's patrons. Since you'll be navigating high society, you will need to make yourself a new identity as the Baroness von Jörger. We've secured you this flat, but you'll also need a maid in case anyone comes to call. Spend at least a little time with Vasily; he can introduce you to French society."

"French society!" Vasily scoffed. "That's the least of it, Molly-my-dear! I'm going to introduce you to M. Eiffel's tower by moonlight—and to those charming little rowboats in the Bois de Boulogne—and to champagne and strawberries at the Pavillon de la Grand Cascade."

"Oh, don't bother yourself on my account," I said. "I've already seen to that. I met a very useful gentleman during the Channel crossing."

Vasily opened his eyes wide in indignation. "Did you, now! Did he give you his card, little mouse? Let me see it. I'd like to get my teeth into him."

"Don't you dare," I told him. "I expect the gentleman to be extremely useful to our investigations; and I can't very well be squired about fashionable Paris by the man I'm planning to divorce!"

"Oh, very well!" he grumbled. "But don't forget that the divorce is only a pretext!"

"So is the marriage," said Mimi, picking up the soda-siphon and shooting a jet of cold water at him. "Stop being so jealous, and show her the dress. It was at least as much my idea as yours."

"Ow! You'll ruin my waistcoat," he objected, but he brought out a large, heavy flat box and deposited it upon my lap. It bore the mark of the House of Worth. I caught my breath;

but when I removed the lid and held up the dress itself, my mouth went absolutely dry.

It was the most extravagant garment I had ever seen—it must have required a small fortune in silk velvet alone. And then there was the craftsmanship: a severely corseted bodice paired with an exaggerated flowing train at the back and great, puffy elbow-length sleeves, which were slashed at the sides to give a glimpse of stiff and heavily beaded undersleeves in ivory. More heavy ivory lace dripped from the neckline.

It was beautiful. It was majestic. Apart from the ivory accents, it was a dark, hot, blood-red colour that no unmarried woman ought to be seen in.

"Vasily," I whispered, as my heart descended to my boots. "It's *wonderful*. But I couldn't possibly wear it."

"Why not?" Mimi demanded. "It will suit you *much* better than that white you always wear."

I shook my head, incapable of explaining. "But it isn't *me*."

Vasily waved a dismissive hand. "Perhaps it isn't—but you can't very well do this job as *yourself*. Why else do you think I dragged Mimi away from her beloved Opera? You need to be made into somebody else entirely."

I realised, then, that the paints and the brushes were for *me*. "Why?" I protested. "Can't I wear my own face and my own clothes?"

"Of course not." Nijam relieved me of the dress and folded it into the box again. Vasily took my hand and made me sit down.

"My dear," he said, "don't you see? Molly Dark is *somebody* now, and one day she might like to visit Paris as herself, and not as the heroine of a scandal."

"Oh," I said. I had not thought of this. Until now it had been no great matter to put on a pretty dress and some sham jewels and go out to the ballet or the opera in Moscow or Vienna, secure in the knowledge that when the masquerade was over I might change back into the sensible, well-worn garb of Molly Dark from Brixton—an obscure little person and perfectly invisible.

Now that I had money, I must take greater care to disguise myself. I have always fancied myself as an actress, and I suddenly wondered very much how I would look in the rôle of the Baroness.

"Let Mimi do your face, and then try on the dress," Vasily said, and I perceived that he had missed nothing in my expression. "It'll be another example of my impeccable taste; just you see."

"I've no doubt of that," I told him. "What luck it is that I met you, Vaska! Every girl needs someone to advise her on dress."

His eyes took on a curious softness. "The luck, my dear, is entirely mine! In former days if I ever wished to speak to a lady—anyone who was not a princess or a show-girl—people would say, 'Get away from her! Find some gainful employment!' Don't blame me if you go to my head a little... Now I'd better get back to the Opera, before Mimi murders me. But don't forget, my dear—the performance begins at nine, and you'd better be late."

I frowned. "Don't you mean that I'd better *not* be late?"

"Dear me, no! You can't possibly be on time—it's frightfully gauche, and as the Baroness you ought to be in the vanguard of fashion. It's a different story for Nijam and Schmidt, of course, as they are mere servants. I'll see you all later."

He collected his hat, gloves, and walking-stick, and away he went. Schmidt, bless him, emerged from the kitchen with a plate of sandwiches, and Mimi seized my chin and inspected my face with a professional squint.

"I hope I won't look *too* painted," I said, feeling nervous.

Mimi snorted. "No fear! The rules are different for a rich Baroness. You shall have a little rouge and a little powder, nothing more than you can deny."

She stepped aside to pick up a sandwich, and I couldn't help noticing that she was limping slightly—that, and the dark circles under her eyes.

"You look tired, Mimi. Is there something wrong with your leg?"

"It's nothing," she said. "My knee is very stupid. I hurt it years ago at the ballet school in Petersburg, and sometimes it comes back to bother me."

Her voice forbade me to ask more, but Nijam sent me a speaking look which told me that this was a conversation she, too, had attempted to have with Mimi.

Then Schmidt, having silently handed the sandwiches about, went to the door to collect his own hat and gloves.

"Where are *you* going?" Nijam demanded. Schmidt heaved a rather put-upon sigh, and I had the odd feeling that in the nearly two weeks I had been parted from my crew, everyone had fallen out of sorts with each other.

"I'm going to tidy up sir's flat," he said.

"For the purposes of this job, you're supposed to be his factotum, not his valet," Nijam snapped. "Let him pick up his own socks. Or better yet, not use them to decorate the parlour in the first place."

"I'm flatting with him," Schmidt protested. "No one at the Opera will know what I do with sir's socks when I'm at home."

"Then you should get a flat of your own," Nijam declared.

"It'll look pretty funny if anyone finds out the Baron is sharing a flat with his chargé d'affaires!"

"It might help us get a divorce," I said, in a feeble attempt at humour, but Nijam and Schmidt sent me a shocked look.

"Out of the question," Nijam said. "Think how Schmidt would look!"

"Shall I move in with you and Mimi, then?" Schmidt asked, as though daring her to agree.

"Perhaps you should!" Nijam retorted. "There's no room for you, but at least you wouldn't be staying with Vasily." Thereby proving that, despite her dispassionate voice, she was perfectly capable of cutting off her nose to spite her face.

And Nijam's nose, like Helen of Troy's, was nothing short of majestic.

Mimi was busy smearing some sweet-scented lotion upon my face, but by dint of rolling my eyes I saw how Schmidt's hands tightened upon his hat. "I'm not going to move in with you," he said in a voice of repressed emotion.

Nijam's lips drew tight, as though holding back cutting words. At this interesting moment, the doorbell rang. Schmidt opened the door in an overwrought sort of way, and I heard a boy's voice saying that he had a letter for Miss Nijam. As Mimi opened a little box of powder, Nijam broke the seal on the letter.

I half expected Schmidt to storm off in the boy's wake—it turned out that he was in possession of a temper, after all! —but instead, he stood as though transfixed by the sight of that letter. His mouth fell open; his hands twitched as though he would have torn it from her grasp.

As for Nijam—having unfolded the handwritten missive, she went about as pale as a woman of her rich complexion could. For a long, awful moment, she stood looking at that slip of paper as though it would bite her.

"Nijam," I cried, starting up. What did this letter portend—some death, or disaster? Schmidt looked equally stricken.

"Is this some kind of joke?" Nijam snarled. She turned towards the open door. "Who gave you this?" she demanded, but the messenger had already departed.

Mimi flitted to Nijam's side and whipped the paper from her hand.

"How dare you?" Nijam protested, trying to snatch it back. But in a single balletic leap Mimi put the sofa between them and snapped the paper flat to read it. Her eyes grew very large, and she gave a shriek of delight.

Schmidt's eyes were glazed in something like terror.

"Wilhelmina Laine!" Nijam thundered. "Give that back!"

"Dark, Dark, you have to hear it!" Mimi shrieked. "It's a *love* letter! *Dear Padma—*"

"Don't you *dare!*" Nijam cried, and before Mimi could say anything else, she snatched a small china shepherdess from the what-not by the door. Thrown with impressive speed and accuracy, it struck Mimi's fingers, causing her to break off with a squeal. The letter fluttered from her hand. Breathless with curiosity, I caught it.

The handwriting was legible enough to be read at a glance, as though penned by a careful and conscientious hand. *Dear Padma—dear dreaded majesty—you must know my feelings. I know that you are too good, too just, and too truly charitable to hold a grudge without cause. If there is any reason—*

Nijam descended upon me and snatched the letter from my hand. She wasted no time, but flung it upon the fire and held it down with the poker until it was reduced to ashes.

I had never seen her more furious.

"How dare you laugh! How dare you read other people's mail! This isn't *funny!*" Nijam turned from the fireplace still brandishing the poker. I am afraid that Mimi was indeed still in fits of laughter. Schmidt had not moved an inch, nor hoisted up his drooping jaw. I hoped the poor man had not suffered a permanent injury.

"Who could have done this?" Nijam muttered to herself. Then a thought must have occurred to her, for she flung down the poker and rushed out into the passage, shouting for the boy.

As her hasty footsteps faded away, Mimi and I turned as one to gaze upon Schmidt, who blushed like a strawberry.

"I never—that letter was never meant to be sent," he whispered, in agonies of embarrassment. "Sir did this!"

"Of course he did!" Mimi proclaimed. "People of his sort always think they know best! This is why he will find a bomb in his morning coffee, one of these days!"

And I recalled the sheet of paper which Vasily had tucked into his pocket when we entered.

"He did *say* he meant to do something about you and Miss Nijam," said I, rather feebly. My thoughts were in a turmoil. *Good, just, and truly charitable*—was *this* the cause of Schmidt's hopeless passion—that he could trust Nijam not to condemn him without *good cause?* Indeed he must be a better, finer soul than I. I would much rather be petted, and comforted, and admired.

All the same, Vasily had treated both of them heartlessly. I felt too sorry for the two of them to laugh; but Mimi was still enjoying herself immensely. "Be a man, Schmidt! You've declared yourself now!"

He shook his head. "It wasn't signed! She can't know it was me, Miss Laine—please don't tell her!"

I knew—as Schmidt did not, for he had lost his memories—that Nijam and Schmidt were old acquaintances, who had once worked in the same laboratory at the University of Heidelberg. Whatever other illusions she might be labouring beneath, there was not the faintest chance that Nijam did not know exactly who had penned that letter. But I could not enlighten him to this, either. Nijam was adamantly opposed to it. Among her most prized possessions was a vial of the bubonic plague, and I have never liked to take unnecessary risks.

Mimi had had nothing but laughter for Nijam's predicament, but now she relented, for she went over to Schmidt and put a sisterly arm around him. "Don't be afraid of Nijam. If she felt nothing for you she would not have been so angry."

He shook his head again, red with mortification. "If Miss Nijam thinks of me at all, it's with disgust. Just today she called me a *coward,* only because I did not want to leave sir."

So *that* was what they had quarrelled about. I felt sorrier and sorrier for both of them. "You'd better hurry away before she comes back," I told him. "But I'll give you some advice, if I may?"

Schmidt sent me a look of pathetic eagerness.

"When you make his bed, you should sprinkle a teaspoon of sugar between Vasily's sheets. That will teach him."

That *nearly* made him smile, but as he hurried away he still looked very crushed. Mimi closed the door with a sigh, and returned to start dabbing powder onto my face. With the excitement over, she looked tireder than ever.

"Why can't people just *talk* instead of circling each other like angry cats?" she complained.

This did not seem to require an answer, so I made none. I was rather uncomfortably aware of the fact that I had myself spent a fair amount of time avoiding conversation with Vasily. We cannot all be as forthright as Mimi.

"Will you be dancing Myrtha tonight?" I asked, and she shook her head.

"M. Christophe says I need more practice," she said. "Also it is a gala performance, and there will be selections from a few different shows. I'll be dancing a trio from *Lakmé*."

By chance I had seen *Lakmé* a year ago in Vienna, the same day on which I met Mimi for the very first time. Had it really been a year since then? Who among us, that night when Vasily and I threw a paper dart at a Russian Grand Duke and were nearly murdered by the Okhrana, could have guessed that a year later we should all still be working together?

It made me wonder whether we should all be together a year from now; and that made me ask the question.

"If *Giselle* does well, do you think you'll take a permanent position here at the Opera?"

"Why shouldn't I? It is what I have wanted my whole life," Mimi said, and there was now something a little defensive in her voice. "Maybe I don't want to be a thief forever."

The words struck a chord in me, too. "None of us became thieves by choice."

"I've never been a respectable woman," Mimi said, dabbing at my eyebrows with a brush. She tilted her head, assessing her work. "Maybe I will try it. Just to see what it's like."

Of course I did not like the idea. Mimi looked so tired! Moreover, if she left the crew—if any one of us left the crew— nothing would ever be the same again. Where would we find another burglar who understood and loved us so well?

But of course I could not say anything so selfish. "Then you ought to try it—and stick with it, if it suits you."

"Of course it suits me," she muttered. "Stop talking; I want to paint your lips."

After that there was no more talking, at least for another half a minute—until the door opened and Nijam marched in, flushed and triumphant, with the messenger-boy squirming and protesting in his grip.

"I ask again: tell me who gave you that letter," Nijam demanded in very bad French, ejecting the lad onto the Persian rug at the centre of the room, and shutting the door none too gently behind her.

"I don't know the one who gave it to me!" the boy responded sulkily. Although he appeared no more than about twelve or thirteen years of age, he must have been older, for his voice was husky.

"Was it one of *them?*" Nijam demanded, with a sweep of her hand towards Mimi and myself. The boy shook his head. "Was it," she added in a voice more ominous still, "a *man?*"

"Nijam, if you want to hunt witches, can you do it elsewhere?" Mimi demanded, slamming down her paintbrush.

"It *was* a man, wasn't it?" Nijam demanded, paying no attention to Mimi's complaint. The boy gave an eloquent shrug. I arose from my seat, thinking it best to intervene before the thumbscrews were applied.

"If you suspect Vasily then you should ask *him* about it, instead of terrifying this boy," I said. There was a bowl of peppermints upon the mantelpiece, which Nijam had thus far been too preoccupied to notice. I offered it to the boy— who immediately emptied the whole thing into his pockets—

shepherded him to the door, and closed it firmly behind him.

"We don't know that it *was* Vasily," Nijam growled, throwing herself onto a couch. "This is a matter of security; we *must* know."

"Of course it was Vasily," said Mimi with withering scorn. "Who else would be such a busybody? Dark, your face is done. Those are the powders I used; keep them for next time. Nijam can help you dress; *I* have work to do."

As she hurried away, her limp became more pronounced, and I felt a sudden pang of premonition. Perhaps, after all, I ought *not* to have encouraged her in her pursuit of her Art!

With a sigh, I sat down beside Nijam.

"Don't tell me you have no idea who wrote that letter," I said, as kindly as I could.

It would be too much to say that Nijam blushed, but I detected a tell-tale dark flush in her cheeks.

"Of course I know who *wrote* it! What I want to know is what joker thought it would be funny to *send* it to me!"

I did not venture a guess—not aloud, at any rate. Vasily had made his bed and now he must eat its bitter fruits, including interrogation and execution at Nijam's hands, if necessary. But we had come to Paris on a mission, and everyone was out of sorts. If I could help straighten them out again it might be the best thing I could do for the job.

"I thought you and Schmidt were getting along better these days," I said. "Did the two of you quarrel?"

Nijam scowled. "You heard him, before. This job requires him to be Vasily's factotum, but he's willing to compromise it by continuing to valet for him. It's a tragedy! Here is Alphonse Schmidt, the brightest mind in bionic chemistry, and he's willing to fritter away his life fetching and carrying for that idiot—no offence meant."

"None taken."

"Anyway, it makes me sick. He might as well be dead."

"You were tremendously impressed when he stood up to Vasily in Moscow," I suggested. "And he did it again in Hong Kong."

She scowled. "So, Alphonse has learned that it isn't always good for Vasily to have his own way. He's still utterly devoted to him."

"You ought to tell him how you feel," I said. Nijam gave me a Look. "No, I mean it! All this time you've refused to admit your feelings, on the pretext that it would impose too great an obligation. But what difference could it make now? Surely you've noticed that he's fallen in love with you again."

Nijam scowled more deeply, but I could see that she was thinking it over—even if only to formulate a rebuttal.

"The problem with Alphonse is that he hasn't changed," she said. "Just like John Grey—well, I grant you, Alphonse would never dare to tell me that I'm sick in the head. But he still insists upon believing the lies they fed him in that place after they took his memories—that he deserved what they did to him, and that if he ever learns the truth about his past he will turn out to be the most frightful brigand. I *know* that it's false—I've tried to tell him—but he won't listen to me. It's pure cowardice, and so I told him." She sighed. "Sometimes I envy you, Dark. Vasily is a trainwreck, but at least he seems willing to *change*."

I asked myself what Nijam would say to *me* in such a predicament.

"Of course Schmidt won't reconsider—not without a jolly good reason to do so. Tell him that you used to know him.

Surely he deserves that much honesty, at least, and knowing *why* you're upset with him."

"I'm not upset!"

It was my turn to give Nijam a Look. That is the problem with people who pride themselves upon their rationality: they don't know a feeling when it's dancing all over them with hobnailed boots. Nijam was, fortunately, sensible enough to see that I was right.

"If I *am* upset," she said, getting up from the sofa, "I think he knows *precisely* why!"

With that Parthenon shot, she stalked off. No doubt it slipped her mind that she was supposed to help me dress. I might have used my transmitter to call her back, but in truth the afternoon's dramatics, in addition to the journey from London, had left me feeling a little tired. Instead, after a quick sponge-bath, I struggled into all that red velvet magnificence on my own. Then, with some trepidation, I peered into the looking-glass.

The sight within took my breath away. Even I could see that Mimi had done excellent work on my face. The powders added no more than a little subtle colour to darken lips and eyebrows, and to impart a flush to my cheeks. I did not look at all like that disgraceful spectacle, a woman who *paints*. Beyond that, there was the dress—and I had to admit that here, again, Mimi had judged perfectly. Those rich warm colours made all the colours in my face more vivid; that heavy sweeping volume of red velvet, which would have overwhelmed a smaller woman's figure, imparted a statuesque nobility to mine.

I did not know the woman in the mirror, but I felt at once that I wished to.

What a shame I could not have Mimi as my lady's-maid! But that was, of course, out of the question. If she had her wish she would at last be a ballerina, and it was my duty as her friend to consider this right and good. Yet, still I could not help worrying. Mimi *did* seem tired; in addition to which, she could barely walk.

I ought not to worry. Doubtless, after two long journeys and much sitting around eating peppermints, it would take a great deal of work and conditioning for Mimi to regain the fitness of a professional dancer. I could sympathise, too, with her wish to be a respectable woman. How often had I myself bewailed the cruel fate which required me to earn my bread as a thief!

And now I did not need to earn my bread at all.

I had begun to steal because I had no other choice—but now it struck me that I could make any choice at all. The sudden awareness of my freedom was intoxicating, almost terrifying. I looked at the strange, magnificent woman in the looking-glass. "Who *are* you, Molly Dark?" I asked, but the image was like an imprint: it had no mind of its own, and could not answer me.

Chapter III.

I arrived at the Paris Opera that evening not a moment before half-past nine. From without, as I stepped from my hired carriage to the pavement outside, I had only the impression of a tall, dark façade overhead, its arches and windows outlined with warm golden light, before my attention was arrested by the sight of a shivering child who crouched in the shadows of the portico, her gaunt hands outstretched pleadingly for a coin. My heart twisted within me, but I did not reach into my purse for a silver franc to give her. The glimmer of pale light that hung about her wasted form, and the pangs of hunger and cold that wracked my body at the sight of her, told me that she was no longer among the living.

What could I do? I stepped into the main lobby and found myself surrounded by a blaze of light and colour. In a dazzle of new electric lights the Baroque magnificence was overwhelming. Every surface shone, glistened, or sparkled, from the polished marble floor to the serried ranks of blazing lamps; from the great bifurcated staircase which swooped to the upper balconies, to the pilasters that reached up the mirrored walls towards the gilded and frescoed roof.

I was by now no stranger to scenes of magnificence and splendour. Yet to my dazzled eyes, the Paris Opera outshone the Maryinsky or the Wiener Staatsoper nearly as far as the Schloss Frohsdorf outshone Brixton. All the same, after what I had seen in the portico, there seemed something rather beastly about it.

Schmidt met me on the stairs and conducted me to the red-velvet-lined box from which Vasily was enjoying the performance. Here, I had the pleasure of seeing my irrepressible lover bereft at once of breath, and words.

"Chin up, Baron; anyone would think you'd never seen your wife in a pretty dress before," I murmured as I offered my cheek to be kissed. I feared that if Vasily meant to gape at me like this, all of fashionable Paris would understand at a glance our true relationship.

"My *wife!*" he murmured, with great feeling; but he recovered himself sufficiently to introduce me to a handsome old gentleman with a pointed white beard and a colourful silk cravat, who sat beside him in the place of honour at the front of the box.

"Dumortier, allow me to present madame la Baronne," Vasily said. "My dear, this is my co-manager, M. Dumortier."

Dumortier arose from his seat and bowed over my hand with an appreciative smile. "Enchanté, madame!"

"And which part of the performance are you most looking forward to, M. Dumortier?" I inquired, thinking it best to commence my investigations at once.

"Chalabi's solo from *Giselle*," he announced. "You know the ballet, madame?"

"I've heard of it—but I admit that I've never seen it performed."

"It was created here in Paris," he proclaimed, "with the great Taglioni in the rôle of Giselle. People today talk of Italian dancers, of Danish dancers, of Russian dancers—but none pure, none original, you understand? For true ballet, as it was danced in Versailles by the Sun King, you must come to Paris." He nodded towards the stage, where a diva with brown curly hair was performing feats of sopranic virtuosity. "The people demand *modern* opera, so of course we must give them Wagner and other rubbish of the sort. But it's in ballet that our national genius truly lies."

I nodded sagely. "It was fortunate, I suppose," I said, "that it was M. Larousse, a mere tenor, who was found hanging in his dressing-room, and not one of the corps de ballet!"

I half expected him to protest. Instead, Dumortier adopted a lofty, judicious tone of voice. "Of course it was a great tragedy," he said, "and it involved us in some difficulties with the police. But in the grand scheme of things, you understand—the money was better spent on other productions."

I wondered what M. Larousse's family would say to this. All I said aloud, however, was: "The police? Was some foul play suspected?"

"Dear me, no! It was quite a simple case of suicide. Nothing at all out of the ordinary. But there were some allegations on the part of the family. It is all settled *now,* of course."

This was very interesting; it would give me a direction to take when I should call upon Mme Larousse the following day. For the present, I gave a sympathetic click of my tongue. "Did it cost you very much to placate the family?"

"Not a sou," Dumortier said, as though he prided himself upon it. "The police agreed with me that the thing was preposterous, and there the matter rests."

Any response I might have made was forestalled by a scratch on the door of the box, and the entry of my old friend, Célestin

Deleuze, with another gentleman.

"My dear Baroness!" he exclaimed with a gallant bow. "I saw a goddess enter the manager's box, and thought, surely I see my friend from the Channel boat! Ah, and you must be the Baron von Jörger. Sir, allow me to congratulate you upon your appointment."

To think that I should live to hear the handsome Célestin Deleuze address me as a goddess!

Vasily arose and bowed to Deleuze rather coldly.

"All the way from the Wiener Staatsoper, Baron, I believe?" Deleuze asked. "How odd that I should not have seen you when I was in Vienna in the summer!"

"Not at all odd; I spent the summer abroad," Vasily replied, somewhat snappish. Now *he* was ill at ease. Deleuze laughed and glanced at me.

"I see what you mean," he said, in a low jesting voice. "What a bear the man is!"

I bit my lip to restrain my laughter. I thought of Vasily more as a house-cat than a bear. "Be careful," I whispered to Deleuze. "He is jealous of you, I think."

"Not at all," said Vasily. His hearing had been a deal more sensitive since he had been bitten by one of his vampire cousins. "Why should I be jealous of *you*, when the lady is *my* wife?"

"That's something only a very jealous husband would say," said M. Deleuze's friend. Even the dignified M. Dumortier smiled at this, while Vasily darted us thunderous glances. I began to feel uneasy. Of course Vasily was duty-bound to misbehave as part of our masquerade. He and I must not seem to be on affectionate terms. But he had been jealous earlier, too, when it was only the five of us.

Perhaps I ought to have tried to soothe him—perhaps it would have better suited the rôle I had to play, of the downtrodden wife. Instead, a spark of the Old Adam entered into me, whispering that carping jealousy had no place in the marriage of true minds, and that if Vasily thought that it did, then he had better be taught a lesson.

Deleuze introduced me to his friend—a gentleman of a similar sort, whom he referred to as M Caillot—and seated himself beside me, where he engaged himself in pointing out and roasting some of the eminent Parisians seated across from us in the dress circle. I, for my part, flirted with him all the more assiduously—laughing shamelessly at all his mean little jokes, and occasionally allowing my fan to tap him upon the arm.

To distract myself from Vasily's air of seething discontent, I also busied myself searching the audience until I spotted Nijam. Seated in the stalls, she was discreetly amusing herself with a book—*Metals in the Service of Man,* no doubt. The Wagnerian soprano finished her aria and was hurried off the stage with a snort of contempt from M. Dumortier. I wondered whether her male counterpart had been assassinated by a disgruntled balletomane.

The irony of this stray thought would occur to me, but not for some time.

With that a much prettier sort of music began, and Mimi and a couple of others ran out onto the stage attired as Indian dancers. I had never seen Mimi dance before, and watching her move through the graceful arabesques of the dance, I caught my breath. Pain and weariness had fallen away from her; she moved with effortless joy. I felt that I had never truly known Mimi until this moment—and knowing, I understood her a little better. Surely it was this for which she was made!

The dance ceased; the theatre erupted in shouts of acclamation; flowers rained down from the boxes, and Mimi and her partners took their bows. At my side, M. Dumortier let out a long and admiring sigh.

"That's Mimi Laine, a dancer from Petersburg," he informed me. "She was a little stiff when she first arrived a week ago, but M. Christophe thinks he can make something of her."

Then Mimi took a step towards the wings, and her knee almost gave way beneath her. "She's about to collapse," I exclaimed, instinctively rising from my seat..

"No doubt she'll see the Opera doctor if there's anything really the matter," Dumortier said. I restrained my indignation at this cool response; Deleuze and Caillot were not even looking at the stage, and Dumortier gave off an air of supreme indifference. I sent Vasily a beseeching glance, for my worry for Mimi had driven any thought of his jealousy out of my mind. He was already moving his hand towards the transmitter in his ear.

"Schmidt, Nijam," I heard him murmur through my own transmitter, "won't you check on Mimi? She'll be in her dressing-room."

Nijam's Alphonse, who had been waiting quietly at the back of the box, left at once, and I reassured myself that Mimi would shortly have a pair of level-headed friends to care for her if she needed them. A moment later, M Caillot took his leave of us and also departed.

"There goes our Dagobert, with his breeches on backwards!" said Deleuze with a snicker.

"Are they really? Oughtn't someone to tell him?"

"It's a figure of speech, my dear Baroness. All the Caillots are inordinately proud, anyway. They say their family line goes all the way back to the Middle Ages, and that is why he has such a ridiculous name—from the days of the Merovingians!"

I put up my fan to hide my smile. Such remarks seemed rather hypocritical coming from a *Célestin*. "Where is he going?"

"He's a member of the Jockey Club," Deleuze replied. "Don't you know what that is? One pays a subscription to be allowed general access to the foyer de la danse, where the corps de ballet gathers during performances. Caillot has a particular interest in the little Allard, who delighted us just now in the trio. She does not care for him, but I've no doubt he will overcome her scruples. They all do, given enough time—or perhaps, enough money!"

I knew that the Russian ballet served up its dancers to the appetites of the noble and monstrous. I did not quite know why I had expected better things from the French, unless perhaps it was that they had cut off the head of their melusine king and now plumed themselves on being a Republic. But that did not mean a lack of monstrosity. After all, the United States was also a republic, and I knew precisely how monstrous their "self-made men" could be.

I took care to conceal my distaste. "You speak from personal experience, monsieur? Why do you not go with him?"

Deleuze laughed and leaned a little too close, so that I saw Vasily's eyes narrow in a look that might have struck the Frenchman dead on the spot, if such a thing was possible. "Why consort with nymphs when one might worship at the altar of a goddess?"

The compliment was a trifle overpolished, as though I was neither the first, nor even the second woman to hear it.

"Why do you keep calling me that?" I whispered, sending Vasily a wink over the top of my fan. I think he actually reddened with indignation.

"Because you are the most beautiful woman I've ever met," Deleuze replied. "Why do you laugh?"

"Oh! I was only thinking that if you saw me in poor and humble clothing, you would never spare me a glance."

"Don't blaspheme! A divinity like yours would grace the most beggarly rags!"

I was obliged to dive once again behind my fan. This was all extremely gratifying, and I did not know how I was to contain myself until I got home this evening and was able to record the whole ridiculous scene for the amusement of my sisters.

I wondered what the co-manager Dumortier thought of all this outrageous flirtation going on beneath his very nose, but he seemed to take it quite philosophically, for at this point he leaned over to me and said, "Now, madame, you shall see one of the great ballerinas of *our* time, in one of the great rôles of *any* time."

"There seems to be some sort of delay," I observed, and it was true enough, for the orchestra was ready, and the audience waited expectantly with an occasional encouraging whistle or cheer. But there was no sign of Mlle Chalabi.

Once again, Deleuze leaned close; his voice was pitched for my ears alone. "If Dumortier had his way, the Opera would only stage endless romantic ballets from the glory days of sixty years ago. That tenor, Larousse, did him a great service in hanging himself before—"

The box door opened, interrupting Deleuze's gossip and admitting a rather agitated-looking gentleman in evening-dress, who approached the managers and quickly bowed to each, wringing his hands.

"Chalabi's disappeared," he hissed. "She should have been waiting in the foyer, but she isn't!"

"Then she must be in her dressing-room," Dumortier said impatiently. He turned to Vasily. "Deschamps, our stage-manager. Deschamps, this is—"

"Forgive me, sir—we've looked in her dressing-room, but there's no sign of her," Deschamps broke in. "Her maid is frantic. Chalabi sent her to fetch a flask of water, and when the girl returned her mistress was gone."

Dumortier's aristocratic old face flushed pink beneath the beautifully-trimmed white beard. "What can the woman be thinking, running away in the middle of a gala performance! Stay here, Baron; I must see to this in person."

"On the contrary—as a co-manager, I think I'd better come with you," Vasily said, rising at once to his feet.

Dumortier seemed reluctant, but of course he could not prevent Vasily doing as he liked. "As you wish," he said, and did not even demur when Vasily turned to me and held out an expectant hand.

"You'd better come too, my dear."

"Surely there's no need for that, my dear Baron," Deleuze said with a wicked glint in his eye. "I would be quite happy to attend the Baroness while you see to business."

I saw that Vasily really wanted me with him—whether for the sake of the job or only his own peace of mind, I did not know; but whether as my comrade or my lover I did not intend to disappoint him.

"You're very kind," I told Deleuze, "but I should go. Perhaps Chalabi's maid will speak more freely to another woman."

Dumortier's face said *Poppycock!* even if his lips did not, but with that it was settled: he and Deschamps led us out of the box, and Vasily and I followed. I gave my lover's hand a reassuring squeeze as we walked, and he returned it as swiftly; after that I felt that all was well between us. As for M. Deleuze, he brought up the rear, strolling behind with his hands in his pockets. I suppose that he scented a tasty morsel of gossip and meant not to let it pass him by.

Our journey to Chalabi's dressing-room took us down magnificent corridors and winding staircases to a door guarded by an attendant whose task it was to deny entry to all but subscribers and Opera functionaries. A word from Vasily secured my entrance, and M. Deleuze, of course, was a Jockey Club subscriber. Having passed the sacred portal to the corridor running behind the stage, we came at once face-to-face with a grisly apparition! My heart stood still at the sight of a tall, fleshy lady with dishevelled hair and with great splashes of blood besmirching her white nightgown. She clutched a shining dagger in her right hand and was glancing impatiently at the silver pocket-watch in her left, as if there was a murder she feared being late for. It was only when M. Deschamps bowed and stood aside, and I heard her humming abstractedly beneath her breath as she passed, that I realised that this was neither a shade nor an imprint, but the soprano from *Lucia de Lammermoor* making her way to the stage from the foyer du chant.

A moment later we came to the foyer de la danse, an enormous and magnificent room placed immediately behind the stage itself. It contained a piano; a shining parqueted floor tilted to the same slope as the stage itself; more gilded pilasters, another gargantuan chandelier, wall-frescoes of the great ballerinas of the past, and at the far end, a set of three enormous gleaming mirrors bisected by a velvet-covered practice barre. In addition to these furnishings, it was crowded with the subscribers, the gentlemen of the Jockey Club and the ladies and even young girls of the corps de ballet. Most of these were in abbreviated white dresses, although others were clad more interestingly in Oriental draperies; so that it took all my self-command not to gawk unbecomingly at the beauties thus displayed. I saw Caillot drinking champagne with the little Allard and glanced about for Mimi, but if she was here she was thoroughly lost in the crowd. Of Schmidt there was no sign, either, and as for Nijam, I believe I was one of only a very few females present not a member of the corps. Doubtless none of the gentlemen present liked their wives or sisters to be tainted by association with the negotiable virtue of the ballet ladies.

M. Deschamps exchanged a signal with a grave and busy-looking pair of other gentlemen, who spread their hands and shook their heads in a decided negative.

"I suppose that means Chalabi hasn't been found," Vasily murmured to me.

"Let's hope that doesn't mean we're about to find her hanging somewhere," I murmured in reply. But I must not have spoken softly enough, because Dumortier heard me.

"Don't be afraid; that's the last thing that is likely to happen," he said. But there was a certain lack of conviction in his voice that I did not much care for. And when he had said it, the nervous Deschamps signed himself rather furtively with the cross.

After that the expedition made its way out at another door and plunged into the warren of staircases, passages and dressing-rooms at the back of the Opera—a dark and cramped little labyrinth, rather bare and serviceable after all the dazzling glory of the public spaces. If the foyer de la danse had been largely undisturbed by Mlle Chalabi's disappearance, a different mood reigned in the rear passages. Perhaps it was the cold, or perhaps a certain oppressive hush in the air, which made me shiver and draw a little nearer to Vasily. Young ballerinas and singers scurried past us in knots, holding hands and whispering. I heard shrieks of terror once as one of the groups was surprised by another. Gentlemen were also present, lurking in the shadows, rarely with a companion. Perhaps on another evening, these darkened passages might stand witness to any number of cruel, debasing little transactions; tonight, they took on the aspect of the Cretan Labyrinth, in which any solitary lurker might be the Chimera.

Up a flight of spiral stairs, and not far down the subsequent passage, we found Demiana Chalabi's dressing-room. It was evident which one of the rooms was hers, for here a thick crowd of ballerinas, subscribers, and functionaries had gathered, whispering and gossiping and making various signs against the evil eye. At our approach, they parted at once to allow the managers entrance to a charming, though untidy dressing-room. There was a dressing-table, the stool of which had been overturned, and pots of greasepaint flung about rather like the inkwell with which John Wycliffe had pummelled the devil in the German castle. There was a painted partition-screen with a fur stole thrown over the corner, a chandelier somewhat smaller and more restrained than those in other areas of the Opera, an array of grandiose bouquets, some of them looking a trifle wilted, and a well-worn sofa with carved wooden legs. It was upon this that the prima ballerina's waiting-woman had collapsed, with a handkerchief pressed with dainty brown hands to her face. Apart from this, very little was visible of her but black hair escaping from a demure bun and a well-starched white cap.

One of the little ballerinas, a girl of no more than thirteen or fourteen, had knelt beside the maid and thrown her arms tightly around her waist. "Don't cry, Khadijah-*ukhti*," she begged, at intervals. "Don't cry, mademoiselle will come back again with a tale to explain everything; you'll see." It was rather like Little Bo Peep, except that there was every reason to fear that perhaps mademoiselle might *not* come back again, tale or none.

"What the devil has happened here?" Dumortier demanded, but the maid was in no condition to reply.

Vasily's arm compressed mine and I followed his glance towards the upset pots of paint and powder. I nodded to assure him that this detail had not escaped me; whereupon I seated myself beside the afflicted maid and put a gentle hand upon her shoulder. "My poor girl!" I said, "it's possible that your mistress is in very grave danger, but it lies in your power to help her, if you can tell messieurs the managers what has happened."

The maid gave another sob and peered over her handkerchief with reddened eyes. I am afraid that the sight which greeted her could *not* have been very reassuring, for M. Dumortier was looking very grim and even when Vasily means to appear reassuring he cannot quite help giving the impression of a cat watching a mouse-hole. The poor girl shrank against me, and I saw that I would need to ask the questions myself.

"When did you last see your mistress, my dear?"

"Tell her, *ukhti,*" the little ballerina insisted.

"Mademoiselle was here in her dressing-room, at her mirror," the maid said, pointing a trembling finger at the vanity. "She sent me for some water, and when I returned there was no mademoiselle and the stool was upside-down."

"I suppose half the Opera has been trampling through and tossing things about," Dumortier said with a sniff.

"The paints and powders?" I prompted. "Were they all tossed about, too?"

"I tell you it was as you see it," the maid sobbed.

"A lovers' tiff, in fact," Dumortier said. "I suppose after all that she ran off with him, whoever he is—lucky dog!"

At that, a titter ran through the crowd at the door, but the maid flared up. "And who would she have run away with, pray tell? Mademoiselle scorned all her lovers!"

"It's true," said a lanky ballerina from the doorway, who held a smouldering cigarette in one gloved hand. There was a pretty brooch in lapis lazuli and gold pinned to the front of her white bodice, marking her out as a woman with a generous lover of her own. "Chalabi fancied herself a saint, you know. She was always going on about Demiana and her forty virgins. Who ever heard of *Egyptians* having saints?"

"That just shows how much *you* know, Gianna," the little ballerina retorted. "In Egypt our saints are older than yours, Christian *or* Muslim, and we honour them better, too!"

"Be quiet, you brat! It isn't as though you've ever seen Egypt in your life!"

"That's enough," Vasily interposed smoothly. "Mademoiselle, your name?"

I squeezed the maid's shoulder encouragingly, and she said, "Khadijah Gobara, and this is my sister, Fatima." The relationship surprised me, for the little ballerina was much fairer-skinned than the maid.

"Think very carefully, Khadijah Gobara," Vasily said, and if his smile had not been likely to inspire confidence, at least he pronounced her name exactly the way she did, with the first consonant softened halfway to an *H*. "Perhaps Mlle Chalabi had no lovers with whom she wished to run away, but had she offended anyone, or made enemies?"

"No, monsieur, none at all! But—"

"Then you can think of no one at all who might have taken her away?" I pressed, aware that time was fleeting and every moment might count. Perhaps there was, among Chalabi's would-be lovers, the sort of man who refused to take no for an answer.

"But yes, madame, that was what I was going to tell you! Mlle Chalabi—it is certain that she was stolen by the ghost!"

An absolute silence fell upon the room, although one of the ballerinas crowding the doorway gave a rather delighted shriek.

"The *ghost?*" I inquired. "Which ghost?" Now, I have met a great many ghosts myself, and I very much doubted that this could be true, for none of them had been able to affect the living world so much as to brew a cup of tea, let alone to kidnap an unwilling woman. So I did my best to keep my scepticism from showing.

"*The* ghost," Mlle Gobara reiterated with a decided nod of her head, "old M. Perrot's ghost, which wanders about the Opera in a mask!"

M. Dumortier threw up his hands in disgust. "They're making up stories about poor M. Christophe again," he told Vasily. "Our ballet-master wears a mask, and some of the dancers are superstitious about it."

"The child has a point," Gianna drawled, tucking the end of her cigarette into a flower-vase. "Don't they say that the Perrot tomb was broken open, and the remains stolen? I would haunt you all too, if that was done to *me.*"

Some of the ballerinas shivered appreciatively at this grisly story. I did not take it very seriously myself. A shade might try to cling to this world if it felt wronged; but for no longer than a day or two before it was moved on, inexorably, to the next.

"Was the body ever recovered?" Vasily asked.

"Of course it was; it had been thrown onto a pile of brushwood the grounds-keepers had made in the cemetery, and set alight," said Dumortier. "Really, the *avant-garde* goes too far! They're all anarchists up there in Montmartre. But it's all superstitious nonsense. The body has been reinterred, and the tomb re-sealed."

"I'd still haunt you," Gianna muttered, not quite softly enough to be overlooked.

"Indeed, monsieur, you don't understand," little Fatima put in. "There are two ballet-masters, not one! There is M. Christophe who wears a mask and never speaks—"

"That isn't true! He speaks to *me,*" Dumortier insisted.

"—and there is old M. Perrot who is dead but cannot leave the Opera in peace!"

"How do you know them apart?" I asked. I might be sceptical of their claims, but I had seen some uncommon things in my life, and thought it best to inquire before passing judgement.

My question was answered with a hubbub of voices.

"M. Christophe carries a white wand," said little Fatima

eagerly, "but M. Perrot's is black!"

"M. Perrot moves like a cat, absolutely silent," said somebody near the door, "but you can hear M. Christophe walking, *thump-tap, thump-tap*, all the way up the passage!"

"M. Christophe lives in the—"

But further revelations were interrupted by a sudden scream from the corridor.

"It's the ghost!"

At that piercing shriek, the hair stood up all over my body. The girl in my arm trembled and sobbed, the people flocking the threshold milled about confusedly, and the gentlemen turned expectantly to the door. Then there came a loud *crack* that made us all jump, and even the lanky Gianna dropped her cigarette in alarm. For a moment absolute silence descended. Then I heard it from the corridor—*thump-tap, thump-tap.* The crowd parted, and a tall cloaked figure stood before us in the doorway. He wore a mask that covered his entire face beneath a smoking-cap of black silk and gold braid, and carried a white wand in his gloved fist!

For a moment I think that no one breathed. The apparition was too unexpected, coming as it did upon the very heels of our conversation! In that shivering silence an odd scent wafted through the room—a little musty, a little like sweet pine and bitumen. Then Dumortier said, "Ah, M. Christophe! Just the man I wished to see!" and dabbed with his handkerchief at a forehead that had suddenly begun to glisten. It was only then that I recalled that the echoing footsteps, and the white wand, were said to be the accoutrements of the genuine ballet-master.

There was, however, a test that needed to be made. I rose to my feet and put out my hand with my most winning smile.

"Ah, M. Christophe!" I exclaimed. "Please, M. Dumortier, won't you introduce us? I have heard so much about your distinguished ballet-master."

But Dumortier had no time for social ceremonies. "In a moment, Baroness," he said, seizing Christophe by the arm. I held my peace, for I saw Dumortier's hand sink into a very tangible sleeve in a grip so strong that the fingers went white, and that provided the answer I sought. Christophe must be very much alive.

"Do *you* know where Chalabi is, Christophe?" Dumortier asked, softly enough that his voice did not carry to the company by the door. Vasily heard, however, and shot me a keen glance. I responded with the faintest shrug. I had not the slightest idea as to why Dumortier should suspect the ballet-master, but I made a note to inquire about this with Mlle Gobara.

While Vasily and I thus communicated by signs, M. Christophe was making some signs of his own—clipped gestures which evidently carried some meaning; which, however I was incapable of reading. Whatever their import, they evidently put the manager at his ease. Dumortier turned to Vasily.

"There's no need to panic," he announced. "Mlle Chalabi is in the wings and ready to begin her solo."

The lanky ballerina, Gianna, threw up her hands and muttered something about *all this trouble for nothing!* I let out a sigh of relief, and it was not the only one, for Mlle Gobara made a sound rather like another sob. Whereupon Dumortier turned to the maid in high displeasure.

"Let that be a lesson to you, young woman!" he snapped. "No more of this nonsense, I beg you! Next time your mistress disappears, have the goodness to wait a decent amount of time before sounding the alarm!"

The maid looked quite crushed, but already Dumortier had stalked out of the little room and Vasily and I were obliged to follow him, or remain and be lost in the labyrinth. I sent my lover another speaking look. It was certain that *something* odd was going on here—but what?

It was, at least, a stroke of luck that Demiana Chalabi had returned, safe and well.

Or so we thought at the time—but this consolation was to prove short-lived indeed.

Chapter IV.

Here I must tell you what Nijam and Schmidt had been doing all this time. As the reader may recall, Vasily had asked the two of them to look in on Mimi after her performance. They had set out at once, met at the door of the foyer de la danse, and requested directions to Mlle Laine's dressing-room. By the time the stage-manager had arrived in the managers' box to inform Dumortier, Vasily, and myself of Chalabi's disappearance, Nijam and Schmidt were deep in the labyrinth, debating whether Mimi's dressing-room was in this corridor, or in the corresponding corridor on a different floor.

"That ballerina said we were to go up one flight of stairs, not two, and that it would be the third door on the right," Nijam said firmly, rapping on the door before them. An indistinct sound informed her that the room was occupied. She threw open the door, and then closed it just as quickly.

"Good Lord," she said. "It's true what they say about the French. Let's try the next corridor up."

"Wait—I see someone," Schmidt announced, gazing towards the far end of the passage, which was cloaked with shadows. "A woman in white."

Nijam looked, and saw no such thing. "Don't tell me you're seeing ghosts, too!"

"It might be someone who can tell us where to find Mimi," he answered, and even Nijam could see the sense in that. The two of them hurried to the end of the corridor and found themselves in a round stairwell with a wrought-iron spiral staircase that seemed to go endlessly up and endlessly down, dimly lit by solitary electric bulbs which cast a sharp and garish pool of light upon each landing.

"I can't see anyone," Nijam murmured. There was a peculiar thick silence on that stair—the sort of silence, Alphonse Schmidt said when he was describing it to me later, that comes before a scream. Even Nijam, in her calm and dispassionate way, noted that her hands had gone clammy, and her heart began to beat a little faster than normal; but she put it down to the fact that she had had certain terrifying dreams as a child, and something about that shadowed staircase reminded her of them.

Then the silence *was* broken. Not by a scream, but by a sound that was barely a flutter—or rather a quick, spasmodic drumming. Schmidt uttered an exclamation and looked down through the iron lace that made up the stair. In the gloom beneath, he beheld a white face with staring eyes and parted lips looking up at him. For a moment the vision made no sense to him; and then it resolved into the figure of a woman in a dress of white gauze, struggling with beating hands against the grasp on her throat.

The sight was so unexpected, and so dreadful, that for a moment, nightmarishly, he was utterly incapable of sound or motion. Then a door banged in the passage behind them.

What went through Schmidt's mind in that moment was scarcely rational. All his horror turned in a moment to deadly fear, and he acted without thought. Turning, he flung an arm about Nijam, crushed her to his bosom, and put himself between her and the threat behind.

Only then did he have the chance to properly assess the threat before him. It was limping a little, wore a navy blue walking-dress that set off its eyes and short-cropped ash-blonde hair, and barely came up to his shoulder.

"Mimi," he gasped.

"Chicken-cage of terror!" Mimi said, rolling her eyes. "Don't say you *believe* the ghost stories!"

Nijam, who had congealed like a block of ice in the crook of his arm, now developed elbows. "Let *go!* For heaven's sake, Alphonse!"

He released her as though she had turned to a burning hot brand. Or perhaps his face had become the burning hot brand. "There's a ballerina down there being murdered," he said, turning again to the stairwell. A glance into the shadowed depths made his heart stand still for an awful moment.

"I don't see anything," Nijam said, joining him on the landing. Schmidt made a strangled sound. Neither did he— *now.*

"Are you sure it was a murder?" Mimi asked from behind them. "People get up to all sorts of things in these passages. The Jockey Club keeps the ballerinas pretty busy."

"Oh, we know," Nijam said. Schmidt was no longer at her side; he had plunged down the stairs. She did not follow him, but she opened her transmitter, watching his progress through the iron lace. "What do you see, Schmidt?"

She hoped he had not noticed the slip of the tongue, a moment ago, with which she had addressed him using his Christian name.

"Nothing," Schmidt replied, breathing hard, perhaps more

from emotion than exertion. "I'll go down and check the next corridor, too."

"All right, but be on your guard," Nijam said. Then, not wanting him to think that she was *worried* about him, she added: "The Baron won't be happy if I let his favourite valet be damaged."

Beside her, Mimi snickered. Nijam sent her a furious glare.

"There's nothing down here, either," Schmidt announced. "I'm coming back up—no, wait!"

A moment later he returned, breathlessly waving a scrap of trimming, done in silver thread and glass beads. "Look! This was on the second landing down! I *did* see something!"

Mimi sniffed. "That's nothing. Anyone might have lost that any time in the last two weeks."

"Likely you did mistake what you saw," said Nijam. It was only logical to think so. Scarcely half a minute could have passed between Schmidt's vision, and his arrival at the scene of what he thought to be a crime. If a woman really had been attacked on the stairs, could she have been subdued and carried away quickly enough to evade detection?

Schmidt reddened. "I know what I saw. Didn't you see it too?"

"I *might* have seen it," Nijam retorted, "had you not been clinging to me like a limpet. But let us look on the bright side! At least Mimi didn't get the chance to beat out my brains!"

Schmidt reddened more violently still, and Mimi said, "Enough flirting. What are you two doing here, anyway?"

Nijam did not dignify the first part of this speech with a response. "We came to see that you were all right. You looked completely done in after the performance."

Mimi sniffed. "I'm perfectly all right, thank you. I was just wrapping my knee and getting changed. What's the matter with you? You couldn't have turned on your transmitter and asked?"

"We wanted to see for ourselves," Nijam replied. Mimi muttered something about busybodies, but Schmidt frowned.

"Perhaps we ought to search the rooms near that landing," he said. "It's the only place where an attacker might hide a body."

"Absolutely not," said Nijam firmly. "We're far more likely to intrude upon an assignation than a murder. Come on; let's go back to the foyer."

They returned to the foyer de la danse to find Vasily and myself still there. Vasily was bailed up talking to a pair of very self-important gentlemen who wanted to tell him, in tedious detail, precisely what they thought of modern opera— "no ballets, just endless caterwauling." I think that they were trying to impress upon him the vital importance of *not* being Richard Wagner. My old friend Deleuze remained attached to my elbow, even sending away a pert ballerina who, I think, would have liked to claim an acquaintance with him. I did not much care for my attendant; so when I saw my friends enter the foyer, I begged him to fetch me a glass of champagne. While Deleuze was thus diverted, I slunk through the crowd and seized upon Mimi.

"Mimi, you're so pale! Did you hurt yourself during the performance?"

"I'm tired, that's all," she said shortly. "Why are you here? I thought Vas—the Baron wasn't going to be presented in the foyer until after the performance?"

"Oh! one of the ballerinas disappeared, and we came down to investigate and couldn't get away."

I could hardly have shocked them more had I tossed a bomb into their midst. Schmidt paled and clapped a hand to his brow. "Oh! my unlucky fate!" he groaned. "I *saw* her! I *knew* I saw her!"

"We don't know that she's dead, Schmidt," Nijam said, with unaccustomed gentleness.

"She isn't, in fact," I said. "Not our woman, at least, who is onstage dancing a solo from *Giselle* at this very moment. But what did you see, Schmidt?"

"I saw a ballerina being strangled on the back stairs," Schmidt said hoarsely. "Then I was distracted for a moment, and she was gone."

I considered this for a moment. Could one of the other dancers have been taken? Or— "Perhaps what you saw was an imprint. It doesn't always take a special talent to see ghosts, you know."

Schmidt snapped his fingers. "That's it!" he cried. "If she died you will be able to see her imprint, won't you?"

"Almost certainly," I answered at once. "Show me, then."

Once more we plunged into that dark and fearful labyrinth, the way newly burdened by the horror of what Schmidt had seen. As we went, I informed Vasily by transmitter of Schmidt's vision, and the necessity of carrying out a census of the ballerinas at once. I knew that he heard and agreed, for he broke off an expansive lecture on the superiority of *Boris Godunov* as compared to *Tristan and Isolde,* and informed his interlocutors of some pressing business that had arisen. After that I switched off my transmitter. I wanted all my faculties for the business at hand.

Deeper we went into those empty corridors, passing Chalabi's dressing-room and taking one or two sudden turns until at last we came to the fateful stairwell. Schmidt led us down two flights to a landing that looked exactly like all the others: dark, empty, and forgotten.

"This is where I found the scrap of tulle," he said.

The others watched me with bated breath. "Do you see anything?" Nijam asked.

Slowly, carefully, I turned to inspect the landing; the corridor stretching away into darkness; the well above and beneath me, dimly illuminated by the weak electric bulbs and scrawled with unlawful messages which generations of passing artists, functionaries, and lovers had etched into the plaster. The place had all the eerie strangeness of the in-between, and there was a certain heavy, oppressive quality to the silence, the shadows, the stillness… I could almost hear my heartbeat quicken its pace; but no ghostly form appeared, and at last I let out a breath of relief. "Nothing."

Schmidt fished from his pocket something white and sparkling—the bit of trimming which I have already described. "Here," he said. "Perhaps this will help."

It might. I took it from him—and all at once, as my hand closed upon the scrap, an icy gust of wind tore through the stairwell. I flung up a hand to protect my eyes; and when I lowered it, a woman stood before me, so that the light of the single electric bulb glowed eerily from the slopes and hollows of her face.

She had pale olive skin, intensely green eyes, and a wealth of curly black hair that rioted from her head for all the world like the carvings on the wall of an Egyptian temple. In that garish light she seemed somehow both too ancient and too wild for her abbreviated white dress, with all its clouds of gauze and silver trimmings.

"He's going to kill us," she hissed. Her voice ran up and down the stairwell in a piercing whisper that made me shiver with pure fear. "All of us. You have to stop him."

"I will," I assured her. There was a red mark around her throat—a ghastly handprint. I could scarcely tear my eyes away from it. "What is your name? And who is *he?*"

"I'm Chalabi, the dancer," she whispered. "And he—God alone knows!"

It was like a candle snuffing out. One moment she was there; the next, she was gone. There was no more wind; no more echoes throwing back ghostly whispers from the walls of the stairwell. There were only my three friends and I. Schmidt had reached out and seized the hands of both Mimi and Nijam; their faces, rigid with something very like terror, stared at me almost in a copy of Demiana Chalabi's own expression.

"What did you see?" Schmidt whispered.

I found my voice. "That was the fresh shade of Demiana Chalabi."

I watched despair settle on Schmidt's face, and a slow look of fear creep across Mimi's. But Nijam only scowled.

"You are quite sure that was Chalabi?"

"She told me her name. Shades can speak, you know— they're different from imprints; they're more like departing spirits than mindless memories."

"I know that," Nijam said, brushing the words away with a flick of her hand. "What I want to know is—if Chalabi is dead, *then who is that dancing onstage?*"

Chapter V.

It was midday the following day before we were all awake and gathered in my parlour to discuss the events of the previous night. I myself had not been to bed before three in the morning, for the gala performance had been followed by Vasily's official presentation to the Opera personnel, and that was confirmed with a ceremonial banquet to which I, as the Baroness, was duly invited.

Vasily was still being fêted by the time I had managed to extricate myself from the festivities. It was extraordinary, therefore, that he should have been the only member of our company looking bright and cheerful the following day. I was barely awake. Mimi threw herself down on the sofa and refused to move, saying that her knee required rest and elevation. Nijam's eyes were swollen half shut from lack of sleep, and as for Schmidt, he was glum and silent—haunted, no doubt, by the murder he had witnessed and failed to stop.

"All right," Vasily said, rubbing his hands together with a briskness that I found quite offensive. "I have to be at the Opera bright and early this afternoon, reviewing contracts and clearing out dead wood—you've no idea how many idle persons are notionally employed in the stables, just on a whim of the Minister of the Beaux-Arts! To business, my friends!"

"Business?" I threw a cushion at his head. "Have the decency to wait until we've eaten some breakfast!"

"Oho, would you!" he cried, fielding the cushion with ease. "Well, then, I have a question: what joker saw fit to iron *creases* into my sheets? I've barely slept!"

"You *look* like it," Mimi muttered.

Vasily's accusing gaze fixed upon me. I thought that this was *most* unjust. "Vasily! I haven't even set *foot* in your flat!"

"We'll discuss your conjugal shortcomings at another date, my dear wife! But then who could it possibly have been? Miss Nijam?"

Vasily laughed, but Nijam sent him a sour look. "What," she asked, "could possibly induce me to iron creases into your sheets, Vasily Nikolaevich? Answer me that."

"You tell *me!*" he replied, with unbridled cheek.

Murderously, Nijam took a peppermint. "Believe me: *if* I had something for which to get my revenge, I would do something a *great* deal worse than creased sheets."

I made a note to beg Nijam for clemency. I hoped she had noticed the diligence with which Schmidt now busied himself about the teapot, asking us our views on milk and sugar, although his ears had gone a little pink. He evidently had no intention of confessing to his crime, but I hoped that his willingness to commit *lèse-majesté* in the form of creased sheets would soften Nijam's heart of adamant.

Vasily, too, was observing Schmidt with a thoughtful air. Having got his attention with a slight pressure of my foot upon his toe, I shook my head. Any more interference, and I was afraid that Nijam really would commit murder. It was not that I thought she would get into trouble for it—if anyone could get away with such a crime scot-free, it was my careful friend—but like most girls, I was fond of my lover and wished to keep him around.

"Stop yapping, Vasily; I need to be at the Opera too," Mimi growled from the sofa, and perhaps that quelled him more effectively than I might have done.

"All right!" he said. "What's this I hear about Demiana Chalabi being dead?"

No one was eager to answer this question; not even Nijam, ordinarily the most practical of us. I cleared my throat.

"She *must* be," I said. "Schmidt saw her struggling with an assailant on the stairs at about the time we were going down to the foyer de la danse with M. Dumortier, and not long after I spoke to her dead shade. She didn't identify her attacker before she moved on, but she did identify herself very positively."

"She was murdered right in front of me," Schmidt muttered, "and I did nothing to stop it."

Nijam's scowl deepened.

Vasily, too, frowned. "It doesn't make sense. I had the roll called, but none of the ballerinas were missing. While you were in the stairwell, Chalabi was on the stage dancing her solo. The papers are calling it her greatest triumph to date."

"Maybe Chalabi has a double," Schmidt suggested. "Someone who might have impersonated her on the stage—"

"Don't be silly," Mimi put in. "Didn't you see the papers? A flawless performance, they say. You can't impersonate artistry like that."

"Mimi is right," I put in. "Impersonating a monster may be easy—it's simply a matter of putting on the right prosthetics. But there can't be any prosthetics to reproduce a ballet." I sighed. "I do have a theory, but it's going to sound quite mad."

"Not compared to the thought of a double who can impersonate Demiana Chalabi herself on the stage," Mimi said, and with that encouragement, I plunged in.

"Well, first of all," I said, "after meeting Chalabi's shade last night, I went back to her dressing-room and waited with the maid, Khadijah Gobara, for her mistress to return. She never did. Gobara was beside herself. I sent her home in a cab, but not before she identified that scrap of trim as being from her mistress' costume." I turned to Mimi. "And you—remember that I asked you to catch Chalabi as she came offstage, after her performance? I gather you didn't manage it?"

Mimi shrugged. "I lost track of her among the other dancers."

"And no one saw her after that? She was not in the foyer de la danse when you were being officially presented, Vasily?"

He shook his head. "She was supposed to make a speech and a toast. One of the other soloists stood in for her."

I nodded. "As far as we can tell, Chalabi was never seen once the performance ended. That confirms my suspicions. We know that I'm not the only person who can see imprints. Most people can, given the proper impetus—like Emperor Nicky or Sir Humphrey Seton or even Griff. Where else do the ghost stories come from? Well, here's what I propose. Poor Chalabi must have spent hours and hours rehearsing that scene on that stage. It's precisely the sort of diligent, repeated work that gets ingrained into a place and produces imprints. Then, once the theatre was full—thousands of people were sitting there, expecting to see Demiana Chalabi dancing Giselle. And that's precisely what they *did* see."

Vasily stared. "You mean to tell me that that performance was Chalabi's *imprint?*"

Nijam sniffed. "You're right. That *does* sound mad."

I turned to Mimi. "Everyone says the performance was perfect. How likely is that?"

Mimi blinked at me. "You mean—literally perfect, with not a single fumbled or mis-timed step? That's impossible."

"Newspapers are given to hyperbole," Nijam said.

"But what if, in this case, they aren't?" I asked. "It would make sense, if Chalabi was dead, that she should be remembered in all her perfection. Mistakes are like innovations: it takes a living creature to make them."

"Don't imprints fade over time?" Schmidt wondered. "In a week, say, will Chalabi cease to appear?"

I shook my head. "Imprints fade as the people who are living forget the dead. But the whole of the Paris Opera is fuelling this imprint, performers and audience alike, and each performance will only reinforce the memory. The managers could let *Giselle* run for months. Perhaps years… with nothing to betray the truth, but the exact conformity of each performance."

Mimi frowned. No doubt the same objection had occurred to her, as has probably occurred to you; but before she could mention it, Nijam spoke. "Well, it's a shame Chalabi didn't tell you who killed her. Schmidt and I went looking for the killer, or at least the corpse, but all we found in the corridors near that landing were empty rooms. After that we followed the stair down into the cellars, and that's where we found something."

"A clue?" I asked, hopefully.

Nijam scowled. "I don't know if I'd call it a clue. But it was certainly evidence of *some* kind of foul play."

* * *

The stair, Nijam explained, ran far beneath the Opera House, deep into the cellars. On their way downwards, she and Schmidt found workrooms and storerooms variously intended for costumers, carpenters, and set-designers; but here they met no living soul and found no sign of the missing artist. The stillness of those empty rooms, which had been abandoned mid-work at the end of the day, made the whole place seem like the scene of some obscure disaster. Nijam took a deep breath and reminded herself very firmly that there was nothing to fear in all this dark labyrinth, except a person who liked to strangle women; but this was somehow not very comforting to her. Meanwhile, the deadly silence reminded her of certain nightmares which had plagued her as a child; so that she had a perfectly irrational feeling that she was walking blindly into some unspeakable fate. She was very glad for Schmidt's comforting presence.

From the foot of the stair they ventured through a warren of storerooms and at length descended one last flight of steps which took them into a place utterly dark, without a glimmer of light from anywhere. Nevertheless, from the sound of their voices, and the movement of the air, Nijam knew that they must have found their way into some vast open space.

"We must be somewhere beneath the stage itself," said she, trying not to allow the irrational behaviour of her pulse to echo in her voice. Taking a candle-stub and a book of matches from her pocket, she struck a light. The flame illuminated very little but Schmidt, who emerged solid and reassuring from the darkness. There was a door set into the masonry wall on their left, but although this looked as though it might be in regular use, it proved to be locked. Ahead, the wall ran on into the darkness, and more masonry paved the floor beneath their feet. Yet this could not quite be the nethermost level of the Opera: before them in the floor was a rectangular opening the width of a coffin and about half as long again, which had been covered over with a grille of heavy iron bars.

Schmidt took the candle from her and held it at arm's-length above his head, throwing a wider circle of light about them. He made a sound of alarm beneath his breath, and Nijam caught her breath with a vertiginous sense of terror. She was almost convinced that she was seeing mirages, for great, dark, heavy shapes hung in the air beside them. Like a street full of impossible buildings they hovered several feet from the ground, perfectly still and perfectly silent and much too large to be illuminated by the flame of a solitary candle.

At last a chill, humid breath of air came from nowhere and set the great blocks a-trembling. Schmidt reached out to catch one of them; it proved to be a heavy canvas.

All at once Nijam understood, and swallowed her terror with a shaky laugh. "I know where we are now," she told Schmidt. "They say there's a vast cavity beneath the stage where the backdrops are lowered and stored when they're not wanted."

Schmidt's throat worked. "Chalabi might be hidden any-where down here. Perhaps she's only hurt, not…" He did not seem able to finish the sentence; instead, he crouched to peer beneath the vast hanging backdrops, but with no result.

"She's dead, Schmidt," Nijam said practically. "We'll find her eventually. The first order of business is to find the murderer himself; or a witness who might have seen him pass."

To this Schmidt assented, and they set off into the darkness, taking the narrow passage between the wall and the hanging backdrops. Nijam kept one hand on the wall, hoping that the rasp of masonry beneath her fingertips would keep her tethered to reality. Schmidt took the lead, peering down the long aisles between each backdrop as though by the candle's weak glimmer there was any hope of seeing Demiana Chalabi's body lying in the shadows beneath them.

Nijam asked herself where that breath of air might have come from. At the moment of arriving in Paris she had of course gone to visit the Bibliothèque Nationale, where she had been able to find some plans of the Opera. They were rudimentary, however, and the original blueprints used by the great Charles Garnier himself had not been made available to her. She ought to ask Mimi to steal them for her, if Mimi could find a spare moment. In the meantime, she racked her brains to recall what had been beneath the cellars. She might ask Schmidt to pry up those bars, of course—

It was fortunate that her mind was on the bars, because at that moment she glanced ahead and saw another of those black openings in the masonry beneath Schmidt's feet.

This one was open, unbarred—and ready to swallow him up!

With a cry of alarm she threw her arms around Schmidt just as his foot descended into the chasm. Nijam was a tall woman, if not particularly well-nourished, and she threw all her weight into the balance against his forward momentum. Schmidt was caught utterly off his guard; he fell back with a cry and sat down very heavily upon her skirts, which brought her down onto his shoulders like the Virgin in a Pietá. In the confusion the candle went out, leaving them gasping in the darkness on the brink of a drop goodness only knew how deep.

"Good Lord," Schmidt gasped. "What *is* it? I wasn't looking down—it's as though the floor gave way beneath my feet."

"Don't move," Nijam said, tightening her grip. She felt keenly aware that there was a great deal of Alphonse, and he was very solid. If he overbalanced, he would most likely drag her with him. "Someone left the bars off another of those floor vents."

For a moment there was silence. Schmidt took a deep breath and Nijam felt the planes of his chest rise beneath her fingers; she felt his heartbeat skittering beneath her palm. The novelty of the experience struck her and for a moment she tasted utter despair. Never before had she held Alphonse Schmidt so close to her heart. She knew with utter certainty that it would never happen again until the sun blasted the earth to atoms and then perhaps for a moment their particles might mix and in passing, touch... Her first and last embrace, and he could never even know what it meant to her.

Then he said, rather awkwardly, "Thanks. Do you have another candle? I think the last one fell through the vent."

Nijam released him hurriedly, but his weight upon her skirts still held her far too close. "No," she said, taking refuge in irritability. "You could have have kept a better grip on it; it would have been extremely useful about now. Have you some small, heavy object about you?"

"Here," Schmidt said. It was so dark that she had to feel his arm from the shoulder to the wrist before she could take the object, which proved to be a pocket-watch, from his hand. That upset her further. If she was inclined to believe in a Higher Power she would suspect it of taking a perverse kind of pleasure in putting her in this predicament of faux-intimacy.

"All right," Nijam said, "keep quiet and we'll see how far down this goes."

There was a splash, followed by rippling echoes.

"Water," she deduced, "and plenty of it, but not far down. I suppose that explains the damp! But why should there be *water* beneath the Opera?"

"Was that my pocket-watch?" Schmidt protested.

On mature consideration, perhaps she ought to have explained that she wanted an object he was willing to sacrifice on the altar of Science. "Don't you think we have bigger things to worry about, Schmidt? Mimi will steal you another."

"You can't just *steal* people's watches. Besides, I was attached to this one!"

"Yes, but only figuratively, which is a very great mercy." Nijam tried to drag the folds of her skirt out from beneath him. "Now, will you get off my skirt?"

The business was a ticklish one, with no light at all and the consciousness of that dangerous drop beneath them; but they managed it in the end. There was no point going forward in that darkness, so they turned and, using the wall as a guide, retraced their steps.

"You'd better let me go ahead," Nijam said as they began the journey, "and hold onto me in case anyone has been playing with the bars behind us."

"But if it's unsafe, surely I ought to go first."

Nijam sighed. "Just do as I ask! If one of us falls the other must catch them, and you are evidently more suited to the task than me. Here: put your hands around my waist."

There was a silence. "Put my hands *where?*"

"Oh, for heaven's sake," she snapped, and after that he made no further objections. She clasped his hands around her middle and set off trying to think of anything but the large gentle warmth seeping through the many layers of cloth and whalebone she wore. Instead she concentrated her thoughts upon their surroundings: the stone floor beneath her cautious feet; the masonry beneath her right hand; the smell of dust; the occasional eddies of moist air, laden with the distant sickly-sweet scent of garbage, that now and again blew past. There was no sound but the sound of their footsteps and the swish of her skirts, and Schmidt's breathing; his hands about her waist were wooden—if wood was warm and soft, with fingerprints one could map through one's underthings.

Nijam put her foot down upon iron bars; hesitated, tested, and moved forward. Schmidt followed. The bars remained in place, and then with a numbing sense of relief she came to the arched door and the narrow stair, with a glimmer of light far off, which had admitted them to this bottom-most cellar.

"All right; you can let go now," she said. Those unmoving hands fell away, leaving her feeling oddly melancholy. Schmidt brushed past her, once more taking the lead.

She did not tell us this until much later, but as he passed her, she glanced over her shoulder into the great cellar. And she saw two minute points of light, close together, gleaming in the darkness from which they had come.

Nijam's body stopped—heart, breath, and motion together. Then she blinked, and the eyes—the points of light—were gone.

It was nothing. Probably an animal had made its home down here, and that faint glow of light ahead of them had caught its eyes for a moment. She ran after Schmidt, and stopped herself with an effort from seizing hold of his jacket.

They went up the steps and saw a lamp bobbing to and fro

in the smaller cellar beyond.

Schmidt reached out as though motioning Nijam behind him; but before he could quite prepare himself for battle, the silence was rent by a shrill barking. A little terrier dog charged up to them and danced about their ankles, threatening murder and fury with his mouth, while his tail expressed transports of joy. The lamp drew nearer and they found themselves in the presence of a thin, stooped, wiry old man with a long beard, keen little eyes and a black silk opera-hat perched very tall and straight upon his hairless head. The dome-shaped cage he carried proclaimed his profession as a rat-catcher.

For a moment, Schmidt seemed at a loss for words.

"Lost your way, monsieur?" the rat-catcher asked in a voice that seemed hoarse with disuse.

"Er—no. We were looking for someone," he said.

The rat-catcher gave them a sceptical look. In the light of his lantern, Nijam became aware that she and Schmidt both appeared somewhat dishevelled. "You should be careful down here," she told him in halting French. "Someone left the bars off the opening in the floor and we nearly fell into the water. Have you seen Chalabi? She has disappeared."

He shook his head, and Schmidt added, "Or have you seen a man in dark clothing?"

"No, monsieur. There's no one down here—no one at all. Except the ghost." And he made the sign of the cross.

Nijam restrained the urge to laugh. After the very particular sort of terror she had experienced in the cellar, a mere ghost would have been welcome to her. But Schmidt said, quite composedly, "And the ghost? Have you seen *him?*"

"Oh, yes. He passed me a little while ago, going *up.*"

"Describe him," Nijam ordered.

"No, no, do not ask me to do that! Everyone knows what the ghost looks like!!" And the rat-catcher whistled to his dog and hurried away from them, down into the echoing vault that must have led the breadth of the cellars.

"Be careful of the bars!" Schmidt called after the man, but Nijam fairly dragged him towards the spiral staircase by which they had descended from the dressing-rooms, and upon which Demiana Chalabi had died.

"Up," she said fiercely. "If the murderer hid Chalabi's body somewhere in the cellars, he might have met the rat-catcher on his way up, and been mistaken for the ghost."

"He might have tossed her into the water through that uncovered vent," said Schmidt.

"We don't know that the same man removed the bars." But the possibility was there, all the same. Had it not been, she would not have insisted upon Schmidt clinging to her waist all the way back through the great cellar.

In all likelihood the murderer had laid a trap for her and her friends, reckless of who fell into it, and absolutely indifferent to the horrible, drawn-out death that might await them down there in the dark. Nijam knew herself to be a clever woman, whom any murderer would have to get up early in the morning to outwit. But this was a foe who knew the Opera far better than she did, and was possessed of far greater cruelty.

* * *

"After that," Nijam now explained, as Schmidt poured the tea, "we searched all the way up the stairs and into the foyer de la danse. But of course there was no sign of Chalabi or her murderer, and none of the other people we met could tell us anything."

"We ought to have sealed the whole Opera and searched it from top to bottom," Schmidt said, frowning almost as ferociously as Nijam herself.

"Impossible," Vasily said at once. "There are limits to the power even of the managers, my dear Schmidt! Can you imagine me trying to convince Dumortier to confine all of fashionable Paris to the Opera until the whole place could be searched from top to bottom, for a culprit you cannot describe, and a murder victim who is in the midst of the most triumphant performance of her career?" —Schmidt was effectively crushed.

"Our best clue is the vent," Nijam said. "What exactly is down there? Some kind of cistern, or underground lake?"

"I've no idea," Vasily answered at once. "But perhaps it can be dragged for bodies. I'll need to speak to Dumortier about it, of course."

I wondered precisely how much help Dumortier would be. He seemed to me quite wrapped up in his own concerns, and disinclined to pay attention to anyone else's. "What about all this talk of a ghost?" I asked. "The ballerinas last night were speaking of old M. Perrot—who is he, Mimi?"

At this Mimi shrugged. "All theatres are haunted," she said matter-of-factly, "because most artists are horribly suspicious. But old Perrot—he was the great ballet-master before Christophe, who danced with Marie Taglioni and with Carlotta Grisi in the days when modern ballet was being created. *Giselle* was his creation."

"But he's dead?"

"Oh yes—thoroughly. It happened four years ago, and until

then he used to come to the Opera every day, a white-haired little man with a tall walking-stick. And now, because M. Christophe covers his face and carries the same sort of wand, he is thought to be M. Perrot's ghost! It's ridiculous."

"If he never speaks," I said, "then how does he teach?"

Mimi shrugged. "Ballet is an art of mimicry. No one will say it, but it's true. If Christophe needs to explain anything, he signs and one of us translates for the little ones. I know the signs very well. At home in Finland, I have a deaf aunt."

"And Chalabi?" Nijam asked. "Was there any bad feeling between them?"

It was Mimi's turn to scowl, which she did with her whole face—bending her brows, and baring her teeth.

"What do you mean?" she demanded. "Do you suggest that M. Christophe would murder Chalabi? That is nonsense! Who told you so?"

"The rat-catcher," said Nijam. "I asked what the ghost looked like, didn't I? and he answered that everyone knows what the ghost looks like. He had to have been referring to Christophe."

"No, he hadn't!" Mimi declared passionately. "Has *he* seen M. Christophe's face? All he meant was that whoever-it-was was dressed and masked like M. Christophe! It might have been anyone! And for shame, that you should accuse a man who cannot speak! M. Christophe cannot defend himself, so you make him out to be a monster!"

Nijam's face became stiff and obstinate. "No, I don't," she said. "I asked only whether he and Chalabi had any reason to be at odds. It is a question that will need to be asked of everyone at the Opera, sooner or later." Mimi said nothing to this, and Nijam turned to Vasily. "What do *you* know about the man, Vasily?"

Vasily shrugged. "Dumortier says he's an eccentric, but a genius when it comes to ballet. He may be. After the Maryinsky; I find all this French ballet to be pretty passé."

Mimi sniffed. "It's *old*, not *worthless*," she said. "And it makes no sense that M. Christophe would be the murderer; why should he do away with his own prima ballerina? M. Christophe *made* Demiana Chalabi, and her contract has still years to run. If you investigate him, you will waste your time, and the real killer will get away."

With that, she stalked towards the door.

"Wait," I said, jumping to my feet. "We ought to discuss our next steps."

"I know my task," Mimi said, tossing her head. "I will inquire of the dancers as to who Chalabi has been seen with, and with whom she might have had a quarrel."

"It's not just that," I said. "Chalabi told me the killer would strike again; we need to keep you safe."

"There are hundreds of people at the Opera. No doubt he'll choose from any of them." But Mimi hesitated with her hand on the doorknob.

"I forgot to tell you," she added. "Yesterday, before the performance, an Okhrana man came to my dressing-room."

It has not happened very often in my life, but my legs suddenly gave way beneath me, depositing me upon the sofa. There was no sound in the room but the roaring in my ears. Then Vasily's hand closed upon mine, and I returned to the moment.

"Looking for me, I suppose," he said lightly, as though the words were not his own death-sentence. The Okhrana were, of course, the secret police employed by his cousin, Emperor

Nicky of Russia.

"No, not for you," Mimi said, rolling her eyes. "Not everything is about you, Vasya! No; it was Schmidt they wanted."

"Do they know he's in Paris?" Nijam demanded. It was difficult for one of her complexion to turn pale, but hers had gone a little grey. During our recent visit to Russia, the emperor's secret police had immediately arrested the lot of us, and it was Schmidt who drew their most eager attention. He had been released only because his memories had been erased, rendering him useless to the Great Powers. Evidently, it was a decision they now regretted.

"Be calm: they only know about me," Mimi assured us. "You know that the Okhrana have an office in Paris? They use it to watch for revolutionaries and runaway Grand Dukes."

"Good heavens," I said faintly.

Vasily squeezed my hand. "Take heart, Molly-my-dear! I'm not the only one of my cousins lying low in this city."

"It turns out the Russian secret police are fond of ballet," Mimi said bitterly. "I am identified as a past associate of Alphonse Schmidt, the bionic chemist, and instructed to report to the Paris office to answer questions about his whereabouts."

"And will you?" Schmidt asked. He had gone pale. Although Vasily's life would undoubtedly be at stake if he was discovered to be alive and well in Paris, Schmidt faced a fate which would be, in my estimation, even worse. Buried deep among his forgotten memories were certain scientific secrets to do with the creation of the horrible revenant gendarmes with which the Great Powers of Europe had once terrorised the populace. Among those Powers, the Russians alone knew that Schmidt still lived, and the Okhrana were evidently keen to secure him for the Emperor. Let him fall into their hands, and he would be kept under lock and key forever—in a laboratory, if he consented to create more of the loathsome creatures, and in the fortress of St Peter and Paul if not!

Mimi snorted. "And will I what—inform on you to the police, you mean? There aren't pearls enough in the world for *that*. I already told them we parted ways in Hong Kong."

"Mimi!" Schmidt cried, deeply touched. Even Nijam looked visibly relieved.

Mimi shrugged. "This time I had the luxury of choosing. With any luck they will send someone post-haste to Hong Kong and it will be months before they pick up our scent again—either of us. Meanwhile, the two of you should take care where you show your faces. It's possible you may be recognised."

"Oh, *Gospodi,* and I was about to audition as a tenor," said Vasily, straight-faced. "I hear there's an opening in the cast of *Tannhäuser.*" I sent him a pleading look, for I found the joke a poor one. At least, I thought, he had altered his appearance. He would be difficult, but not impossible to recognise.

"We're obliged to you, Mimi," Nijam said. "Tell us if you see the Okhrana again."

With that Mimi left us. Schmidt took out a handkerchief and mopped his face. Vasily attempted to release my hand, but I held him like a drowning woman and said, "Be careful, both of you. Try not to show your faces unless it's absolutely necessary."

"I blame myself," Vasily said, vexed. "If I had been thinking straight I would have arranged to fake Schmidt's death in Moscow, as well as my own. They were happy to let him be so long as he was safely attached to a Grand Duke inside Russia, but now they think the secret to revenant-making is wandering the earth without a master. Whether he remembers or not, they'll do anything in their power to get him back."

"They won't be the only ones, if the thing becomes generally known," Nijam put in. "The French used revenants a great deal, especially against the anarchists. And the Germans were about to train them for the military."

There was a moment's silence. I shuddered to think of the revivified corpses being pressed into the army, incapable of being killed or stopped. And where would the necessary bodies be found? In prisons, among the inmates? In far-flung colonies, among the colonised? Since I took up thievery, I had begun to see the ugly side of life, and could no longer put much trust in the goodness of the rich and powerful.

The rather bleak silence was broken by the chime of the clock on the mantelpiece striking one o'clock.

"Is that the time?" Vasily exclaimed, getting to his feet. "Really, I ought not to be late on my first day managing the Paris Opera. I suppose I shall see what I can get out of Dumortier regarding M. Christophe—and I'll interview Christophe as well, when I review his contract."

"Good," said Nijam decidedly. "With all deference to Mimi, our only clue points directly to Christophe. Either he is the murderer, or there is a very good reason for the murderer to want us to think so."

"And don't forget to ask about those vents," I put in.

"No," Vasily agreed. "I'll ask Dumortier what's down there, and perhaps insist upon retrieving Schmidt's pocket-watch. And a body, if one can be found."

"As for me, I'll visit the Larousse family," said I, "and oh, I suppose the Chalabi family also. Poor things!"

"What about me?" Schmidt asked. His hands had clenched into fists. "Please don't tell me to stay out of it, now that the Okhrana are looking for me. I'll wear a mask myself if I must."

"You ought to be safe enough in the Opera as my chargé d'affaires," said Vasily. "You're under an assumed name, after all. There can't be more than one or at most two policemen in the whole of Russia who'd know you to look at you, and we may safely presume that *they* have been dispatched post-haste to Hong Kong, if they were ever in Paris at all. … Besides, we have work for you. You and Nijam must continue investigating the Opera. As the manager, I won't have time to question the stable-hands and furnace-men, the seamstresses and the box-ladies. I'll provide you with a list of the Opera employees, and you must try to speak to as many of them as you can about where they were last night during Chalabi's performance, and what they saw there."

Nijam raised her eyebrows. "You don't believe that Dumortier will help us? The thing might be done more quickly with his assistance."

Vasily stroked his beard, which, although unfashionably square and long, was also thick and rather soft-looking. "I don't believe he will," said he. "As Miss Dark noticed last night, M. Dumortier is quite disinclined to be useful."

"We'll have to rely on Mimi to gather information among the corps de ballet," Nijam said.

"Let us not depend upon her too much," I said. "She is so tired and busy."

Nijam scowled as she and Schmidt made ready to depart. "I don't like her being in that corps de ballet, and I don't trust that M. Christophe. He's no ghost: he's a killer. Mark my words."

"For the moment we must trust to Mimi's infinite resource and sagacity," said I, and with that they took their leave.

Now that the others were gone, Vasily seemed in no hurry to leave. Taking up his hat and his sword-stick, he raised my hand to his lips in a gesture that was half courtly, half affectionate. His lips did not *quite* touch my skin, for he had been strictly forbidden to take liberties, and he was adhering to that injunction with a quite unaccustomed zeal. But I repressed a little sigh of happiness all the same. Vasily as my acknowledged lover was somebody to whom I could speak frankly. I had never before been able to tell a man how much I admired him, and it was a topic upon which Vasily was willing to listen without interruption or demur, for hours at a time if I wished. The arrangement was one that suited us both admirably.

"Do you know that you're far too charming for anybody's good?" I asked him now. "No, what a foolish question. Of course you know."

"My dear, you cannot conceive how it puts me at ease to hear it. Where *are* you playing at, with that young exquisite, Leuze?"

"Deleuze," I corrected. "He's thoroughly bourgeois, you know; he just doesn't like to spell it that way. When I met him on the boat from London, and he was most obliging and gallant in his attentions. Naturally I thought he might be useful in the future. He's quite taken with the Baroness, which is a tremendous joke."

"Indeed! I don't find it funny at all. Shall I challenge him to a duel?"

"Don't you dare!" It was a joke—of course it was a joke—but I could make such jokes, myself. "Do you know that *I* used to be quite taken with him, once upon a time, in the days when I first came to the Continent? He has no notion at all that I'm Molly Dark, his sister's governess! What do you think of *that?*"

Vasily was affronted, but not outraged. *"You* fancied *him?* Why, he's the worst gossip in Paris and more than half in love with himself."

"Of course he is," said I. "I thought my bad taste in men was an established fact."

"The things I have to endure! Well, don't encourage him too much, my dear, or I shall be obliged to shoot myself and then Deleuze. Don't laugh! What do I have in life to give me joy, but you?"

I did laugh at him, because it did him no good to think that he could win sympathy in such a manner. "What indeed, but good friends, warm clothes, fine food, and a whole Opera to play with! Good heavens! what more could any man want?"

"Someone to love me," he purred.

"I would love you just as much if you were a ghost," I told him. "So if you ever feel inclined to shoot yourself, don't hold back on *my* account."

"Divine condescension!" he murmured, and although he wrinkled his nose, there was a ring of sincerity to his voice. "Tell me, my angel, *why* do you love me? I can't make any sense of the thing."

My first impulse was to say that I had never had the opportunity to love anyone else. But I could imagine how those words might sound, once they were spoken. They would not be a very great compliment to either of us.

"Well," I said instead, "you are very good-looking, Vaska, and very charming. You know how to have a good time, and you are smart and elegant."

"So is Deleuze."

That much was true. "And you care for other people's feelings," I added. "You *pretend* to be careless and flippant, but it is all show, to protect your reputation. M. Deleuze doesn't truly care for anyone but himself, and it's his manners that are all show. Now you must tell me why you love me, even though I am only a governess, and a bourgeois, and I tease you to distraction."

His eyes gleamed with affection. "But that's precisely it, Molly-my-dear: you *are* a governess, and you've always been firmly convinced that you could make a better man of me. You see me as I *could* be and not as I am. How could I possibly resist? I have the most desperate desire to prove you right."

He paused, but, seeing that I was too overcome to speak, he added in a hopeful sort of voice, "Now, what about a kiss?"

That helped me tremendously: I recovered my countenance at once. "Don't be an opportunist, Vasily! And don't plume yourself upon your reformation, for I have a bone to pick with you. How could you have embarrassed poor Schmidt like that yesterday—to say nothing of Nijam herself?"

Vasily sniffed. "*Something* had to be done for them. They're even worse than dear old George and May."

Some old acquaintances of his, no doubt, or perhaps servants he had employed in London. I made a note to ask him about them later. "Just be careful you don't ruin things entirely! For one thing, I don't think either of them much care to have things *done* for them."

"Never mind! I won't do it again," Vasily said, once more

kissing the air half an inch from my hand. He went away to the Opera leaving me to feel, amidst the glow of his compliments, a little dissatisfied. He seemed quite unrepentant. Perhaps it was my fault, for not putting my objections to him more strongly. Had he seen Schmidt's face, or Nijam's outrage, he would have understood how thoughtless his actions had been—or would he?

I did not like to be the only person Vasily treated with respect. It struck me that if I was the only person he treated with respect, then he had not really changed at all. His respect would be short-lived; his jealousy would only increase; and then I would have the dickens of a time trying to put an end to our courtship without causing a terrible scene and possibly needing Nijam to carry out that murder.

I might have accepted Vasily as my suitor, but I had not yet made up my mind to accept him for better or for worse; and if I did, I was quite determined that it *should* be for the better, and not for the worse.

As for Nijam and Schmidt, while I had been bidding my lover farewell, they made their way up the Boulevard Haussmann to the Opera. At first Nijam set a brisk pace, for after the undignified scenes in the Opera cellars last night she was feeling rather skittish. No sooner did she make a fresh resolve to discourage Schmidt's attentions, than she was receiving his love-letters and exhorting him to lay hands upon her person. It was enough to make anyone believe in a mischievous Deity.

Schmit had no trouble lengthening his stride to keep up with her. He did not seem talkative, however. A sidelong glance informed Nijam that his brows were knitted, and Discontent rode upon them.

At length he said, "I can't get it out of my mind, you know—the fact that she was murdered before my very eyes, and I did nothing to stop it."

Nijam herself had spent a bad night contemplating the same thing.

"I wasn't *afraid*," Schmidt added, in a rather defensive tone of voice. "Only shocked. For a moment I couldn't believe what I was seeing, and I couldn't seem to *move*."

"Of course not," Nijam said, biting her lip. "According to Dark, her shade predicted more murders. We were meant to find out if someone murdered Larousse and catch the man who did it, and instead the murderer struck again right under our noses. We might as well have stayed in London playing croquet, for all the good we've done."

"Do you think it really was Christophe?"

Nijam thought on this for a moment. "Mimi's right," she said at last. "I could understand somebody trying to sabotage *Tannhäuser* in favour of *Giselle,* but it doesn't make *sense* that such a person would murder the prima ballerina."

"The only alternative is that the killer is trying to sabotage the Opera itself. Perhaps we're looking for a culprit outside the Opera."

Nijam shook her head. "No. There's one more possibility, which is much worse, because such men are far more difficult to find and stop."

"What do you mean?"

"I mean that he might be the sort of man who murders for no motive at all, but the simple pleasure of killing." Nijam glanced up at the beautiful man beside her, and her throat clenched with worry. "Stay hidden in the Opera, Schmidt, but don't mistake it for safety. The Okhrana aren't the only danger in Paris."

Schmidt stopped walking so suddenly that Nijam got ahead of him and had to turn back.

"Stay hidden?" he asked in a low voice. "*I* was the one who stood by and let him kill Chalabi. It's *my* duty to stop him. No—stopping him isn't enough. I want him caught and guillotined, so that he can never do this again."

His voice shook with emotion, and Nijam's heart smote her. Oh, what did it matter? She couldn't treat the man like a leper if they were to be working together, protecting each other from the killer. If he got the wrong idea she would simply have to tell him straight that she would never be his.

She let out a sigh. "I'm sorry I called you a coward. I didn't mean physically—no one could accuse you of that. So for the love of God don't throw your life away on a sense of false guilt." She put out her hand. "Call it Pax?"

Alphonse Schmidt grasped her hand, flushing a little. "Pax," he agreed. "Let's solve a murder."

Chapter VI.

Having put on one of my new London afternoon-dresses, I was ready to go about the day's business. As I waited for a cab to appear, I sorted through the calling-cards which my concierge had collected in the course of the morning. I expected cards from Deleuze, Caillot, and Dumortier, of course. But there were cards from other people, too; mostly gentlemen, but a few ladies as well, paying their respects and asking me to attend various salons, soireés, and even balls. The Opera itself had sent an invitation to a bal masqué occurring this evening, at which I knew it was Vasily's intention to secure his escape from the terrible burden of Opera management.

Once again I found myself scarcely able to believe my good fortune. For seven years I had been firmly excluded from such events, watching enviously from the shadows as my employers and their friends enjoyed a whirl of gaiety. Recently, of course, in a variety of assumed guises, I had begun to venture out into society and enjoy myself—but always with a job to do, and always in the consciousness that I was only an intruder upon that society, and not properly native to it. All that had changed now: one day soon I would be free to take my place in the world, with no assumed names, no jobs to do, no complicated deceptions to carry out. And this was a foretaste of it.

I paid my first call of the day to the House of Worth—a brief, but exhilarating visit. As I came away, I reflected that it would be wise for the sake of my masquerade to follow Nijam's suggestion and engage a real lady's-maid. Indeed, now that I was a woman of substance, such an attendant might become an absolute necessity, for it had taken me a deal of time and trouble to clothe myself and dress my hair for the Opera last night, and I could see a great many other such appearances in my future.

That thought was also exhilarating. With professional assistance, I might spend every day of my life looking as ravishing as I had the previous evening. Oh, I *liked* having money!

My second call was more serious. Madame Larousse, the tenor's widow, lived not far from the Opera in the Rue du Faubourg St Honoré. As the cab drew to a halt, I took a moment to compose myself. My fortunes might be rising, but the unfortunate Mme Larousse must still be overcome by fresh grief.

I was surprised, therefore, upon being shown to an airy little sitting-room where the widow was taking breakfast, to find her in the company of a gentleman.

Neither of them were very young. The lady's hair beneath her black widow's cap had once been gold but was now touched with silver, and the gentleman, who was perusing a newspaper in companionable silence, did not much resemble the hero of an affair, being tubby and spectacled. Well! thought I. It was France; they did things differently here, and things that in England would have been hushed up and smothered over were dealt with quite matter-of-factly here. But was it delicate to ask a lady questions about her husband's untimely death in the presence of her lover? My years as a governess in this city had not prepared me for such social dilemmas.

"Good morning," I said, trying not to appear at all discountenanced. "Madame Larousse, I presume?"

She had been studying the card I sent in, and now rose to make her bows. "Madame la Baronne von Jörger? To what do I owe this very great honour?"

I sent the gentleman another covert glance. He did not seem embarrassed at all. How I envied him! "It's a rather delicate matter," said I. "You may know that my husband, the Baron, has very recently been appointed to manage the Opera alongside M. Dumortier?"

"Of course. I congratulate your husband."

She looked rather hopeful.

"I heard of your sad bereavement, and…" It was no use. I glanced once again towards the gentleman. "Do you think we might speak alone, madame?"

She glanced about the room and turned back to me in gentle perplexity. "Are we not alone, madame?"

The words were struck from my lips. I saw my mistake at once, of course. The gentleman was the imprint of M. Larousse himself, and had I been paying attention to the table setting before him, which was perfectly untouched, I might have guessed the truth. I blushed to think of the unseemly behaviour I had imputed to the lady.

Then in a flash I saw how my faux pas could be turned to some use. "Oh!" I cried. "I thought—I beg your pardon, but I saw a gentleman in that chair, reading his newspaper."

For a moment Mme Larousse only looked more deeply puzzled still. I saw I would need to help her a little.

"Is it possible, madame, that your husband was a man of about forty-five, with a dark moustache and kind eyes?"

At that the lady went so pale that I feared she might faint. "You—you *see* him?"

"Some of us are particularly sensitive to the Beyond," I said, looking as spiritual as I knew how. "Here, be seated; you look pale."

She gripped my arms as I helped her into a seat, and did not let go, even when I attempted to straighten. "Is it true, then? Did he really kill himself, and leave his wife and children to go begging?"

Her words, and the piteous tone in which they were spoken, went through me like a knife. The police must have told her that it was a case of suicide; and now she, as we had been, was left to break her heart twice—once for her loss, and again for the cruel betrayal of the husband and father who had left her destitute…

Ah, how well I understood her feelings!

"Ask him," she begged me. "If you can really see him, surely he will answer you!"

I cast a glance at the imprint, who seemed entirely unconscious of his wife's distress. I could not ask *him*, of course: he was only a relic of Mme Larousse's grief, and would not respond to my questions. But to one question he had already revealed the answer: Mme Larousse had no more idea of the reason for her husband's death than I did myself.

I wanted to give her some comfort, if I could. "You shall not go begging for your bread," I told her. "I think he has sent me to ensure that you will not endure that, at least."

She seized my hand. "Madame, you are an angel! Do you really mean it? The Opera has given us nothing—nothing."

"What! nothing at all?" I prompted. Not that I would have expected it; Larousse could not have completed his contract, and was unlikely to merit a state pension on that account.

"You will think that I am greedy, madame, but indeed they should have, for it was partly the Opera's fault. My poor Pierre was driven to his death. I will show you."

So saying, she jumped to her feet again and ran from the room. A moment later she returned and thrust into my hand a sheaf of papers, many of them scrawled upon Opera letterhead. I leafed through them, and my whole body went cold. They were nasty, bullying things—threats and insults, telling M. Larousse to leave the Opera, that he had no place there and that he sang like a toad.

"These used to arrive every day," she told me, watching my face hungrily for any sign of sympathy. "When it was already too late I showed them to the police—but that did no good at all."

"Have you any idea who might have sent these?" I inquired, shuddering a little over the vitriol they contained.

The widow bit her lip and hesitated. I saw that she had an answer for me, but feared to speak it.

"My father died when I was a girl," I said gently. "I know what it is to be in straitened circumstances, and to wonder what we might have done to make him abandon us with so little. As it turned out, the truth was quite different. Perhaps the truth will be kind to you, also—if you are brave enough to seek it."

Mme Larousse drew a great deep gulp of breath. "I'll trust you, then," she said, "but if you cannot believe me, I ask only that you bury my folly unrepeated in your heart. Madame Baroness, this paper is only found in the managers' office of the Opera! It was this that most injured my poor Pierre!"

"The managers' office!" I repeated, aghast. "But then is it M. Dumortier you suspect, or the former manager?"

"Oh! *you* know who it is that hates modern opera, and only wishes to stage endless Romantic ballets from sixty years ago!"

"M. Dumortier!" I repeated. "But surely the police commissioned an expert to compare this handwriting to M. Dumortier's?"

"Not in the least," said the widow sorrowfully. "He drove my poor Pierre to kill himself, and he drove old M. Mandrillon to Baden, and he paid the police to overlook the evidence. And now there is nothing to prevent him showing nothing but *Giselle* and *La Sylphide* and *Thaïs* and *Lakmé* until we all perish of stultification! And to think that the Paris Opera was once the avant garde!"

I did not much care for the avant garde myself. *Lakmé* and *Thaïs* I liked, because I could understand them. But I suppose that art is like anything else; it benefits from new blood. And at any rate it seemed hard, if artists were never to be allowed to innovate.

"It would be very shocking," I said, "but I have heard stranger things in my time."

"People with money can get away with anything at all," said Mme Larousse, "and who will hold them to account?"

"I will do what I can," I assured her, "and if you will entrust me with one of these letters, I will have a sample taken of the handwriting of all the Opera managers and secretaries, so that the Baron and I may get to the bottom of things."

Having modestly decried her gratitude, I went downstairs in

a thoughtful mood. I would be a fool to rule out M. Dumortier from my list of suspects. Yet presumably there were a great many secretaries and acting-managers and under-managers at the Opera, with free access to the official stationery. If M. Larousse really had been hounded to his death by one of these, I was sure that Vasily would ferret out the culprit, whoever it might be.

I had not paid my cabman to wait for me in the street. It was an extravagance I had never been able to justify in the past, and I could not quite bring myself to do it now. Someday I might want that handful of sous to buy myself a pinwheel or a cup of tea, or to endow an orphanage.

As I waited to hail a new cab, therefore, I considered the motive Mme Larousse had suggested. If her husband *did* kill himself under a campaign of bullying conducted by somebody in the Opera management, then it seemed the likeliest thing in the world that the motive was artistic. Somebody did not like Wagner. I thought of the handsome old gentleman I had met upon the previous evening. Dumortier seemed the sort of person who liked to have his own way: in the very polish of his manners was that self-conscious magnanimity—that noblesse oblige that was itself a mode of self-congratulation. He would bow to a lady, not because he reverenced the lady but because he liked to think himself a gallant gentleman. And he might very well decide that the bourgeois masses of Paris needed to subsist forever on an artistic diet of aging French Romanticism; and anyone who was unlucky enough to stand in his way might feel the iron hand within the velvet paw.

A rich and powerful man, accustomed to having things his own way, need not consider the Paris Opera too small a kingdom to conquer.

I did not think, however, that Dumortier would have a ballerina strangled on a back staircase. Certainly not the prima ballerina in one of his pet productions. Even if Chalabi had rebelled or otherwise threatened his rule, it made no sense to do away with her at the height of a gala performance, when the crime would almost certainly be discovered at once.

All the same, perhaps what I found at the Chalabi house would surprise me. I hailed a passing cab and gave them the address, which was not far away. A few minutes later I dismounted outside a row of tall, thin townhouses all huddled up together like the dancers in an ill-assorted chorus line. Anything more different to the tall, uniform tenements of the Boulevard Haussmann could scarcely be imagined: of these houses, some were tall, some short, some extremely thin, and all of slightly varying colours of cream and slate. The house I wanted was particularly short and squat, comprising only three levels—basement, entry, and attic—with three columns of windows, a charming little pair of spiral-moulded pilasters to either side of the front door, and a horseshoe-shaped staircase to get you across the sunken area to the door. When I tell you that the attic dormer windows had round arches, so that the house looked like nothing so much as a sleepy infant blinking placidly at the passing world, you will understand why I fell in love with the place at once. I wondered whether I could convince the Chalabis to sell the house to me, for it looked like the perfect place in which to install Vasily and his figured-silk dressing-gown.

In front of the house a carriage was waiting at the foot of the stairs. It was a private carriage, for the coachman was in a smart livery. That gave me pause, and instead of knocking at the door I passed on and pretended to be buttoning my gloves. After a little more time the front door to the Chalabi house opened and M. Dumortier emerged.

This was very interesting! I waited until the manager had entered his carriage and driven away, and then I went up the horseshoe steps and knocked on the little door. When it opened a moment later I found myself face to face with Khadijah Gobara, Mlle Chalabi's own lady's-maid. She was evidently surprised to see me. I was less surprised to see the redness of her eyes, as though she had spent much of the night weeping.

"Good morning, Mlle Gobara," I said gently, proffering the card of Baroness von Jörger. "I wonder if I might visit the family."

She gulped. "They aren't at home, madame."

I did not believe this, because M. Dumortier had evidently been with them quite recently. Still, if the family did not wish to see me, I could scarcely intrude upon them.

"I take it that Mlle Chalabi did not return home last night, then?" I inquired, thinking that the maid might speak to me if the family did not.

Mlle Gobara's lip trembled. "Oh, madame, I *am* so afraid!" Just then a voice called indistinctly from within the house, and the maid threw a nervous glance over her shoulder. "I'm sorry," she added. "I can't tell you anything more."

"Keep my card," I said. "I am looking for a good lady's maid, if you find yourself in need of employment." Then she closed the door and I returned, mystified, to the street.

After a moment's thought, I hailed another cab and had myself returned to the Opera. My assumed name opened my way to the managers' office, which was situated to one side of the great, gilded entrance lobby near the sweeping staircase that led upwards to the theatre itself. I was astonished to find a long line of people in the antechamber, all waiting to go in and see the Baron. I quailed and nearly retreated—but then it occurred to me that I was a Baroness and could throw my weight around. Therefore, I marched up to the secretary at the desk and demanded to see my husband.

A moment later the prima donna who had been expressing herself shrilly within that hidden sanctum emerged and sailed past with the brown curls atop her head bouncing energetically—I recognised her as the soprano from last night's selection from *Tannhäuser.* Then the secretary got up and ushered me deferentially into the office.

The office, of course, was no common pigeon-hole for obscure clerks and musty stacks of paper: it was a kaleidoscope of gold leaf and polished marble. In the midst of it, enthroned behind a gleaming desk like a modern-day Louis XIV, Vasily was hunting through a sheaf of papers with a red pencil and evident relish, humming jubilantly under his breath. I believe it was the climactic trio from *Faust.*

"Madame la Baronne," announced the secretary, and Vasily dropped his red pencil as though it had burned him.

"My dear!" he exclaimed, arising from his seat. "What a surprise! What a pleasure! …What are you doing here?"

The secretary retreated and closed the door behind him, allowing me to speak freely. "I wanted to tell you what I've discovered this afternoon visiting Mme Larousse and the Chalabis. I think we may have a new suspect. Is it a bad time?"

"What? Oh, no! Not at all! I'm bored out of my wits," he said, lying through his teeth. "All the same, you'd better be quick about it. I have about three dozen more artists to see this afternoon, and this preposterous contract of Mlle Saunders-Britton's to amend. The work is overwhelming. I'm absolutely swamped."

"You and Mimi both," I said affectionately. Then I showed him the poison-pen letter, and told him of Mme Larousse's suspicions of Dumortier, together with the coincidence that I should have caught that gentleman visiting the Chalabi house.

"That's very interesting indeed," said Vasily, frowning at the letter. "I have been asking a few questions myself, and I don't much like how Dumortier responded. He's absolutely refused to allow anyone to drag the cistern beneath the Opera. He says that it's too deep and too dangerous to send workmen down, and that there's no reason to meddle with it. But it's not merely that. He *looks* guilty, as well as suspicious."

"What do you mean?"

"I can't explain it—it's in the way he looks and moves. I haven't noticed anything else odd about the man, except that I saw him in the Place de l'Opéra with a raven riding on his shoulder."

"A raven! Perhaps it's a pet?"

"If that's so, then where does he keep it when he's at the Opera? I've seen his office; there's no perch or birdcage there." Vasily touched his face. "It's this new prosthetic eye, I think. It's very sharp and clear; it gives me too much, sometimes. I keep noticing things I never did before."

"Then it might be useful," I said, "but I think Miss Nijam will want a little more hard proof before she's willing to approve making Dumortier our target."

"He ought to be," Vasily said thoughtfully. "But, my dear, even if we can prove that M. Dumortier wrote these letters, I doubt that it would be enough to condemn him in the eyes of society, let alone the law. He might have carried out a mean-spirited campaign of bullying, but unless we can prove that he actually put the noose about poor Larousse's neck, we might be best advised to make the Chalabi case our first concern."

"Naturally," said I, "but if we *can* solve the mystery of the poison-pen letters, it might provide a helpful clue for the Chalabi case."

"Very well: I shall collect the handwriting samples. The other question is, what should be done for the bereaved families? If the Opera is responsible for either of these deaths, then the Opera should do something towards their support."

I could not resist softly clapping my gloved hands. I was not like Nijam: I did not revel in the process of piecing together evidence into a chain of ghastly misdeeds. I much preferred the part where the wrongdoer was tricked into betraying himself. "I've been thinking about that," I said. "Everyone says that Dumortier practically worships the great ballets of the past. What if we could find an artefact of the past—a shoe of Taglioni's, say, or a memoir of M. Perrot's? We could sell it to him at some inflated price and use the proceeds to support poor Mme Larousse."

"Oh, yes!" Vasily said, laughing. "And if we can't find one?"

"We'll find one," I said. "At worst, I'll bet there's any amount of likely things lying forgotten in the Opera archives."

With an admiring look, Vasily raised my hand to his lips. "Mimi's had a bad influence on you, my dear."

There was a rap on the door, and I quickly distanced myself from the man I was supposed to be in a bitter dispute with. Just in the nick of time, too, for the door opened at once and Dumortier himself stalked in.

"Baron!" he cried. "What can you mean by letting half the

stable-hands go?"

"Forty per cent. of them, to be precise," Vasily responded coolly. "Useless people who I can only presume are state clients looking for a sinecure. What's wrong with giving such people a pension, if they must be supported? We don't want them here. Anyway, do you mind, my dear fellow? I have some pressing business to discuss with the Baroness."

"Please don't worry, monsieur," I said to Dumortier, settling my hat a little more firmly upon my head. "I don't see the point of discussing anything further with the Baron. Don't forget that legal matter I spoke to you about, monsieur!"

"Yes, yes; that's tonight. I remember," Vasily said carelessly.

Dumortier held the door open for me to depart. As I made a show of putting on my gloves, I said to him in my most winning voice, "By the way, monsieur, I meant to tell you last night, but all the excitement over Mlle Chalabi drove it from my mind. I would have *loved* to have met the great M. Perrot! Tell me, does he have any family still living? Perhaps I might pay my respects."

"A niece, I believe," Dumortier said. "Amélie Perrot. She will be attending the bal masqué tonight—but pray don't let us keep you, Baroness." I gave an elaborate curtsey and tripped lightly away.

Chapter VII.

The *legal matter* which I had exhorted Vasily not to forget, was, of course, the arrangement of our divorce—though perhaps not in the way that Dumortier took it. Of course, that evening there would be a bal masqué at the Opera. I had never attended such an occasion, although I had heard them denounced from the pulpit as sinks of vice and infamy, where principle and identity alike were discarded and the revellers indulged themselves in every sort of dissipation!

Needless to say, I would not have chosen to attend such an occasion now, had it not been for the grave necessity of catching Vasily betraying me with a ballerina—or, at least, *seeming* to do so. The thing must be done; and it could not possibly be done in the same dress in which I had visited the Opera last night. Despite the lateness of the hour, I once again made myself known to the good people at the House of Worth, for the purpose of collecting the gown I had ordered for the evening. The necessary alterations, to be made in such a rush, had cost me a fabulous sum of money; but I was shortly once again beholding myself in the gilt-edged mirror with a dazed awareness of having been transformed into an entirely new creature.

This was once again a severely simple red dress in silk velvet;

but this time the red was as bright as holly-berries. A band of red velvet crossed the bodice from one shoulder, passing almost beneath the opposite breast; which, together with its corresponding shoulder, was clad in ivory satin with a gauzy overlay. A heavy red tassel hung from the band. That was all the ornamentation the dress needed: it was otherwise starkly sculptural. There had been other dresses, too, frothing with lace and embroidery, but the modiste assigned to me had, like Mimi, been of the opinion that my tall frame required something simpler. With one look at the glass, I knew the woman understood her business.

"Will that be all, madame?" the woman asked, and I cleared my throat and admitted rather bashfully that I would also require a domino-cloak to go over the dress.

She clicked her tongue. "Ah, madame, you are going to the Opera bal masqué! That is always a very fine occasion. And one of the most democratic of our traditions, for it is open to anyone with the price of a ticket. Here, madame, let us see how this fits you. It was commissioned by a lady who no longer wants it." Still chattering, she helped me to draw on a long black cloak with a voluminous hood, made of a crisp silk so fine that the slightest gust of air caused it to billow out revealing all the scarlet magnificence beneath. By the time I departed, carrying a small fortune's worth of the most magnificent garments that money could buy, and with the name of an equally prestigious mask-maker written down upon a slip of paper in my pocket, I felt that I was rather looking forward to the ball than otherwise. It sounded like a very brilliant affair, and if the fun *did* get a little wild, at least I was unlikely to meet any vampires, werewolves, sirens, or assorted other monsters while I was there!

Vasily had counselled me to arrive no sooner than midnight, when the festivities would be reaching their height. I went home, therefore, and found a note awaiting me from M. Deleuze, asking whether I meant to attend. I returned another asking him to be my cavalier for the evening, and directing him to meet me in the grand foyer ten minutes before midnight. Then I had a little supper and a nap.

Promptly at the time appointed, I alit from my carriage and climbed the steps to the great porch, where a stream of masked and dominoed merrymakers were still climbing towards the great doors. The foyer itself was crowded with gorgeously dressed people, some of them already very merry, wielding champagne-coupes and raucous voices. Upstairs could be heard the strains of a small orchestra and the rhythmic tap of shoes; the dancing must be happening in the great crush-room directly overhead. Reaching up to settle my transmitter a little more firmly into my ear, I looked about me for M. Deleuze.

Instead, abruptly, I was accosted by a short, burly man in a black robe that looked as though it had seen better days, for the dye was fading in patches and it was generously besprinkled with the hairs of some domestic animal. All I could tell of the man beneath the half-mask he wore was that it had been some time since he had last shaved.

"Madame la Baronne?" he asked, in a voice that indicated how little he cared for baronesses.

I wondered whether I ought to encourage him. But in any case Deleuze would be along in a moment, and in the meantime I might trust my wits to keep me safe. "Yes, my good man?"

I thought that his lip curled a little at that. But he adopted a wheedling tone that sat rather ill with his gruff voice and said, "You have a kind face, Baroness. I know you'll help a poor devil with an ailing wife and ten children to support, won't you?"

I smiled serenely, despite his impertinence in addressing me as "Baroness" rather than the more respectful "madame". "Is it money you want?"

"In fact, I wondered if you'd put in a word for me with the Baron. I know a lot of men were let go from the stables yesterday. Nobody knows horses like me. I was a peasant before I was a coachman, but now I have no work at all."

I do not think that he can have been a very good actor, for he recited the story as though he had it by heart. Really! The audacity of the man! No sooner had Vasily cleared out one set of sinecured idlers, than a new cohort presented themselves!

"No work, and ten children!" I said sweetly. "How unfortunate! What are their names?"

His mouth dropped open. I had caught him completely off his guard. "Er," he said. "There is Jean, and Jacques, and Jeanne, and Jacqueline—"

"My good man," I said with a kindly air, for he was doing his best, "I should advise you to prepare your story a little better if you wish to fool anyone."

For a moment he was completely out of countenance. Then he rallied, and his voice was sincere when he spoke again. "I see you're cleverer than I took you to be, Baroness. In fact, I need this job desperately, and more than one person's life may depend upon it. Put in a word for me with the Baron, there's a good woman, and I'll be most devotedly in your debt."

I regarded him thoughtfully for a moment. The ring of solemnity in his voice troubled me, and I felt instinctively that if I wished for peaceful days I ought not to help him.

"I'm afraid you overestimate my power over the Baron," I said at last, grateful for the loophole provided by this part of my masquerade. "These days he and I are not on the best of terms."

My interlocutor held out a scrap of paper with a name and address written upon it. "I don't have a card, but if you ever need something done for you, you will know where to find me. I'm a useful man and I play by my own rules."

The offer put a bad taste in my mouth. If he had had money he would probably have tried to bribe me, but since he did not, he was offering services, of any dubious nature. No doubt this was another of the peculiar privileges of wealth—being beset by petitioners who desperately wanted something and were not too nice about how they got it. I felt that I ought to draw myself up to my full height and spurn what he offered; but I hesitated, for I felt quite alone in that glittering crowd. Then suddenly Deleuze and Caillot came up on either side of me and Deleuze said in tones of raillery that identified him at once despite his mask and domino, "Why, madame, you look puzzled! But of course you must accept! One never knows when such an offer may come in handy!"

Evidently this was quite a common occurrence for Deleuze, so that he felt no trouble at all in demanding services from people driven by desperation to desperate measures. I must not seem to be naïve; so I cleared my throat, hoped that the warmth in my cheeks was not too visible, and said with dignity, "Thank you, monsieur. If it is within my power to do you good, I shall certainly call upon you."

The little man gave me a curt and businesslike nod before retreating into the crowd, and Caillot scoffed a little. "Delightful manners," he murmured.

"Probably an anarchist," Deleuze agreed.

At that word I shuddered, recalling how much the French anarchists loved their bombs and assassinations. During my last sojourn in this city it seemed that there had been a dynamite outrage in the newspaper headlines every second week. Was that the reason for the strange intentness of the man's manner? Glancing down at the paper I held, I read the name *Jacques Dupont* and the address of a flat in Montmartre. Neither of those was very reassuring.

Still, I had bigger business to attend tonight. Tucking the scrap of paper away where it could be investigated later, I turned to Deleuze with my brightest smile. His friend Caillot, I observed, already had a lady on his arm, although her face was obscured by a mask. "Don't let us speak of such things!" I said. "How shall we enjoy ourselves first?"

Deleuze laughed. "Well, there is champagne and supper in the Rotunda, and dancing in the crush-room, and as you see there is the grand staircase, where the best costumes can be seen."

"And then there are the theatre boxes, if you want a little privacy," said Caillot, with a smile I did not like. His fair companion tittered.

Thanks to Vasily and Mimi I knew about the boxes, and the unsanctioned use to which they were put at such events. They were indeed about to be very useful to us, though not quite in the way M. Caillot meant. In the meantime, I had another end in view.

"I'm told that Mlle Perrot is expected to attend," I said. "The niece of the great ballet-master, I mean. I'm anxious to pay my respects."

"Oh! la petite Perrot!" Deleuze said with a laugh. "She ought to be in the Grand Salon, holding court with that Dargent woman. Of course you must see them—Dargent and Perrot, the female Damon and Pythias, whom everyone worships. Onwards!"

He offered me his arm and forged a way up the grand staircase. Caillot and his friend followed, and little as I trusted any of them, I was glad not to be alone in that crush of painted faces. Strange, glittering costumes lined the steps, preening and displaying themselves like the mannequins in a shop-window. Some blew kisses or performed contortions, told jokes or flung handfuls of confetti. Then I looked into *one* masked face and caught the ruby glow of a vampire's eyes. My heart leaped into my throat at the thought that one of Vasily's horrible family might be here, and still thirsting for his blood. Man or vampire, it wore a black domino, and swept an arm about a pert-looking girl in blue, snatching her into the shadows. I pressed a hand to my heart, hoping devoutly that I had been mistaken—or that one of the revellers had chosen, as a prank, to dress himself up with red lenses.

All the same, when suddenly the transmitter in my ear crackled, the sound of Vasily's agitated voice filled me with the liveliest alarm.

"*Bozhe moi!* What is *he* doing here?"

"Be more specific," Nijam responded on her own transmitter. "*Who* is here?"

"Anton Lupei!" Vasily nearly wailed, "the anarchist who tried to murder me in Paris! And again in Hungary! And again in Coburg!"

Evidently, I was not the only member of our company catching glimpses of old enemies.

"It's fortunate that we are all wearing masks," I murmured, for now that Vasily was wailing in my ear I felt a little steadier. Deleuze gave me an inquiring look, but in that crush he could not have heard me clearly. I made myself smile at him. "Half of Europe must be here. I'm *almost* certain I just saw one of your cousins."

"Oh, I expect the place is thick with disgraced Grand Dukes, but—"

"Dark is correct," said Nijam brusquely. "You'll be perfectly safe as long as you keep your mask on."

"—But I recognised Lupei even *with* a mask!" Vasily protested. "And what is Anton Lupei doing in *Paris?*"

"It doesn't matter in the slightest," Nijam said, "because the chance of the two of you meeting again after tonight is practically nil."

Vasily muttered something, but he must have been reassured, or at least content that we were aware of the danger, for he switched off his transmitter.

At the top of the stairs the crowd was thicker and more riotous. The crush-room was loud with music and dancing and cheers. We were accosted by passers-by; strangers asked me to dance or pressed flowers or goblets of champagne into our hands. Deleuze put a hand out to fend off their attentions, but I accepted a hot-house rose to tuck into my hair, and a champagne-glass because I thought it made me look festive. At last we found our way to the Grand Salon, a round pavilion with a great domed roof and windows on three sides, curtained against the chill of the December night. Here it was still crowded, but a little more blessedly quiet, for the conversation was not conducted at the top of everyone's voice. Deleuze led me through the press until we came to the great west window, where two ladies in masks and blue silk dominos sat to either side of a small table. A crowd of people were gathered around them, some sitting at their feet and others leaning forward as though to hear their conversation. They were drinking, but not champagne: amidst the perfumes clogging the room I caught the faint sweet scent of hibiscus tea.

"Each of you must say one very striking thing touching upon something in this room," declared the taller of the two ladies, whose domino was the rich dark blue of a sapphire. I could see very little else of her, except for a brown curl or two and a pair of very shrewd brown eyes that peeped through the eye-holes of her simple white mask. "Let it be wit, or pathos, or verse, or epigram; and Mlle Dargent shall judge which one pleases her best."

Mlle Dargent, a small, dainty, blonde person in sky-blue silk and a mask of black velvet, clapped her hands eagerly. "And the prize shall be a bonbon from my own hand!" she added, exciting the onlookers to cheers and laughter.

"That is Mlle Perrot," Deleuze said to me in a low voice, as the lady in sapphire blue began to point out one or another of the ladies and gentlemen gesturing for her attention. "As you can see, they are grand intellectuals. I don't care for such games myself, but for your sake I'll try for the prize."

At first I wondered what he could mean. The crowd now hushed, and with each gesture from Mlle Perrot, someone stood forth and declaimed a few words. The crowd clapped or booed each; indeed many of them were little more than flattering tributes to the ladies themselves, or cruel little remarks about others. Either way, the two ladies accepted them with a show of grace, finding something pleasant to say about each one. Then Deleuze put up his hand and was selected: and with a straight face declaimed:

And lately, by the Tavern Door agape,
Came stealing through the Dusk an Angel Shape,
Bearing a vessel on his Shoulder; and
He bid me taste of it; and 'twas—Hibiscus Tea!

That startled genuine laughter from the ladies.

"Ah! Célestin, do you not know? Look upon the hibiscus tea when it is red, but never the wine of the grape!" Mlle Perrot cried, raising her glass as though to toast him.

"I think we must reward this one," Mlle Dargent put in, selecting a bonbon from the plate before her. "Even if it *is* mostly Khayyam, it is both witty and apt."

I decided at once that I liked them. Witty or not, the joke had been at their expense, for choosing to remain sober at the party. No rank flattery or poisonous little remarks for *them,* and no excess or indiscretion, either.

"I will accept the bonbon," said Deleuze, going down on one knee to receive the boon, with a gesture like a knight accepting a favour from the lady of his heart. "But, mesdemoiselles, you will reward me more richly by permitting me to present to you my friend, madame the Baroness von Jörger, who has asked most humbly to be presented to your ladyships!"

"But of course!" said Mlle Perrot, getting up to offer her hand. "Why did you not present her at once, Célestin? Madame, I think that it is partly your husband's hospitality we are enjoying! You must congratulate him and M Durmortier for their princely generosity, and thank them for inviting us!"

"I wish I knew whether it was for the sake of our wit or *your* uncle, Amélie," Mlle Dargent put in.

Mlle Perrot laughed wryly. "What about you, my dear madame? Do you prefer Romantic Ballet above all else?"

"In fact I rather enjoy literature," said I. No sooner were the words spoken than I wondered whether this would make me seem rustic and unworldly to these sophisticated people, but what else could I say? Although I thought I could happily learn to become a connoisseur of the modern stage, I had never had the opportunity to do so.

And there was something frank in the very guardedness of these ladies, which had charmed the confession from me. I found them both very attractive; particularly Mlle Perrot, who was precisely the sort of elegant, self-contained person I could never manage to be.

"What sort of literature?" Mlle Dargent asked, leaning forward. "Do you like poetry?"

"Very much."

"We have regular poetry readings at our house on Monday mornings. You ought to come," said Mlle Perrot. "We are reading Greek lyric poetry at present: Pindar, Simonides, and Sappho. Are they familiar to you?"

I did not know how to confess that I did not speak Ancient Greek at all. "I'm very fond of Christina Rossetti," I said, almost apologetically. "But I should very much like to attend next Monday. Perhaps I'll find that I enjoy Sappho."

"Perhaps you will," said Mlle Dargent, and her blue eyes crinkled up merrily behind her mask.

For a little while, just now on the stairs, I had half wished I had not come at all. Amidst all the febrile cavorting of the bal masqué, who would have expected to find a small haven of rational conversation on *polite* topics!

I was just about to ask Deleuze if he knew the time, when the transmitter in my ear crackled once again. It was Nijam.

"Mimi?" she asked.

There was no answer. "What is it?" Vasily asked at once, sounding as though he was about to go off into another fit. "What's the matter? She's supposed to meet me at twelve-thirty in Box Three! Do you mean to say that she's vanished? I caught a glimpse of her a moment ago going upstairs towards the crush-room!"

"Don't panic," said Nijam. "It's not quite twenty minutes past. Schmidt and I will find her."

I switched off my transmitter. The whole plan depended upon Mimi being in Box Three at twelve-thirty, but even if we had run into a hitch, I could not possibly lend my assistance.

"In fact I wondered if you might have some mementoes of your late uncle," I said to Mlle Perrot. "Journals, sketches, choreography; anything like that. I suppose you get pestered for such things all the time."

"Not at all," said Mlle Perrot, most obligingly. "I don't think anyone has been through his belongings since he died four years ago. I've always meant to look through the stuff myself, for it's possible there may be something of value. If you come half an hour early on Monday, we'll look through it together?"

I thanked her with a slight twinge of conscience, for if my search turned up anything particularly valuable, I was not sure I liked to steal it from her. Perhaps, on the other hand, if something valuable *did* turn up, she would agree to make it a charitable donation.

"What pleasant ladies," I observed, returning to Deleuze, who had withdrawn a little from the knot of admirers and was talking and laughing with Caillot and the other domino.

"Everyone *says* so," Deleuze said, with a meaning smile. I perceived that he had gossip to relay, but not even to preserve my masquerade could I indulge him now.

"Monsieur," I begged him, "I feel a little weak. Will you take me for some supper?"

"By all means!" said Caillot. "We didn't come here to spend the entire evening in a graveyard!"

We left the "graveyard" behind us and plunged once again into the crush outside. I stole a hand to my ear and switched my transmitter on again. "What news?" I asked, *sotto voce.*

"We haven't found Mimi yet," said Nijam. Now even she was beginning to sound worried, and I felt a cold hand tighten around my heart.

"Delay ten minutes," said Vasily, "and then go ahead anyway, my dear. I have an idea."

"You're sure?" I asked, dubious.

"Perfectly; leave it all to me and proceed according to the plan." With that he ended the transmission. I bit my lip. How Vasily meant to betray me *without* a ballerina, I did not quite know. As for Mimi, what could her disappearance possibly mean? Had she fallen afoul of the killer—or was she busy on some more important investigation of her own?

As we made our way through the crush, I set myself to letting my nerves show in the deathly grip I kept upon Deleuze's sleeve, and the way I allowed myself to lean more heavily upon his arm in the jostling crowd. Eventually we found our way to the supper-room, which was in the counterpart of the Rotunda at the other side of the Opera.

Just inside the door, Deleuze bent down towards me and asked, "Madame, are you well? You seem overwhelmed. Do you need air?"

"No—no," I said faintly, making a show of rallying my courage. "I'll have a bite to eat, and a glass of champagne, but then I must leave you."

"Do you mind, Caillot?" Deleuze asked, and his friend began forging a way to the table. Deleuze turned to me, smiling. "You'll leave me, eh? What am I to make of that? Have you an assignation?"

It was time to execute the plan; I could only put my trust in Vasily, who had not disappointed me above once or twice in the course of our acquaintance. I adopted, therefore, an air of tragic resignation. "Not I, monsieur—my husband!"

"No!" Deleuze cried, making a manful effort to conceal his delight. "I am shocked! What a fool the man is!"

"His valet warned me it would happen tonight, here, at the Opera," I whispered. "No woman of spirit could bear it. I must have my revenge upon him." Then Caillot returned. I kept an eye upon the clock as I sipped my champagne, nibbled at my caviare, and pretended to be returning shudderingly to life. "There: I must go. No! Do not follow me! I cannot bear anyone to witness my shame!"

I took three steps and then in the doorway, I faltered and put a hand to my forehead as though I might be about to collapse. Gratifyingly, Deleuze was there at once, putting an arm around me.

"Madame, you can scarcely stand upright. Come, you had better let me attend you."

Since everything was now proceeding according to plan— at least on *my* end—I made no further protest, but led the way out of the crush-room to the empty halls and staircases around the theatre itself. At once we caught sight of Vasily's tall form swathed in a long red cloak; he was arm-in-arm with a much smaller figure. He bent his head to murmur in her ear. Laughing, the woman threw a glance over her shoulder towards me; and the sight of the dark unruly curls that haloed her face within the hood of her domino struck me speechless.

It was Vasily, going to keep his assignation—with another accomplice, who was not Mimi.

But then—where was Mimi? and what could Vasily mean, betraying me with a woman who wasn't Mimi?

It was scarcely rational, I know. But he had gone and altered the plan without warning me; and in the heat of the moment I suddenly recalled his jealousy, and wondered whether he meant to pay me back with a little jealousy of my own.

"Hush," I exhorted in a whisper, as Caillot and his friend, who was stifling her laughter, flocked into the corridor behind us. Vasily and his fair companion went up a flight of stairs, and we hurried after, and saw them going into Box Three!

"I must know the worst," said I, starting forward. I was in a great hurry, for now I was at least a little in earnest.

Deleuze caught my hand. "Wait," he said. "You can listen more comfortably from one of the adjoining boxes. You'd better go, Caillot."

Caillot turned, but with a quick movement I caught his sleeve. "You saw them enter the box, M. Caillot!" I whispered.

"Ah, I suppose I did!" he said, resigned. "Don't tell me I shall have to swear to it in court!"

"You'll do whatever the lady asks," said Deleuze with that fulsome gallantry of his, "including keeping it quiet if she prefers."

"Oh yes—yes, if you would be so kind," I murmured, and with that he and his friend went away downstairs again. Even amidst all my fears I felt somewhat bereft. It was not that I *liked* Caillot, but in this heightened atmosphere I was suddenly not sure that I liked to be left alone with Deleuze.

Yet the show, as they say, must go on. Deleuze scratched on the door of Box Two, and opened the door to lead me within. I brushed past him and pressed an ear against the thin partition between the boxes; whereupon the indistinct murmur of Vasily's voice condensed into words.

"No, my dear, I'm perfectly serious. This is only to give my wife a reason to divorce me! I'm madly in love with her, if you want to know."

I pressed a hand over my mouth, for fear that my true emotions would betray something I did not intend. Of course he was only following the plan we had made. No girl should accept as a lover a man she cannot trust, and I really ought to trust Vasily—but he *had* been jealous!

Deleuze had the delicacy not to listen in, but he had settled himself into the nearest chair in a posture of splendid indolence. I became aware that he was watching me with a peculiar expression which was somehow both sleepy and alert, the eyes narrowed hungrily upon myself.

"There's a very pleasant way for you to revenge yourself, you know," he said in a murmur even softer than Vasily's own. "All without setting foot in the courts."

And he drew off his glove and extended his hand.

It took me a long moment to understand; and then the infamous suggestion rendered me utterly speechless. As far as Deleuze knew, I was an injured wife bleeding with the wounds of freshly-inflicted betrayal, and his idea was to make a quick profit from her. What a horrible, low sort of mind the man must have, if he thought one's first impulse in such a situation would be to give herself up to the embraces of another!

"How could I bear to do such a thing?" I asked him, quite sincerely. Only the depths of my astonishment prevented me in that moment from telling him precisely what I thought of him. Then I recalled my masquerade and fetched out my handkerchief. "All I ask is that if ever I call upon you, you'll swear to the truth of what you have seen this night!"

Deleuze smiled, a swift flash of predatory teeth in the dim light. "Upon my honour as a gentleman," he said, and I restrained the laughter that rose to my lips. What honour? What gentleness, either of manner or of mind?

Then we both heard quite clearly Vasily's uplifted voice from the box beside us. "Now, don't be shy, my dear!" It was the signal we had arranged between us ahead of time.

"I cannot bear it," I said wildly. "Quick—come!" Catching Deleuze by the hand, I drew him out of the box again, and into the corridor that ran the circumference of the theatre. Perhaps he thought that I meant to flee. Instead, I caught the door to Box Three and tore it open; there was a gasp from within, and Vasily and the ringleted ballerina stared up at me in alarm. They had removed their masks. The ballerina was sitting on Vasily's knee and his mouth was all over red with her lip-paint.

"Baroness!" Deleuze protested, trying to close the door again. I fought against him to keep it open. For a moment the voice of reason was nearly drowned out by the emotions the sight of Vasily kindled within me. Then I succumbed without a struggle to that madness, knowing that it would give the ring of truth to what I must do next.

"I knew it," I hissed. "I knew from the first it would come to this. The fool I have been!" And I let myself believe it.

Vasily got up, disentangling himself from the ballerina, who snatched up her mask, gave a breathless curtsey as she sidled from the box, and rushed away. For a moment he was silent, and his mobile face went through the practised motions of surprise, guilt—and defiance.

"Don't look so shocked!" he said silkily. "I don't know if you recall, madame, but I once offered you the chance to have as many of your own affairs as you pleased."

He *had*—once. I allowed myself, for a moment, to remain speechless. "And I refused! I knew you only meant to justify your own affairs by permitting me mine."

Vasily threw a meaning glance at Deleuze. "Forgive me," he said, "for doubting whether you meant it."

That look was a step too far. He *was* jealous—and what! after all he had done, did he dare to be jealous of *me?* The *opera buffa* we had scripted had now blundered perilously close to the truth. Perhaps we had been foolish to play at such a thing, with love so young and tender and easily bruised.

We were rescued by a sudden crackle of the transmitter within our ears. It was Nijam.

"Mimi is gone," she said breathlessly. It sounded as though she was hurrying somewhere. "We found her with M. Christophe—and now they've both vanished without a trace."

There was something in Nijam's voice, a note almost of panic, that purged every other thought from my mind. I drew in a sharp breath and said to Vasily, "It doesn't matter. You must come at once. The child has been taken ill."

"Why didn't you tell me?" Vasily asked at once, playing up to my improvisation. *Now* I could hear the false note in his voice—perhaps it had been there all along! "Where is she? Take me to her."

I caught his hand and we rushed away, leaving Deleuze in the corridor looking thoroughly befuddled.

"Molly-my-dear, I beg you not to think I *meant* any of that," Vasily panted as we descended the stair leading towards the foyer de la danse.

I found myself suddenly incapable of brushing it off with a laugh. "I didn't expect you to *kiss* the girl," I said.

There was a moment's silence. "You told me to make it look convincing!" he protested.

"You *changed* the plan," I said. "It was supposed to be *Mimi.*" Mimi would never have agreed to kiss him. *She* would have too much regard for me.

We entered the foyer de la danse, which was dark and deserted save for a band of imprints that made my heart jump for a moment: gaunt, ragged, and desperate as they were, and one of them waving a red petticoat on the end of a rifle. I guessed these must be the famous Communards. In that moment they felt a fitting complement to my own feelings.

"I couldn't find Mimi," Vasily said, dragging my attention back to himself. "I had to make do with one of the corps de ballet, and it's a mercy she's employed at my whim, or we might have her telling tales about it."

"Oh! so that makes it all right! You may kiss a ballerina and it doesn't mean a thing, but heaven forbid I exchange two words with Célestin Deleuze!"

"Oh, *slava,*" he groaned, pulling me to a stop. "I'm not a fool, my dear—I know that you could have any man you liked, with a snap of your fingers. Perhaps that frightens me into saying things I shouldn't. What can I do if you send me away? I've always been a coward."

And that was the problem, I thought, looking up into

his shadowed face. Far though we had come, Vasily still wanted me the way a drowning man wants a life-line. And he would never be at peace until he had chosen me, not out of desperation but simply and fearlessly, out of love.

"There are plenty of fish in the sea, Vasya, for you as well as for me," I said.

The moment I said the words I knew that he misunderstood. For a moment his face showed the stillness of utter desperation. Then he held up a trembling hand. "Look," he said hoarsely. "Look at the colour on my fingers. My lips never touched her; I swear it on my mother."

Something that was pulled tight within me unspooled, just a little. Still, I caught his hand without looking at it. "Vasya," I said, half-choked, "why did you not say so to begin with? Does it please you to torment me?"

"Never! I would have cut off my own hand before touching her." His grip tightened almost painfully on mine; then, just as suddenly, he released me, and his voice sank to a whisper. "Still, I am afraid, and fear makes me jealous. How could I be otherwise? For me there is no other fish in the sea, or fowl in the air, or angel in heaven."

It was a perfectly ridiculous thing to say, but he seemed so much in earnest that it would be cruel to laugh. I only shook my head. "You misunderstand me," I said. He opened his mouth to protest, but I shook my head. "Later, when we know that Mimi is safe."

Then we hurried on towards the dressing-rooms, and Vasily followed at my heels in silence like a faithful dog. My thoughts reeled a little. *You could have any man you liked,* Vasily had said, and I felt with bewilderment that it was true. I had money now. I did not *have* to choose Vasily, any more than I must choose Célestin Deleuze. The thought half horrified, half intoxicated me. I did not *want* anyone but Vasily. But if I did—I could have him. If Vasily broke my heart, there would be other chances at love. I was no longer merely a governess, or a confidence-trickster. I could choose.

My thoughts swam. Who would I have chosen, if not for circumstances throwing me into Vasily's society? Who was I really, without the constraints of poverty? Did I truly know myself?

Chapter VIII.

Now I must tell you what Nijam and Schmidt had been doing while all this was happening. Nijam had spent a rather fruitless afternoon in the netherworld at the back of the Opera, interviewing scene-painters and seamstresses, cobblers and goldsmiths, carpenters and decorators. Meanwhile Schmidt had been doing the same among the stage-hands, the stable boys and the furnace-men who operated the boilers that kept the Opera warm. The business was slow and tedious and not remotely sufficient, for it excluded the artists, the box-women, and the various managers and assistant managers of each department. As for the firemen, the gendarmes, and the doctor attached to the Opera, interviews with them must wait for a future date.

By midnight most of these denizens had either gone home or joined the revelries, either as servants or participants. Nijam went up to the empty foyer de la danse and found Schmidt waiting there with his hands in his pockets, scrutinising the great murals of past dancers.

"Why aren't you at the party?" Nijam asked, as he turned towards her. He looked particularly earnest just now, and there were times when offence was the best defence.

"It's a ghastly crush up there," he said. "Why don't I see you home, and we can compare notes."

"There isn't much comparing to do," Nijam said briskly. "As far as I can tell, no one has seen hide nor hair of the real Demiana Chalabi, and no one saw a man on the back stairs last night during the imprint's performance."

Schmidt nodded. "I had much the same result. As to motive, Chalabi made no enemies and took no lovers, and she was M. Christophe's special pet. M. Dumortier paid her well but otherwise took no particular interest in her."

Nijam must have been frowning terribly, for she felt more certain than ever that the very lack of clues pointed in a direction that might be deadly. "I don't like it," she said. "The sort of man who kills with no motive is the sort of man who will kill again and again until he is stopped. We ought to warn Mimi, if not the whole Opera."

Tapping her temple to open the transmitter embedded beneath her skin, she called Mimi's name but received no response.

"What is it?" Vasily asked, instead, via his own transmitter. "If it's Mimi you want, I caught a glimpse of her a moment ago going upstairs towards the crush-room. There was a black domino with her—a great raven, with a beak like a plague-doctor."

Nijam sighed. The last thing she wanted to do was to join anything that could be described as a *crush*. Too much light, sound, scent, and motion always made her feel sick and overwhelmed.

"What was Mimi wearing?" Schmidt asked. "A white silk domino? That ought not to be too difficult to find."

Resigned to the ordeal, Nijam led the way towards the state-rooms at the front of the Opera. When they emerged at last into the atrium at the head of the grand staircase, it was like running headlong into a wall of sensation. Nijam found herself gripping Schmidt's sleeve very tightly.

"Look there," said Schmidt, pointing towards the supper-room, which lay to their left. Amidst the crowd they both caught a glimpse of a tall, sinister figure with a long hooked beak. It was visible only for a moment before the crowd closed in and hid it from sight. They started in that direction, but the going was slow and they had not made it very far through the crowd when Schmidt stopped moving altogether.

"What?" Nijam hissed. She was wild to get out of the crowd, or at least to put her fingers in her ears. It was not merely the sensory assault that bothered her. A mob like this was just as explosive as thermite or paraffin, and far more volatile.

"There's another raven in there," Schmidt said, pointing across the atrium to the rank of immeasurably tall entrances that led into the crush-room. "That one has a woman with him."

Nijam hesitated. Common sense urged the two of them to split up and pursue the ravens separately. But she did not think she could get far in this madhouse without Schmidt's solid arm to cling to.

"Follow the woman, then," she said, and they changed their direction. After an endless struggle they made it through those immense doorways into the grand crush-room at the front of the Opera, a magnificent apartment with a polished floor and great windows that gave onto the loggia overlooking the Place de l'Opéra. Above, the chandeliers and the painted and gilded ceiling seemed dizzily far from the crowd gathered upon the parquetry below. The whole room was full of hectic music and breathless dancing. Just looking at them made

Nijam feel sick and dizzy.

The raven galloped past them with his partner clasped in his arms. Her domino was not silver-white, but pale gold; a mass of chestnut curls spilled from the hood and she was certainly too tall to be Mimi.

Schmidt gave a hiss of disappointment. "I'm sorry. Under the lights, it looked white from a distance… There! Over by the windows. A third raven!"

Nijam lost her temper, but not with Schmidt. "There is something very odd about this," she said. It felt as perilous as crossing a busy street with carriages flashing to and fro; but she moved faultlessly into the flow of the dance, laid a hand on the second raven's wrist, and said sternly, "May I cut in?"

It did not occur to her in that moment that this was something a man might do, but never a lady. At any rate the dancers did not refuse her: few people ever did, especially when she spoke in such forbidding tones. The lady in gold relinquished her partner, and Nijam took his hand.

"Who are you?" she demanded, resisting the raven's attempts to continue the dance. That point of contact was a poor substitute for the comfort provided by Schmidt. "Where is Mlle Laine?"

The man said something about masks, doubtless protesting that it was not yet time to remove his. In all that noise, and in a language in which she was not perfectly at home, Nijam abandoned any attempt to understand. Action must suffice. She tore the mask from his head to reveal the perspiring features of the assistant stage-manager. Then he snatched it back and replaced it, quivering with indignation.

Nijam waited for his spate of angry words to subside before repeating her question. "*Where* is Mlle Laine? Have you spoken to her this evening?"

He shook his head vigorously and went off into another torrent of French.

"Where did you get that costume?" she asked next, but he had evidently had enough; he turned his back and went in search of the gold domino. Well; the answer to *that* question could wait until the morrow. But some dreadful premonition was now brewing like a storm within her, and not merely because of the overwhelming sensation of light, sound, and motion that assailed her. It was like a nightmare. Mimi had vanished; no one could say whence she had gone, and the Opera was full of ravens!

Nijam turned in search of Schmidt and then had a particularly horrible moment, for he was not there. He had abandoned her, and she was marooned in the midst of a nightmare throng of flash and glitter. Someone shrieked in her face. Someone else thrust a brimming glass of champagne beneath her nose and demanded to know where her mask was.

It was all too much. Nijam acted in self-preservation, squeezing her eyes shut and clapping her hands over her ears. "Once twelve is twelve," she chanted in pure desperation. Demanding hands plucked at her elbows, demanding voices shouted in her face, but she shrugged them away and went on, faster and louder. "Two twelves are twenty-four, three twelves are thirty-six, four twelves are forty-eight, five twelves—"

There was the sound of a scuffle and then a tiny bubble of stillness seemed to enfold her.

"Miss Nijam," said Schmidt, using his transmitter, so that his quiet voice was delivered directly to her ear. "Are you hurt?"

Nijam cracked an eye open and peered between the elbows that caged her face. Schmidt stood before her, looking flushed and worried. His arms hovered about her, guarding her without touching.

"No," she gasped. "I'm all right now."

"Come," he said, taking her hand. A white domino at his side, with black hair and olive skin a few shades lighter than Nijam's own, took the lead, whisking them directly out of the crush-room by a low door in the panelling and into the blessed quiet and comparative solitude of a corridor.

Nijam put a hand against the panelling, focusing for a moment on taking long, slow breaths. When she was sufficiently collected, she nodded towards their guide. "Whom do we have here?"

"One of the corps de ballet," Schmidt said. To Nijam's relief, he made no reference to the weakness that had beset her in the crush-room. "She says she's seen Mimi."

This gave her mind something to cling to. "Where?" Nijam demanded.

"She went up the stairs with M. Christophe," the ballerina volunteered. "I think they were going to the roof. Though why she likes him so much, I can't imagine! If *we* make mistakes, he switches our ankles with his wand."

Nijam darted a glance upward at the gilt-encrusted ceiling. A cold shiver of worry crawled over her. Mimi up there, alone, with one of their main suspects! "Take us to the stair at once," she commanded, and the little ballerina gave a brisk nod. She evidently knew her way around the Opera, for in less time than Nijam had thought possible they gained the stair at the western end of the theatre, which gave access to all the boxes, from the dress-circle to the "gods".

"This is where I saw the raven and the white domino," the girl proclaimed cheerfully. "I know it was Mlle Laine because I heard her ask if they were going up to the roof. And I knew she was with M. Christophe because of the signs he made in reply."

"We're indebted to you," Schmidt said fervently, bounding two or three steps up the stair.

Nijam hung back only long enough to ask, "Your name?"

"Fatima Gobara," the ballerina said, dipping into a curtsey. She beheld Schmidt with an admiring and speculative gaze. "Are you her lover? Are you going to fight M. Christophe?"

Schmidt opened his eyes very wide. "Never mind about that," he said, and such was his haste that he actually snapped his fingers at Nijam before turning to pelt upwards.

Nijam sighed and followed on his heels, leaving the enfant terrible to her own, doubtless lurid, conjectures. With a pang of nostalgia she remembered the old days at Heidelberg, when Alphonse Schmidt was rumoured to be in love with a new girl every week, only because he was not standoffish around young ladies and liked to cultivate friendships with them. It was one of the things she most respected about him.

This was the moment at which I opened my transmitter and asked for news.

"We haven't found Mimi yet," Nijam answered, "but we have a lead." As Vasily and I made plans to continue without Mimi's assistance, Nijam switched off her transmitter, satisfied that she and Schmidt could now focus their entire attention on the far more important business of keeping Mimi alive and well.

"We'll go up to the roof," Schmidt panted as they passed each landing and corridor, "and then work our way down if Mimi's not there." This was such manifest sense that Nijam made no reply. Up they went and up—past each level of the boxes that ringed the theatre, past the "gods" on the uppermost levels where the students of Paris gathered at cut-price rates to jostle and cheer and heckle the performances, and finally up one final, narrow flight to a low door that gave onto the roof. The handle turned quite easily, allowing them out into the chill night air. Here on the rooftop, the midnight sky was dark and mottled with clouds; but the city was an electric pool of light about them, throwing the vigilant shapes of the statues of Poetry and Harmony at the front of the Opera into dark relief. Most of the roof was taken up by the pyramidal shape of the great atrium skylight, but a flat, paved path led from the doorstep, curving about the great green copper dome of the theatre immediately to their left.

Slowly, silently, they circled the dome until two figures came within view upon the pavement. Schmidt drew back when he caught sight of them, and Nijam followed a moment later, keeping close within the shadow of the dome.

For a moment they only watched as the white domino and the black danced a silent pas de deux. Without music, it was possible to hear the scuff of their shoes on the pavement, the flutter of their garments, and now and again a gasp of pain or effort from Mimi. The raven domino made no sound. In the darkness he seemed little more than a shadow, occasionally visible eclipsing the white robe of his partner.

Schmidt thought they looked like ghosts. Nijam only knew that the dancing was marvellous: perfectly in time despite the lack of music, and so expressive that as the dance unfolded she almost began to hear the music in her mind, swelling and ebbing like a dream.

"Leave them be," Schmidt murmured in her ear after a moment, and Nijam nodded. Mimi had been short-tempered of late, and would not relish being dragged away from her impromptu lesson to hear that the rest of the crew half suspected her ballet-master of planning to kill her. No doubt she would be safe so long as she was watched over.

"Christophe is working her too hard," Nijam murmured beneath the cold breath of the wind, which whispered through the strings of Apollo's lyre high on the green dome above them. "Mimi must have been rehearsing all afternoon. Surely she ought to be given a rest."

Schmidt evidently was not thinking of Mimi. "Are you cold?" he asked, seeing that she had her arms wrapped about herself for warmth. Nijam was still trying to settle on a reply when he took off his jacket and put it about her shoulders. She accepted with silent despair. One day soon, she must tell Schmidt quite plainly how things stood between them...

"Sir thinks Dumortier is the murderer," Schmidt added in an undertone, much to Nijam's relief. She had much rather discuss the murder than the great chasm between them. "But Dumortier is a manager of the Opera and a rich man with everything he wants. Why should he murder his own artists? If he wanted to be rid of them he could easily send them away."

"A man who kills for his own amusement is harder to find, because he has no enmity which can be traced," Nijam murmured. "Our best hope is to catch him in the act."

"That will need vigilance indeed."

"The only clue is that he is killing Opera artists." Nijam brooded for a moment. Whatever choice they made, if they chose wrongly she might find herself with another death on her conscience. But it was hard for even the five of them, even working together, to watch the entire Opera. "We may take it that the next victim is likely to come from among the singers or dancers, as the first two did. That narrows things down a little. If I had any better idea what links Larousse and Chalabi, we could arrange someone to use as bait. Mimi, for instance."

Schmidt gave her a look of alarm.

"Don't be shocked," Nijam said. "If we knew for certain that it would be Mimi, then we could devote all our time to protecting her. I'd use myself as bait if I could, but can you imagine *me* as a ballerina?"

"Yes," he said, as though the thing was obvious—as though he had imagined it often, despite the dark skin that no ballet-company would ever accept. Nijam felt herself go hot. After a moment, however, Schmidt continued. "Perhaps there's a way for *me* to pose as—as a tenor, for instance."

"Can you sing?"

"No, but otherwise I'm the best person for the task; I'm the most expendable. You have the brains, and sir and Miss Dark have the wiles, and Mimi has the agility. I only hit things."

There was, Nijam thought, a very easy way for him to repair *that* shortcoming. Then he added under his breath, "And I don't always do that in time, either."

"The best person for the task is the one who the killer takes an interest in next," she said as kindly as she knew how, "and that's far less likely to be you, than Mimi."

"I know," Schmidt said, and there was still an ocean of regret in his voice.

Nijam's heart plunged. She did not want to be cruel to Schmidt. It was one thing to wound him when they were strangers, but now the idiot had gone and fallen in love with her a second time.

Perhaps she had been a coward, too. She might not be able to love Schmidt, but she could at least be kind to him.

She took a great gulp and said, "I never thanked you for giving me the plague."

"You *knew?*" He looked down at her with something halfway between terror and hope. "You didn't *say* anything."

She had not said anything, precisely because she *did* know that it was Schmidt. It was not that she didn't love the man; she did, horribly. She would have given anything to be able to return his feelings—and that she could not do, while he was too much afraid to face his past, and to recover his memories.

When she did not reply, Schmidt reddened and looked away. "That letter, the other day," he said, with every sign of embarrassment. "It wasn't me—I didn't send it."

"Oh, I know," she responded. "*That* was Vasily. It was a dirty trick, and I'll make him suffer for it."

If Schmidt reddened any more, his ears might spontaneously combust. "All right! I wrote the letter. I meant every word. What do you say to it?"

Nijam felt that an alarm-bell had gone off in her head. *Fire! Fire! Evacuate the laboratory! What the blazes, Nijam, didn't you know you were bound to get such a retort?*

"I *said* you were a coward. I meant moral cowardice, but I meant every word of it." She shuffled away from him, scanning the pavement where it curved before the dome. "Where's Mimi?"

There was no sign of the dancers.

Fear went through her like a lance, overwhelming any other considerations. Nijam darted out from their hiding-place, seeing at a glance that the pavement was empty. A door at the far end of the horseshoe-shaped path emitted a thin ray of golden light. She tore it open and was greeted only by the silent corridor at the head of the eastern stair.

"Gone," she said blankly.

"God in heaven," said Schmidt at her elbow—strong language for Alphonse, but she sensed the theological significance he imparted to the words. "D'you think they overheard us?"

Nijam stared unseeing at the downwards steps. "The next victim," she breathed, slapping at her transmitter. "Mimi! Mimi! If you're there, answer me!"

No answer came. Nijam and Schmidt exchanged glances—he was still flushed from their conversation—and then rushed down the steps. "Vasily! Dark!" Nijam cried into her transmitter. "Mimi is gone. We found her with M. Christophe—now they've both vanished without a trace." There was a confused sound at the other end of the transmission—Vasily and I making our hurried excuses to Deleuze. "Meet us in her dressing-room," Nijam added, before silencing the device.

At each landing they stopped to scan the corridor girdling the theatre, and to glance within the nearest boxes; but there was no sign of the dancers. "It was Christophe," Nijam panted. "I ought to have known. I ought to have had him crawling with bugs and trackers."

They reached the foot of the stairs and made their way through the foyer de la danse. In the corridor beyond, the ubiquitous Fatima was gathered with a knot of other ballerinas her own age, cracking nuts and chattering. Nijam caught the words *le fantôme!* and turned peremptorily towards them.

"Have any of you seen Mimi just now?" she asked. "Or M. Christophe?"

They shook their heads. Nijam wanted to gnash her teeth. Up a flight of stairs they went towards the dressing-rooms, and flung open the door to find Vasily and myself.

* * *

I had spent a fruitless minute or two engaged in trying to raise an imprint. If, heaven forfend, we were too late and Mimi had died, then something in this room—the hairbrush, still thick with ash-blonde hair, or the negligée of white lace which had been tossed carelessly over the screen in the corner—ought to recall her. Indeed it ought to be easy, given how well *I* recalled her: but there was not the slightest flicker of an imprint in the room. When Nijam burst in looking as wild as I had ever seen her—that is to say, mildly bilious—with Schmidt bringing up the rear, I turned towards them and said, "Calm yourselves. I trust she's still alive."

"Can't raise an imprint?" Vasily asked, fully alive to the meaning of this. "That does it. I'll have the whole Opera sealed and searched from top to bottom."

"You'll never get Dumortier to agree," Nijam said. "If you ask me, they'll have gone down to the bottom-most cellar, above the cistern. If we start now we may catch them."

"There's another possibility," said I, "which you have all forgotten. Mimi may have been snatched up by the Okhrana."

"That's highly unlikely," said Nijam. Vasily opened his mouth to disagree, but she silenced him with a wave of her hand. "If by some wild chance she *is* in the hands of the Okhrana they will keep her alive, at least for the moment. The killer is the greater threat; we should assume she has been taken by him and respond accordingly. To the cellars!"

She turned abruptly towards the door and nearly ran bodily into Schmidt, who stood between her and the exit.

Schmidt, pale with worry, held up a hand that hovered about Nijam's shoulder in a soothing sort of way. "Wait," he said. "Let's try one more thing."

He tapped his transmitter and his voice resounded in our ears. "Mimi," he said with commendable calmness. "If you're there, answer if you can. We only want to know that you're alive and well."

His voice died away, leaving a great echoing silence behind. For a moment we all held our breath. Then, just as Nijam looked ready to cut Schmidt to the ground and storm over his expiring corpse—I imagined her producing a battle-axe or scimitar for the purpose, from some hiding-place within her skirts—we had a reply.

"Ugh! What are you bothering *me* for?" Mimi sounded sulky and very tired. "Where did you think I *was*, Schmidt? I went home. I'm tired. I've been working on the case all day."

Nijam gripped Schmidt's sleeve. I allowed myself to collapse with graceful breathlessness upon the sofa, an attempt complicated by the fact that Vasily had done the same thing at nearly the same moment.

Schmidt patted Nijam's hand and spoke with feigned calm into his transmitter. "We only wanted to warn you that we believe the Opera killer will strike again, probably another artist. Be careful, Mimi. We haven't come to any conclusions, but you must remember that our only clue points towards M. Christophe."

(It was not so bad, after all, sharing a sofa with Vasily. He had a very comfortable shoulder and his arm was pleasantly warm. Perceiving his subtle attempt to put a polite distance between us, I reclined a little more insistently.)

"We need your help, Mimi," Nijam said, in a voice that had gone gruff with emotion. "You must help us to keep track of M. Christophe."

"Well, you'll have to do without me," Mimi said. "I'm quitting."

She could not have startled us more had she thrown the golden apple of discord into our midst, like Pyramis with the three goddesses. Seeing Nijam open her mouth, I hurriedly tapped my own transmitter.

"Are you sure, Mimi?" I asked. "There's still a murderer at large, and you might help us. If you were to prove Christophe innocent—"

It was the wrong thing to say. Mimi erupted.

"I'm not interested in proving him one thing or another! Don't imagine you can interfere with *my* life, Molly Dark, the way Vasily does with Nijam and Schmidt! I only have time for one job, and this is the one I've always wanted—so you can consider this my resignation!"

I sent a shocked glance towards my confederates; yet, to my surprise, Nijam and Schmidt betrayed no embarrassment whatsoever. They had already aired their feelings on the roof, and nothing Mimi said could be worse than *that.*

"Of course, Mimi," Schmidt said, with perfect calm. "This rôle is the sort of chance that only comes along once in a lifetime, and we'd never forgive ourselves if you lost it. Take all the time you need—but do take care. No matter who it is, someone at the Opera is a danger to you."

"I heard," Mimi said sullenly, and there was a distinct *snick* as her transmitter switched off. For a moment there was only silence in the dressing-room as the rest of us followed suit.

Schmidt and I exchanged a troubled look.

"I don't know that he's a murderer," Nijam said in a low growl, "but that Christophe is doing her no good at all."

"That's something she'll have to figure out for herself," Schmidt said, soothingly.

Nijam scowled. "Fatima told us that Christophe switches his students when they make mistakes. If *that* doesn't worry her, what will?"

"We can't interfere," I said. I felt the return of that premonition from yesterday; the fear that I had done wrong in encouraging Mimi in the pursuit of her Art. Yet, what else could I have said? I felt stung by the accusation that I wished to meddle in her affairs the way Vasily did with Schmidt and Nijam. "She's right, you know—we can't rescue her from a high-handed ballet-master by being high-handed ourselves. At least she answered her transmitter, and she knows where to turn if she's in trouble. There's nothing else we can do, except to give her her privacy."

"I hate to admit it, but you are right," said Nijam. "We should let her cool down, and then she will see things differently. I'll stay at your flat tonight, Dark. Come on, let's go. It must be past one o'clock."

In a warm vibration beneath my shoulder, Vasily said something about the evening having scarcely begun. I sighed. I myself was very comfortable, and besides, I owed it to Vasily to finish the conversation we had begun in the foyer de la danse. But Nijam already stood by the doorway, giving the distinct impression of a cat on tenterhooks. I sighed, squeezed Vasily's hand in a manner that I hoped he found reassuring, and followed her.

A cab was easy to find; for the evening, as Vasily had said, was scarcely begun, and very few had yet attempted to depart the festivities. All the short way home, both Nijam and I remained silent. With Mimi accounted for, I could not help reverting to the false quarrel with Vasily. I reflected sadly that I ought to have regarded my first instincts, that marriage was far too serious a matter to play at. Then I found myself wanting to laugh, for we had proceeded directly to divorce without even managing to get properly married in the first place! What a cockeyed way we had of doing things, to be sure!

Well: we had passed through stormier waters, and no doubt we would pass through these, also. Only I could not stop thinking of the choice I had suddenly, for the first time, perceived that I had.

Nijam betrayed the tendency of her own thoughts by saying, "Perhaps I ought to have gone to Mimi's, after all. Just to be sure she had really gone home."

That brought back all my premonitions. "Do you think she might have been fibbing?"

"No, but she hasn't been herself lately, and this way I could be sure."

Possibly we ought both to have listened to our misgivings; but I could not help imagining Mimi's indignation if she felt that we were in any way breathing down her neck.

"Let her alone for tonight," I said, "and go to see her in the morning, when she's cooled down a little."

With that we reached the tenement on the Boulevard Haussmann. In the corridor the final surprise of the night awaited us: for there was Khadijah Gobara, with a carpet-bag and an expression that was both tired and worried. She straightened hurriedly when we approached.

"Madame, pardon the hour, but I had nowhere else to go. Are you still in need of a lady's maid?"

It had been but a few hours since I had last spoken to her, yet most of those had been spent in an effort to make myself look the part of the Baroness von Jörger attending her twentieth bal masqué. "I'll say I do," I said with feeling, unlocking the door to my little flat. "At least for a week or so, until business takes me away from Paris. We shall be very cosy tonight, but I dare say you will be comfortable on the sofa, Nijam."

Nijam allowed her silence to pass for assent. We spoke little more that evening, but unpinned our hair and went gratefully to bed. It was not a peaceful night. I lay awake for many hours, worrying about Mimi. Once I heard Nijam cry out, and put my head into the sitting-room to see if anything was wrong. She was fast asleep. I think she was having nightmares.

Chapter IX.

Nijam was already gone by the time I arose a little before midday on the following morning, having been summoned from my couch by a distinctly buttery scent drifting from the kitchen. Gobara must have been up for some time, for the flat had been straightened and the blankets which I had provided Nijam on the previous night had been tidied off the sofa.

Upon hearing my footsteps, my new servant emerged promptly from the kitchen with a cup of tea and a piping hot croissant. I fairly wept to see them.

"You are a treasure, Khadijah," I told her. "Do you mind if I call you by your Christian name?"

Gobara regarded me gravely. "It would be very—friendly," she said, carefully, and as though she did not know whether she liked the idea of being friends with her employer. I understood. I should not have liked it much, either, if Mme Chardigny or the Countess von Hügel had announced that she meant to call me Molly. I could not very well object when the lady was paying my salary; and then she might expect to presume upon the relationship in other ways, too.

"Then for the present I'll just call you Gobara," I said, "and you can decide later whether you want me to change it."

"Thank you, madame," she said, a little less reserved. "I don't have a Christian name," she added. "I'm a Moslem."

"I ought to have guessed," I said. To make up for the faux pas, I added, "I suppose your observances are different to mine. In the normal way of things I would give you Sunday off, but if it's a different day for you—"

"Please don't mind," she said. "Here it is easiest to do as the rest of France does, and see my family on a Sunday. I don't usually attend Friday prayers. God is merciful, and knows that women have much work to do."

I listened to this with great interest, for she was the first Moslem I had ever met. "Wasn't your former mistress Egyptian, too? Did she also miss prayers?"

"Mlle Chalabi is—" She caught herself, and gulped before going on. "Mlle Chalabi *was* a Christian—a Copt. She was named after a Coptic saint, you know, and was very proud of it. That's why she refused to change her name when she went on the stage."

"Is that common?"

"Oh, yes, madame. People take you more seriously as a dancer if you sound like you might be French, or Italian. If Mlle Chalabi had not kept her name, my little sister Fatima might be performing as a Carlotta or a Gianna today."

"That strikes me as a shame," said I, warmly. "Fatima is a lovely name—wonderfully romantic. I suppose she wanted to become a ballerina because of Mlle Chalabi?"

A warm flush spread across Gobara's cheeks. "No, madame. She wanted to become a ballerina because of me. But I was not permitted to join the Opera school."

"Why not?"

"My skin," Gobara said, simply, spreading out her lovely brown hands.

I had noticed that Fatima's skin was lighter than her sister's, but I had not connected this with their respective choice of occupation. Now that I thought about it, it struck me that the corps de ballet *was* very pale. "Oh, Gobara," I said, unhappily.

"It's the way of the world," she said, and turned the conversation back to other matters, such as her wages, her half-day, and so on. By the time we were done, Vasily and Schmidt arrived and I sent Gobara to fetch more tea and croissants.

"Where is Nijam?" Schmidt asked, when we were alone. I was about to answer when the door opened and Nijam herself entered, with a frown a little deeper than normal.

"I went home," she announced. "Mimi's bed hasn't been slept in."

"Are you sure?" I asked, feeling my heart drop into my stomach. "Perhaps she made it when she got up this morning."

Nijam gave me a withering look. "Perhaps an angel dropped from heaven to return her bedroom to precisely the state of disarray in which I last saw it, with the pillow beneath the dressing-table."

"If she didn't sleep at home last night, then where was she?" Vasily asked. No one had any answer to that question.

"Maybe it's not M. Christophe. Maybe the Okhrana has her," I suggested. It would not be the first time that Mimi had told fibs to prevent us learning of her entanglements with the Russian secret police, albeit with the best intentions in the world. "Do you think we ought to do something, after all?"

"Stop worrying," said Nijam. "Mimi's told us everything she wants us to know, and we must trust her." From the tone of her voice I perceived that she was not particularly happy with Mimi's fibs, all the same.

Then Gobara came in with the tea. She and I had not

merely confined our remarks, that morning, to the terms of her employment. Now I thanked her for the tea and added, "You must tell these gentlemen and this lady what you told me this morning, Gobara, about what brought you to seek employment with me."

Gobara looked abashed, but pleased. Perhaps she had not really thought that I would help her.

"Well," she said eagerly, "it's as I told madame yesterday—Mlle Chalabi has vanished clean away, and no one knows where she is. And instead of making a report to the gendarmerie, Monsieur Chalabi her father has turned away all the servants, and has taken the entire remainder of his family to Egypt."

"To Egypt!" Schmidt exclaimed. "But why?"

"I do not know," Gobara said. "Yesterday morning he announced that it would be so, and by evening they were gone."

"Surely they mean to return," Vasily suggested.

"But no, monsieur. They will have an agent pack up the house and deal with the property."

"And they left their Egyptian servants behind?"

Gobara shrugged. "Only me, and I would not leave. Someone ought to remain in case Mlle Chalabi should return. In any case, my family has been French since the days when Napoleon withdrew from Egypt with all of his men and his allies. My sister is a dancer at the Opera. What would I do in Egypt?"

When the door closed behind the young woman, Nijam said in a low voice, "Mlle Chalabi will never return, and her family knows it. That is why they have gone to Egypt."

"I'm not so sure," Schmidt put in. "How could they know?

We do, but only because of Miss Dark's gift."

"If only they hadn't gone away, we could question them," said I. "Can we spare anyone to follow them?"

"Not you or me," Vasily said. "We're society figures now; if we run after the Chalabis it will attract attention all over Paris, and then the killer will certainly be upon his guard."

"Not Schmidt or me, either," said Nijam. "We have to watch over Mimi and try to find the murderer, and it's dangerous to do it alone."

Reluctantly, I conceded that this was true—we were spread thinly enough, especially without Mimi to call upon. "At any rate, I've scraped an acquaintance with Mlle Perrot, and I have an appointment with her tomorrow to look through her uncle's papers," said I. "With any luck, we'll find something that can be sold to the Opera for a sum large enough to recompense the families of the dead."

"What, the laundry-lists of a superannuated ballet-master?" Nijam asked, with contempt.

"*You* may have no sentiments regarding relics of the past, my dear Miss Nijam," said Vasily, "but M. Dumortier, I assure you, does."

"Don't worry," I said. "If there's anything of value I'll find it and get full price for it. But the more important thing is to catch the killer. If only we had Mimi to call upon! Then she might burgle Dumortier's house, and Christophe's, and we should have some hard evidence to go upon."

"We have plenty to go on without that," said Nijam with energy. "Vasily, have you finished collecting those handwriting samples?"

"Very nearly."

"Excellent," said Nijam. "Let Dumortier and the rest of the

managers' office be Vasily's responsibility. I will keep an eye on M. Christophe, and Mimi too if she attends rehearsals today. Schmidt will assist me. What about you, Dark?"

I had been thinking furiously. I might not be able to go in person, but it had occurred to me that there was one person I *could* send to Marseille. "I have an idea for retrieving the Chalabis," I said. "It isn't a certain thing—but it might help."

That satisfied them, and off they went to the Opera, leaving me to sip tea and meditate upon my next steps. The longer I thought about it, the more certain I felt that we *must* speak with the Chalabis. Nijam was right: why should they pack up and run away, so precipitately, unless they knew their daughter had been murdered? They might be able to clear up the whole mystery, and the sooner we questioned them, the sooner we might catch the killer.

It was a risk, and it made me feel that I was dirtying my hands. But then it might save a life—perhaps several lives; and that made it absolutely necessary.

When my tea was no more, I rang for Gobara, who emerged from my bedchamber with her sleeves rolled up in a very business-like manner.

"Dear me!" I said. "Was my room in such a shambles?"

"It was dusty, madame," she said. "I don't think much of your landlord, if he let it to you looking like this."

"All right; you may go and put the thumbscrews on him another day. I have another errand for you today. There was a paper in the pocket of my domino last night—"

"I found it, madame," she said, producing the paper at once.

"So you did!" I said in astonishment. "Well, just put on your hat and pop around to that address, and ask M Dupont to come and visit me. I have a job for him."

* * *

I felt a little nervous when Gobara announced Jacques Dupont, but indeed the interview went far better than I had feared.

It was the first time I had got a look at the man's unmasked face. Dupont reminded me more of the bearlike men whom I had seen in Petersburg and Moscow—round-faced day-labourers with pugnacious stubbled chins and hamlike fists—than of the leaner, darker French variety of navvy. I wondered how many days' wages had gone into purchasing a ticket to the bal masqué last night, merely on the chance of getting my assistance.

"What do you want?" he asked by way of greeting.

His impoliteness, I thought, was more a matter of habit than of hostility. "I want you to run an errand for me. It may take you as far as Marseille, though hopefully not further."

He considered this for a moment. "All right, I'm game."

"I'll understand if you refuse," I said, observing him thoughtfully over the rim of my teacup. "As a father of ten you must have other responsibilities."

I saw a twitch at the corner of his mouth, and a glint of humour in his eyes. "My wife's a capable woman. What do I do in Marseille?"

"Last night an Egyptian family, the Chalabis, departed Paris for Egypt," I told him. "You may know of the prima ballerina at the Paris Opera, Demiana Chalabi. She is their daughter, yet they travel without her. I must know what caused them to make this journey."

By the time I finished this little speech, all the humour had left Dupont's face, and a scowl replaced the smile. "I see," he said. "Has something happened to Chalabi?"

It was an odd thing for him to say, unless he already knew of Chalabi's disappearance. For a moment I wondered whether I had stumbled upon the killer! But how could a man like Dupont have gained access to the managers' letterhead, or the back stairs of the Opera? And if he had, then why should he beg me for a job? No; we were all quite certain that the murderer must be somebody already in the Opera's employment.

All the same, I could hardly tell the man that I had seen her ghost. "Nothing is yet confirmed," I said. "That is why I must send you to Marseille. Believe me: it is no whim, but a matter of life and death."

"I believe you. I'll go," he said, quite solemnly. "Will I report to you here when I return?"

"Yes; or if I'm not at home, go directly to the Opera. If you cannot find me there, report to the Baron von Jörger."

Dupont looked stubborn. "I'll make no reports to government agents. I'll report only to you, Baroness."

"What! I can assure you that the Baron is not an agent of the French government," I said, trying not to laugh.

"What else would you call a man who's been appointed by the government to run a government institution?" he asked. "An institution, moreover, which is funded by the state to the tune of four million francs a year while the lower classes die of cold, hunger, and misery—and all of it designed to glorify a corrupt and oppressive class structure!"

I suppose he made a persuasive point. Vasily had certainly been *engaged* as an agent of the French government; but whether he meant to act as one was another question entirely. I was not, however, about to enlighten Dupoint as to this point; and indeed I was beginning once again to wonder if I had made a mistake in confiding in this man.

"Jacques Dupont," I said thoughtfully. In English one might say *John Smith* or *Jack Everyman*. "Is that really your name?"

"Is von Jörger really yours?" he responded without blinking. *That* was a nasty surprise; I opened my eyes and gave him my most innocent look of perplexity. Dupont grinned and got out of the armchair, in which he had been lounging in an attitude of elaborate defiance. "Wait for me, Baroness. I'll be back in a day or two. And don't worry about the money. I've enough to take me to Marseille, but I'll keep account of everything I spend."

I saw him to the door, which was not perhaps what a real baroness would have done, but seemed appropriate given the odd sort of camaraderie he had shown me. Before he left, he said something that struck me fairly amidships.

"Keep your eye on the corps de ballet," he said, "because Chalabi isn't the first to disappear."

I knew at last precisely what it feels like to have a handful of snow dropped down the back of one's dress at a Christmas party. Not that I have ever done this to anyone; that is, not more than once.

"What do you know about it?" I asked.

"That rich people can get away with anything, and probably will," was all the answer I got. Then he put on his cap and went away despite my protests, saying that he must hurry to the train station if I wanted him to catch the Chalabis. I was left, therefore, in a state of wild surmise.

Chalabi not the first ballerina to vanish! But no one had mentioned other disappearances! Had Dumortier concealed them from us? Would Dupont tell me more if I asked? As these new questions thronged me, I felt newly uneasy about

Mimi.

I touched my transmitter. "Has anyone seen Mimi?"

"Not yet," Nijam replied. "She isn't at rehearsal, and she isn't answering her transmitter."

"And that doesn't worry you?" I cried.

"Of course it does, but I don't mean to lose my head about it."

"*Giselle* opens tonight," Vasily put in, no doubt from the marble-lined splendour of his office. "Mimi's supposed to take a major rôle in it. She will be there."

"Yes, and Demiana Chalabi is supposed to dance the lead rôle," I said, "and we know for a fact that *she* is dead!"

"Stop fretting, Dark. We're doing all that we can do," said Nijam.

"At least we may comfort ourselves that Mimi is not entirely helpless," Vasily told me, and then I knew that he was worried, too.

After that, wild horses could not have kept me away from the opening performance of *Giselle* that evening. I had Gobara do my hair, and watched the whole thing from the managers' box, seated between Vasily and M. Dumortier. The performance was a raging success. Mlle Chalabi gave a performance that even I understood to be a triumph, it was so ethereal and effortless. The crowd went into fits of adulation at each bravura display of skill.

But when the queen of dead spirits appeared at the commencement of Act Two, I sent Vasily a look of blank dismay. For this did nothing to resolve our mystery. Mimi's rôle was danced by an understudy.

Chapter X.

The significance of Mimi's non-appearance was not lost upon Nijam and Schmidt, who at the commencement of the second act had gone to wait in the wings in the hope of catching our burglar before she succeeded in stealing herself away once more. Schmidt held a small posy of flowers, which Nijam had instructed him to bestow upon Mimi as she emerged from her performance. If she accepted them, it would prove that she was alive and well. Incorporeal spirits cannot carry flowers.

Now, as the queen of the dead appeared, gliding with slow movements from the opposite side of the stage, it was Schmidt whose keener eyes first pierced the gloom. Hissing softly under his breath, he bent down to speak in Nijam's ear. *"That's not Mimi."*

Nijam did not bother to ask whether he was sure. All night, she had been plagued by nightmares; and all day, she had been bracing herself for some disaster. That it had now come upon them seemed perfectly natural and fitting. She touched her transmitter.

"Mimi would never have missed this performance of her own volition," she announced. "She may be alive, but something has most certainly gone wrong."

In the managers' box, I exchanged another glance with

Vasily. He leaned forward to address Dumortier, who sat at my right. "Isn't Mlle Laine performing the rôle of Myrtha tonight?"

"Unfortunately not," Dumortier said, quite unconcerned. "I meant to let you know that she has taken a few days' sick leave. Her understudy will fill in, meanwhile."

Backstage, Nijam and Schmidt heard Dumortier's words through my transmitter. Nijam said, "Then she must be expected to return."

"Let's hope that he knows what he's talking about," said Schmidt. Then Chalabi's partner, the dancer who played Duke Albrecht, came leaping springily offstage. Schmidt called out, "Catch," and tossed the posy. It sailed through the air and passed completely through the dancer—who vanished from view entirely!

Schmidt went over to tidy up the flowers, which had fallen to the ground. Nijam stared.

"What?" she demanded, as he returned. *"Duke Albrecht* is an imprint, too?"

"So it seems."

"But how did you *know?*"

"I didn't," Schmidt admitted, gazing down at the bruised roses. He had, of course, identified the one flaw in the theory I had proposed to explain how Chalabi was able to go on performing *Giselle* as an imprint. "It only struck me to wonder how a living man could dance with a ghost and never notice. The only possible answer is that both of them are dead."

Had Nijam bothered to attend the ballet's first act, she might have guessed herself. She touched her transmitter and in a few terse words informed Vasily and myself of their discovery.

In the box, I excused myself and stepped outside. What I

had to say could not risk being overheard by Dumortier.

"I suspected this since this afternoon. Listen: someone told me that Chalabi wasn't the first dancer to disappear."

"Who?" Vasily asked in a low voice.

"I don't know," I admitted. "He came to me at the bal masqué with a cow-and-hen story…"

"Cock-and-bull," Nijam snapped. She began to say something else; but broke off suddenly with a cry of alarm that left my ears tingling.

"Alphonse!" she shrieked.

But I am ahead of my story.

The second act of *Giselle* takes place in the pale moonlight, and the area backstage must remain darker still for fear of spoiling the effect. Nijam, in the midst of her dissertation upon the correct usage of English idioms, was arrested suddenly by some whisper of movement in the air above—a soft and swift sound, unmistakable despite the music welling from the theatre. The sound, in that darkness, saved a life. Looking up, Nijam saw a dark shape descending from one of the distant gantries that criss-crossed the rear of the stage. A heavy weight—and it was plummeting directly towards Alphonse Schmidt's golden head.

Schmidt heard her warning cry and congealed, not understanding what he was being warned of. There was no time to think; only to move. Nijam flung herself towards him and sent him staggering backwards. The next moment a punishing blow felled her.

Had the weight fallen on her head it would certainly have killed her; but her momentum was already carrying her away and it only struck a glancing blow to her shoulder. Nijam found herself gasping on hands and knees. Dust had spilled all over the floor, pooling around her fingers. *A sand-bag,* said a cool part of her mind that was not addled with pain. No doubt it was one of the counterweights used in the mechanism for raising and lowering the backdrops. It must have burst upon impact with the stage. Meanwhile, the backdrop remained stationary, meaning that this was no mechanical error. Some malicious person had detached the bag from the mechanism and carried it up the gantry—poised, aimed, and then released it at the moment it might do most harm!

Gentle fingers probed her shoulder, making her gasp with pain. Nijam looked up to find Alphonse crouching before her. His hand touched her cheek. She had never seen him look so pale and frightened. "Miss Nijam, Miss Nijam"—he kept saying her name again and again, begging her to tell him that she was all right.

What the blazes did he think he was doing, having a breakdown at a moment like this? Nijam caught his wrist, tearing his hand away from her face.

"The killer," she choked. Her throat wasn't working properly. "Up there. In the gantry. Trying to murder you."

He ought to have been up and running after the man they had come to Paris to catch, at great trouble to Nijam herself, who would have been quite happy to stay in London experimenting on a new idea she had for improving the transmitters. Instead he was simply congealed to immobility and staring at her with enormous eyes. Nijam raised her eyes to the shadows above. She saw the gantry; she saw a dark shape moving upon it. If the Paris Opera was anything like the Bolshoi in Moscow, there would be a ladder or stair—yes! There, in the corner!

She wrenched away from Alphonse, scrambled to her feet,

and tottered towards the ladder. Her whole being was fixed upon the need to catch the attacker before he could hurt Schmidt or anyone else…The whole theatre seemed to be reeling in an earthquake, but she made her way up the ladder to the first landing before her body betrayed her altogether and she found herself lying on the rough iron of the gantry, panting hard and sick with pain.

Schmidt reached the gantry a moment after she did, but instead of going on, he knelt down and raised her head from the cold iron. "Alphonse," she said, with volume and insistence, *"you have to go after that creature."*

"And leave you fainting in a dark corner?" he asked, as if the thought was too preposterous to be entertained for a moment. "He tried to kill you!"

"Tried to kill *you*," she mumbled, but Schmidt peeled her off the floor, put his shoulder into her stomach, and straightened until she was draped over him like a wet towel. As he carried her down the ladder again, she dimly heard him speaking on the transmitter, telling the others what had happened and asking where he might be able to find the Opera doctor. Nijam ground her teeth together, only partly to keep any whimper of pain from escaping her. The killer had been there, right above them, and once again they had let him get away.

* * *

The doctor pronounced nothing wrong with Nijam but a bad bruising, and after keeping her for an hour to ensure that she was recovering well, sent her home with instructions to apply ice, arnica, and rest. With that, Schmidt helped her out to the cab he had waiting in one of the side streets that ran the Opera's circumference and settled her within so tenderly that Nijam scarcely knew herself. She had long made her peace with the knowledge that she was too foreign, too dark, too low to be treated with the tenderness and gallantry afforded to the fair and golden. Not for Nijam any affectation of weakness, any touching reliance upon the gallantry of a gentleman. From a coloured woman these would only be viewed as an invitation to an exploit, something to be recounted with laughter in the clubs of white men... Since she could inspire no tender feelings of protection, she must provoke terror instead.

Or so she had always believed, and so she had always conducted herself, choosing rather to be cursed for her severity, than exploited for her weakness. Even Alphonse himself, in the old days before he lost his memory, had treated her with a certain cautious reserve. ...Of course, in the old days, she had never been sandbagged by a homicidal maniac.

Nijam was well accustomed to fits of melancholy, in which unhappy thoughts chased themselves ceaselessly through her mind. The thoughts that took possession of her now were different and altogether unexpected. How different was Schmidt from any other man she had ever met! How much he had changed for the better, even since the days in Heidelberg when she first formed the opinion that he was the best of men! She knew very well that she had made him fear her; yet despite this he still found the courage to treat her as someone infinitely precious—someone whose moments of weakness called for tenderness, rather than brutality.

Opposite her, Schmidt heaved an unhappy sigh. "Perhaps you were right," he said. "Perhaps I ought to have gone after him."

"Oh, without a doubt," Nijam agreed. She was still lost in a rosy haze. Schmidt, who always conscientiously did what he believed to be right, had set aside the greatest good for *her* sake. The hope she felt was as poignant as grief and as blinding as the sun. Perhaps he would give up other things for her, too, if she only confessed everything, as I had advised her. Perhaps both of them deserved her candour.

At that moment they arrived at the narrow townhouse she shared with Mimi. The cab drew up behind a brougham waiting there. Schmidt opened the cab door and said, "Don't move; just give me your key and I'll help you in." Nijam was fumbling in her pocket among the candle-ends and notebooks and pencil-stubs for the key, when the door to the house opened and Mimi emerged carrying a valise.

Such was their surprise that neither Nijam nor Schmidt moved or spoke as Mimi briskly descended the steps and handed her valise into the brougham. Then Schmidt shouted, "Mimi!"

Turning a startled face upon him, Mimi leaped into her brougham. Schmidt darted after her, protesting, "Mimi, Mimi, a moment!"

"I'm not ready to come back yet!" Mimi retorted. Her coachman cracked his whip and the brougham began to move. Schmidt leaped to the step of the carriage, seizing the door and wrestling with the handle. Then he seemed to recoil, losing his grip just as the carriage picked up speed. It sped away; and Schmidt tripped in the gutter and sat heavily upon the curb, staring wordlessly at the departing vehicle.

Nijam eased herself out of the cab. Her heart stood still when she saw the look of terror upon his face.

"Are you hurt?" she cried, imagining goodness knows what.

"That face!" he cried hoarsely. "I know that face; I've dreamed it!"

"What face?"

He staggered to his feet and put a hand against the nearby lamp-post. The other he passed across his eyes. Nijam inspected him for blood or bruises, but there was no injury that she could see. A hurt, then, of the mind. When that occurred to her, her blood ran cold again.

"There was a man in the carriage," he said slowly, as though the thing needed explaining to himself as well as to Nijam. "You never saw such a face! Black and withered and shrunken, with protruding teeth—and sunken cheeks—and his eyes!—Great staring eyes, and a cold blue light burning within them."

Nijam reached out blindly to steady herself against the same lamp-post. Faces like the one he described had been plaguing her dreams all night. It was impossible, she thought. How could one of *them* have survived?

How could Schmidt's doom have come upon them like *this?*

"It looked like a dead thing," Schmidt said dully. And then his voice changed. "Look at me," he said, seizing her hand. "Look at me, Padma Nijam."

She raised her eyes and watched the look of inquiry on his face harden into certainty.

"You *know*," he breathed. "You know what that *thing* is!"

How could she know anything? Events had left their known path and marched beyond the realm of possibility. She had no explanation for this.

Schmidt looked at her as though she had tried to stab him in the back.

She tore her hand away with such force that she pulled her bruised shoulders. Tears of pain sprung to her eyes. "I don't," she said hoarsely. "What you saw cannot possibly be what you have described." The door-key was still clutched in her hand. Somehow, she made it to the door, got herself inside and shot the bolt behind her. Once inside, she fell back against the bolted door, breathing hard as though she had just finished a race. In her head, her transmitter crackled. Schmidt calling her, begging her to explain. She switched the device off.

Explain? She could not explain any more than she already had. He could not have seen what he had described. What he had described was a memory, that was all.

And she ground her teeth. *Now? Now* Schmidt was ready to remember? *This* was what he remembered? Why could he not have remembered *anything* else?

Why could he not have remembered *her?*

A stranger, observing Nijam in the grip of this emotion, doubtless would have considered her to be pondering some abstruse mathematical equation. The entry-hall echoed to the blows of Schmidt's fists and his muffled pleading. At last the dull ache in her shoulders reasserted itself, and Nijam moved slowly up the stairs. There was some chloral in the case in her room: that would dull the pain and put her to sleep.

But if Schmidt had not seen what he described, then what *had* he seen? What had Mimi got herself into?

It was not a question she could answer; not in this condition. Nijam paused only to take her dose and kick off her boots before pitching into bed, where blissful oblivion soon descended.

* * *

When it became quite clear that Nijam meant not to answer him, Alphonse Schmidt turned his back on the house altogether. At first he did not think of going anywhere in particular; he only roamed through the streets of Paris, plaguing himself with questions. *How* did he know that nightmare visage, with its glowing eyes and its bleached locks? What did Nijam know of the creature—and how did Mimi come to be in its company?

Once more, Schmidt felt the past breathing hot and accusing down his neck, for all the world like a hound with molten eyes. Once more, he felt the formless guilt of some long-forgotten wrong committed by himself against heaven only knew whom…

A horrible thought struck him. Schmidt recoiled. No! He *had* sinned, he was sure of it—but surely not against Miss Nijam!

Still, he could not help the thought taking possession of him. A thousand small pieces of evidence flocked to reinforce it. Miss Nijam had been struck all of a heap the first day they had met at the Schloss Frohsdorf, demanding to know whether he was an acquaintance of hers in Heidelberg. Miss Nijam had always been unrelentingly hostile. When the Okhrana arrested him in Moscow, it was Miss Nijam who explained that Schmidt had once worked with his elder brother, Stefan, to create revenants.

Most troublingly of all, that glimpse of the man with the flaming eyes had upset Miss Nijam quite as much as it had upset himself.

Schmidt wished that he might flee, that when the secret of his past was revealed he might be far away on the other side of the world, ignorant and happy as he hitherto had been. But that was impossible. He, no less than his master, *needed* his friends: without them he would be defenceless, easy prey for the Russians or whoever else might still dream of using him to create monsters… Besides, he could not leave Miss Nijam. Everything within him revolted at the idea.

He was caught in the horns of an intolerable dilemma.

The clock of a nearby church struck two o'clock. Schmidt looked up. He had made his way somehow to the Boulevard des Capucines. It was not very far to the flat he shared with Vasily, and he knew that he ought to go home, to rest if he could not sleep, and to prepare himself for the day ahead.

He turned up the Rue Scribe towards the Boulevard Haussmann, and a few minutes later was unlocking the door, when the tail of his eye caught a dark shape fleeting towards him. Turning to face his assailant, Schmidt saw a long glinting blade drawn back for a thrust. He parried the blade with a sweep of his left arm, which was protected by a thick woollen overcoat, before shooting out his right and dealing the attacker a stunning blow upon the point of the jaw. Schmidt was surprised when this hardly seemed to bother his assailant: who, staggering backward, caught Schmidt's wrist and used it to steady himself for a riposte with the sword-point. Schmidt twisted, feeling a scorching pain as the point pierced his waistcoat and shirt and grazed his ribs. Whereupon, feeling that enough was enough, he seized his assailant in both hands—the latter was much lighter than he looked—and hurled the fellow bodily over the railing into the area. There was a loud clangour from below as the garbage-bins were bowled down. The attacker was evidently still attempting to extricate himself when Schmidt opened the door and slipped within, closing it gently behind him.

It struck him as merely fitting that a day of such extraordinarily bad fortune should have ended with a second episode of random violence. Now he had a gash in his ribs and, worse still, bloodstains in the lining of his best winter coat. Heaving a sigh, Schmidt pressed a hand to the wound and climbed laboriously up the stairs to his rest.

Chapter XI.

Nijam awoke late the next morning with throbbing shoulders and a foggy head. Downstairs, someone was apparently making renewed efforts to batter the door down. She groaned and got up, moving stiffly, to look for a glass of water. Mimi's room, of course, was in nearly the identical state of disorder it had been left in.

She switched on her transmitter with a tap at her temple. "Go away, Schmidt," she croaked.

"Miss Nijam, thank God," he said. "I was afraid something had happened to you. May I have a word?"

"I'm not the one you should be worried about; Mimi is," said Nijam disagreeably. Her back ached abominably, and she was in no fit state for confidences. She switched off her transmitter and went back to bed.

* * *

Alas! I myself did not overhear this exchange because at the time I was not wearing my transmitter, being nose deep in my bath. After a leisurely brunch about one o'clock, I had Gobara do my hair and fit me out in an afternoon-dress of a tyrannical emerald-green colour, which suited me nearly as well as the red velvets had. Strong colours, my mother always told me, were unsuitable for unmarried girls in general and myself in particular. But the Paris modistes kept producing dazzling jewel-coloured reds and blues and greens for me—colours that suited me so well, I barely needed Gobara's subtle powders to emphasise the colour in my cheeks.

Then I ordered a cab and went to visit Mlles Perrot and Dargent, who occupied a town-house nearly as charming as the Chalabis'. Some two hours later, as I was finishing off a slice of cake and my third cup of tea in the merry hum of Mlle Perrot's impeccably appointed drawing-room, the transmitter in my head crackled and I heard Vasily saying, "But my dear fellow, you ought to have told us *hours* ago! Molly-my-dear! Stop what you're doing and pay attention!"

"A moment," I said, over the sound of Schmidt protesting that he would have informed sir of recent developments if sir *or* madam had been listening at all. Excusing myself reluctantly from the conversation—for the poems being discussed contained some rather provocative ambiguities—I asked the parlour-maid to show me to the water-closet.

"All right; go ahead," I said, closing the door behind me. I looked for a place to sit, but the porcelain necessary was so intricately embossed and gilded with swooping Art Nouveau motifs that I hardly liked to profane it.

"It happened last night," Schmidt said, "when I was seeing Miss Nijam home after somebody tried to sandbag her. We saw Mimi."

"You saw Mimi!" I exclaimed. "Where? Was she all right?"

"Perfectly," he answered. "She had evidently been collecting some belongings from the house. We saw her from our cab and called out to her, but she hurried into a brougham that was waiting for her and called out that she was not yet ready to return. Then I ran after her and tried to peer into the cab." For a moment he fell silent, as though summoning up the courage to continue. "There was a man in there with her—I don't know how to describe him. I thought I had strayed into a nightmare. He had a head like death, and flaming eyes. He leaned forward and hissed at me. I was so startled that I fell from the step and the brougham dashed away."

Vasily was silent a moment, as though even he had not expected this. "Flaming eyes? I don't suppose *you* have ever come across such a thing, Molly?"

"Never," said I. Later, it occurred to me that perhaps Schmidt's description was a trifle overdone; but then, the poor man had had a dreadful shock. "I say—you don't suppose that might explain why M. Christophe goes about in a mask?"

"Indeed, I've always presumed he had some sort of—ah, condition, that made him unpleasant to look at," Vasily said. "I don't suppose, Schmidt, that this person might simply have been rather ugly?"

"No," Schmidt said at once. "No ordinary man could look like that."

"Curious," Vasily murmured thoughtfully, half to himself. "We shan't know until Mimi comes back."

"*If* Mimi comes back," I said, for I was full of foreboding upon the topic, "and *if* she is willing to speak to us when she does."

"In any case we know that she was alive and well last night, and that if she is staying away, it's of her own free will," Vasily said.

"Are we sure of that?" Schmidt asked, voicing my own unspoken worry. "That creature might have any sort of hold over her."

"That's true," Vasily said, "but remember that this is Mimi we're talking of! The man doesn't live that could hold Mimi captive wholly against her will. We must just trust her judgement, that is all. Anything to report, Molly-my-dear?"

I risked a glance into the passage to assure myself that no one was waiting impatiently for the use of the facilities. Finding it empty, I told them where I was.

"There isn't much to tell, except that you've dragged me away from a very pleasant party. Everyone is eating very small cakes and reading poetry and discussing which Greek philosopher they would name a cat after. I've never felt like such an intellectual in my life. Oh! And one of the gentlemen is putting on a reading of *Phèdre* next week, and he has asked me to take a leading rôle! I can't even recall the last time I had the chance to do some real acting!"

"As I recollect, you put on a rather decent performance the other night as the injured Baroness von Jörger," Vasily said, a mite unhappily. "Didn't you have other business there, my dear, rather than taking parts in French tragedies?"

"Oh! You mean old Perrot's papers? Mlle Perrot and I had a look through them before the salon began. I'm afraid it's not good news. They are mostly private, family documents, and it seems that anything of value was already purchased by the Opera after M. Perrot's death. There's an old journal of Marie Taglioni's, but *that* is probably worthless, for it was written after she retired from dancing and chiefly concerns what she had, with whom, for dinner. But Mlle Perrot said there's a Degas painting upstairs, a portrait of her uncle in the foyer de la danse. I suppose old Dumortier may be interested in *that*. But she doesn't want to sell it, and we can't very well rob Mlle Perrot, a perfectly innocent third party, in order to right Mme Larousse."

Besides which, I couldn't imagine stealing the thing without Mimi's expert assistance.

"You might as well cut upstairs and take a look at it, anyway," Vasily said. "Dumortier has a passion for Degas, and has collected a number of his paintings to display at the Opera. The greatest danger is that he may already have commissioned a copy of this one. Do you think you can find it?"

Once again, I wished devoutly that Mimi was here. *She* would have no trouble climbing in at an open window, taking a look at the painting, and deciding at a glance what it was worth. Myself, I am not cut out for burglary. I become nervous, and I don't know how to ferret out what I want. Still, with the ladies of the house and all their servants thoroughly occupied in the salon, the upper floors must be more or less deserted. If I was to do the job at all, I would never have a better chance.

"All right," I said, "but if anything goes wrong I shall tell them I was following *your* orders, Baron."

I now switched off my transmitter, stole past the drawing-room door and tiptoed up the stairs, which I thanked Providence were solid enough not to creak. To tell the truth, my mind was mostly taken up with happiness at the thought of acting again. Mlle Perrot's friend said that he often put on home theatricals, in which ladies and gentlemen whose appearance on the public stage would cause a scandal were able to pursue their art. If I did well in reading *Phèdre,* I might be able to take another rôle later. I might be a *real* artist again!

Then I recalled that my job was of the sort that was likely to take me away from Paris before I could do more than attend a reading or two, and I heaved a sigh of regret. I recalled an exchange that had occurred the first time we were all in London together on the Noor-Jahan job—Vasily asking my sisters what sort of artist I was, and Mimi answering "Confidence" under her breath. She and I had both, I thought, begun with other ambitions.

Upstairs, I began opening doors in search of the painting. The first two on either side of the corridor led to spare rooms and a cosy little upstairs parlour that was partly sitting-room, partly study. None of them contained a Degas painting, and none, apart from the sitting-room, showed any sign of human habitation. The fifth and final door led to a bedchamber which *was* inhabited, being splendidly decorated in a state of bohemian disarray. The wardrobe stood open and since the sky-blue domino from the night of the bal masqué was flung over the door, I judged the room to belong to Mlle Dargent. Two windows opened onto a high balcony at the front of the house, sheltered beneath the eaves. There was a writing-desk, a multitude of potted palms and Persian carpets—and there on the wall above the writing-desk was the Degas.

The painting was larger than I expected and showed M. Perrot as a white-haired little old man standing in the foyer de la danse, wearing a suit of pale-coloured summer flannels and surrounded by fashionable young ballerinas whose dresses of white gauze were accessorised with coloured sashes, flowers pinned in their upswept hair and black ribbons tied rakishly about their necks. It was a comfortable scene, the sort of picture a camera, which requires its subjects to sit stiff and formal for a deal of time, could never capture. M. Perrot's attention was taken up by a ballerina on the far side of the room, who was demonstrating her steps; nearer the viewer another, perched idly atop the grand piano, had reached around herself to scratch at her back.

I may not be very good at burglary, but I have a decent idea of a painting's worth, since my mother and my sister Emily are both successful artists. I could see at once that this was a magnificent work. Moving quickly, I seated myself at the desk and took up a sheet of letter-paper to create a rough sketch of the painting and its chief figures. This did not take me very long, and I was returning my pen to the blotter when I saw another sheet of paper tucked beneath the one I had taken up. This proved to be the rough draft of a poem that bore some startling similarities to the ones we had been reading this afternoon—except that in French, certain turns of phrase within it lost all ambiguity. It was signed *Amélie Perrot*. I stared at it for a long time in amazement. Surely not!

But then the entire pattern fitted together in my head. The taste for Sappho and Pindar—Deleuze's hints that there was gossip or scandal to share—the unoccupied rooms, except for this one. Clutching my sketch, I arose from the desk and gazed about me. There was a case for spectacles on one of the bedside tables. Only Mlle Perrot wore spectacles—and now that I could see within the wardrobe, I also saw Mlle Perrot's darker domino folded upon one of the shelves.

In all the space and comfort of this house, the ladies were sharing a room—for all the world like a married couple! I was truly shocked. It was not, as the reader will know, that I found the notion odd or repugnant—how strongly I felt the charms of my own sex!—but I had always believed that by and large people did not *act* upon these inclinations. After all, when Vasily's father was caught embracing a male dancer on the stage of the Bolshoi Theatre, it had exposed him to the scorn of the world, so that he was exiled in disgrace to the Crimea!

Now I saw at a blink how the ladies covered their unconventional household arrangements beneath the respectable mantle of friendship. I saw, too, that I had all unwittingly stumbled upon a secret that could ruin them forever. I liked them both; I shared some of their inclinations; I did not wish to see them subjected to all the vicious penalties that hypocrisy could visit upon those who erred in such a fashion. Imagine what Célestin Deleuze would do with such a tidbit!

Perhaps I did not reason it all out like that, in that moment. But it ran through my head in a single flash of intuition: so that a moment later, when I heard footsteps coming up the stairs and Mlle Dargent calling out that with the visitors gone she meant to lie down for half an hour, I lost my head entirely. I could *not* be caught in this room, in the guilty possession of such a secret! In the guilty possession of a *painting,* now, I might have dared to brazen it out; but the secret was too much for me. I stuffed the sketch into my pocket, opened the French door as softly as I dared, and slipped out onto the balcony. There was as little room to hide here, as there had been upon a similar occasion upon a similar balcony in Moscow. And on that occasion, although it was midnight, I had been discovered!

Quick, I asked myself—what would Mimi do? There was a trellis at one side of the balcony, supporting a creeping vine positioned to screen the little platform from harsh sunlight and prying eyes. I swarmed up it and got my hands onto the gutter of the roof. The sound of the bedroom door opening below lent me agility, and in a mad scramble I made it onto the steeply sloping slate tiles. The trellis gave way beneath my foot just as I got my right hand around the corner of the chimney-stack. For a ghastly long moment I clung precariously to that slope, slicing open my palm on a ragged edge of slate as I sought a hold with my left hand. Then at last I pulled myself up and wedged myself safely between the slanted roof and the great solid brick chimney.

For a moment I hugged myself and listened.

I must have made some slight sounds, for the French door to the balcony opened, and I heard Mlle Dargent call sharply—"Is someone there?" But she must not have found the tell-tale signs of my passing. After a moment's stillness she only sighed and closed the door again. For a moment I felt extremely clever. I had asked myself what Mimi would do, and it had proven easier than I expected. True, I had cut my hand, and the roof was not particularly comfortable; but I had a handkerchief with which to stanch the flow of blood and at least I had avoided discovery. Now I had only to wait until Mlle Dargent finished her nap, and then I might climb down and steal out of the house.

Then I peered around the chimney, and that was the end of all my fine plans. With my eyes fixed upon the next hand-hold, going up had been very little trouble. Going down would be impossible. The roof sloped sharply away to the gutter, and the trellis beneath was now wavering in the wind, held in place only by a few strands of creeper. Tucked beneath the eaves, the balcony could not catch me if I fell; and then there was a dizzying drop of three storeys to the pavement below, the mere sight of which made me feel weak and dizzy. I was completely stuck!

There was nothing else to do. I touched my transmitter.

"Vasily?"

"Little mouse," he answered at once. "How did you know I was thinking of you?"

"Oh, Vasily," I repeated, for I was in no mood either to bill or to coo. "I've got myself into a dreadful fix, and you must promise not to laugh."

"Would I do such a thing? What has happened?"

I told him. Vasily said blankly, "On the *roof?*"

"I asked myself what Mimi would do," I wailed.

Vasily then proved himself entirely heartless and also untrustworthy, for he went off into gales of laughter.

"You promised you wouldn't laugh!"

"But how can I help it? The roof! My dear! If God had meant mice to fly He would have given them wings! Have you a safe place to sit?"

"Yes, and pretty well hidden too. Do you think you can get me down?"

"Never fear: you won't escape me so easily. I will fetch you down or perish in the attempt. But it might be best done after darkness falls. Do you think you'll be safe for two hours until sunset?"

I shivered, for the day was cold and I had come upstairs without a coat, or a hat, or a pelisse. When Mlle Perrot found my things still hanging in her hall, she would be terribly puzzled—though that would be nothing to her puzzlement if she was to learn that I was at present perched behind her chimney-pots! I felt extremely grateful for the masonry that concealed me from any servant who might happen to peer out one of the nearby windows.

"I'll have to be," I said mournfully, surveying the sea of sloping roofs, chimneys and little dormers that surrounded me. "I may catch my death of cold, but just now I'd prefer uncertain to certain death."

"All right," my lover said. "Stay there; I'll be with you the moment it's dark enough to conceal me." His transmitter snicked shut and I buried my face in my hands. I felt a frightful duffer, but at least I had Vasily. He had been an idle fellow all his life and did not have many accomplishments to recommend him, but he had climbed in at windows of mine on previous occasions and I felt that, in Mimi's absence, he was the next best person to retrieve me from my ridiculous perch.

For some time, then, I sat uncomfortably wedged against my chimney, watching the sun go down behind M. Eiffel's great tower in the west. Now, with my rescue secured, my thoughts reverted to the startling discovery that had sent me scrambling up onto the rooftop.

So, this was the meaning of the Greek poetry reading circle! I shook my head, thinking now that I ought to have understood sooner. Did I like Sappho, indeed! In fact, they had taught us very little about Sappho at school, except that she had been a poetess. We did not, of course, *read* any of her verse. Only the veiled discussion in the salon downstairs this afternoon had opened my eyes to the real meaning of the poetry, but even then I had thought little of it. These days, surely, people did not live as the Ancient Greeks had lived!

Yet the ladies had seemed so very respectable! I understood now the meaning of the circumspection with which they carried themselves, and why they took care to offend no one in the exercise of their wit. True: Deleuze and his ilk might sneer and gossip, but there was no *proof;* and what was more natural, or more ladylike, than two quiet, sensible spinsters sharing a house as each other's companion? Never having been capable hitherto of imagining such a ménage, I was now struck all of a heap by how utterly simple the thing was—and how perfectly respectable! It would not be like living with a *male* lover. Indeed it would not be half so bad as getting married to a layabout like Vasily!

The day grew colder as the sun declined. The light became slanting and golden, yet still I could not expect Vasily for another hour at least... It struck me that some, at least, of the people I had met in Mlle Perrot's salon this afternoon must know of her domestic arrangements, and share in her inclinations. It was that thought which entirely overbore me. I could never confess *my* secret, either to my family, or to my crew. There was no one to whom I could speak of the things I thought and wished. Even Vasily, who had guessed at it, did not *really* understand—his experiments had been just that, a passing whim. Now it occurred to me to wish for the company of another person like myself—someone to whom I could, at least, *speak* with perfect freedom. I had never had such a friend in my life; for a moment I was nearly sick with wanting one.

A chill wind blew upon the rooftop. I hugged my knees with a shiver, thinking how society and religion both frowned upon my inclinations, until I sometimes felt very wicked, merely for having them. It had, after all, taken the wickedest person I had ever known to see the inward desires of my heart. But was Vasily the best I deserved? I did not *want* to feel wicked. I did not think that Mlle Perrot felt herself to be wicked, and oh! how I wished I might feel the same!

It struck me more forcefully than ever that I had money now, and choices. I did not need to marry at all, if I did not wish to. If I found that I did not get on with Vasily...

I recoiled from the idea, and then fell into a rather feverish conversation with myself.

Careful Molly pointed out that the ladies in this house might be strong-minded enough to live without the sanction of God or society, without the protection of vows or the solace of offspring. But I was not made in such a heroic cast. *I* liked to be approved of.

Curious Molly said that I could not know until I had tried it, and after all it would be a very easy thing to try. I had barely lived enough to know what I really wanted. Now that I was free, I could try anything at all—or any *one*. Perhaps it was my duty to try it. Then I would know whether Vasily really was the man for me—just as Vasily needed to understand that he had other choices, too, before he could be at peace with me.

Careful Molly insisted that this was confounded sophistry. If Vasily ran about paying court to other people in the name of making informed choices I should feel angry and betrayed, and I must not play the same tricks on him.

But I needn't go very far, said Curious Molly. Whenever Mimi turns up again I could give her five pounds to kiss me and no one would be any the wiser.

But this was a step too far, and then I felt half sick. Mimi had been bought and sold all her life, and I had sworn to myself that as a member of my crew she should at last have her dignity. And now my thoughts enticed me to trample upon that dignity—to use my money against her, and have her kiss me when I knew perfectly well she didn't care for it.

I could not reach for what I wanted by trampling upon my friends. And then, I wondered, how was I to square such a thing with my religion? Was not God, as I had begun to think of him, my Friend in Heaven?

Always, before, I had been able to answer that quite easily. Religion was religion; it was the guide that restrained
my actions precisely when my inclinations most conspired
against me, whispering that I had the right to be impatient, or
grasping, or unkind. This evening, I turned to that guide and
found it suddenly lacking: for what kind of Friend would see
fit to burden me with such a secret, and such a load of guilt?

So far I had come, when my transmitter crackled and I
heard Vasily say in a low voice, "All right, Molly-my-dear—
I'm coming to get you."

"I'm waiting," I said in a small, subdued voice. I leaned
forward and shuddered once again at the dizzying drop
beneath me, so far in the darkness that I could not tell which
of the dim shapes coming and going in the street beneath me
might belong to my lover. "Oh, Vasily! I can't imagine how
you'll climb it!"

"My dear, are you forgetting that I was bitten by my cousin
Cyril several months ago?" He sounded quite calm, though
somewhat short of breath. I leaned out a little further and
saw a dark shape perched upon the pediment of the front
door, reaching for a fresh hand-hold. "I am now a good deal
stronger than most men, if not quite what I used to be. Second,
thanks to your beau Griff, I also have a prosthetic eye that
can see in the dark. I am, in fact, the very model of a modern
Opera-manager."

I stifled a giggle and felt better at once. "Does the prosthetic
eye help with Opera-managing?"

"Oh, immensely," he said with a little gasp, for he was
now scaling the second-floor balconies. "You have no idea—
how useful it is—to know when one of the sopranos is
bamboozling one." He disappeared into the balcony, but his

voice went on. "Third—you don't know many vampires, I take it, but we are all very good at climbing things. We have to be. There used to be a connection of the family in Roumania who fairly crawled about the walls of his ancestral castle like a lizard."

"Well, be careful of the trellis on the second right-hand balcony," I told him. "There's nothing but a few vines holding it up anymore."

This did not trouble him, however; and a minute later Vasily got himself onto the tiles and crouched before me. How he kept his footing on that dizzy slope I shall never know. In the fading light I could see that he was in his shirt-sleeves and carried a pack on his back.

"There," he said, between breaths. "I told you you couldn't get away from me." Then he stopped and sniffed the air, and said in a sharper tone, "You're injured!"

"It's nothing, really."

"My dear, I can smell the blood."

I put out my hand, and he unwrapped my handkerchief and looked down at the oozing cut for a long, silent moment.

"What's wrong?" I asked. Perhaps with his prosthetic eye he could see something I could not.

He drew in a deep breath. "It's nothing. It's like the old days again; that's all—scaling a house, and fresh blood at the end of my climb. What I wouldn't have given for a taste, back then!"

I watched him through the twilight, and then said, "You may taste, if you wish." What was a little blood between lovers? Since I had spilled the blood already, he might as well have it, if he liked it.

Vasily hesitated; but then he shook his head with an air of decision, and wrapped up the hand in the handkerchief, tucking in the ends, before pressing a kiss upon it. "Tempt me with your kisses, my sweet, but not with your blood. *You* might be willing, but it is not good for *me* to treat you as a thing, as food."

"I *am* sorry," I said, vexed with myself for offering him the same sort of temptation I had spurned myself a moment ago. Perhaps, for a moment, I had forgotten that consciences are tricky things; that a thing might seem perfectly harmless to one person, and yet be poison to another.

"There's no harm done. Now, let's see what might be in this pack!"

Vasily loosened the draw-string and opened the knapsack. "Hmm," he said, coming out with a brown-paper bag that smelled tantalisingly of butter and hot, crisp pastry. "I know that I had a rope-ladder in here somewhere. Hold this for me."

I accepted the paper bag with a giggle which probably would have scandalised my sisters, could they have heard it. There was a croissant within, still warm enough to make my numb fingers tingle. "Oh, Vasily, you shouldn't have!"

"I didn't," he said, straight-faced. "That's my dinner."

"Too late; you ought to have mentioned it sooner," said I, through a mouthful of the hot pastry.

"What a future I have to look forward to!" he sighed. He took a second pastry from the pack (of *course* he did) and then produced a bottle of wine and a pair of glasses. At this point I was laughing so much, it is a wonder that someone didn't come around to investigate.

"Please tell me you have a cushion in there, too."

Wordlessly, he produced it.

"Ah," he added, happily. "I've found the rope-ladder. Sauvignon blanc?"

"Vasily," I protested, "you can't really imagine we ought to be drinking wine on a roof-top."

"My dear, it's Paris. What else are we going to drink on the roof-top?"

"Can't we drink it somewhere else? *After* we have climbed down?"

"I could ask nothing more," Vasily said, "than to deck you in red velvet and garnets, and take you out to Maxim's for the best dinner of your life. But it's useless. We're supposed to be divorcing."

"It *was* your idea," I reminded him. "Come on. Let's climb down and find a nice warm room to picnic in, perhaps with a Persian rug and a fireplace."

With that Vasily packed the food and drink away again, before making the rope-ladder fast to the chimney. "Schmidt will anchor it, down below," he assured me. "Are you sure you don't want a nip of something to steady your nerves?"

"Quite sure," I assured him. "Do you mean to say Schmidt has been waiting all this time in the cold street?"

Vasily looked surprised. "Why shouldn't he? *You* have been waiting on a cold rooftop."

"Only because I had no choice," said I. "You understand, don't you, Vasya that that's part of the trouble between Schmidt and Nijam? She sees the way you treat him, and she thinks he ought to stand up for himself."

Vasily frowned over the complicated knots he was making about the chimney. "What is the matter with the way I treat Schmidt?"

"Oh—*you* know. Like a servant."

"But he *is* a servant."

I thought about it a moment, racking my wits in vain for a person whom Vasily might recognise as an equal. If I mentioned one of his brothers or cousins, he would very truly insist that they outranked him. Apart from Schmidt, he had no other male friends. I was his lady-love and everyone else he knew, he treated as an inferior—save, perhaps, one:

"You don't treat Miss Nijam the same way."

"Miss Nijam is a *lady,*" said Vasily. "Moreover, she would have my head if I tried it."

"Miss Nijam is the illegitimate daughter of a bigamous marriage between a coloured man and a lady whose grandfather was a stevedore," I pointed out. "If she gets treated as a lady it is only because she insists upon it. Schmidt doesn't. That's the only real difference between them."

Vasily tested the rope-ladder, first by a few sharp tugs, and then by trusting it with his entire weight and *bouncing.*

"You think I ought to treat Schmidt as a gentleman?" he asked, when he was finished. He spoke quietly, as though the thought was a startling one.

"I think you might eventually work up to considering him an equal," I said.

He was silent for a moment. "I don't think I've ever considered anyone my equal," he said at last. "Everyone I've ever known has been either my inferior or my superior."

I did not tell him that this was clear to anyone who had known him. "You aren't a Grand Duke any more," I said, quietly. "You must learn new ways of doing things now."

"And you really think it would help the two of them?"

"I think," said I, "that Schmidt has been taught not to respect himself, and that it will be very difficult for him to learn better, while you treat him as though he is nothing."

Vasily gave a rather forced laugh. "Enough! I am chastened," he said. "But I ought to have expected it. I could never stop at treating *you* like a person. Now I must go on and do the same for the rest of the world, too."

I allowed him his flippancy; it was his last shred of princely dignity. But I said wickedly, "Do you regret it? Don't forget that you might have had Princess Zlata instead."

He shuddered. "I'd let Schmidt play the master and I the man, sooner than go back to Russia and kiss Nicky's ring."

Then he helped me extract myself from the chimney and creep onto the rope-ladder, which swung and twisted quite alarmingly, even with Schmidt's heavy weight affixed to the end. My heart was in my mouth the entire way down, particularly when my journey took me past the sitting-room windows. I vowed that if I survived the climb, from this moment forth I would leave the burgling to Mimi!

At last—trembling, but safe and undetected—I reached the ground. Schmidt assisted me to disentangle myself from the ladder and to my great delight returned to me the same hat, gloves, and warm coat I had left in Mlle Perrot's hall closet. It is possible that I shed a tear or two upon his shoulder— but Schmidt was the sort of person who did not mind such familiarities. Then the rope ladder was loosed from its place around the chimney and fell in a slithering heap at our feet, and I watched with my heart in my mouth as Vasily made his way from the roof to the ground.

"Safe at last!" I breathed, when Vasily too had returned to *terra firma*. "At least, the three of us. I say, has anyone heard from Nijam today? Was she that badly hurt last night at the Opera?"

"She's at home," Schmidt said quietly, "but she's not answering her door—or her transmitter."

Not answering her door—to *Schmidt,* thought I. The entire crew was a little out of sorts; and when that happened it was doubtless *my* job to smooth things over. Sighing, I touched my transmitter and said, "Nijam, are you there? We just want to know that you're all right."

"Of course I'm all right," Nijam answered at once. "Yes, I'm up. No, I don't need a doctor. We ought to meet; I have something to tell you."

"Oh," I said in surprise. "I'm delighted to hear it. Shall we come over to your house?"

"Don't bother; I'm already within sight of the Opera. I'll see you in Vasily's office in two minutes."

"But we're in the Rue de Grenelle," I objected. "We'll have to catch a cab. Never mind; we'll be on our way at once." So much for the cosy little picnic before the fire!

"The Rue de Grenelle?" Nijam repeated blankly. "What are you doing over *there?*"

"Rescuing Miss Dark from a rooftop," Vasily said promptly. Of *course* he did!

There was a brief silence, during which I could *feel* Nijam pinching the bridge of her nose. "I don't want to know," she said with decision. "All right; I'll be waiting for you in—"

Abruptly her voice stopped, and then sharpened. "Something is happening in the Grand Foyer," she said. "Mimi—it's Mimi!"

For a horrible instant my heart stood still. "Dead?" I asked.

"Good God, Dark, what an imagination you have. Mimi— you look terrible! What has happened to you?"

I exchanged a glance with Vasily and Schmidt. Then Schmidt sighted a cab and fairly flung himself towards it.

Chapter XII.

Having impressed our cabman with the need for haste, we were not long on our way and soon found Mimi with Nijam in her dressing-room. My first thought was that our little friend looked a great deal better than I had feared, for my imagination had summoned up the picture of a Mimi reduced to a quivering heap and covered in her own gore. My second was that nevertheless I would very much like to have a word with whoever had put her into her present state, for that was quite desperate. Wet and bedraggled, clad only in her underthings, she stalked about the room with great staring eyes, pulling at the furnishings and up-ending lamps and pounding her fist against the walls.

"Calm yourself, Mimi; it's highly unlikely that anyone has bugged the room." Nijam had seated herself upon the sofa, which was placed there for the purpose of entertaining the soloist's guests. She appeared to have gone through a harrowing experience of her own, for her brown skin had a slightly ashen tinge and her fingers were laced together so tightly that the knuckles had gone pale.

"Dark!" Mimi cried hoarsely as she saw us enter. She seized my shoulders in a grip of painful intensity. "Dark, you were right—it's M. Christophe. I know his secret!"

Her hands were trembling. I dug into Vasily's backpack for the wine-bottle and a glass. "All right," I said, as soothingly as possible. "Sit down, Mimi, and let Vasily pour you some wine while you tell us where you've been."

As Schmidt found a warm coat to put around her dripping shoulders, Mimi drank a brimming glass of wine in a single gulp. Then she began her story. I will put it down more or less as she told it to us.

* * *

From the moment she was hired by M. Dumortier, M. Christophe had taken Mimi under his wing. It was he who believed she had the makings of a fine soloist, and he who began teaching her, step by step, the rôle of Myrtha in *Giselle*. He seemed to understand the part as though he had written it himself. At the time, Mimi presumed that he must simply have learned it from his great teacher, the originator of the ballet, M. Perrot.

Christophe wanted her always working, and because it had been years since Mimi had had any proper teaching at all, she grasped desperately for everything he was willing to teach. Even when he suggested giving her a lesson on the memorable evening of the bal masqué, she was eager to accept. They went up to the roof, where on the pavement before the dome, they began practising the pas de deux from *La Sylphide*—another very old rôle, but one with which Mimi was somewhat familiar from her Petersburg days. Even without the music, Christophe kept time as rigidly as a metronome; so rigidly, in fact, that Mimi wondered whether the dance might be more artistic if he allowed greater latitude.

But then he drew her to a pause, rigid with indignation. Mimi followed his gaze to the narrow pathway where it curved around the green dome. There, just within view, was the shape of a man's shoulder. A moment longer and she heard the murmur of Nijam's voice.

Perceiving that they were being spied upon, Mimi felt nearly as offended as did M. Christophe. When he signed to her to be silent, therefore, and led her around the dome to the second door, Mimi obeyed. Once inside, she expected Christophe to depart in his usual manner, with an imperious flap of the hand to tell her she was dismissed. Instead, he beckoned her towards the stairs.

"I think I'd better stay," she said with her customary bluntness. "Those are my friends, and they'll be anxious if they can't find me."

But Christophe, seizing her wrist, insisted she follow; and Mimi presumed that it was for good reason. They descended only a few flights of the great stairs connecting the different tiers of the theatre before he hurried her to the east end of the dress circle, to a hidden door opening onto a little spiral staircase much like the one on which Demiana Chalabi had been murdered.

Down, Christophe gestured—down further! Mimi was beginning to feel uneasy, but she told herself that she had little to fear and much to gain. It was *so* unlikely that Christophe was a murderer! And she knew him for a very great teacher… Down they went, therefore—down beneath the theatre, down beneath the subscribers' lounge, down into the great muffled cavity where the backdrops hung. Here it was perfectly dark; but Christophe drew her to a halt. A moment later, and a match hissed as it was struck. The flame flared up, making their shadows leap out of the darkness against the wall of dirty masonry beside them. Here was a narrow shelf, with a little lantern set upon it, the glass shutter open. Christophe lit it.

It was then that her transmitter crackled, and Schmidt begged her to speak to him.

Mimi hesitated. If she did not reply, she knew the rest of her crew was quite willing to tear the Opera apart in search of her. "Give me a moment," she told Christophe. "My friends are calling for me. I'm carrying a transmitter, so if I don't answer they'll be worried. Let me send them away."

He signed his permission, and Mimi turned away, hoping to conceal the location of the transmitter as she switched it on. The reader knows how she answered, telling us that she had gone home. Then Nijam asked her to keep a watch on Christophe, and Mimi's impatience boiled over. All she asked of life was to dance; she did not *want* to be a thief, and she did not want Nijam and the rest of us breathing down her neck like a whole flock of mother hens, either.

"Well, you'll have to do it without me," she said. "I'm quitting."

Of course we had protested and begged her to reconsider, and all the while M. Christophe had stood there before her with his lantern held high, shedding a stark light upon his masked face, and watching her with an almost oppressive vigilance. At last she extricated herself from all our cloying solicitude and switched off her transmitter.

"Sorry," she muttered. "I've told them not to bother me, now."

Good, Christophe signed. Then he startled her, for he reached out and tore the transmitter from her ear, dropping it into his own pocket. After this he turned, beckoning Mimi to follow him.

It was at this moment that Mimi began to wonder whether she was making a mistake, for even if she had wanted to call for help, she was now unable to do so. But at the same time, it seemed preposterous that Christophe could mean her any harm. Ballet-masters were famously dictatorial, and likely Christophe was only anxious to avoid interruptions during her lesson. Moreover, he had said himself that she was the only woman in the world who could possibly dance Myrtha the way she ought to be danced.

Repressing her doubts, therefore, she followed him through the bowels of that deep and disremembered place to a dungeon-like door in the furthermost corner. Christophe opened the formidable lock using a key attached to the fob-chain of his watch. At once, a golden glow of candlelight welled out. Mimi caught her breath to see a dim, spacious room which was fitted up as a studio. A dusty chandelier, encrusted with wax drippings, hung from the stone arch of the ceiling. This illuminated great long mirrors whose gilt was flaking off in the musty air of the cellar, and whose surface had become spotted with age and damp. The barre was dark, worn smooth and oily by constant touch. But the dusty grand-piano was a Blüthner, and the parqueted floor was pitched at the same slope as the Opera stage itself.

There was also, to her mystification, a perch to which a sad raven was attached by a fine chain about its leg, pecking listlessly at its cup of seed.

"Is this your own studio?" she breathed. Gloomy and secret though it was, she loved it at once. She would have given her eye-teeth to possess just such a room, in all its seclusion—

although she might have done without the pitiable raven.

The door closed behind her with a loud bang. Mimi jumped, and saw Christophe turn the key in the lock. He tucked it into his pocket and turned to her, beckoning with a gloved hand; no doubt he meant them to finish their interrupted pas de deux.

Mimi was not afraid—not consciously, at any rate; that was to come. But the room seemed suddenly less charming with the door shut and locked. She did not like the thought of being chained up within it, like the raven on its perch.

"Not now," she told Christophe. It was perhaps the first time she had ever refused him anything. "I've been dancing all day and my knee is tired. I ought to go home and rest."

Christophe nodded, and she thought he would unlock the door for her. Instead, he crossed towards another door in the right-hand wall, the one not hung with mirrors. This was a heavy affair—oak reinforced with steel, with a little steel shutter covering up an opening set at eye-height. Mimi thought it looked exactly like a prison-cell; and then she remembered that the revolutionaries of the Paris Commune had once used the Opera cellars as their headquarters, and had kept prisoners locked up here!

Having unlocked the door with a second key, Christophe seized her reluctant hand and placed the key within. This door led to a small room fitted up as a bedroom, complete with a looking-glass, an armchair, and a narrow bed dotted with cushions.

There was a faint lingering perfume in the air, and Mimi knew at once that this room must have been occupied by some other woman, and not so long ago. But by whom? and what had become of her? Her unease by now was intense.

Perhaps Christophe was in the habit of giving secret lessons in his secret studio to his secret protégées; more likely he expected Mimi take him as a lover in exchange for his tutoring. And if she refused—what then? Was *this* the reason for Chalabi's disappearance? She was no longer able to deride our warnings.

She considered her situation for a moment in silence. She felt weary. She had taken lovers before for things she wanted not a fraction as badly as she wanted Christophe's lessons: for food and shelter and clothing. She did not want to take another, not even Christophe. Still, if that was the price she paid to become a great artist, then of course she would pay it.

But she did not mean to become Christophe's pet raven, tethered down here in the darkness. If he wanted a mistress he could put the thing to her outright, like any other business proposition, and then he could instal her in a pretty flat or townhouse with a generous allowance and the freedom to go wherever she pleased; he certainly should not cram her into a secret dungeon in a forgotten corner of the Opera cellars.

No, Mimi decided; first she must get herself out of his power, and then she must speak to him frankly about what he expected from her, and what she meant to demand in return.

"It looks very comfortable," she told him, affecting an air of diffidence, "but I haven't had any dinner, and I won't get a wink of sleep without it."

In answer, he indicated a little trolley that stood beside the door. There was a covered plate upon it, and Mimi understood that this was her dinner.

Beholding the trolley with resignation, she found herself treading through a wearily familiar calculus. Of course she must submit. Christophe had made up his mind; and it would no doubt be easier for her to steal away in the night, than to defy him outright and perhaps get herself murdered for her pains. In the meanwhile, information was paramount and might be her best protection. She must make the best of her time by searching the room for clues of its previous occupant.

"Do you mean me to stay here some time, then?" she asked, scarcely able to conceal her reluctance.

He nodded his head and signed *Yes—but only to practice. That is all.*

Mimi felt sharp embarrassment. What a little fool she was, attributing such depraved motives to a man who so evidently cared only for art! "Oh, of course," she said, and then added, "I beg your pardon," because she felt that he *must* have perceived her hesitation and known precisely what it meant.

His hands flew. *You are not afraid? Down here, alone?*

Afraid—no, but uneasy, and unreasonably, wretchedly suspicious. "I'm not alone," she said. "But won't you show me your face?"

At that, the man took a sudden step backward. *No, no, no!* His hands moved in vigorous, unmistakable signs. *If you see my face, I must kill you.*

Mimi's throat went absolutely dry, and once again her fears seemed less unreasonable. Well, if she wanted to see his face, she must do it without his knowledge.

"Then good-night, monsieur," she said, snatching up her plate and the cutlery that went with it.

Christophe took a small leather-bound book from his pocket and pressed it into her free hand. *Take this and read,* he signalled. Mimi fled into her cell; she shut the door behind her and, very softly, turned the key in the lock.

She seated herself at the dressing-table and uncovered the

plate. The food was still warm—a simple but hearty ragout, and a roll of fine white bread to go with it. Someone in the Opera kitchens must have sent all this down—which meant that someone up there must know the location of these rooms, and their purpose. Perhaps that was a comforting thought; or then, perhaps it was not.

She put her head in her hands, wondering what kind of pickle she had fallen into. Still, perhaps she should not call it a pickle. It was not as though Christophe had actually threatened her. The only thing he had offered her was the thing she wanted more than anything else in the world. In the meanwhile, she might snoop about a little and satisfy her curiosity.

There had been a bottle of wine upon the trolley as well, but Mimi did not want anything clouding her wits tonight. Instead, she amused herself by opening the book. It was full of handwriting in French, and what appeared to be tables and diagrams, very neatly copied out. Mimi, who had been taught the language at the Imperial Ballet School in Petersburg, and spoke it like a native, saw at once that the book contained a description of a training schedule—supremely punishing, but detailed and comprehensive. She paged back to the beginning of the journal and read the name printed tidily at the head of the first page.

"Pour flour in my mouth!" she whispered. The name was *Marie Taglioni.*

Everyone knew the great Taglioni, she who more than anyone else—perhaps more than Perrot himself—had created modern ballet. Taglioni—the original Sylphide, the first Giselle, the mother of French Romantic ballet, whose shoes her devotees had cooked and eaten—had gone away to Vienna and created her legend in the Wiener Staatsoper when Paris would not enthrone her; and her training schedule, long thought to be lost, had been the secret to her success.

A secret which now lay in the hands of Mimi Laine!

Eagerness and delight banished all fear. For the next few hours Mimi devoured the little well-thumbed journal from cover to cover, and at last laid it down with a sigh. Perhaps, after all, the schedule was not so very revolutionary. With slight modifications, it was much the same as what Christophe already had her doing. All the same, it gave her confidence. If only her knee would allow her to spend all the time practicing that she needed!

Then with a jolt, Mimi recalled her immediate purpose. She glanced at her watch. She was very sleepy, but it was now about three in the morning, the ideal hour for a burglar to ply her trade. There was no sound from the outer room. She had a vague memory of hearing a door close some time ago, and after that all had been silent. Christophe must be gone, or asleep—or so she hoped. In the meanwhile she must make the best of her time.

The room was so small and bare that it did not take her long to search. Mimi was thorough, peering beneath the mattress and holding a candle to the walls to see if any words had been scratched upon the rough masonry. One clue only, she found in the shadows beneath the dressing-table. This was a fine silver chain with a little cross hanging from it, but a cross rather different to any other she had seen, for in place of the top arm was a circular ring or loop. Mimi put it into her pocket, thinking that it was distinctive enough to offer a clue as to who might have been here before her.

After this she unlocked her door and peered out into the

studio beyond. The candles of the chandelier must have been snuffed or allowed to burn out, for the room was cloaked in darkness. Mimi removed her shoes and ventured out. The place looked exactly the same as it had before, with one exception: the raven's perch was empty.

She went, of course, directly to the door that led out to the main cellar. It would not open, and Mimi's heart sank, knowing that this lock was of the sort that would take her days, if not weeks, to pick. Feeling more trapped than ever, she pressed the back of her hand against her mouth. Well: it simply meant that instead of the lock, she would need to pick Christophe's pocket, either for the key or for her transmitter.

Mimi looked over the room a little more closely, seeing nothing that could help: there was only the dust, the mirrors, and the piano—and the three doors at the side of the room. One of these led to her own cell; but when she approached the middle door, she saw that it was secured with a more primitive lock, which should present her with little difficulty. Picking a lock would be awkward to explain, however, if Christophe proved to be within. She knocked.

The sound was magnified in that echoing studio, so that Mimi's heart jumped into her mouth. When, after a suffocating period of time, no answer came, Mimi knocked again— loudly enough (she thought) to wake the dead. The whole room rang like a bell; she felt the cold sweat break out upon her brow. But again there was no answer.

He must be gone. Mimi may have been forced to give up her transmitter, but she habitually carried a little pack of lock-picks in her pocket the way other women carried smelling-salts. Out they came, and she worked almost by touch, for the candle settled on the floor at her feet scarcely illuminated the scene.

In two minutes she heard the last click of the tumblers and found that the latch would turn. Stowing the lock-picks safely back in their pocket, Mimi picked up her candle and silently opened the door.

She found another little cell, as small as her own but bare and unfurnished. It took her a moment to realise that the oblong black shape in the centre of the floor, about the length and breadth of a man, was another opening like the ones in the cellar outside, into which Schmidt and Nijam had so nearly fallen. There must be a row of them across the breadth of the cellar, and this one happened to fall within this room. There were no bars across it: they had been lifted out and placed against the wall.

Apart from this, the only thing in the room was a second black oblong near the wall. Mimi stole nearer and saw that it was a box—no; it was genuinely a coffin. For a moment she stood motionless, for a powerful urge was upon her to turn and flee back to her own room. Then she got a hold of herself. Ignorance could not help her now. She tiptoed nearer—it was the bravest moment of her life and more than I could have done in her shoes—and raised her candle.

The coffin was open. Within lay M. Christophe, his black mask gleaming in the candlelight.

Instantly, Mimi snuffed the light. The wick glowed a moment and then the whole cellar was plunged into such darkness and silence that it was like going into a swoon. She herself did not move; she did not breathe. It was so silent that she could hear her own heartbeat.

Nothing moved—not so much as a breath.

If the man in the coffin was asleep, Mimi thought, he should surely be breathing!

An interminable time later, Mimi screwed up her courage. She *must* know what was going on in this hidden cellar—knowledge was life to her just now. She found the paper of matches and struck one of them. The figure in the coffin lay absolutely lifeless. Was it a corpse? Was it a mannequin? There was only one way to tell.

Mimi reached out, shuddering, to touch the thing's head. It was like touching a corpse, cold and lifeless. That gave her a little courage, and she took hold of the mask, easing it from the grey and waxen face.

It *was* a corpse. It looked like a mummy she had seen whilst casing the British Museum—the skin fragile and papery, shrunk against the bones of the skull and drawn back from the teeth; the eyes sunken, the scanty locks lank and dusty. She experienced a momentary instinctive protest against the evidence. *This* could not be her ballet-master. He wore the same clothing—down to the last detail—of the man who had danced with her tonight on the rooftop; he grasped the same white wand in the same black-gloved hands. But he must have dressed this corpse in similar clothes, as a kind of *memento mori*…Then she saw the little black thread that had come loose in the seam that attached the thumb to his glove, and her heart stopped. It was the same, the very same glove.

There occurred within Mimi then a sort of upheaval. She had thought she had to do with simple daylight things; a threat from which she could bargain or steal herself away. Now she saw that this was not the case at all. She had no experience of the dead. For a moment she wished passionately that I was there, for she had a feeling I would understand at once what to do. This is flattering; but indeed I cannot say that I would have known what to do any better than she did herself.

The first thought that occurred to her, once she acknowledged that I was *not* present and could not help her, was that it was probably a good time for her to get religion. Mimi had no illusions about herself: she was a thief and a dainty who did not like to bother the supernatural more than she could help, and she had always hoped that the supernatural would be content to leave her in peace and overlook her little faults. Manifestly, this pleasant state of affairs had now broken down. She had no silver on her person, nor garlic—either of which might or might not be of any assistance; but in lieu of that, she made the sign of the cross and offered a silent bargain to the heavens.

Sir, I won't insult you by offering more than I'm willing to pay, she thought, *but if you'll get me out of this I swear I'll sell my favourite pearls, and give the proceeds to the poor.*

Then, being a practical soul, she drew a deep breath and began gingerly to pat the corpse's pockets in search of her transmitter.

She had not got very far in this unpleasant business when a sound interrupted her. Mimi's heart leapt once again into her mouth and she recoiled from the corpse in time to see a black shadow swoop up from within the yawning hole in the floor. It was the raven. It settled upon the rim of the coffin and fixed her with a beady eye—an eye that glittered with cold, blueish fire. Mimi made a choking sound, finding herself pinioned in the glare of a cold and malicious intelligence…Then she must have blinked, for suddenly the raven was only a raven, sidling away from her, afraid and no longer accusing…

A withered hand darted from the coffin and fastened upon her wrist!

Mimi screamed in earnest then and flung herself away. She fell upon the floor and very nearly toppled through that great, open hole. But the bony grip on her arm only tightened; her convulsive movement had raised the corpse from its bed and now it bent over her with blue fire smouldering in its angry eyes.

She could see its withered visage quite close to her own, could smell the peculiar sweet-pine scent that had always clung about M. Christophe. Its grasp upon her wrist held the candle steady and upright between them. Then its other hand came into view, holding a thin cord.

Mimi saw at once what it intended. All had come to pass as she had been warned: she had torn off the mask and now she must die. The white wand had fallen on the ground at her feet; she managed to claw it into her fist, and instantly rammed the silver-tipped ferrule directly through the creature's ribcage.

There it stuck, having had all the effect of a sneeze in a thunderstorm. The creature never faltered; it looped the cord over her head. Mimi felt numb and utterly at a loss. The silver knob at the top of the wand winked at her from the creature's torn shirt-front. She saw, with an almost painful sort of clarity, that it was etched with a monogram; one she recognised.

"Jules Perrot," she gasped. "You're—you're Jules Perrot."

The hands stilled. Mimi looked up. If a corpse was capable of looking surprised, this one did.

A moment divided her from death. Mimi said the only thing she could.

"Teach me," she sobbed. "No one can dance Myrtha like I can. Let me live, and I swear I'll never betray your secret. Let me live, and I swear your art will live on."

It seemed that a momentary indecision had grasped the creature. Then it took her candle away, and without a word or a gesture, dragged her back to her own cell. Her own key lay where she had left it, upon the dressing-table. The creature that had once been Jules Perrot took it up and departed, locking the door behind him.

Mimi was alive—but utterly alone. Her candle had been taken away, leaving her plunged in Stygian darkness. The cord still hung about her neck. She tore it away, sank onto her bed and surrendered herself to a fit of the horrors.

Chapter XIII.

Mimi did not sit there long, for she was naturally an active and practical person, and she had not yet given herself up quite for lost. It occurred to her that she *did* have a bit of silver in her pocket; and she quickly dug out the little chain with its odd little cross, and hung it about her neck. Perhaps it would protect her; perhaps it would not. Perhaps it had done the former occupant of this room no good at all—but she was no expert; she was only Mimi Laine from an out-of-the-way village in Finland.

She did not, as Nijam might have, set herself to think furiously about how she might rescue herself from this predicament. Instead she found herself thinking of something quite different altogether: of the Skeleton Room at the British Museum. There, in a shadowy store-room in quite a different sort of cellar, she had run across creatures of dry and rattling bones, creatures so angry and so stubborn that they clung to their mortal remains long after they ought rightly to have moved on. Mimi supposed that M. Perrot—or the thing that he had become—was one of these; a kind of natural revenant created by its own obstinate fury… Certainly it could not be a man-made revenant. *That* secret was lost; and besides there was more of intelligence and willpower to this creature, than the revenant policemen had ever shown. It was only now that she fully understood the impulse which had saved her life. Perrot had ruled the Opera so long as its ballet-master that not even death could force him to relinquish his grip upon it. Command of the living was what he wanted; he would allow her to live so long as she submitted.

Doubtless the tenor Larousse had been killed because he represented something the creature could not control—an opera with *no ballet.* But what about Demiana Chalabi? Had *she* discovered the revenant's secret? Is that why she had to be killed? Or was her death part of some larger game?

Mimi did not know how she would begin to gather answers to these questions; but perhaps she did not need to. If she could find her way back to the rest of her crew, she could leave the thinking to people who were better at it. Instead, she turned her thoughts towards prolonging her own existence. For the present, the creature had decided to let her live. How could she defend herself against it for the future? She knew a little about revenants, of course. One could not be born in the Russian Empire and grow up without a decent working knowledge of the police and their tools. Incendiaries were the generally accepted method for dealing with the creatures, but Mimi would as soon have considered incinerating the Paris Opera itself.

She had known a great many ballet-masters, and all of them had been a little like this revenant—demanding and authoritarian. The art of ballet always had been strictly hierarchical. And Perrot had been the last of the great French Romantics. He had so much to teach her. He had driven her mercilessly, it was true; but she was dancing like never before in her life.

Knowing that she could not dance like this forever, Mimi burned with the urge to dance now, as fiercely as she could. She knew that it was a dangerous game she played; she knew that she might pay for it, eventually, with her health or her life. She knew that the Perrot-revenant could not be allowed to go on its way forever, terrorising the corps de ballet, or killing the Opera artists. Still, what a treasury of secrets it must hold! And Mimi Laine had always prided herself on her talents as a thief…

* * *

Deep in the Opera's cellars, no busybody disturbed Mimi's slumbers until late the next morning, when the sound of the piano playing in the next room roused her from her rest. Mimi got up and tried the handle of her door, which—to her dismay—had been unlocked as she slept. Peering out into the studio, she saw by the flicker of the lighted chandelier that the revenant was seated at the piano.

On the little food-trolley by her door a new plate had appeared, fragrant with the scents of butter and coffee. The revenant fixed its burning eyes upon her—it wore no mask this morning—and signalled her to eat.

Mimi, never one to beat around the shrubbery, demanded, "Aren't you going to kill me, then?"

The revenant shook his head and made a series of gestures.

"Yes, of course I'll keep my mouth shut," Mimi responded, very subdued. "I must have been out of my wits last night. But don't worry: I won't tell a soul."

The creature gave a wave of its hand. Mimi felt bold enough to help herself to the pastry and the cup of coffee that awaited her on the trolley; and then to say, "Oughtn't I to return soon? The managers will miss me if I don't attend rehearsal."

The revenant indicated a sheet of the Opera's own letter-head that lay on the trolley, together with a pen. Mimi considered her next step. She *must* write something; that was clear. But what? The new day, and the bargain she had made with the revenant, had revived her spirits. If she wrote something to alert the rest of her crew to her whereabouts—receiving special tuition from M. Christophe, for instance—then there was every chance that they would sweep in and incinerate her tutor before she was ready to say farewell to him; if, that is, he did not intercept and stifle the message himself. In the end she merely wrote a request for sick leave, saying that she would return in a day or two. She signed it with her name and let the revenant glance it over. He seemed perfectly content with the missive, and slipped it into his pocket. After that she hastily swallowed the remainder of her coffee, and the day's work began.

Hours passed in a kind of fever; the revenant driving her to repeat the same passages of the ballet again and again, until they became second nature. He himself played the piano as only a dancer could, with an innate understanding of the difficult passages, and a muscular kind of assertiveness that lifted her up and became the wind beneath her tiring wings. Mimi felt that there was nothing she could not do with that music supporting her. She lost all count of time; until suddenly the weakness in her knee crept up on her unawares. Attempting a jeté, the leg gave way and deposited her unceremoniously upon the ground. She tried to stand, and found that she could barely hobble.

Even the revenant could see that she was incapable of

further effort that evening. Signing to her to cease work, he arose from the piano, fitting on his mask.

"Are you going out?" Mimi asked. "May I come?"

He shook his head, pointing to her knee.

"I know," she replied, "but I want fresh clothing, and a toothbrush, and a comb, and a bath. Won't you let me go home for them?"

Later, he signed.

Mimi sighed, feeling again the oppressiveness of her own captivity. "What's behind that third door?" she asked. Her room and his accounted for only two of the rooms that led from the studio.

His only answer was to shake his head. Then he went away, and Mimi heard his key turn in the lock behind him. She bit her lip, wondering whether she dared to open that third door. It was difficult to know how long she would be left in peace, and she thought that if there was some secret concealed in that room, she would prefer to investigate at a time when she felt certain of not being interrupted.

Moreover, she now felt utterly exhausted. Mimi looked at her watch and saw that they had been working with scarcely a pause for hours; it was now evening. Tonight was *Giselle's* first performance, and even now she supposed her understudy would be performing Myrtha. Somehow that was the most upsetting thing about this enforced absence—that she should have missed opening night. Of course the revenant knew his business, and they had spent the day working little unevennesses out of her performance. But she resented each delay. She felt that she had spent her entire life waiting in the wings.

There was no point in asking the revenant to let her dance

tonight. Perhaps it was the previous night's lack of sleep, or perhaps it was the constant nervous strain, which she now recognised only because it had suddenly lessened with the revenant's departure. Now she had barely the strength to do anything but stagger to her bed.

Mimi slept until the revenant returned around midnight and signed her to follow him.

The rest had restored strength to her knee, although it still twinged as she climbed the endless stairs from her dungeon. The revenant remained close beside her all the way, leading her out by a side-door into the Rue Scribe where a brougham awaited them.

It now became clear that the creature meant to accompany her. Mimi settled into the brougham opposite him and contemplated the masked visage. If he would not leave her alone, then it would serve him right to be pestered with questions.

"M. Perrot," she began, "are you really dead?"

In answer, he removed his mask. The gas-lamps lighting the street flickered past them, throwing glaring light upon his withered face. Mimi shuddered, feeling that she would never accustom herself to that horrible sight.

Perhaps he meant to stifle her questions, but Mimi was of the opinion that if people wanted things they should ask honestly and not be cowards. And that if people didn't want to be pestered with questions, they ought not to take other people prisoner.

"Do you remember everything from your previous life?" she asked.

Yes, he answered, a trifle impatiently.

"And did you kill Demiana Chalabi?"

She thought he hesitated a little at that; but then he nodded. *Yes.*

Mimi swallowed, finding her throat suddenly dry. "Because she saw your face?"

This time he did not deign to answer, only keeping his baleful, death's-head gaze fixed upon her. Mimi saw his game at once and resented it. He would boast of murdering Chalabi, because he wanted her to be afraid. But he would not tell her why, because he wanted to keep her compliant, too frightened to do anything but what he expressly commanded.

Had the real Perrot been like this in life? Or did she now face some evil creature wearing his skin and memories like a cloak? ...For a moment she was too frightened to say anything at all. If she asked too many questions, he might really kill her, as he had Chalabi. But just as she could not burgle a house without some idea of the building-plan, she could not protect herself from Perrot without some idea of his purpose.

All my pearls, she reminded the Almighty, *if you get me out of this alive.* Then she cleared her throat.

"If you died, why did you come back? Are you angry about something?"

No.

"But you must have unfinished business," Mimi guessed.

This time, a nod. *Yes.*

"What is it that you want?" she asked. "Are you trying to ruin the Opera?"

An emphatic shake of the head—*No, no*—and a gesture she couldn't quite understand.

"Or save it?"

Yes.

"Save it—from what? Wagner?"

Yes, he signed again, with utter solemnity.

Mimi almost wanted to laugh; but perhaps he had killed Demiana Chalabi for laughing when he told *her* that he wanted to save the Opera from Wagner. Well: a person so stubborn as to return from the dead could not be in a very well-balanced state of mind. That did not matter to Mimi, so long as he was willing to teach her.

Presently the carriage came to a halt before the house she shared with Nijam, and the revenant indicated with a jerk of his head that she should go in and find what she wanted. He evidently meant to remain in the carriage; but Mimi did not push her luck too far. Once inside the house, she quickly gathered her things. She did leave a note upon her dressing-table for Nijam, explaining where to seek her if she had not returned in a day or two. She half hoped, as she left the message, that Nijam would *not* find it. But at least, if her friends became worried enough to search her room, there would be this record of her whereabouts…

She regretted leaving the note almost at once, for she was ambushed by Alphonse Schmidt as she descended the steps. "Mimi!" he cried, hurling himself out of a nearby cab. Not yet ready to be rescued, Mimi darted for the brougham. The revenant drew the door shut behind her; but before he could get the shade down, the carriage lurched as Schmidt leaped upon the step.

"I'm not ready to come back yet!" Mimi cried in a sudden agony of terror. Bad enough that her friends should wish to drag her home, without their getting a glimpse of the revenant's unmasked face. She rapped frantically upon the partition, crying to the cabman to hurry. The door rattled; Schmidt was trying to get it open.

Then the revenant took a hand. A low, malevolent hiss escaped him as he leaned forward and presented the horror of his un-dead countenance to his assailant. Mimi saw Schmidt's eyes grow wide with the shock. Then the creature that had once been Perrot thrust the ferrule of his wand through the small window and struck Schmidt upon the collar-bone. The carriage lurched a second time as his not-inconsiderable weight fell away. Then they were whisked off down the empty midnight streets at a hard trot.

Mimi fell back against the cushions, breathing hard. The revenant seated himself and replaced his mask; and Mimi had the sudden horrible feeling that he had shown himself to Schmidt on purpose. "That was one of my friends," she said. "He means well—he is only worried for me. So long as I return soon, and safe—"

The revenant turned upon her again with another sharp hiss. Mimi fell silent; but she felt the hairs standing upright upon the nape of her neck.

At length the brougham drew up in the Opera stable-yard. The revenant arose, seized Mimi's wrist, and hurried her once more into the cellars. She did not try to speak again; not until they returned to the cellar, and the revenant stalked into his room. He returned with a black walking-stick, the silver head of which he unscrewed. Mimi saw then that it was a sword-stick encasing a long, slender, horribly sharp blade.

The sight made her feel dizzy and sick, so that for an instant she thought something she had eaten must have disagreed with her.

"Are you going to kill him?" she whispered. "Only because he has seen your face?"

He turned upon her with a series of savage gestures. *Your*

lover, he signed. *No lovers.*

"He isn't!" she cried, fairly offended by the thought. "Schmidt is like a brother to me!"

The revenant only shrugged, as though to say that it made no difference to *him.* Mimi threw herself on her knees, with that instinct for self-abasement that had preserved her skin under the rule of other masters.

"Don't do it," she gasped, snatching at his coat. A stroke of inspiration came to her, and she added: "Think of your duty to the Opera! You don't know what he's like—he'll destroy you."

The revenant made a contemptuous gesture—seized her by the arm, flung her into her room, and closed the door behind. Mimi heard the key turn in the lock; and then he went out by the main door before she could get her own lock picked.

Her hands were trembling as she worked. Curse Schmidt for ten kinds of fool! Sticking his nose in where it wasn't wanted—and now, if he got hurt, Nijam would never forgive her. For that matter, Mimi did not know if she would be able to forgive herself… She got the door open and staggered into the studio. If only she had found her transmitter! On her knees just now she had made a desperate attempt to pick the revenant's pocket, but all she had found was a fob-watch.

She glanced at the main door in despair. There was no escape that way; not tonight, at least. Perhaps the third door led to a way out? She attacked it with the lock-picks, made the tumblers click, and threw open the door.

From the darkness within a ghastly smell rolled out—sickly-sweet and rotten. Mimi pressed a hand over her mouth and nose. For a moment she stood in an agony of fear upon the threshold. She felt again, as she had the previous night, that she only wanted to close the door and run away. That stench certainly meant nothing good. If she took a single step further she would discover some fresh horror.

Mimi knew, as she had last night, that there was no help for it. She must *know.*

She lifted her candle from where it sat at her feet and stepped into another cramped little cell, bare and unfurnished. All the hairs on her body rose, as though her skin was trying to crawl off her, to escape.

There was no escape, of course. There was only death.

She recognised Demiana Chalabi first—laid out nearest the door, still wearing the dress of white gauze and the toe-shoes in which she had died. Her dark, curly hair was a spreading shadow about her white face, which stared sightlessly towards the ceiling. There was a mark around her neck, the place where the cord had choked the life from her.

Beside her lay her partner, the male dancer who had taken Duke Albericht's rôle. Of course, Mimi thought: that explained how he could dance with a ghost, night after night. He was himself a ghost.

Four or five other bodies lay like discarded puppets in the darkness beyond. All of them were dancers. Mimi knew them—had been working beside them for days without realising that they were already dead. No wonder they had always danced so perfectly… Her stomach turned with revulsion and she stumbled out of the room, slamming the door behind her. For a moment she leaned against it, breathing hard and struggling to keep her gorge down.

It had to be a nightmare. Mimi pinched herself until her fingernails printed crescents in her skin. Then she took a deep breath and opened the door again.

They were all still there—all still dead and decaying. Mimi forced herself to carefully inspect each corpse, committing their names to her memory. She calculated that they had all been dead varying lengths of time; those furthest from the door were most decayed. All showed signs of strangulation.

She raised her candle and swept the light over walls, floor, and ceiling. A stout wooden ladder lay against the wall, for which purpose Mimi could not guess. Otherwise there was no sign of any way out; no sign of any of the dead having been kept here when alive. That was what her own room must have been used for!

Mimi beat a hasty retreat, shutting the door behind her. The raven beheld her from its perch with dim, unseeing eyes as she used her lock-picks to seal the door behind her.

Seven dead ballerinas, she thought, and herself the eighth. A ghostly corps de ballet, perfect in every step, unchanging, unaging, undead… In English one might call it a *corpse* de ballet. A cackle of laughter escaped her, ringing feverishly in that echoing room. Mimi shivered and fell silent.

The truth was now inescapable: she had been brought here to die. She must escape. But how? Mimi flung a glance at the raven. The bird had escaped the cellar through the opening in the floor of the revenant's room. Either she must try to follow it, or she must try to pick the lock to the main door. If she threw herself down that opening, she knew nothing of what she might find there. Perhaps the sewers of Paris, a free passage out of the Opera and thence into the streets. Perhaps a heap of rubble at the bottom of a hole, and a slow death by inches in the dark…

But if she stayed here, death was certain. And this way she might save Schmidt.

Her fingers were already at work while these thoughts fleeted through her mind. Mimi threw open the middle door and searched the empty coffin, hoping against hope that she might find her transmitter. It was nowhere to be found, and she had an idea that it might have been tossed down that great, empty opening. Lying on her stomach at the edge of the hole, she reached her candle down as far as her arm would stretch.

The light reflected a dull yellow off water as still as a mill-pond, barely two yards beneath her. From that glassy surface, great, shadowy piers of masonry arose to support the floor she lay upon. She should at any rate be unlikely to break any bones. It occurred to her that this was the purpose of the ladder in the third room.

Mimi's heart was in her throat. If there was a hatch here, then there had to be other hatches, and a way for the raven to get out. It was only a case of finding her way in the dark. If there was an opening, then there ought to be sounds and air-currents to lead the way.

She was still hesitating when she heard the key in the lock of the outer door, and knew the revenant had returned.

She could no longer delay—not even to retrieve the ladder.

I'll give all my jewels to the poor, she promised. And then she rolled from the edge and dropped like a stone.

Chapter XIV.

Having reached this point in her story, Mimi shuddered and fell silent, drawing Schmidt's coat a little more tightly about her shoulders.

"That must have been early this morning," said I, with a shudder of my own. Mimi was still dripping filthy water into the sofa cushions. "Good heavens, Mimi, how many hours were you down there?"

She shook her head, evidently exhausted. "How should I know? I hoped that it was a sewer, but it seems that it's a closed cistern. If I hadn't found a niche in the masonry to cling to…There's a ladder, you know, and another hatch to let you out at the other end of the cellar. Who knows how often I blundered past it in the dark? Chicken-coop of horror! I never want to see darkness again…"

"All's well that ends well," said I, "but, *Mimi!*"

"I *know,*" she said, a little sulkily. "And I know that Nijam warned me, too. Do you want me to beg *your* pardon, too? I've had a little too much of *that,* these days."

I folded her in my arms. "Oh, Mimi, of course not! We're just glad you're alive."

She shivered a little, and then actually nestled into my shoulder. "Now you know the truth. Christophe is a revenant."

"Yes," said Nijam, who had listened to the whole story with the uncanny calm of an automaton. "That is what I meant to tell you. Christophe is a revenant. From Schmidt's description, it could not have been anything else."

"That is why the revenant had to try to kill him," said Mimi in a muffled voice. "I *tried* to warn you, Schmidt…"

"It's all right," Schmidt answered. He looked a little dizzy, like a man who has been pole-axed. "You shouldn't have worried about me. He did come after me, but I heaved him into the area and locked the door between us."

Vasily opened his eyes very wide, and Nijam exclaimed, "*What?* When did this happen?"

"Last night, after I took you home," Schmidt said, turning red. "I never saw his face. But he had a sword-stick, so I suppose it must have been the revenant."

"Do you mean to tell me," Nijam said with some heat, "that someone attempted to *murder* you in the small hours of the morning, and you never thought to *mention* it?"

Schmidt reddened. "But you weren't well, and I didn't like to trouble sir over something so—"

"Sir begs to inform you," said Vasily, before Nijam could get her own words in, "that an attempt upon *your* life, Schmidt, is as serious a matter to me as an attempt upon my own."

I was gratified to see how both Schmidt and Nijam gaped at these words.

"There, now," I said, before tempers could rise any higher. "It's all settled: next time someone tries to murder one of us, the others shall be notified at once. We don't want any more bodies being stockpiled in the Opera cellars."

That caused a silence to fall upon the dressing-room.

"I found Demiana Chalabi, didn't I?" Mimi asked, from where she was nestled within my arm. She removed the silver chain, with its pendant, from about her neck. "I'd bet anything that this belonged to her."

"I'll show it to Gobara and make sure of it," said I, pocketing the little jewel. "Heavens above! This must be what that odd little man, Dupont, meant by telling me that Chalabi wasn't the first ballerina to disappear!"

"Dupont?" Nijam asked, putting on her *pince-nez* in a rather reproachful fashion.

Vasily threw up his hands. "Another secret! I wish the lot of you would pull yourselves together and *talk* to me!"

This was rich. "I *was* about to tell you, when somebody tried to brain Schmidt with a sand-bag! Dupont was the little man who came to me as the bal masqué, and tried to bribe me to get him a job at the Opera."

"But Mary Angelica, my sweet, why haven't you questioned this man?"

"Because there wasn't *time,* Vaska, my pet!" And I explained how Dupont had tossed the words at me on his way out the door to catch the Marseille train, in pursuit of the Chalabi family.

"Pay attention to the main thing we have learned," Nijam said. "At last we know *who* is murdering people, and *why.* Mimi is right. Perrot, or whatever he is now, is some sort of revenant; and he's come up with a plan to create the perfect corps de ballet. One by one, he's training ballerinas—and then, once their performance is sufficiently embedded within the memory of the Opera and of the public, he kills them. Then the imprints go on dancing the perfect *Giselle* forever…"

"It's what we've always dreamed of," Mimi said, and there

was an odd, wistful look in her eye. "That is the tragedy of ballet. It cannot be recorded; it can only be passed down from master to student. No system of notation we have is sufficient. Always, change creeps in. But this—Perrot is not just creating the perfect *Giselle.* He's making it immortal. It's priceless."

There was something in her voice that struck a shaft of horror into me. "Mimi!" I exclaimed, seizing her hand. "However priceless such a thing might be, it's not worth your life—or anyone else's!"

"He won't *have* anyone else's life," Nijam said. The light of battle was in her eye. "Or his perfect *Giselle.* We've got him now."

Mimi looked a little apprehensive. "What are you going to do?"

"I suppose natural revenants burn as easily as the unnatural ones," Nijam said, with a shrug.

Schmidt cleared his throat. "I don't suppose it's possible the revenant could have been man-made?"

"We'd better hope not," said Nijam, and Mimi shuddered.

"There may be another way," I put in, speaking slowly. "Shades—the dead spirits, I mean, as opposed to the memory-imprints—are usually moved on pretty quickly to whatever lies beyond. A natural revenant must be created when the shade sticks closely enough to the body to escape attention..."

"So?" Nijam asked, levelling a sceptical gaze through her *pince-nez.*

"So," I said, "if we could decoy the shade away from its body for just long enough to be moved on...Or, perhaps, if we could *convince* it to move on..."

"You won't convince it," Schmidt said with conviction. "It wants so badly to go on controlling the Opera that it hasn't even allowed death to stand in the way."

"Schmidt is right," said Mimi in a low, exhausted voice.

"Fire, then," said Schmidt.

"Explosives are better," Nijam put in. I think we all must have given her a funny look at that, because she said, rather defensively, "What? It stands to reason, doesn't it? It's a reanimated body; you have to thoroughly destroy it."

"What about the sigils?" Vasily put in.

Nijam scowled. "What about them?"

"Don't they all—or the man-made ones, at any rate—have some sort of mark drawn or carved on their bodies? As I understand it, if you deface the sigil, the revenant loses whatever animating spark it had."

"They *say* so," said Nijam, "but I've never tried the thing myself. And I wouldn't, except in a last resort."

"What do the sigils look like?" Schmidt asked in a low voice. He had a hand to his heart, and looked rather as though he was having indigestion.

"It doesn't matter," Nijam said testily. "The sigils were always an unscientific affectation. A creature can't be re-animated by the use of some occult symbol. The natural revenants don't have them, anyway. Much better to use incendiaries; that way we can be sure of destroying the creature."

"Then we will," I said. "Oh, Mimi! Does this mean that you're part of the crew again?"

Mimi went a little stiff. "You ought to let me continue my lessons," she said in a stubborn, defiant tone.

"Why? Do you *want* to die?" Nijam asked.

Mimi flushed. "If I don't, he will know we are onto him. I'll be safe enough; he won't kill me until I'm perfect, and..."

She caught herself before she could say more, but I thought I could hear the words she didn't say. Poor Mimi! She wanted so badly to be perfect!

"Please don't," said Schmidt, quite evidently distressed. "I've already watched one woman die, and been unable to help."

Mimi shrugged. "What other option do we have?"

"Let me think," Nijam retorted, with biting sarcasm. "*I* thought I might waylay the creature in a dark corridor and cover him with flaming naphtha!"

"I beg your pardon! Do you have any naphtha at hand?" Mimi asked, with a spark of her old audacity. "Or a means of delivering it?"

Nijam scowled. "I'll need to find some. And build a—a pump of some sort."

"Well, then," said Mimi triumphantly. With that she fell back upon the sofa, and the angry colour faded from her face, leaving her very pale and weak-looking. "At any rate, I *have* to go back to him. I left Marie Taglioni's journal down there under my pillow."

I understood at once what she meant. "Taglioni's journal! That would be the perfect bait for Dumortier."

"He'd be willing to pay a small fortune for that book," Vasily agreed. "That is—unless it's already listed in the Opera archives. The revenant must have got it from *somewhere*."

"That's easily found out," said I. "But we have now a great many victims. The Taglioni journal might provide comfortably for Mme Larousse, but what about the dancers?"

"We'll cross that bridge when we come to it," Vasily said, frowning slightly. "I've a notion that if we can get to the bottom of this revenant business, we can find a way to provide for the other bereaved families, too."

"Then it's settled. Mimi will retrieve the Taglioni journal. Vasily and I will sell it to Dumortier. Nijam will make a fire-spout—"

Nijam had a far-away look in her eyes. "I'm thinking of calling it a flame-thrower," she said dreamily.

"Flame-thrower, then," I said. "And Schmidt, you must guard Mimi. It's dangerous, for I don't suppose the revenant will like it much; but whatever he says, he can't be allowed to have her to himself."

Mimi, now visibly wilting, had not much to say to all these plans. I remember saying something about getting her home and putting her to bed. Then Schmidt went out to call a cab, and Vasily gathered her up in his arms, and the upshot of it was that we all took her home together. As we crammed into the cab, Mimi murmured something about a pack of mother hens, and Schmidt told her not to be silly.

"We want to make sure that you're safe," he said, and then Mimi actually kissed his cheek.

The house was dark and very cold, but I ran ahead and turned up the gas in Mimi's room, so that when Vasily carried her in it was nearly as bright as day. Schmidt could be heard downstairs instructing Nijam to light a fire so that he could heat some food and water. Having ferreted a clean nightgown out of the wardrobe, I picked up the basin and ewer.

"I'll fetch you water for your bath," I told Mimi. "Get out of your wet things while I'm gone."

"No! Stay with me," Mimi begged.

I gave the basin and ewer to Vasily, along with another whispered errand. He went away, and I sat beside Mimi where she huddled shivering on her bed. "You'll catch your death, you know."

Wordlessly, she began undoing the busk of her corset; she must have stripped off her over-dress in the cistern in order to save her life. I wondered what part of her ordeal had put that haunted look into her eyes, but I did not like to intrude. Instead I said, "I'm so glad you've come back to us, Mimi. You'll never believe the lengths we have been driven to without you. I tried to burgle a house today, you know."

That got her attention. "But you can't climb!"

"Believe me, I know!" I said. Then I told her the whole story, leaving out what I had learned about the ladies who lived in the house.

"You tallow-head!" she cried, as I wrapped her in a dry blanket. "That settles it! I must teach you to climb!"

"Heavens above, *no,*" I said. "I have had enough climbing to last me two lifetimes!"

Mimi slipped with a shiver beneath the bedcovers and pulled up her knees to create warmth. It was pretty rough to spend all of a December day in a cistern, and then to come home to a cold dark house; but at least she was laughing. "But Dark, what made you *do* such a stupid thing?"

I bit my lip. It was not that I didn't *trust* Mimi; but some things are private. And the day's events were still too raw for me. I was conscious of having done Mimi a wrong, even if only in my thoughts. Yet, in seeing to her needs, there was something healing for me, too.

"I was afraid," I said at last. "You must promise not to tell a soul—but I know I'm not mistaken. The two of them were sharing a room…and a bed."

"Oh!" Mimi exclaimed, clearly shocked and delighted by the gossip. "I thought that was the sort of thing only aristocrats did!"

"I was mortally afraid of being caught prying into their secrets. And then, sitting on the roof, I began to think…I am rich now. I could do anything I liked and make it respectable—even something like that."

Mimi gave a vigorous snort. "No, you couldn't. Not even if you *liked* women. You're much too religious."

I laughed; and to my own ears the sound was strained and wild. "I believe that you're right," I said. I *was;* just too religious for my own peace of mind. Once more I felt myself caught in an impossible dilemma. I wished, as much as ever, to be what the apostle once called *a friend of God.* But I was now caught in a terrible doubt as to whether God wished to be a friend of *mine.*

Mimi gave me a smile. "I am always right," she said. "People are always surprised by that. They think that to be right is the same thing as to be good, when it is not the same at all."

A moment later the door opened and Nijam brought in a bowl of soup, a basin of hot water, and Mlle Gobara. That was the errand I had given to Vasily—to go and fetch my maid. Nijam is a splendid woman, but I did not trust her, in the throes of invention, to care for an invalid.

"Here is Mlle Gobara to take care of you," I told Mimi. "You don't mind staying here tonight? Excellent. What's that, Mimi? Oh! The cross! Take a look at this, Gobara."

I drew out the silver pendant which Mimi had found in the Opera cellar. Gobara took one look at it and went as white as paper.

"This was Mlle Chalabi's necklace," she whispered. "Oh, madame! Where did you find it?"

I exchanged a look with Mimi. "Beneath the Opera," I said. "My poor Gobara, I'm afraid that your former mistress is certainly dead."

* * *

Schmidt drove Vasily and myself back to our lodgings on the Boulevard Haussmann. At first the journey was silent. I thought of Gobara, who had taken Chalabi's death pretty quietly. She had to have already prepared herself for the news, but my heart ached for her, all the same.

Apart from this we had great cause for thanks. Mimi had been returned to us safe and sound. We now knew the identity of the killer, the location of his subterranean lair, and—most likely—who his next target would be.

All this ought to have put my mind at ease. Of course, it did no such thing; it only allowed my mind to return like a querulous old woman to the one consuming question. I could not, of course, make experiments with Mimi—or indeed at all, while I had Vasily to think of. But then, he and I might part ways. I might meet a Mlle Perrot of my own; and then what should I do?

"How quiet you are!" Vasily remarked. "Is it Mimi who worries you?"

I returned to myself with a jolt. "Oh! No, not Mimi." And I heaved a sigh, because he, too, would be affected by my choices.

"I think that Mlle Perrot and Mlle Dargent are lovers," I said, "and it—made me think."

There was a silence.

"That you might do the same, do you mean?" There was something wary in the tone of his voice. My face warmed. How easily he had seen through me!

"You knew this about me, didn't you?" I asked, softly. "Are you very shocked?"

Vasily seemed to weigh his words with great care.

"You were right, the night of the bal masqué," he said at last. "What right have I to be shocked? God knows how often I've toyed with others and thrown them away. If the same thing happened to me it would be no more than I deserve."

"Vasily," I whispered. I believe it was only at that moment, hearing the fear in his voice, that I truly saw how he had injured, not only others, but also himself by his past faithlessness.

In the darkness of the carriage his hands found mine and clung, but his voice was all supplication.

"I knew it would happen," he said. "You are too good for me. It was only a matter of time before you knew it…Be at ease, my love. I've tried to buy you with pity and pleasure and power, and I won't offer them again. I only ask that if you take your own freedom, you'll not try to give me mine. Let me be your footman if you won't have me as your lover."

Overcome with emotion, I gripped his hands more tightly. Only at this moment did I realise how frightened I had been to broach the thing aloud with him, or how much it meant to me that he did not seem to think any the worse of me because of it.

"Vaska, you're a perfect ninnyhammer, and I certainly won't let you be my footman," I said, trying to conceal my tears with laughter. "For one thing, you would make a rotten footman; and for another, I refuse to be your one reason for living. It isn't healthy, and it isn't right."

"I don't want any other reason," he said, a little sulkily. "I haven't the heart for it. I am tired."

"Never fear—I'm not going to throw you lightly aside."

"I cannot be thrown," he said with dignity. "I cling much too tightly for *that*."

I knew that, despite his funning, he was honestly touched. Yet his words left me with more questions than answers. If even Vasily would not stand in my way, then the choice was thrown back upon me. Society could be hoodwinked, and my lover only wanted me to be happy. What, then, should I do?

In that moment of stillness, the choice came to me. After all, one did not get to have everything one wanted in this life. One could not serve every god. I recalled, now, why I yet clung to mine. In the hour of my distress, He had seen the crimes committed against me, and had shared in my anger. *This* God had chosen to stand my Friend, and I did not like to grieve Him.

I knew then that it would not be the last such choice I would have to make; nor, perhaps, the hardest. Had it not been Vasily before me, but Vasilissa, so to speak, then the thing would have been as bitter as death. Still: for the moment, it was enough to go on by.

Vasily was still waiting, silent, for me to speak.

"Mimi was right," I told him. "I think I'd rather be true to my religion than to my temptations."

He said nothing, but he squeezed my hand.

"You said once that for you it was a—a phase," I added. "I don't think it's a phase for me. I think I'll always find other women as attractive as I do men. But I want you to know that I mean to go on as I always have—not pretending to be something I'm not, but doing what I believe to be right. And I hope," I added, after a moment, rather uncertainly, "that that suits you, too."

"It's more than I could ever hope for," Vasily said. I wished he did not sound so pathetically grateful. "May I kiss you now?"

"Oh," I said, and I came over all fluttery. "I don't know. I think virtue should be its own reward, don't you?"

"Absolutely not," he said. On neither of the two previous occasions upon which Vasily had kissed me had he consulted my views upon the subject. Now he said, very softly and utterly irresistibly, *"Please?"*

I found that I did not think that virtue should be its own reward, after all. I slipped across the space between us and perched upon his knee, and found his lips by touch in the dark. This time he let me kiss him at my own pace, soft and gentle, and it was a little less like being eaten alive. When Schmidt drew the carriage to a halt I was extremely sorry for it to do so. I drew back and caught my breath, and for a moment rested in Vasily's arms, feeling exceedingly warm and content.

"There's another reason I couldn't follow Mlle Perrot's example," I said sleepily.

"Oh? What's that?" Vasily asked, as though he was only halfway paying attention.

I kissed the top of his head. "I've always wanted to have children of my own some day."

And then Vasily went absolutely rigid. "Children!" he said. *"Gospodi,* with whom? With *me?"*

"Or with someone better," I said wickedly. I reached for the door-latch; he grasped my wrist with sudden desperation.

"I can't," he said in tones of absolute horror. "How can *I* be a father? I don't know how!"

"Ninnyhammer!" I said, affectionately.

"I mean it!" he protested. "Imagine *me* trying to be stern—and wise—and all-knowing—"

"I see your point," said I. "Then they'll just have to have a father who's soft in the head."

"Bozhe moi." He was silent a moment. "You know that I would do anything for you, Molly."

"Even this?"

"Even this," he said, and his voice was that of a man who had been condemned to death. I laughed and kissed him again, because virtue was not its own reward. Then I bade him good-night and went up to my flat.

Gobara had left the gas burning and the place was wonderfully warm and cosy. I closed the door behind me and stood a moment hugging myself. The room was so bright and pleasant, limned with gold despite the shadows gathered in the corners. My lips tingled and I felt rather as though I had been drinking champagne. A weight had rolled off my shoulders. I felt that I had for days been lost in a gilded hall of mirrors—shiny, reflective surfaces like a kaleidoscope, in which all vision seemed hopelessly confused. Who was I to be, now that I was rich? Which was my true reflection? Now, at least in *one* respect, I had caught a glimpse of my true self.

Nor was that the only thing that had been weighing me down. Ever since I arrived in this city, people had been telling me that the rich could do as they liked without any fear of consequences. I saw now how the thought had oppressed me, until I had half despaired of bringing either the murderer or M. Dumortier to justice, in the face of a world that allowed money and power to dictate what they ought to believe.

But it was not so—it had never been so. Money could not entirely overwhelm one's conscience. This glittering world of masks and facades had still a sense of right and wrong; could still be shamed or shocked into upholding the one, and condemning the other.

I had only to find the right leverage; I had only somehow to engage their consciences, and the evil would be defeated.

Chapter XV.

Obedient to his instructions, Alphonse Schmidt presented himself at Mimi's house the following morning in order to escort her to her rehearsals at the Opera. He found the soloist pinning on her hat in the foyer. The night's sleep appeared to have restored her spirits, although she still appeared tired and pale.

"Do you think you're quite ready for this, Mimi?" he asked.

Mimi gave him a look of blank incomprehension which he thought she might have learned from Nijam. "I'm supposed to be dancing Myrtha," she told him. "Should I be lying about at home?"

Schmidt cleared his throat. "No, but don't forget that *you* are more important than the ballet."

"The ballet is important to *me*," she said, stubbornly. "I'm the only one who can dance Myrtha, but I can't do it without practice. He may be a revenant, but he's right there."

She brushed past him, out the front door and up into the carriage. Schmidt followed reluctantly.

"Where is Miss Nijam?" he asked, as the carriage got underway. He had rather hoped to catch a glimpse of her.

"Nijam is working on her flame contraption, of course. I don't even know if she's had breakfast."

Of course Nijam could not spare the time to come down and make small talk—if small talk was really what he wanted. Schmidt had lain awake all night brooding over the news: that the thing he had beheld in the carriage with Mimi—the thing that had awoken so many guilty feelings—was a revenant.

Of course it was a revenant. The Schmidt name had always been associated with revenants; he had known that since Petersburg. Now Alphonse felt himself caught in an inexorably closing trap; his past had not forgotten him, and would soon close its jaws about him. He might have been able to wait passively for the approach of his fate had it not been that Nijam evidently *knew* something. She knew—she was keeping it a secret—and for some reason he could not comprehend, she would not tell him.

No, it was not *small talk* he desired with Miss Nijam.

Mimi was engaged in powdering her face. As she pressed the puff to the dark circles beneath her eyes, Schmidt told himself not to be a busybody; but it was impossible to say nothing.

"That *thing* does not have your best interests at heart," he said. "Why do as it tells you?"

Mimi glared at him, as indeed he had expected she would. "Why do as Vasily tells *you*? Don't tell *me* who to mind when *you* run about at the beck and call of a vampire."

Schmidt's face reddened; he had not expected his own words to be turned back on him. It hardly seemed fair.

"Sir is not a vampire any more. Nor did sir end up in a prison for criminals so dangerous that they needed their memories removed. That," he added, bitterly, "was me."

Mimi snapped her compact shut. "Nijam was right about you. You think you're some terrible monster, but you don't even know whether it's true or not. And you don't have the guts to find out."

Schmidt put a hand to his heart. Even beneath the starched shirt-front he could feel the ridges of the scars there.

"I know that it's true," he said, soft and stubborn.

Mimi relented a little. "I am tougher than you are, Schmidt. Don't worry about me."

After that they relapsed into silence. Schmidt felt torn, for he wished never to reawaken that dreadful, dimly-perceived shadow-self, which he had escaped only by giving up his memories. Yet, if it was possible that he had ever harmed Miss Nijam, surely he must make amends. If she would agree only to *tell* him what their past connection had been, without insisting upon his recovering his memory entire!

Upon arriving at the Opera, Schmidt followed Mimi to the foyer de la danse where the girls of the corps de ballet waited, pert and gossiping, for M. Christophe's appearance. To his surprise, a gaggle of the youngest dancers immediately left their place atop and around the piano, flooding Mimi with squeals and hugs.

"Mademoiselle! You came back!" cried a dark-haired ballerina whom he recognised as Fatima, the little dancer who had shown him and Nijam where to find Mimi on the night of the masked ball. *"Alhamdulillah,* now you must take us through our steps before M. Christophe comes and canes our ankles for getting them wrong."

"If you brats practiced when you ought, you wouldn't get them wrong," Mimi said. "All right, line up over there. Schmidt, move yourself. You're in the way."

Mimi gave him a shove towards the piano, and the ballerinas giggled. "Oh, I wish I dared!" one of them cried, looking at

Schmidt in a manner that made his ears uncomfortably hot. "It must be love," Fatima added in a stage whisper. A third bit her lip wickedly and said, "Mademoiselle, I hope you had a *lovely* time while you were away."

Schmidt opened his mouth to protest, but in the nick of time realised that anything he said would only add fuel to the fire.

"Look at him *blushing!*" one of the ballerinas whispered, behind her hand, to her friend.

"That's enough," Mimi snapped. "Don't you know this gentleman is the personal chargé d'affaires to the new manager? Treat him with respect." Then they all stopped tittering and stood to attention, while Mimi began to drill them like toy soldiers.

Schmidt retreated into a corner, wishing the floor would open and swallow him up. It was bad enough being made the butt of sir's jokes in his genuine feelings for Miss Nijam. Now the whole Opera corps de ballet was going to laugh at him for a completely imaginary liaison with Miss Laine. If Miss Nijam was to hear of this…!

No, he was daydreaming—hopelessly, as usual. Miss Nijam would not be bothered in the slightest by the news that gossip had linked his name with Mimi's. She knew them both much too well.

Putting the daydream aside, then, he turned his attention to the rehearsal. Here was a side of Mimi he had never seen, for she was utterly absorbed in her work. With a snap of her fingers she would halt the dancers before demonstrating the steps herself; the little ballerinas hung on her lips and followed her lead and wrung from her smiles and words of praise. It struck Schmidt that the colour had come back to her cheeks, and the light to her eyes. He had never seen her so happy.

"Oh, mademoiselle!" Fatima exclaimed at last, with shining admiration in her eyes. Just then the pianist stopped playing and rose to his feet, and the other soloists and members of the corps de ballet, who had gone on smoking and gossiping and lolling about the edge of the room while Mimi's little rehearsal went on, suddenly stood to attention; but the young girl saw none of this. "You are *ever* so much better a teacher than M. Christophe!"

"Mind your tongue, Gobara!" cried Mimi, going in an instant as white as a sheet.

Then Schmidt heard what the little ballerina's prattle had disguised: the *clack* of a white wand against the parquetry as the revenant himself advanced into the foyer de la danse. He was once again masked and gloved, wearing his smoking-cap and an impeccably cut coat; but now Schmidt had seen beneath the mask, and he wondered that he had ever thought this creature a living man. His clothing hung loose upon a cadaverous frame, the scent of the embalmer was heavy upon him, and those eyes—ah! those eyes, even with their fire banked, still glittered uncannily within the holes of his mask. They settled upon Schmidt for a moment, and he found himself nearly breathless with the sense of malice that suddenly beat against him.

Schmidt moved a step or two away from the piano, to where he would have a clear path to Mimi if one should be needed.

At the centre of the foyer, Mimi held her ground as the revenant advanced towards her. In preparation for the rehearsal she had stripped down to the abbreviated dress of white gauze worn by all the ballerinas; and above the low-cut back Schmidt could see the tension in her shoulders.

In the cloying silence that had fallen upon the room, the revenant made a series of brusque gestures. Schmidt could not quite interpret them, but Mimi could.

"Yes," she answered in a low, submissive voice. "Please don't be angry, monsieur."

The revenant turned his back upon her.

"I was afraid for my friends," she added."Of course I had to leave you."

As the ballerinas whispered to each other, the revenant turned again, with another sign, angrier.

"Yes, I know," Mimi said with downcast eyes. All the life seemed to have been sucked out of her. Schmidt had been half afraid that the creature would try to strangle her on the spot, but this, somehow, was worse.

The revenant stomped away, halting before a ballerina who had quickly snuffed out a cigarette when he entered. She straightened eagerly as the revenant's pointing finger settled upon her.

"Oh yes, monsieur," she said. "I'll dance Myrtha for you, if you like."

"No!" Mimi gasped. "She's already danced Myrtha twice, and I haven't even danced her once, though the rôle was given to me!"

The revenant turned upon Mimi with an angry gesture, and this one, even Schmidt could interpret: *It was I who gave you the rôle, and if I please I can take it away!*

Mimi grasped the revenant's sleeve to prevent him turning away. "*She* hasn't been taught to do it. *She* doesn't understand you like I do. Please!" And she threw herself down on her knees.

"Oh, for God's sake," said the smoking ballerina in disgust. "You had your chance. Now it's mine."

Mimi did not for an instant take her eyes from the revenant. "You know the way Moretti dances. She's careless. She'll *never* be perfect. I can be perfect. I can work day and night. I'll hold nothing back; not my body, and not my soul. That's why you chose me, isn't it?"

Moretti scoffed, but otherwise there was perfect silence in the room, and a horrible ring of absolute sincerity in Mimi's words. And Schmidt, watching, felt his flesh crawl.

"Mimi," he whispered, the plea forcing its way out of him.

Mimi never turned to look at him; but the revenant did, and for a moment the banked-down fire in his eyes flickered up. Schmidt ground his teeth together, for the creature's attention was like a blow across the face.

The revenant made another sign; gestured first to Schmidt, and then to himself.

"You," Mimi said at once. "Always, you."

Another gesture. Mimi turned curiously lifeless eyes upon him, and Schmidt had the horrible feeling that he was watching another slow, strangling murder. Only this time the victim was Mimi, who for all her brutal honesty had always had a kind word for him; Mimi, who had once said that he was the most important person in the whole crew; Mimi, who for all her toughness was not invulnerable.

"Leave us," she told him.

Schmidt clenched his fists. Sir had once told him that he displayed his emotions upon his face for all to see, and he had no doubt that his feelings in this moment were thoroughly betrayed. All the same, he forced himself to move deliberately and speak clearly: he bowed and said, "Mademoiselle, I've been sent to watch over you on the orders of the Baron von Jörger himself. I dare not obey you."

The corps de ballet held its breath. The revenant looked naked murder at him. Mimi transferred her attention to her un-dead master.

"You see that he will not obey me," she said. "Forgive me."

Moretti spoke, desperately. "Don't listen to Laine," she said. "I too can work. I'll prove it. Give me a week—no, three days and I'll be—*ow!*"

She broke off as the revenant delivered a stinging blow with his wand to her ankle. He turned his back on Moretti, signing to Mimi, who leaped to her feet. She was trembling, perhaps with eagerness, or perhaps with desperation.

"He wants us to begin from the start of Act Two," she cried. "Music, please!"

The ballerinas flocked to the edges of the room. The piano began its eerie melody; and Mimi, hearing her cue, turned up her face and cradled her arms and began to drift across the sloping floor on her toes, a spirit gliding across the ground and no longer a mortal woman at all…

Schmidt, now that the moment of crisis was past, retreated to the corridor where he might have a little privacy whilst still keeping an eye upon the rehearsal. Mimi might have sworn that she knew how to handle the revenant, and surely she did—yet, just as surely, there was a part of her that remained beneath his spell.

He touched his transmitter. "Miss Nijam," he began, and then stopped. He hardly knew whether he and the inventor were on speaking terms. But surely Mimi's safety was the overriding consideration.

"What is it, Schmidt?" Nijam asked crisply, as though she

had no time to waste.

"I'm sorry," he said, "but I was going to ask how that flame-thrower is coming along."

"How do you think?" she snapped.

"I'm sorry," he repeated. "It's only—I've never seen Mimi like this before. She was down on her knees to that thing just now, and—"

"Put yourself at ease, Schmidt." That was sir's voice. "Mimi is never subtle when she's playing a part, but revenants are simple creatures. He'll fall for it."

"No, that's not what I mean," Schmidt insisted. "I've never seen that look on her face before. She has a weakness, and anyone can see it—even a revenant."

Listening on my own transmitter, I understood his perturbation. "I know, Schmidt. Mimi's always had ambitions as a ballerina, and she would have to be more than mortal to resist the temptation now. That's why her friends must watch over her. Remain vigilant, and call on us if anything happens."

I switched off my transmitter, and Vasily must have done the same; but Nijam, perhaps, was too busy with a delicate bit of machinery to silence her own transmitter at once. Perceiving this, Schmidt screwed up his courage to the sticking-point.

"Are you still there, Miss Nijam? Will you spare me ten minutes of your time this evening, when I bring Mimi back?"

He thought he heard a sigh. "Look, Schmidt, *do* you want me to finish this contraption or don't you?" Then the connection was cut.

Miss Nijam might not wish to give him an explanation, and Schmidt himself would almost have done anything to avoid demanding one. But they were bound together by the people who depended upon them—by Mimi and Vasily and myself—

and for the sake of the mission they must sort out all these tangled unsaid things.

As he returned to the rehearsal to take up his guard duties, Schmidt heaved a deep inward sigh. Miss Nijam must have that conversation with him. If necessary, he would take a leaf from Miss Dark's book, and resort to trickery.

Chapter XVI.

No doubt the reader is agog to learn how I had been amusing myself while all this was going on. In fact I had had a rather exciting afternoon running some errands for Nijam. In addition to a number of pipes, tubes, pistons, and heaven knows what else, she also required me to order quantities of kerosene, creosote and shale oil. The men at the fuel depot greeted this request with suspicious looks. Only the sight of my very modish afternoon dress, in a shade of brown so lively that it was almost red, which I had recently collected from the House of Worth, must have persuaded them not to call upon the services of the gendarmerie.

Money might be no substitute for virtue, but it certainly gave one the right appearance.

My errands for Nijam discharged, I made my way to the Opera. "Any news, Schmidt?" I asked via transmitter, as I crossed the Place de l'Opéra. "Does Mimi have the Taglioni journal yet?"

"Not yet," Schmidt replied softly. "She is having a lesson in the cellar. I've been told to wait outside the door, but she's wearing an open transmitter."

Indeed, I could hear the tinkle of a piano and Mimi's hard breathing as she worked.

"How much longer do you suppose it will take?" I whispered so as not to disturb her.

"Who can tell?" Schmidt answered. "That creature drives her like a machine. It's not right."

Mimi gave a sudden gasp of pain, and the piano stopped. Although she was not speaking to us, her voice came over the transmitter quite clearly.

"No, I'm sorry! It was my knee. I was distracted. No, it won't happen again; I *promise.*"

Those last words were very pointed, no doubt at us. "Sorry," Schmidt muttered. I turned off my transmitter without speaking again, feeling a little guilty for having distracted Mimi at a time when she was working so hard.

I continued, however, and found Vasily in his magnificent office, clearly having a wonderful afternoon. "My dear!" he greeted me, leaping up from behind the gleaming marble expanse of his desk. "Who do you think just came to see me, but M. le President himself!"

"Indeed! Does he have views on ballet too?"

"No, on comic opera! Can you imagine it—a mistress of his fancies herself as a singer, so he wishes me to put on that *Cosi fan Tutte* Mozart nonsense, with Mlle Sorel in the lead. I turned him down flat, of course."

"How so? Isn't Mozart rather well thought-of?"

"Yes; but my dear, I find your sex too charming to endure hearing them slandered as that opera does."

Having closed the door of the office behind me, I perched myself upon the edge of the desk and observed him fondly. "No wonder you're enjoying yourself, Vaska! It can't fall to everyone's lot to send away a head of state with a flea in his ear!"

"Enjoying myself? Hardly!" He kissed my hand.

Perhaps the solution to all my worries had been staring me in the face all along. "What a shame you'll have to resign in disgrace after another week or two!" said I. "Are you quite sure you want to? The Baroness might relent."

Vasily's laughter faded, and he searched my face with an expression of dawning hope. "Do you mean it?"

I shrugged. "Perhaps I was mistaken about you and that ballerina, after all. And perhaps you *do* have other reasons to live, besides me."

At that, he drew himself up to his full height and hauteur. "You aren't seriously proposing that I, Grand Duke Vasily Nikolaevich Romanov, should stoop to the level of a common impresario—"

He was wearing a very convenient cravat with a ruby pin winking in the centre of it. Seizing the knot, I drew him down until his face was on a level with my own, which ruined the hauteur but made it easier to press a fleeting kiss to his lips.

Vasily stopped talking for a moment. His face softened. "Witch," he murmured. "Very well, since you'll have it so, I *am* enjoying myself."

I rewarded him for that admission with another kiss, this one not so fleeting. I am afraid that it was imprudent to do so, for a moment later the door opened without warning and in order to keep up appearances I was compelled to deliver a stinging slap to his face.

"There!" I cried as he recoiled, "let *that* teach you to think of winning me back in such a manner!"

I could not resist a glance towards the door as I did so. Jacques Dupont stood there, having entered without announcing himself. My messenger had returned from his errand.

Then Vasily caught my wrist and showed me his teeth in a theatrical snarl, which was perhaps half habit and half play-acting. And then Jacques Dupont responded in a way that I found wholly unexpected, for he panted, "Ha! *Vasily Nikolaevich!*" —swept the door shut behind him with an echoing slam, and in the same motion levelled a *revolver* at my lover's head.

Glancing at the intruder for the first time since the door had opened, Vasily abandoned his play-acting at once. "Oh, *slava,*" he said in a tone of resignation. But he put himself before me, as though to shield me from the firearm. I suppose he was not wrong to do so, for bullets may go astray, like letters, and do more damage. But indeed we would have been far better off had I thrown myself before *him. I* was not the person half of Europe wished to murder.

Dupont had gone pale, but he was grinning with a rabid sort of exultation that made me feel very nervous about the revolver. "Baron von Jörger! My foot!"

"Anton Lupei, on my life," Vasily drawled.

Well. I had *never* believed that his name could be Jacques Dupont.

"Oh, for heaven's sake keep your voices down," I said, in that tone of governesslike authority which has so rarely failed me in moments of crisis. "If you expose each other as frauds then you'll both be in trouble. And put that revolver away, Lupei! Do you fancy yourself the hero of a shilling shocker?"

Lupei's revolver wavered a little at that, but he, too, was showing his teeth. Quite likely he had never had a governess. "Tell him to keep his hands to himself if he doesn't want to die like a dog."

"Tell me to keep *my* hands to myself?" Vasily objected. I had never heard him sound so injured, and even at that fraught moment it was a struggle to keep my face straight. Hell hath no fury like a man who has been accused of annoying a lady after having learned to behave with restraint for the first time in his life.

Lupei, still threatening Vasily with the weapon, hardly seemed to hear this. The look of triumph faded from his eyes, leaving implacable wrath and utter contempt. "I suppose I have no further to look for the one who has been making ballerinas disappear."

I stepped boldly before the muzzle of the revolver, making Vasily draw in a hissing breath. "Explain yourself, Lupei—or Dupont, or whatever your name is. I thought you agreed to be my servant."

That got his attention. Lupei raised the muzzle of his revolver to point at the ceiling. It was still ready to use; but at least it was no longer pointed at me or my lover. "Baroness, do you have *any* idea who this man is?"

"Indeed I do."

"This is Vasily Nikolaevich Romanov," he told me, anyway. "Traitor—murderer—*vampire.*"

"Former vampire," Vasily said, very quietly, from behind me. "You were there the night I gave up my fangs."

"Still? A few months ago all the gossip was that you'd received them back." Lupei spat on the floor. "Then they said you'd been blown up by the Moscow anarchists. I wasted a good bottle of wine drinking to your death. I should have known a pest like Vasily Nikolaevich would not die so easily."

"Yes, still!" I insisted, trying to keep Lupei's attention on me. "If you've heard otherwise, it was only a story we invented for one last job in Moscow. I'll swear to it, if you like."

"Will you?" Lupei looked at me with dawning curiosity. "Who are *you?*"

"Allow me to make the introduction," Vasily said, drawing me gently but insistently to his side. "Molly-my-dear, this is the angry little man I told you about, who flayed the skin off me on the Orient Express. Lupei, this is Miss Molly Dark of Brixton, a lady of impeccable respectability and awe-provoking accomplishments, who has seen fit to receive me as her suitor."

Whatever he might have expected, this caught Lupei entirely by surprise. His mouth dropped open—and thank God, at last he lowered his weapon.

"You're courting a *bourgeois?* A lady? From *Brixton?*"

"I'm not really a baroness," I said apologetically.

"No! My God, when I saw you with *him* I thought you were a *dainty.*" It was much to Lupei's credit that he accepted my assurances to the contrary. But then he let out a forced laugh that rang madly in that room. "And Ioanna? Did he tell you about my cousin?"

Suddenly Ioanna was in the room with us—the peasant girl who had been Vasily's first love, and had died at his hands. She was everywhere in a dozen different guises: bloodied and dead, laughing and alive, rotting and skeletal in the crown of flowers in which she had been buried. It was impossible to tell which were Vasily's memories, and which Anton's; but Vasily's arm tightened about me and I knew that he, too, felt her presence.

I drew in a little sharp breath at the sense of so much grief. For the first time I had an inkling of who Ioanna might have been—not just dead, not just an aching memory, but a living person: sturdy, tall, cheerful, unconquerable. She had been *so* certain of cheating death—so certain that she could win the boy she loved. Life had always bowed to Ioanna; death alone could have defeated her.

"You were her cousin?" I whispered.

"I was Ioanna's cousin," Lupei confirmed, "and also I was Liz's lover. He has told you about Liz Sharp?"

Vasily's arm about me had become almost crushing. He said in a low voice, "Miss Sharp is the woman I told you about, the one to whom I gave Missy's diamonds as a wedding-gift."

Still, I must have looked puzzled, for there had been no Liz Sharp among Vasily's collection of ghosts.

At the sight of my face, Anton gave another mad peal of laughter. "She doesn't *know*? She doesn't know what you did?"

And I recalled with a pang what Mimi had told me in Hong Kong—that the truth about the woman who came before me, the woman who had refused to be Vasily's salvation and had taken away his fangs, was not so pretty as he had made it sound.

Vasily said, "I have no secrets from Miss Dark. I mentioned her accomplishments. One of them is this: that she sees memories of the dead. My past is an open book to her. What about yours?"

Lupei sent him an uncomprehending look; but even in the midst of my own preoccupations I saw what Vasily was about.

"He's telling the truth," I told Lupei, still in that soothing, matter-of-fact voice. "Ioanna was here just now. She was tall and dark-haired, and you buried her with red flowers in her hair. I am sorry."

Lupei looked at me and turned as white as a sheet. Then

the room was full again, full to the overflowing with other people—other peasants, women in head-scarves and aprons and men in short vests and cloth caps—all of them grim and bloodied and terrified, looking as though they had been savaged by wild beasts. The sight was so unexpected, and so overwhelming, that I staggered against Vasily with a cry as though I had been struck.

Instantly, Lupei cried out also and fell to his knees, dropping his revolver. For a moment he gazed upon me in horror.

"You see them? The ones I killed?" His throat worked. "Then you know why I must see justice done for others."

Overwhelmed by death, I was incapable of answering. Vasily guided me to a chair and scooped up the revolver, putting it into his pocket. Had it been me, I should have been inclined to turn the weapon upon Lupei himself, just in case he felt inclined to run amok, and add us to his ghastly collection.

But then, perhaps my lover had not been the only one to give up his sanguinary habits.

"Depend upon it, if I was the one killing ballerinas, Miss Dark would know about it," Vasily said, going to the sideboard and pouring out a dram of cognac for Lupei, and another for himself. He handed the brandy to Lupei, who drank it in a single gulp. "I don't marvel at your thinking I was the culprit. But imagine, for a moment, that I might feel some of what you feel—that I, too, might wish to devote myself to justice."

The ghastly vision faded as Lupei calmed himself. When Vasily returned to me, I gratefully accepted his steadying embrace, but I also helped myself to the cognac.

"In fact," I said, a little breathlessly, "I believe we can help each other. We have discovered the real killer, and he—or I should say *it*—is something else entirely."

* * *

After that Lupei was willing to believe our story, and the meeting went a little more smoothly. Vasily explained what Mimi had discovered in the cellars, although he was obliged to take some time about it; for he kept having to stop to answer the man's questions. I gathered Lupei had little idea of how Vasily had been spending his time since relinquishing his fangs. He kept looking to me for confirmation, and then shaking his head and muttering oaths when I confirmed that Vasily was telling the truth. Given the elasticity of my own loyalty to the truth, I found this trust in me rather touching.

Then Lupei explained how he had come to interest himself in the case. A friend of his—a factory-labourer who had sacrificed much to send his younger sister to the Opera's academy of ballet—came to him in alarm. His sister, now a successful member of the corps de ballet, had cut all ties with her family. She still appeared every evening at the Opera, but her flat was empty and her few servants had been turned away. In the course of his investigations, Lupei had borrowed a black cloak and gone to the bal masqué in hope of securing work that would grant him access to the Opera and its denizens. The rest the reader knows.

Better yet, he had tracked down the Chalabi family before they returned to Egypt.

"It was Dumortier," Lupei declared. "He visited them the morning after Mlle Chalabi's disappearance, when they were about to go to the police, and made them a proposition. Either he would pay them to return quietly to Egypt without their eldest daughter—or, if they wanted to stay and make a fuss, he would expose the youngest sister, Irina, as an anarchist."

"Irina Chalabi is an anarchist?" I asked, fascinated.

"She! No," Lupei said with a snort. "But such is the law, you understand, that merely passing the time of day with an anarchist is as good as being one. Irina once attended a suffragist rally. It is enough to get a whole family in trouble, especially if they are not of French blood. The Chalabis had lost one daughter; they chose not to risk another."

Vasily, now seated behind his desk, snapped triumphant fingers. "I *told* you that Dumortier had something to do with this!"

"You did," I admitted, "and I ought to have believed you."

"No, you oughtn't," Lupei told me. "A person like that should be disbelieved on principle. It is good for him."

I regarded the little man with wonder. "Lupei, there's someone you ought to meet. I think you and she would get on very well together."

"Perish the thought!" Vasily murmured. I paid no heed to this, for my mind was working on something else.

"Mimi was certain that the revenant had accomplices," I said. "Someone to send food to the cellar—to say nothing of fitting it up as a studio, with piano and mirrors and floor and all. Someone to hound M. Larousse into leaving—or killing himself. Someone anxious to see the Opera reliving the glory days of Perrot and Taglioni and *Giselle.*"

"Someone," Vasily said pointedly, "who was seen conversing with a raven one morning in the Place de l'Opéra."

"I had forgotten that! How clever you are, Vaska-my-pet!" Lupei made a stifled sound.

"Please don't call me that in front of the gun-slinger," Vasily said, before adding: "I wonder if that's why the previous manager left. Perhaps he was getting poison-pen letters, too."

Lupei became solemn. "Then it is Dumortier who is responsible for the death of Pierre's sister—and seven other people. What is it you mean to do about it?"

I hesitated, thinking that it might be a little difficult to explain this in a way that an ordinary, reasonably honest person might accept. "Well, we don't mean to go to the police."

Lupei scoffed. Vasily cleared his throat. "Have no anxiety on that account, my dear. Lupei won't insist on police. He's an anarchist."

I was going to protest that this sounded like a rather harsh judgement of the man, who had surely now seen the error of his ways. But Lupei forestalled me by saying, "What we want is an incendiary bomb. I can get you one of those, if you like."

It took me a moment to recover from this blithe pronouncement. "Oh! there's no need for *that*," I said. "Our inventor, Miss Nijam, is working on what she calls a flame-thrower. The plan is to eliminate the revenant, and then to arrange compensation for the bereaved families."

Lupei scowled. "It's more than they'd get if they went to the police. But Dumortier should die for what he's done."

"We aren't executioners," said I, hastily.

And Vasily added, "We'll make sure he can never cause any other deaths. —How? My dear fellow, you'll have to trust us. We're professionals." Lupei looked murderous, but Vasily, despite my sore misgivings, placated him by taking the revolver from his pocket and sliding it across the desk towards him. "Now, do excuse me. I'm afraid that I have an appointment with the government representative in ten minutes."

"Boot-licker," Lupei grumbled.

"Even I can't compete with the representative of the French government, charm I never so wisely," said I, earning myself a melting look and a kiss on the hand. "All right: come along, Lupei, and I'll introduce you to the rest of the crew."

Lupei pocketed the revolver, but he fixed Vasily with a black glare. "You'd better tell her about Liz," he said, "or I will."

Vasily's mouth tightened, and I felt my stomach contract. What on earth had he done to the poor woman? And why had he not told me? I could feel impending revelation thickening over my head like a thunderstorm.

Before any of us could say anything more, however, there came a brisk knock at the door. Vasily broke off the glare he had been exchanging with Lupei as the door opened and Mimi entered, Schmidt following close behind. She looked utterly weary, but she held her head high with an air of triumph.

"I told you I could get the creature eating out of my hand," she declared. Then she saw Lupei. "Who is this?"

"A friend," I put in hurriedly. "His name is Anton Lupei, and he's been trying to investigate the disappearances himself. Lupei, this is our ballerina, Mimi Laine."

Lupei looked her up and down. "Your ballerina is limping. How can she dance with a duff knee?"

"Better than you can with two good ones," Mimi answered without hesitation. Then she slammed down a slim, leather-covered journal upon the marble desk. "Here: Taglioni's journal, with the training schedule that made her a legend. Dumortier will sell his eye-teeth to get his hands on this."

"Mimi, you're a marvel," I told her, picking up the journal and leafing through it. The carefully-copied tables and annotations made little sense to me, but I was pleased to see it for two reasons: first, that we had what we needed to provide for the families of the dead, and second, that we could now extricate Mimi from her dangerous task.

Schmidt cleared his throat. "If you don't need me, sir, I'll escort Mimi home. I want a word with Miss Nijam."

"Oh, what an excellent notion," I said. "Why don't you take Lupei with you? He has a lot of experience with incendiaries, and Nijam will want to meet him."

It was only later, of course, that I understood why Schmidt appeared so crestfallen at this suggestion. He could hardly enjoy a tête-à-tête in the presence of a small but noisy anarchist. All the same, he assented manfully and beckoned Lupei to follow him.

Vasily gave Mimi a crooked smile. "That's the angry little anarchist I told you about. What do you think of him?"

Mimi sniffed. "He's rude," she said. Then she followed the others, leaving Vasily and myself in fits of stifled merriment.

"I knew it," said I. "It would be love or hatred, and nothing between. Perhaps it's best this way. He claims to have a wife and ten children."

"That's highly unlikely," Vasily said. "Three years ago when I knew him, he was a bachelor and devoted to…to Miss Sharp."

The laughter faded from his eyes. I said softly, "Hadn't you better tell me?"

Perhaps he would have told me, then. But the clock struck five o'clock, and Vasily started from his chair.

"That's my appointment," he said. "I'll tell you next time— you have my word." Then he kissed my hand and showed me out. I went biting my lip, for I did not like to go about my day with this hanging over my head. It did occur to me, as I went to take the cab which one of the secretaries called for me, that the Baron von Jörger might have begged off his appointment in favour of a little pressing business with his Baroness. But quite possibly it had not occurred to Vasily to do so.

Returning home, I told my maid that I wanted a quiet evening in.

"I suppose you had a busy night," Gobara observed, snatching my hat and coat before I could stow them away myself. "Oh, madame, I'm so happy that Mlle Laine returned safe and sound. I was so worried for her!"

"That's very kind of you," I said, a little puzzled. "Do you know Mimi?"

"No, but my sister Fatima speaks well of her. She says that Mlle Laine is very kind to her, and helps all the ballet brats learn their steps, so that M. Christophe does not beat them."

"Of course she does," said I, thoughtfully. Mimi always did have a kind heart beneath her pugnacious exterior.

"I'm grateful to her on another account, too," Gobara added. "You've heard of the Jockey Club?"

"Yes, and I believe I've met one or two of them," I said, thinking of Deleuze and his friend Caillot.

"Well, you know what men are like," Gobara said, with a knowing shrug. "There are ladies enough in the corps de ballet to entertain them, without their going after the younger girls. And the ballet school has rules which ought to protect them until they turn sixteen and begin their careers. But sometimes, in the back passages, or at the bal masqué—well, they say that rules were made to be broken. But Fatima says Mlle Laine has been watching over them, making sure that the gentlemen don't find them alone."

I felt a little sick at the thought of how vulnerable those bright-eyed young girls might be, to a man sufficiently lacking in scruples. And then I remembered how unscrupulous Vasily had been, once. I did not know what to imagine. The Vasily I knew was capable of admitting to his faults, and of seeking to mend them. Yet the wrong he had done to Miss Sharp had not, after all, killed her…

"You are quiet, madame," Gobara observed. "I beg your pardon for prattling on."

"Oh, no," I said, forcing myself to smile. "It wasn't you, I promise. Only something ominous happened today."

"Is it the Baron, then?" she asked.

She had put her finger uncomfortably close to the truth. "In a way," said I; and then, to keep up appearances: "You know that I am thinking of divorcing him."

Her face fell. "Oh, madame, how can that be? When you love him so much!"

And *that* was such a blow to my clever schemes, that I was forced to stifle a laugh. "You're very perceptive, Gobara," I told her; and there I left it, feeling that perhaps the less that was said, the better.

Chapter XVII.

Nijam was not usually an early bird, no doubt owing to a lack of interest in worms for breakfast. She was, nevertheless, up early the next morning. A prototype flame-thrower was nearly ready for testing, and she had awoken thinking of some finishing touches which she hoped might prevent it setting fire to Paris. Mr Lupei had proposed an empty warehouse in the factory district of Saint-Ouen, which would allow them to test the invention in safety and privacy. All the same, it was Nijam's very first flame-thrower, and she had little notion of how it would behave, given any of the fuels she proposed using with it.

She was in her bedroom beating the prototype with a hammer, and Mimi was beating on the other side of the wall to express her dissatisfaction with this aubade, when her transmitter crackled.

"Miss Nijam?" asked a diffident voice. Nijam sighed. What did Schmidt think he was doing, awake so early in the morning?

"What's the matter?"

"I've been talking to Lupei," said Schmidt, after a period of time in which his tongue seemed to have become entangled with his vocal cords.

Nijam permitted herself to breathe a little more easily. "And?"

"He's agreed to take on my rôle, protecting Mimi."

Nijam took off her pince-nez and rubbed her eyes. "You'll need to explain a little better, Schmidt."

"So that I can go to Heidelberg. That's where we first met, I presume."

Nijam blinked at the wallpaper. How the blazes could Schmidt know about their time in Heidelberg? Then she remembered the day when she had first stumbled across him at the Schloss Frohsdorf, and had expected him to remember her. Her hand tightened upon the little hammer, but she was incapable of speech.

"It's just that you don't seem to want to explain," Schmidt added. "So I'll just have to go to Heidelberg and find someone who will. There's a train—"

It had never occurred to her that he might do something like this—that if she hid from him, he might take action on his own account. Nijam found her voice. "Where are you?"

"I'm at the Opera."

"Stay there," Nijam ordered, dropping her hammer and checking to see that her soldering-iron was safely cooling. "I'm coming."

It was not far to the Opera and she took the journey on foot, thinking furiously the whole way. When she entered the grand foyer she paused to catch her breath, glancing into one of the great mirrors lining the walls. She had come out without her hat, and the walk had whipped a faint flush into her cheeks. Her black dress was marked with a burn on one sleeve and a spatter of oil down the front. She rubbed at the stain uselessly with her cuff.

It wasn't that she particularly cared how she looked—it was only that when she was done with the mirror, she was going to have to go and find Alphonse Schmidt and he was going to ask her about revenants. The answer, if she chose to give it, would crush him. And then, what if he wanted to know more—what if he wanted to know about *her?*

For a moment she wanted nothing more than to run home, to let him take that train to Heidelberg alone.

But that would be impossible. There was no more perilous place on earth for Alphonse Schmidt than the place where he had once lived, studied, and worked. Even if the Okhrana happened not to be watching the University, he might easily be recognised by some other old acquaintance. Then he would be sold to some Power that would pay richly for the secrets locked in his brain…

Nijam took a deep breath and tapped her temple, where her own transmitter was embedded.

"I'm here," she announced.

Schmidt was in the theatre, a lonely figure waiting on the rim of the stage before the lowered curtain. The great auditorium was empty and dark, the velvet box-ledges swathed in holland covers and more calico thrown over the chairs in the stalls. It occurred to Nijam, not normally a fanciful person, that the place looked like the corpse of a theatre, wrapped in its shroud. Even so had looked the bodies, when they were brought into the laboratory at Heidelberg to undergo revivification.

She shivered, trying to shake off the old, unsettling feeling that there were eyes watching her from the darkness.

It must have been somewhere around eight o'clock in the morning. A cleaning-lady was sweeping the aisles, and there was a faint sound of the piano being played in the foyer de la danse, just behind the stage. Otherwise the place, normally swarming with stage-hands, dancers, and musicians for the day's schedule of rehearsals and performances, was quite empty.

Empty, save only for the glimmer of gold from Schmidt's hair against the dark velvet of the stage-curtain. Slowly, reluctantly, Nijam ascended the stair at the side of the pit and crossed to meet him. It was perhaps the first time in her life in which she had been on a stage. Alphonse, in his own quiet way, always did have a sense of the dramatic.

"Well?" she demanded.

He gulped. She recognised the tension in his jaw and his shoulders, and knew that he was very nearly as terrified as herself.

"I ought to have thanked you for saving my life," he said.

Nijam was still sore from catching the sand-bag, but she scowled and said, "I would do the same for any of the crew."

"Yes," he said, with faint weariness, "I *know*. Allow me to thank you, all the same." He was silent a moment, not meeting her eyes. Alphonse never could look you in the eye when there was something personal to be discussed; he became too conscious of himself. Then he managed to say it:

"Why didn't you tell me?"

"I did tell you," she said. "In Moscow."

"In Moscow you told me about the *revenants*. You never told me that you *knew* me."

Nor had she. She had always been very careful to keep that from him—and now, how the blazes had he guessed?

"I feel like a fool for not seeing it sooner," he added. "You've always known about me—about my brother—about the revenants. I thought at first that it must all be common knowledge among men of science. But then, the other night—you knew at once what I had seen. You had to have been there, in Heidelberg. You had to have worked with the revenants yourself."

He raised pleading eyes for her answer. Nijam could make none. Once again Schmidt had taken a few miserable pieces of evidence and leaped unerringly to the truth. She wished he would not be so clever, sometimes; it made him impossible to predict.

"I'm a fool," he said, unconsciously contradicting her, "but even I can tell that you've been keeping this from me for a reason. That's why you've never liked me… Don't spare me, Miss Nijam. If I've injured you—"

"No," she said flatly. Again, he had thoroughly misunderstood her. "I've never had any grudge against you, Alphonse Schmidt."

"Then why?" The word hung in the air a moment before he went on: "Why must I *trick* you into speaking with me? I can understand your concealing yourself from me if we had been enemies—but if we were *friends*—"

"I offered you your memories back, if you recall."

That silenced him.

Of course he didn't want his memories. What Schmidt wanted was a nice, neat, pretty little explanation, which would absolve him of needing to look their past squarely in the eye.

"Do you," she said, "or do you *not* want to know?"

His throat worked. He shook his head. And she tasted the bitterness of defeat, because despite everything, he still lacked the courage. Perhaps he had never really meant to go to Heidelberg, after all. Perhaps he was only trying to trick her into telling him the truth.

Two could play *that* game.

"Perhaps I'll tell you anyway," she said, "as your friend who owes it to you. I can tell you every bad thing you ever did."

"No," he whispered, backing into the great curtain. "Not like that. Please."

"No?" she repeated, following him through the heavy velvet folds into the darkness beyond, which was lit only by a faint grey beam of light from some opening far above. "Why are you so frightened of the truth?"

"Ought I *not* to be?" He let out a shaking breath that might have been a sob, or might have been laughter. "I don't want to remember the evil I have done—all I want is to know what you and I meant to each other."

"What makes you think that it is possible to tell you one, without the other?"

This side of the curtain, the sound of the piano was clearer as it moved to a new tune—not the *Giselle* programme music, nor even *Lakmé.* As Fate would have it, the pianist was playing not for dancers, but for himself—one of Strauss's waltzes, pensive and yearning. Nijam felt her face become stiff, like a mask. She had reason to remember this tune.

Schmidt dragged in a breath, almost as though he had been stabbed. *"Roses from the South,"* he whispered. "I know this music. Don't I?"

It never occurred to Nijam to break her resolve. There was no way she could speak; and so she did not. But it had become an absolute impossibility not to do *something*.

In a moment of surrender that carried with it an almost physical sense of relief she reached out and put her right hand in his, and her left on his shoulder. She let the music move through her the way it once did long ago in a Heidelberg dance-hall. Schmidt made a soft sound in the back of his throat—surprise, perhaps—and then his free hand came hesitantly up to her back.

He was clumsy, at first, stumbling a little over both their feet, losing the beat and then finding it again. Nijam waited patiently. And then suddenly he caught the trick of it and knew what he was doing; and they went gliding through the shadows together like birds.

Nijam closed her eyes, giving herself up to the moment and to the music. She had never danced with anyone but Schmidt: it was a thing she had done only to please him, though she had taken to it far more deftly than he. Now once again she felt all the pleasure of two bodies moving in synchronicity: motion, time, and gravity in miraculous accord. And she wished that it might be like this forever—Schmidt and herself, flying and swooping on the wings of a buoyant music...

The music faltered and stopped, the unseen pianist having stumbled. With it Schmidt stumbled too. Instinctively, Nijam moved forward to steady him. His forehead pressed against her own, damp with exertion. His hand made a tiny unconscious movement against her back, and for a moment Nijam felt like a building that has been electrified for the first time—all lit up like a torch.

Then—she was surprised to find herself still standing—Alphonse whispered, *"Why do I feel like this?"*

She pulled back and opened her eyes, pathetically glad that he could not have recognised the effect he had upon her. Her face was stiff again with the effort not to speak. If she spoke she would give everything away.

Schmidt let go of her, and Nijam shivered at the cold where

his hands had been. He touched his own face and looked at the wetness on his fingertips. "I can never remember what I once knew," he said softly. "No one, not even I, should know how to create such monsters."

Nijam felt the mask of her face slacken in surprise. *That was why he feared to remember?*

He retreated a step and took a deep breath. "I won't go to Heidelberg," he told her. "I have all the answers I need. Thank you."

He nodded to her—it was almost a bow—and swiftly fled. Perplexed, Nijam watched him go. Answers? What answers could she have betrayed? Had the dance been a mistake?

Chapter XVIII.

Had I been aware at the time of this interesting scene, I might have arisen earlier, instead of lazing about in bed, drinking tea and reading my novel. Alas! It was some time later before I learned what had passed on the Opera-stage that morning. It is sadly disappointing, this propensity of the human race to conduct its love-affairs in private.

As a result, I reached the Opera at the usual time, early in the afternoon. I asked Anton Lupei to accompany me, for I was not feeling quite easy about the Taglioni journal. Once I offered the journal to M. Dumortier, it was possible that the revenant would learn what had become of the priceless gift he had made to Mimi, and then hers would not be the only life in danger.

"Dumortier has an appointment in the Île de la Cité at two," Vasily informed me via transmitter as we crossed the Place de l'Opéra. "Be quick about it, and you ought to catch him in the grand foyer."

We reached the Opera in good time, and Lupei closed the umbrella with which, in his guise as a footman, he had shielded me from the rain.

"Has the bloodsucker confessed?" he asked.

"He isn't a bloodsucker any more," I retorted mechanically.

I had lost sleep that night, recalling the brutal details of the crimes I knew about and conjuring up increasingly horrid ideas of the one Vasily had left unconfessed.

Lupei snorted. "Evidently not," he muttered, in answer to his own question.

I had half an idea to march Lupei directly into Vasily's office and demand the truth then and there, and to let this impudent little man see just how my lover had changed. But then I caught a glimpse of Dumortier approaching from behind the grand staircase, which rose in a graceful forking arch towards the galleries of the second floor.

"Try to play along, M. Dupont," I instructed my footman, before setting an interception course.

I met Dumortier at the foot of the grand staircase and accosted him with my most breathless, open-eyed charm.

"Baroness! What a pleasure!" he said, bowing. "Are you here to see the Baron?"

"I *was*, but indeed I'm more pleased to meet you. Have you a moment? I shan't keep you long, but I'm sure you will be interested."

Dumortier looked a little uncertain and reached for his pocket-watch. I laid an arresting hand on his arm. "You know about Marie Taglioni's sojourn at the Staatsoper in Vienna, of course?"

That got his attention. "But of course. It was there that she began her career in earnest."

"Yes, and some of her things were left behind there. As it turns out, I'm in need of a little ready money, so I am trying to liquidate a few old curios. One of them is a journal kept by Taglioni during her stay in Vienna. I thought at once that it might be of interest to *you*, monsieur."

"I'm sure the Opera has one or two of Taglioni's journals in its possession already," Dumortier said. Yet, despite his dismissive tone, I could see the light of avarice in his eyes.

"This one contains the training schedule she followed in order to gain her first triumphs," said I. "I've received an offer of five thousand francs from M. Petipa in St Petersburg."

Dumortier raised his eyebrows. "Marius Petipa is after it too?"

"Oh, he's dying to have it," I said, reaching into my pocket, and taking out the forged letter which Vasily had prepared for me. "Look, he wants me to bring it to Petersburg. But have you ever been to Petersburg? It's ever so far away, and not a nice place to visit. So I thought I might offer it to the Paris Opera."

"*We* would certainly know how to give it the respect it deserves," said Dumortier. As he read the missive, his lips pursed almost unconsciously in a whistle. Vasily, writing above the carefully-forged signature, had been sure to include an offer to outbid any competitor.

"And M. Petipa would not?" I asked, hoping to distract him from a closer inspection of the signature. After all, Dumortier probably carried on his own correspondence with the master of the Russian Imperial theatres.

Dumortier re-folded the letter with a sniff. "Petipa may *pretend* to respect the old masters, but he merely wishes to introduce his own *improvements,* as he thinks of them! Madame, I should very much like to see this journal. I'd be willing to offer you as much as ten thousand francs for it."

"Oh, but of course!" I assured him. "Shall I bring it to the Opera tomorrow?"

Dumortier looked at his watch. "I had an appointment in

the Île de la Cité—but that is unimportant. If you're at liberty, I might pay you a visit at once."

This was moving a little too fast, since we had not yet completed our plans for dealing with the revenant. "Alas! I have some pressing business of my own," I told him, with feigned regret.

"I can have the ten thousand francs ready by this evening," he said. "You'll be watching *Giselle* tonight? Of course. Bring the journal then; the money will be waiting for you."

He bowed and hurried away towards the portico. Lupei gave a low whistle. "Ten thousand francs for an old diary!" he whispered. "Think how many poor families *that* could feed!"

"And that's precisely what it's going to do," I said. Still, I was left feeling ill at ease. Expecting the capture of M. Dumortier's gold to be a somewhat more delicate affair, I had been prepared to spend several days on the operation. Immediate success made me worry.

"We'd better go and see Vasily," I declared, hurrying towards the managers' office. To this inner sanctum we were admitted at once: Vasily, for a wonder, was not lost in feverish activity, but lying back in his chair with folded arms and a distant frown.

"You heard?" I asked, switching off the transmitter which I had kept open for his benefit. "I don't like it at all. It was far too easy."

"Eh?" Vasily straightened. "Oh, I shouldn't worry, my dear. Dumortier loathes Petipa. I knew he would cease to see reason if he thought there was a chance his rival might be interested in the journal. And speaking of Dumortier, you were quite right. His handwriting *does* match the poison-pen letter. I have the evidence here."

He handed me a sheaf of papers, and I made a mental note to look in on Mme Larousse on my way home.

"But he didn't even ask if I could swear to the journal's authenticity," I said, tucking the papers into my pocket. "And he means to give me ten thousand francs for it at the performance tonight. Why should he trust me so unquestioningly?"

"Well, my sweet, you aren't just anybody: you're the Baroness von Jörger. You're perhaps the best accredited woman in Paris—to say nothing of the best-dressed."

Indeed I was feeling particularly dashing today, wearing a blue the colour of lapis lazuli. Vasily kissed my hand in a mawkishly sentimental manner, and I judged that the time was ripe.

"Didn't you promise to tell me about Liz Sharp, next time we met?"

"Ah," he said, and from his wry look it suddenly struck me that he meant to wriggle out of his promise.

"Vasya," I whispered pleadingly.

Then he did something I did not expect, for he turned to the anarchist. "Lupei—"

"Do you expect me to go away?" Lupei asked, all truculence.

"Not at all," Vasily said. "Yesterday, you gave me an ultimatum. I must confess what I did to Miss Sharp, or you would tell Miss Dark yourself." He swallowed hard, then looked directly into my eyes. "Only I've been thinking about it, and I don't know that a villain should be allowed to tell the story of his own villainy. For one thing, I would undoubtedly be too kind to myself. Perhaps Mr Lupei would be good enough to tell the story."

Lupei opened his eyes very wide, but he was not left speechless very long. "Well, then, let's see how long your good intentions last." He turned towards me. "The facts are simple. We of the People's Vengeance had captured Vasily Nikolaevich and drained him of his blood. He was in no danger of dying, of course, but it kept him weak and unable to escape. Miss Sharp was with him. She'd already been attacked by a monster once, and she had no inclination to become the dainty of another." Lupei sent Vasily a simmering look. "The bloodsucker knew full well that she would never consent to give him her blood—so he took it against her will. And that is why Elizabeth Sharp would never have him, though he gave up his fangs for her."

At that Vasily looked up, with a face that was somewhat flushed with indignation. "I didn't give them up for—" He caught himself. A muscle twitched in his jaw.

I stood there feeling sick. It was nearly as bad as the worst I had imagined. So there was the truth of it—the meaning behind all Vasily's loud self-recriminations for having betrayed the women he cared for and rendered himself incapable of trust.

Lupei shrugged. "I had my own part to play in the business, of course. It's my fault she was in that dungeon with him at all. But I'm not your suitor, Molly Dark. *He* is."

"Thank you, Lupei," said Vasily softly.

"It was my pleasure," the little anarchist snarled, but I knew that it had given him no real joy, from the way he patted my shoulder as he left the room.

The door closed and Vasily stood, thrusting his hands into his pockets and looking down at my feet. "I have nothing to add," he said, gloomily, "except that there was no misunderstanding, no delirium. I knew precisely what it meant to her, and I was fully in possession of my wits when I did it. And now you know everything."

At that I found my tongue. "No, I don't," I said fiercely. "In Hong Kong, you said that she offered you forgiveness. You must have done something to merit that."

"But I didn't," he said bleakly. "I knew Miss Sharp didn't care a fig for me. She only ever had eyes for another man, a bourgeois with a long face. *I* never expected to win her over; when she offered me her forgiveness I was in the very act of delivering her into the hands of her enemies."

"And then what happened?" I prompted, when he fell silent.

"Well, after that I could hardly go on with it, could I?" He managed a sickly-looking smile. "If she had been anything like you, my dear, I might have suspected her of playing me like a fiddle, saying the precise words to heap coals of fire upon my head. But she always was as straight as an arrow. I was incapable of repaying such divine compassion. All I could do was free her for the one she truly loved."

I bit my lip to conceal my smile, for I had my own doubts as to whether he could have resisted the kindness, even coming from me. "And steal Missy's diamonds to take with her?"

"Yes—and give up my fangs," he added. "But I suppose Mimi would tell me I'm making a modern play about losing something I ought never to have had in the first place."

"You ought not," I agreed. My first impulse had been to comfort my lover; but now, belatedly, I was thinking of that other woman, and what she must have had to endure at Vasily's hands. I shuddered. I had seen how Mimi was treated on account of the scars around her neck; I knew how I had been tempted to treat her, myself. Elizabeth Sharp had already suffered one attack, and must already have been marked out as a fallen woman when she suffered the second. I could never know what that must have been like—I, who had so freely offered Vasily a taste of my own blood. I could only dimly guess.

"That might have been me," I said, half to myself. And I thought of the moment in the British Museum, when Vasily might very easily have taken the Noor-Jahan diamond and left me to the tender mercies of Mr Vandergriff. Miss Sharp had faced a far worse predicament even than that—and Vasily had not spared her then. "And she to bear all the blame. Oh, Vasily."

There was a long silence. I glanced up at him and found the corners of his mouth pulled down, almost in pain.

"*Bozhe moi,* if you cannot bear the sight of me, Molly, then tell me so and I'll go away at once." He took a deep breath. "Forever, if you insist."

Again, I had the feeling that to be easy on him now would be his ruination. So all I said, as sorely as it went against the grain, was, "Would you? Truly? You'd never permit it before."

He caught his breath as though I had struck him.

"Don't answer at once," I said, turning towards the door. "Hasty vows are soon broken. And I have much to consider also."

Before I could depart, however, the door burst open and Mimi entered. Lupei, behind her, was grimacing with pain and shaking a hand in the air, and although I can't swear to it, I would be willing to wager that he had attempted to deny her entry and been bitten for it.

"What's wrong?" I asked, startled entirely out of my sombre mood.

"Perrot won't teach me any more," she announced. "He says I'm *ready*...I'm to go home and rest before the performance tonight. Oh, Dark!"

She might have bitten Lupei, but she was pale and limping, barely a shadow of herself. I saw at once the terrible meaning of her words. Perrot had finished his creation: if Mimi played her rôle tonight as she was meant to do, she would deliver a flawless performance, and then she would die at his hands…

I seized her trembling hands in mine. "Don't be afraid, Mimi. We won't let you die."

She snatched them from my grasp. "I'm not afraid of dying! I'm disappointed I couldn't make him give me any more lessons!"

Despite her words, I think all of us knew that our preparations were over, and the game must now begin in earnest. Schmidt, who had followed Mimi into the room, touched his transmitter. "Miss Nijam, did you hear this?"

I switched on my own transmitter to hear her reply. "Yes, and of course Mimi must not appear tonight. If she does, the revenant will certainly attempt to kill her."

"Don't be ridiculous," said Mimi with a frightful scowl. "If I don't appear then how can you be certain of catching the creature?"

"We'll simply substitute your understudy at the last moment," I suggested.

"He'll know," Mimi said, with complete finality. "I *must* dance, or you'll never catch him. You have a working flame-thrower, don't you? Just be sure to deal with him by the end of my performance."

"Dark and Nijam are right," Lupei said, for he had been fitted with a transmitter of his own. "There must be another way. This one is too dangerous."

I could have warned him that this would not be persuasive.

"What other way?" Mimi demanded. "If I'm not there he might kill somebody else instead. Little Gobara, or one of the other ballet brats. No! This is *my* task and I won't be cheated out of it. Not when I've waited my whole life for such an opportunity!"

"And you shall have it," Vasily said smoothly. "She's right," he added to the rest of us. "There's no one better suited to the task, and we'll only get bitten for our pains if we try to make her stay home. But Mimi, my dear, try to make some mistakes, for Nijam's peace of mind if nothing else."

"For all of us," Schmidt put in, settling a comforting hand on Mimi's shoulder. "I don't want to watch you die, too."

Perhaps Mimi might have argued with the rest of us, but when Schmidt put it like that, of course she unbent. "Don't worry," she said. "I won't put myself in any more danger than I must." And despite the gruffness in her voice, I thought that she was touched.

After paying a visit to Mme Larousse, I had to go home and let Gobara dress me for the evening's performance. As she combed my hair and began pinning it up again atop my head, I watched in the mirror without quite seeing myself.

The day had left me with much on my mind. Mimi in danger—the trap in which we were to catch M. Dumortier—the story I had heard from Lupei and Vasily. Why did I feel so shaken? I had never thought Vasily any *better* than this. This Miss Sharp had suffered no more than any of the other people Vasily had injured and killed. That he had not told me a little sooner *did* sting, a little. But I think it was mostly because I could so easily imagine myself in that other woman's place. If Vasily ever forgot himself…

But he had not forgotten himself. He had known precisely

what he was doing: had acted in cold calculation.

Just as cold and just as calculating as he had been earlier today, when he refused to tell the story himself and submitted to the telling of his enemy. Vasily, I thought, was not the man he used to be. But could I forget what he had once been? He had promised to go away if I sent him, and that had shaken me too: I had accustomed myself to thinking that I could not rid myself of Vasily, even if I wished to. I had been prepared to fight him for my liberty, if needs must; but I had never imagined him giving me up without the fight he had promised me.

"Jewellery, madame?" Gobara asked me. She held up two necklaces—a string of pearls and a garnet pendant, both gifts from Vasily.

I made myself smile. "You choose for me, Gobara. I've had such a number of decisions lately, and I'm weary to death of making them."

Chapter XIX.

Anton Lupei escorted me to the Opera that evening. The Taglioni journal was tucked safely into the breast-pocket of his smart jacket, which had been requisitioned from Alphonse Schmidt for the occasion. With a little tailoring, the garment fitted Lupei none too badly—for although he was at least eight full inches shorter than the German Adonis, the anarchist was correspondingly broad across the chest.

As we took our seats, I scrutinised the managers' box through my opera-glasses. Vasily sat there alone. There was no sign of M. Dumortier, and for a moment I feared that we might have overplayed our hand. But then the box door opened and the man himself appeared.

My sigh of relief was lost in the little ripple of sensation that ran through the theatre at his appearance. Everyone stared at Dumortier, and there was a cry of "Shame! Shame!", quickly suppressed. I hid a smile behind my fan. Mme Larousse had wasted no time in carrying her evidence to the offices of *Le Soir* for inclusion in the evening paper; so that by now all Paris knew that M. Dumortier had hounded one of his own artists to kill himself. The law might not hold M. Dumortier accountable; but society—as I had hoped—was profoundly shocked.

Dumortier pretended to take no notice of the stir his appearance caused, but a dark figure arose behind him in the box. M. Larousse's imprint now looked quite different to the comfortable, happy gentleman I had seen at Mme Larousse's breakfast-table: he was now an awful, sunken-cheeked, grim-visaged figure, who bent over Dumortier like an avenging Nemesis! —if that's the chap I'm thinking of.

I could breathe more easily now. We had put Dumortier off his stride for the evening, as intended, without entirely driving him away. I could not help feeling a fierce satisfaction that the man who had treated M. Larousse so cruelly was now at last feeling the censure he so richly deserved.

The curtain rose on the first act. Lupei had clearly never attended the ballet before. Chalabi may have been a ghost, but Giselle's story held him spellbound.

"The Duke has a woman already?" my escort inquired, as the first act unfolded. "Why doesn't she take up with the huntsman instead?"

"That's love, I suppose," I said, thinking of my own unaccountable romance.

"If the Duke doesn't love her then I don't see how *she* can love him. Oho! Why's she taking her hair down?"

"Because she's about to go mad, very properly, in white gauze."

"I don't see why she should be considered mad, only because she's been disappointed in love and wants to stab somebody!"

"How right you are!" I murmured, thinking with feeling of my own adventures in lunacy.

"*Mon Dieu!* Why's she fallen down? Is she dead? Why is she *dead?* Did she stab herself when I wasn't looking?"

"Hush!" I begged him, laughing. "She hasn't stabbed

herself—she has a weak heart!"

"How do you know that?"

"It's written in the program notes."

Lupei sniffed. "I do not think this story is very well written. Oh, and now the Duke is blaming the huntsman for exposing his villainy! Of course he is! …Is it over already?"

"No," I said as the curtain went down and the lights went up. "That's the end of Act One. Now all the great people of Paris will visit each other's boxes for the next quarter-hour. Take care not to give yourself away."

"You mean I ought to shut my mouth," he said wryly. "Very well; I'll be silent as a stone. I will laugh at them later, when we have ten thousand francs to give away."

Our first visitor, in fact, was Vasily. He stepped into the box and said, "Hide me!"

"Good heavens, where?" I asked, sending a glance about the narrow space. But then the door opened, admitting an elderly gentleman I had never seen, wearing a diamond cravat-pin and some very impressive-looking orders pinned to the breast of his impeccably tailored coat.

"I beg your pardon, madame," he said with a handsome bow. "Allow me to introduce myself. I am Prince Lvov."

A Russian name—and a familiar one, too! Vasily appeared to be trying to melt into the shadows of the box. "Enchanté," I said, rather weakly.

"Forgive me, but I saw an acquaintance of mine enter here." And the prince turned towards Vasily, who managed a sickly smile.

"Enchanté," he echoed. "But I don't believe I have the pleasure, monsieur. Baron von Jörger, at your service!"

"Oh, I beg your pardon!" the prince exclaimed. "When I first saw you I thought that you were one of the Grand Dukes—now, which of them did I think of? But I see now that I'm mistaken. I was thinking of a *much* younger man."

At this, Vasily opened his eyes very wide indeed. Hurriedly, I observed to the prince that I had recently been in Petersburg, on which occasion I had heard excellent things about his work on behalf of the Russian peasantry; and having charmed him thoroughly, sent him on his way.

Vasily was in a ferment. "Younger?" he exclaimed once we were alone. *"Younger?* I'm only thirty-five!"

"Thirty-seven, if he's a day," Lupei muttered in my ear. "I ought to know. I grew up on his estate in Moldova."

I pretended not to hear this. "Yes, Vaska, but we've made you up to look old and staid, precisely to avoid this kind of embarrassment."

"Old and *staid?* I beg your pardon! *I* made myself up to look grey and distinguished!" For a moment he brooded upon his wrongs. "I was coming to see you in any case, my dear. I think you may be right about Dumortier. He—"

But we were interrupted by another knock at the door, and the opportunity was lost—for who should enter but my old friend, Célestin Deleuze!

"I'll take care of it," Vasily told me, hastily excusing himself. As Deleuze bowed over my hand, I watched my lover depart with a sense of foreboding. So I was right about Dumortier? Did this mean that he *was* planning to double-cross me, somehow, over the journal?

"Ah, Baroness, it's been too long," Deleuze reproached me. "Have you forgotten your faithful Célestin?"

I dragged my attention back to him. Indeed I *had* more or less forgotten the man, for he had served his purpose and I no longer had any use for him. Nor had I forgotten that when I had last seen Deleuze he had insulted me in a way that no woman of spirit could endure.

Of course, I said none of this. Instead, I fluttered my fan in pretended distress.

"Oh, forgive me! but I have had so many important affairs to occupy me! You know how life crowds in upon one. Let me see, when did we see each other last? It was at the bal masqué, was it not?"

"Indeed it was; and I made an oath to assist you in the future."

I did not like the way he said this, as if it was a bargain I had failed to honour.

"Indeed you did, and I shall be eternally grateful for it," I said, with a conciliatory tap of my fan upon his wrist. "Moreover, you introduced me to Mlle Perrot and her friend."

"So I did! And did you go to their salon? You must tell me all about it." He lowered his voice. "Is it true what they say about the two of them?"

I knew without the shadow of a doubt what he was getting at. How had I ever been able to bear the sight of this man? A low toady, and a gossip, and one who wanted to know everybody's business, even though he would only use it to cause mischief!

I opened my eyes very wide and candid.

"Oh, I couldn't possibly say," I told him. "But I *can* tell you that your friend, M Caillot, attended also. And *he* said something that was very surprising indeed."

"Oh! What was that?"

"It was during a game, you understand—we were each supposed to say something very shocking and witty."

"And?" Deleuze asked in a fever of impatience.

"Why, he said that twenty years ago, at university…you used to spell your name differently; as Deleuze, without a space."

I had the satisfaction of seeing him look thunder-struck. "What! Caillot said that?"

I felt a twinge of conscience. Caillot had not offended me, although I did not think that he deserved much better than I gave him.

"I'm afraid that he did," said I sadly.

"What a nerve! Doesn't he know that we're a *very* old Picardy family! And I was at university ten years ago, not twenty! Why, the cad!"

He excused himself quickly and went off, doubtless seeking revenge upon his friend, just as the lights went down for the second act of the ballet. Turning back to face the stage, I found Lupei beholding me with admiration.

"Nicely done!" he murmured.

I felt my face warm, though not entirely with pleasure. I had merely given Deleuze a nice little taste of the medicine he so often dispensed to others—a poisonous tid-bit of gossip which would eat away at his peace of mind and sow discord betwixt himself and his friend. All the same, I felt a little uneasy. I did not want to become another creature such as Deleuze. He was not merely a gossip; he would ridicule anyone who did not behave as badly as himself. Seeing this, I had begun to make high-minded resolutions, never to hide the light of my true convictions beneath the bushel of social acceptability. Yet, for all my noble intentions, I had in the heat of the moment reverted to the ways of the shyster and the confidence-woman!

I had not become what I was by choice, but only because

I had been forced into it to keep body and soul together—that is the story as I had always told it. It struck me then that I did not have to be a confidence-woman any longer. I was now rich enough to say nearly anything I liked without fear of consequences. If I wanted to I could have stood up and demanded M. Deleuze explain to me why Mlle Perrot's domestic arrangements should be any of his business. I could have told him precisely what I thought of people who meddled maliciously in other people's affairs. Moreover, I could go down to the gendarmerie tomorrow and demand them to investigate Mlle Chalabi's disappearance. I could give interviews about it to the Press. I could make myself such a public nuisance that M. Dumortier would have to give up the creature he was harbouring and admit publicly to his own collusion.

I could, in a word, give it all up—my wiles, my subterfuge, my bald opportunism—to become a second Josephine Butler, a crusader for truth and justice. And surely it was my duty to do so!

No doubt it is a mark of my bad and weak nature that merely the thought of doing such a thing made me feel horribly tired. I had faced hungry werewolves, vengeful prosthetes, and tormented shades with the greatest goodwill. I felt quite prepared to face them again, if I must. But I could not set myself up before society at large as a mark to be shot at.

Once again, I found myself in the grip of an impossible choice. I had pined for my liberty when I was poor; and now that I was rich, I found that it was too much for me.

Chapter XX.

At this moment Alphonse Schmidt was waiting in the shadows of the stage wings for the curtain to go up on the second act. One might have said that he was *concealing* himself in the aforesaid shadows, but let us not deceive ourselves. Schmidt was far too good-looking to successfully conceal himself in anything short of a ghillie suit or an uncommonly large cupboard. He was waiting, as I say, in the wings for Mimi's appearance; it was fortunate that he was known in the Opera as Vasily's personal factotum, or the stage-hands and managers flocking about him would certainly have sent him about his business.

As for Nijam, a little last-minute modification to her flame-thrower had kept her late at her lodgings. She had only a moment ago switched on her transmitter to say that she had got the contraption loaded into a cab and would shortly arrive at the Opera.

Meanwhile, Schmidt could see no sign of the revenant, either in the foyer de la danse, or up in the shadowed gantries that ran above the stage. Schmidt could not help feeling uneasy about this: it was certain that the revenant would be present at Mimi's performance, but where? It must be somewhere with a decent view of the stage. Then it occurred to him that the creature might have reserved one of the boxes in the dress-circle, so that he and Nijam would be obliged to burn it to a crisp before the eyes of all Paris. That would lead to uncomfortable explanations and a great deal of unwanted scrutiny. Besides, he thought the red-velvet furnishings of the boxes looked uncommonly flammable.

Before Schmidt could go around to the box-office to ask the names of those who were renting boxes for the season, however, Mimi entered the wings, surrounded by her little cloud of young ballerinas. She walked slowly to favour her bad knee. At once Schmidt approached her, doing his best to overlook the whispering and giggling that greeted his approach.

"Will your knee hold up?" he asked her.

"It will come right when my aspirin takes effect," she told him. "Don't look at me like that! Aspirin helps the swelling as well as the pain."

Schmidt hoped that she was right. "I came to ask which side of the stage you will come off at the end of the Act."

"Stage left—opposite," she said.

"Then that's where I'll be waiting with Miss Nijam," he said. "You have only to get through the night, you know, and then you can rest with a clear conscience."

He expected a retort, but instead she glanced about her, wistfully biting her lip as though bidding a silent farewell to the place. Schmidt knew then that Mimi had come to accept what he and I and the rest of the crew had been trying to persuade her of: the impossibility of continuing as she had been.

"Don't look so sad," he said, very gently. "Perhaps it need not be adieu but au revoir—till we meet again."

Fatima Gobara must have heard his words, because she turned up a face to him that was a mask of horror. "What are you saying, monsieur? Mlle Laine, don't tell me you are leaving the Opera!" She threw her arms around Mimi. "What will become of us? We all love you so much better than M. Christophe! You must stay!"

The others flocked about her with beseeching eyes and similar words. Schmidt retreated into the shadows again. Mimi was left in the midst of that crowd of little ghosts, looking surprised and a little wary.

"Promise! Promise you'll come back!" little Gobara begged, and Mimi shrugged.

"If it will make you happy," she said.

Then Schmidt's transmitter went, and Nijam said, "Come and help me carry this confounded fire-spout, Schmidt." He left Mimi in the midst of her ballerinas and went to do as he was bid.

Chapter XXI.

The lights went down, and the curtain rose on the second act. This is the forest scene, of course, in which the village maiden's two rival lovers visit her grave. At first Duke Albericht came in and mimed passionate grief over the tomb of his beloved.

"How did a village maiden get a marble monstrosity like *that?*" Lupei muttered.

"Of course the Duke had it built, to show how sorry he is," said I. It was precisely what Vasily would once have done, in place of true repentance.

"Oh, and off he goes," said Lupei. "To seduce another village maiden, I suppose." Possibly I was not the only one of us thinking of Vasily.

Then the music became soft and eerie, and a white shape glided onto the stage. The lights were dim, and it took me a few moments to recognise in this serene and ethereal figure the resourceful and burglarious Mimi Laine. Lupei whistled very softly between his teeth.

"Is that your ferocious little friend?"

I had known Mimi more than a year and had never seen her dance—not like this! She seemed to have left solid flesh behind, to have ascended to a bodiless and spiritual plane of existence. For an instant the horrible thought struck me that we were too late—that what I saw was only her ghost, for how else could she waft about the stage in such a manner, as light as a feather and as graceful as a swan? There was a twitch in my fingers, urging me to reach for my transmitter.. I restrained myself, of course, for if Mimi was alive she would not thank me for interrupting her, and if she was dead it was already too late to do anything about it.

Off she went, and on came the corps de ballet to dance their ensemble piece.

"What are those little white puffs on their waists?" Lupei muttered. "Oh—I suppose they're supposed to be a sort of vestigial wing. They're some kind of fairy?"

"They're the souls of brides who died of betrayal before their wedding-day," I informed him.

"But there must be dozens of them! Why has no one investigated the Duke? Look, he must have killed half the maidens in all the nearby villages!"

The handsome huntsman came back onstage and Mimi reappeared, inciting her ballet brats to set upon him. The music became more intense; in a flurry of white gauze the poor huntsman paid with his life for his part in Giselle's death.

"Why must the *huntsman* die, when he has only told the truth?" Lupei folded his arms in disgust. "Wait until they get their hands on that Duke."

I did not think to disabuse him, for I was entranced by the performance. Somehow, even within the strictures of the dance with all its elaborate prettiness—somehow Mimi now became a fury, a she-devil. In one thing the revenant had told the strictest truth. No one else could possibly have married grace and savagery like this.

The huntsman done away with, off went the furies with their queen, and Duke Albericht returned to reunite with the ghostly Giselle. "Oh, *mon Dieu,*" Lupei muttered in absolute disgust. "She died for his lies, and now he gets to dance with her and play the grand hero, only because he is a nobleman!"

As for me, I could pay no attention to the story just then. For I knew that Giselle *was* a ghost, that Demiana Chalabi and her partner were dead; and with that knowledge I could not see past the eerie, almost the mechanical, virtuosity of their performance—a performance that was in truth no performance at all, but merely the image of all their rehearsals. And as perfect as it was, I could not forget that there was not a single living being upon that stage.

It struck me how absolutely soulless the thing was. I felt as you would feel if you were promised the return of a long-departed sister or lover, and were given a photograph instead.

At last Mimi returned with her furies and commenced the execution of the hapless Duke. Then I was happy to see my friend, for I recognised in her the imperfections, but also the fire, of a real living soul as she descended upon Albericht like an avenging angel. The music and the dancing became wilder. The Duke staggered within a ring of frenzied white spirits. How many of them were dead in truth, and how many alive? and how many, if the revenant had his way, would yet perish? Then the ghostly Chalabi broke into the ring to seize her lover, protecting him from Mimi's wrath. The light upon the stage turned rosy, signalling dawn and the end of the story.

"That's our cue," I said, jumping up. "It's ending. Give me the journal."

Lupei seemed utterly absorbed by what was happening on stage. "Go on," he said, handing me the brown-paper parcel I had made of the Taglioni journal. "I want to see what happens."

"The Duke lives," I said, slipping away from the box. If Lupei answered, I did not hear him in my eagerness to be away. The ballet might end badly, but real life need not. I had witnessed a desecration, and now I was eager to see justice done to the one who had murdered Chalabi and stolen her art.

Chapter XXII.

In the darkened wings, Nijam wore a ferocious scowl. Even a determined philistine like herself could tell that Mimi was giving the performance of a lifetime. The audience responded in kind, with outbursts of applause and cries of *"Brava!"*

"Is she *trying* to get herself killed?" Nijam hissed. "Where's that dratted revenant? Can't you see it, Schmidt?"

Schmidt was carrying the flame-thrower, a heavy piece of iron tubing nearly as long as himself, which was connected by a sort of flexible hose to an even heavier pack on his back. Nijam had designed the thing for efficiency rather than comfort, and the straps galled his shoulders. Shifting the weight in an attempt to make himself more comfortable, he said, "No, and it worries me."

Nijam scowled fiercely. "Vasily says everyone in the boxes is accounted for, so he's not likely in the audience. He must be lurking in the dark here somewhere."

She touched her transmitter. "Vasily, there's no sign of the revenant yet. Try to keep your gendarmes out of sight until Schmidt and I have sighted him."

"All right, but be quick about it," Vasily murmured. He was stationed in the passage at one of the stage doors, holding it ajar so that he and the men with him could peer in at the performance. It was very dark within, but his prosthetic eye, which caught heat where it could not catch light, saw Nijam and Schmidt as green silhouettes in the shadows. Of anyone else besides the dancers there was no sign at all—but then, there might be any number of revenants lurking in the darkness, and his wonderful eye would never catch them. A dead body gives off no heat.

Nijam and Schmidt set off on a circuit of the wings, moving slowly and quietly for fear of tripping over some stage-property in the darkness. The artificial dawn began to shed some light upon their way; yet still there was no sign of the revenant.

"When all this is over," Schmidt whispered into his transmitter, very daring, "might we go dancing again?"

"Absolutely not," Nijam responded, crushingly. "Where is that dratted revenant? Maybe he's watching from the gantries."

I, meanwhile, had joined Vasily in the passage. He had with him a plain-clothes detective and three gendarmes, as well as a short, slight gentleman who was all muffled up in an opera-cloak and wearing a mask which concealed his whole face. He looked for all the world like a masquerader who had fallen asleep in a corner at the bal masqué and only just awoken. Seeing him there, I knew that another part of our scheme had fallen neatly into place.

M. Dumortier arrived a moment after I did, panting a little with haste and still trailing M. Larousse's grim imprint as evidence of his guilty conscience.

"What the devil does this mean?" the old gentleman demanded, observing the little gathering of policemen as though he found it a personal insult. He brandished a scrap of paper in a kid-gloved hand. "I received your note, Baron. Mlle Laine in danger? Preposterous!"

"Not at all, my dear M. Dumortier," Vasily said, very urbane and deadly. "I'm afraid that Mlle Laine has become the object of some rather sinister attentions from an unknown quarter, and we have reason to believe that the man will show himself at the end of the performance."

"What reason? If there was a threat, why didn't you tell me about it sooner?" Dumortier sailed through the gendarmerie as though they didn't exist, and threw the door open. Beyond, in the rosy light of the artificial dawn, Nijam and Schmidt were visible returning from their fruitless search.

"My man, Schmidt," Vasily murmured, by way of introduction.

"What is that Persian doing here? And what the blazes is that contraption?" Dumortier demanded, pointing at Nijam and the flame-thrower.

His words were just loud enough to be heard over the sound of the orchestra. Nijam approached, taking off her pince nez. "Allow me to explain," she said. "This is a little innovation of my own. The pack contains a small motor, which, when it turns, creates a gentle vacuum. Since nature abhors a vacuum, as we know, surrounding matter rushes up the pipe and into the pack to fill it: air, dust, and small discarded items. I expect it to be of remarkable assistance in cleaning floors, carpets, corners and the like." She smiled at the confused faces before her.

There never was anyone like Nijam. Her explanation was so dry—so unexpected—so prolix that it left Dumortier utterly befuddled. He simply stood there, blinking.

"But what the blazes is it doing *here?*" he demanded.

"Hush!" said Vasily. "The ballet is ending!"

Such was the tone of his voice that Dumortier, in all his confusion, obeyed. The vengeful brides came flitting off the stage, dropped their arms, and transformed in the blink of an eye into a company of very ordinary working girls with foreheads to be blotted, itches to be scratched, and aching toes to be rubbed. A moment later Mimi, too, crossed the stage, leaving the ghostly lovers to their final farewells.

"Schmidt," Nijam hissed as the wings filled with chattering ballerinas. "Keep an eye out."

There was no need for her exhortation. Impeded though he was by the rush of bodies, Schmidt stood poised to spring, his eyes roving the shadows in anticipation of the enemy. Yet, even as Mimi stepped into the wings—silently and without the least fanfare, she promptly vanished from our sight!

For an instant my heart stood still within me, for I remembered how Chalabi's imprint disappeared after *her* performances, and the horrible truth this might signify. Then Schmidt, despite his weighty accoutrements, made a panther-like leap to the spot where Mimi had stood. As he began to pound against the floor with his fist, Nijam struck her forehead with an angry hiss. "A trap-door! She's fallen through a trap-door!"

She followed Schmidt towards the place where Mimi had vanished before our eyes, employing her elbows and scattering ballerinas left and right. In the passage, consternation reigned among the gentlemen. "Quickly," Vasily proclaimed. "How does one get beneath the stage? Laine must be found at once!"

"Pull yourself together!" Dumortier snapped. "One of the stage-hands has left the trap-door unsecured, that is all! Wait a moment and I'll call one of them."

"Don't you know the way yourself?" Vasily demanded.

"Naturally I do; but I see no reason to spoil my digestion by having hysterics."

Vasily went absolutely white with fury and I almost expected him to strike the older man down on the spot. "You'll take us down at once," he breathed, "and if Laine is dead when we get there there'll be a second murder. We have no time to lose!"

"A murder? Don't be ridiculous!" Dumortier cried. "There is no murderer at the Opera! There *is*, however, a thief! Inspector, I have to tell you that a crime is about to be committed, and not against a mere ballerina, but against the Opera itself!"

Vasily, with a violent gesture, seemed ready to brush past him, but Dumortier raised a peremptory hand.

"No, Baron, don't move! This business requires your presence!"

I put a hand on Vasily's arm to restrain him from bolting, for I saw that Nijam and Schmidt were already on their feet again and hastening away from us. That set my heart at ease. Having spent the past week scouring the Opera from top to bottom, the two of them would surely find their way quickly enough to the other side of the trap-door.

"Come after us when you're able," Nijam told us via transmitter as she and Schmidt disappeared into the shadows.

In the passage, Vasily recovered himself with an effort. But he bit savagely at the fingertips of his gloves, as though there was something else he would have liked to have bitten just then.

"Indeed," the police-inspector was saying doubtfully, "unless it's an urgent business, M. Dumortier, shouldn't we see to the ballerina first?"

"I insist," Dumortier said haughtily, dabbing at his glistening brow. "There's no danger to Mlle Laine; I give you my word of honour that she will be dancing tomorrow just as she did tonight." Then it was my turn to wish to bite something, for I saw that he knew quite well what he was about, and meant to prevent any help getting to Mimi until it was much too late.

In any case we were a captive audience, unless we meant to give away our real identities and motivations. Thank heaven, we could rely upon Schmidt and Nijam to do all that was mortally possible to succor our friend.

"Gentlemen," Dumortier said with impressive force, "a shocking crime has been committed against this sacred institution of the French State! A priceless manuscript has been stolen from the Opera Archives!"

Ah! I had *known* that Dumortier had agreed too quickly to purchase the journal!

I did not, however, lose my head. Such embarrassing moments had come my way so often of late that I was beginning to be used to them.

"Good heavens!" I gasped. "Stolen! By whom?"

"By you, my dear Baroness," he said, quivering with triumph. "Do you deny that you attempted to sell the journal back to me at a price far beyond its worth? Inspector, kindly arrest this woman!"

All at once I found myself the unwilling centre of attention. One of the policemen gasped and the short man in the opera-mask gave me a startled look.

Vasily raised a protective arm before me. "You forget yourself, Dumortier! This lady and I do not always agree, but she is still a lady and my wife!"

"I'm sure there's been a misunderstanding," the Inspector agreed. "Not everyone in possession of stolen goods is a thief, you know!"

"I have proof!" Dumortier cried. "Come to my office and you shall see it!"

The Inspector took off his hat in an apologetic sort of way. "I'm afraid I must ask the lady and yourself to come with us, M. le Baron."

"For heaven's sake," I burst out, unable to keep silence. "I'll go to the Bastille if you like, but first go down and look for Mlle Laine, who for all we know is dead by now!"

The Inspector drew himself up, a picture of offended French dignity. "The Bastille has not been a prison for a very long time, madame! It was razed to the foundations more than a hundred years ago!"

Vasily put a steadying hand on my shoulder. "We had better go with him, madame, or the whole thing will have to be litigated here on the stage." Indeed, the corps de ballet, having finished its bows, was hurrying back into the wings with noses outstretched for the scent of somebody else's business.

Off we went towards the managers' offices, and I could have wept with frustration. Vasily and I should have been joining in the search for our missing friend and seeing to the revenant's capture or destruction. Instead we were to spend the next goodness knows how long trying to evade the perfectly justified suspicions which had fastened upon us— and who could say that we would escape them? Dumortier said that he had proof—but what proof?

Then it struck me that after all, I held *one* force in reserve, which I could send down to help my friends in the maze-like darkness of the Opera cellars. I opened my transmitter.

"Lupei," I breathed. "We have an emergency. Mimi was swallowed up by a trapdoor, and Vasily and I have been detained by the police."

Lupei swore in a colourful manner that, delivered directly to my ear, rather made me start. "Do you want me to come for you or for Mimi?"

"Mimi first," I murmured. "You can come for us later, if you must."

Then we came to Dumortier's office, which was the match of Vasily's, all gleaming marble and gold leaf. He took his seat behind the desk and Vasily and I found ourselves standing before it, for all the world like prisoners at the bar.

"I must say that I am being treated in an infamous manner," said I with a haughty sniff. "I told you that I bought the journal in Vienna, where it was written. How could it ever have been in the Opera archives?"

Dumortier gave me a thin and furious smile, quite at odds with the charm he had employed with me on former occasions. "You also told me that you had been in communication with M Petipa in Petersburg," he declared. "I wired him this afternoon and learned that he had never heard of you." And he handed a piece of blue flimsy to Vasily.

Vasily read the telegram and tutted. "My dear," he said, reproachfully, "you didn't *really* tell him you knew M Petipa, did you?"

I raised my eyebrows at this rank betrayal, but could only play along. "Oh, very well! Perhaps I *did* only pretend that M Petipa had offered me five thousand francs for the journal! But that is only because of *your* cruelty! How else am I to keep myself in the manner to which I'm accustomed, when you cut off my allowance and tell me I must make do with my own money!"

The gendarmes sent each other knowing looks. Dumortier scowled.

"Madame," Vasily said loftily, "I beg you'll remember that our affairs are between ourselves. If you had made the retrenchments I proposed—"

"Then I should be reduced to poverty in that draughty Tyrolean castle," I said, taking a moment for some bosom-heaving. "Very well! If the Paris Opera is not interested in the Taglioni journal I shall take it to Petersburg, where I am sure that M. Petipa will pay handsomely for it!"

"You'll do nothing of the sort!" Dumortier cried. "That journal is still the property of the Paris Opera, and I insist that the police should take it into custody as evidence!"

"M. Dumortier," Vasily said, before the bewildered Inspector could make any reply, "I must really insist that you present some evidence before depriving my wife of what may, after all, very well be *our* lawful property."

"Your lawful fiddlestick!" I cried.

The masked man kept his eyes on his watch, like a man in an agony of anticipation. Outside, there was a hum of noise in the grand foyer as the crowd flooded from the theatre, gossiping and sipping champagne. There was no sound from the transmitter, which I had left open in case Nijam or Lupei should have news for me. Confound this Dumortier!

"Let's see the journal," the Inspector said, with a sigh.

"She has it with her," Dumortier declared, as though he thought I might deny it. "She was going to sell it to me for ten thousand francs!"

"That's because I thought you were an honest man, and

not a highway-robber," I retorted, for I was now thoroughly absorbed by my rôle. "Here you are, Inspector. I have nothing to fear and nothing to hide. If this book ever belonged to the Opera there will of course be a record of it in the archives!"

"That's true!" Vasily exclaimed. "There's no need to let this go on a moment longer than it must. Let us step into the archive and see!"

"I should be delighted," Dumortier said, showing his teeth. Vasily offered me his arm and we set off decorously for the Archives, which were housed a few steps away beneath the round room in which I had first met Mlle Perrot.

As we walked, I could not resist opening my transmitter to broadcast. "For heaven's sake, Nijam, what is happening? Have you found her?"

"Not yet," Nijam replied at once, in an undertone. "There was no sign of her beneath the trap-door. We are approaching the studio in the cellar—*what's that?*" There was a moment's silence, and then she shrieked: "Schmidt! Trap!"

A sudden confused rush of sound came to me over the transmitter—cries of alarm from both Nijam and Schmidt; a clatter that might have been the flame-thrower, and then a horrible loud fizz of interfering sound that hurt my head. I slapped at my ear to turn off the transmitter.

What had happened? What did Nijam mean by a *trap?* Horrorstricken, I turned to Vasily, who had paled. He must have heard it all too.

"You should leave me," I murmured.

He shook his head. That was all the communication we could make, for Dumortier and the gendarmes now shepherded us into the archive. The rotunda itself was an elegantly appointed room mainly comprised of a magnificent chandelier and several table settings, with low bookshelves around the perimeter. But the other rooms connected with it were lined with a double level of bookshelves in some warm dark wood. The catalogue was a massive ledger near the door, and Dumortier went to it at once, planting an unerring finger upon the open page. I thought that this was an omen, for it suggested that he had already been to the library to do a little detective work.

"Here it is—*item, a journal of Marie Taglioni.* Do your duty, Inspector!"

"Oughtn't we to check the shelves?" I asked. "You'll look very silly, Inspector, if you arrest me for a book that was in the archive all along."

Dumortier threw up his hands, but the Inspector doggedly made a note of the shelf number and ventured into the stacks. A moment later he returned, holding a small brown leather-covered journal in his hand.

"I believe," he said, "that this is your Taglioni journal, M. Dumortier."

"What!" Dumortier cried, incensed. He snatched the volume from the Inspector and leafed through it, the colour mounting to his face. "But this one is worthless! A social journal from her retirement!"

Vasily sent me a startled look. I concealed a smile. I *did* think it was good sense to help myself to the journal I had found among old M. Perrot's belongings!

"This is ridiculous," Dumortier protested. "The Opera would never have acquired such a useless item!"

"The record says it is a brown-leather-covered journal of Marie Taglioni, that's all," said Vasily, recovering his wits at once. "I really don't think you can arrest my wife or confiscate her belongings on the strength of such shaky evidence!"

Dumortier was in agonies. "Someone has made a substitution," he breathed. "Someone has taken the Opera's journal and returned *this* nonsense."

"Indeed?" Vasily said, with withering contempt. "M. Dumortier, it seems very much as though you're trying to cheat my wife out of her lawful property. Is the Opera too poor to pay what this journal is worth?"

Dumortier turned white with fury, and the Inspector returned the more valuable of the two journals to me with a bow. "Madame," he said, "I apologise for inconveniencing you."

"You must do your duty, I know," I said prettily, returning the journal to my pocket. "And now, M Inspector, perhaps you might turn your attention towards the matter of the missing woman?"

"Hear! hear!" muttered the masked man, who betrayed greater impatience with each passing minute.

Dumortier forced a smile onto his face. "Inspector, it is late, and the Opera has its own gendarme, who can investigate anything that needs looking into! I am covered in shame for having detained you so long on this business. You must be eager to return home."

"If M le Baron requires our assistance, we shall remain," said the Inspector, with a bow in Vasily's direction. I was tempted to suspect that he felt it incumbent upon him to curry favour with the wronged party.

"Good," Vasily said, becoming brisk. "The facts, gentlemen, are these. For some time Mlle Chalabi has not been returning to her home at night, and neither have some of the other dancers, which has caused their friends great alarm. I therefore decided to employ Mlle Laine as my agent in an attempt to get to the bottom of the matter. She disappeared in turn, and only returned to us two days ago, saying that she had been held in the cellars, in a cell where she found this trinket, which has been confirmed as belonging to Demiana Chalabi." He produced the silver necklace.

The masked man started forwards as though to say something, but he was silenced by a commanding gesture from Vasily.

"And whom do you suspect?" the Inspector asked. "I take it that Mlle Laine beheld the face of the man who held her prisoner!"

"If we catch him, you may see for yourself," Vasily said. "As for me, I have only Mlle Laine's words to go upon, and I know better than to make accusations upon little proof!"

This charge did not pass Dumortier by. He opened his mouth to protest, but Vasily turned upon him with bared teeth.

"What is the meaning of this, monsieur? Are you trying to protect the culprit by throwing so many obstacles into our way?"

"For God's sake let us be going," the masked man burst out. It was he, in the end, who led the way. Vasily, myself, the gendarmes, and last of all a pale and anxious-looking Dumortier followed closely on his heels.

At last, we were on Mimi's track! But, good heavens! what scenes of disaster awaited us in the cellars of the Opera?

Chapter XXIII.

Nijam and Schmidt, meanwhile, were hot on Mimi's tracks. They went at once to the area beneath the stage, riddled with trap-doors, where stood the great "organ" that operated the foot-lights—the reader already knows with what result. The gas-man, in the dark little box beside the prompter's hutch, swore that he had seen nothing; all his attention had been upon his lights, and the task of gradually simulating a sunrise. There was no prompter to corroborate his story, because of course there are no speaking parts in a ballet to be prompted.

Nijam fixed the man with a distrustful glare as she lighted her little dark-lantern. "Are you quite sure you saw and heard *nothing?*" she asked in a softly menacing voice, with some idea of telling him what her invention really did if he proved recalcitrant. But Schmidt attached himself to her arm.

"For heaven's sake, you can see that she isn't here," said he. "And in that case we know precisely where she ought to be."

"The studio," Nijam muttered. Then they left the organ-man and descended deeper into the cellars; past the furnace-men whose boilers kept the Opera warm and heated, and down the long stair that plunged into the depths where the great backdrops were stored. Schmidt led the way, expecting at every turn to come upon the nightmarish sight of Mimi, like Chalabi, struggling in the grip of a dangerous lunatic.

At last the bottom came in sight. It was then that Schmidt did something which, at the time, seemed unlucky. He took the final two steps in a single leap and landed upon the stone floor with a jar that snapped one of the straps holding the flame-thrower pack to his back.

"Ah! great God!" Schmidt exclaimed, which was about as near as he ever got to using bad language. He shrugged off the pack, and that was when Nijam heard me on the transmitter asking about their progress.

She informed us that they were approaching the studio, when they heard a woman's cry from somewhere ahead in the darkness of the cellar, and knew that it was Mimi.

Schmidt threw down the flame-thrower, said, *"She's alive,"* and charged towards that distant voice.

Nijam darted after him, her lantern throwing a drunken pattern of light and shadows ahead. Schmidt's shadow was an inky pool of black on the floor before them. Then Nijam felt the cold, damp puff of wind coming from the cistern below, and realised that it was not only shadow: it was an unbarred opening directly before Schmidt's feet.

"Schmidt!" she shrieked, abandoning her lantern and snatching at his coat with both hands. "Trap!" —but it was already too late. The ground opened up beneath his feet. His head went back, and he threw up his arms. Both of them cried aloud. Then Schmidt fell like a stone, and Nijam, who could neither arrest his fall nor bring herself to let go of him, was dragged after him into the depths…

Toppling like a stone, they plunged deep into cold water until the soft silt closed around their ankles. Nijam extricated herself at once and pushed her way back to the surface, emerging into black darkness, noisome with foul-smelling water. She spat in disgust.

Above, there was a clang as the heavy iron grille was replaced in the opening!

"Perrot! A moment!" she shouted, but there was no answer from above. Nijam swept her arms through the water, desperately seeking a ladder, a wall, anything that might be of assistance to her. It was only then that Schmidt surfaced, gasping.

"I'm sorry," he gasped. "Oh, Mimi! How could I not mind where I was going?"

Nijam's hand smacked masonry. The wall! "Stop apologising," she said, hastily emptying her pockets of candle-ends, peppermints and a particularly beloved wrench. Her pocket-knife she retained just long enough to relieve herself of her boots and her long, clinging black dress. "We've no time to lose," she gasped. "Mimi found a ladder out of here. Where?"

"There," Schmidt said, pointing. A dim ray of light appeared shining down from another hatch some distance away, illuminating a ladder—just as it was drawn up, out of reach.

"You *blackguard!*" Schmidt shouted, but Nijam, though treading water, had kept her head. She tapped her temple—her implanted transmitter was still in working order, although Schmidt's must be ruined—and hissed, "Mimi? Mimi, can you hear me?"

"No answer?" Schmidt panted.

"The revenant must have taken it," Nijam whispered. "Quickly—follow me!"

She struck out at once for the studio end of the cistern, using the wall as a guide in the darkness. There were other hatches above them, and the furthest was in the revenant's own chamber. Where there had been one ladder at one end, there might possibly be another at this. Of course, it was also possible there was not. In that case they would simply have to listen to Mimi being murdered at leisure before themselves drowning by inches in the dark. A pleasant notion!

At length she stopped swimming. Beside her, Schmidt came sputtering to the surface and Nijam said, "If my calculations are correct, the hatch above us leads into the room with the coffin."

"We can get to it," Schmidt panted. "If you climb onto my shoulders—"

"Don't be ridiculous," said Nijam, treading water. Then she raised her voice as far as she dared. "Mimi! Mimi, can you hear us?"

"Mimi! We've come to get you!" Schmidt bellowed, his voice making the whole cistern ring.

There was a glimmer of light above, and by it—to their great relief—they saw Mimi's white dress and pale face looking down at them. "I already heard your voices," she said calmly. "Now I suppose *he's* heard you, too."

"Just throw us a sheet or a rope or something," Nijam said, ever practical.

"There aren't any sheets here," Mimi said, pulling lock-picks out of her hair. "But I can open this door up again, and fetch you something a good bit better. ...I shut myself in here because he went away and I thought that if it came to the worst I could jump into the cistern again. Do you have the flame-thrower with you?"

There was a little tremble in her voice, just enough to make Schmidt dream fondly of punching the creature that had put it there. Nijam, on the other hand, was so staggered by the idiocy of this last question that she could only take refuge in sarcasm.

"What do you think?" she asked. "It weighs a mere thirty kilograms, and we're neck deep in water."

A moment later Mimi returned. "Mind your heads!" she called, and fed a ladder down into the opening. The thing was heavy and unwieldy—more a stair than a ladder. Above, a sliver of wood must have run into Mimi's hand, for she suddenly let go with a hiss of pain, and the whole heavy assemblage slipped into the water with a great splash.

"I hear a key in the lock!" Mimi hissed down at them. "He's coming back! I'll go and buy you time, but for God's sake don't be long."

Then she ran out of the room above into the studio, and Schmidt and Nijam heard the door shut between.

Beneath, Schmidt and Nijam clung awkwardly to the floating ladder. "Help me raise it up," Schmidt panted.

Treading water as they were, it proved nearly impossible to get that ladder into position. At last they managed it, and a moment later—cold, wet, and exhausted—they were lying on the floor of the revenant's cell.

"I thought for certain we were going to drown," Schmidt gasped.

Nijam snorted. "I knew that if Mimi was alive she would be busy securing her escape."

Schmidt sat up, becoming solemn at once. "Please God she will not pay for our escape with her life."

"Careful," Nijam hissed as he got to his feet. "We don't have a flamethrower—"

Her warning was too late: already Schmidt had flung himself at the door and tried to wrench it open. But the great heavy door only rattled in its frame.

"Locked!" he cried.

There was a little shutter in the door at eye-height, which now shot open, revealing a horrible, unmasked face—the revenant, which Schmidt had last seen hissing at him from the shadows of a brougham. He recoiled with a cry at the sight that had haunted his nightmares ever since. A slender arm went about him and steadied him.

Nijam faced the revenant coolly. If the sight of the revenant put Schmidt into a dither, it rather had the effect of steadying her. She much preferred to look a revenant in the eyes, rather than to imagine it lurking in the shadows. "Go on," she said. "Open the door. You mean to kill us, don't you?"

Then they heard the welcome sound of Mimi's voice. "Won't you show me that passage again, monsieur?"

She came into view, putting a gentle hand on the revenant's sleeve; but she never looked through the shutter. Schmidt gave a soft hiss at the sight of her drawn, doubtful face.

The shutter closed, and presently the sound of piano-music began in the next room.

"She must have convinced him she still needs lessons," Nijam muttered, releasing Schmidt and attempting to wring out her wet petticoats. "What the blazes, Mimi! If he'd opened that door, we could have hurled him down into the cistern! Now what?"

"She can't open any doors," Schmidt said in a voice of concentrated fury, stripping off his waistcoat and wrapping it around his fist. "Don't you see the look on her face? That's what I tried to tell you about, the other day—he's crushing the life out of her."

He took a deep breath and then drove his padded fist at the

shutter in the door.

The door jumped in its frame, and Nijam in her wet underthings followed suit; but in the studio the piano-music went on, almost mockingly. Schmidt hissed with pain, adjusted the folds of the waistcoat, and struck again—one, two, three! On the third blow the shutter sprang away from the door and clattered to the stones without, and Nijam and Schmidt crowded eagerly to the opening.

The scene that met their eyes had something of the quality of a dream, for neither of the two on the other side of the locked door seemed to have noticed Schmidt's assault upon the shutter. The revenant sat at the piano, playing with a single-minded absorption; and Mimi was dancing with her eyes closed.

Nijam could have told him it was useless, but Schmidt reached an arm through the opening and felt for a key in the lock. Of course there was none. The music stopped. Schmidt withdrew his arm and Nijam, rolling her eyes, peered out the opening again. The revenant had arisen from the piano and approached Mimi, who went on dancing in a kind of trance.

A cord swung from the revenant's fist.

"Mimi!" Schmidt shouted, making the door rattle in its frame. "Look out!"

Mimi opened her eyes and saw the approaching threat: she stopped dancing at once.

"The lock-picks!" Nijam cried. "Throw us the lock-picks, Mimi!" She was vaguely aware of Schmidt darting into the centre of the room and hauling the ladder from the cistern.

"Stand aside," he panted, raising the ladder like a battering-ram.

"Don't be an idiot! It opens *inwards*," Nijam snapped. "Mimi, the picks!"

Mimi hardly seemed to hear: she reached into the folds of her white gauze skirt and came out with a pair of tiger-claws on her hands.

"*No,*" Nijam groaned, as Mimi threw herself upon the revenant.

The revenants with which Nijam was familiar had responded to physical resistance by going into a murderous rage that ended only with death; but those had, after all, been created expressly to function as policemen. This one, to her astonishment, merely collapsed flat beneath Mimi's onslaught. She landed uppermost, claws flashing as she plunged them in quick succession into the creature's body. Then she tore them out and scrambled backwards across the floor, breathing hard, until her back was against Nijam's door. For a moment she sat there, claws poised for a renewed attack.

"Is it dead?" Nijam breathed, trying to make some sense of the scene. "Did you deface its sigil?"

Mimi gave no answer. For a moment the only sound in that room was the tormented sound of her breathing. Then an unearthly voice broke in upon them.

"Foolish girl!" it croaked. "Why resist, when I would make you immortal?"

All three of them—Mimi splayed inelegantly against the door, and Nijam and Schmidt behind it—must have jumped. Mimi gave a shriek and scraped at the air with her claws.

"The raven!" Nijam breathed. The big black bird on its perch had escaped her notice until this moment; now she spied it in the shadows, marked out by the minute blue fire in its eyes. Beside her, Schmidt had gone absolutely still. Nijam wondered whether he had forgotten to breathe.

She felt sick herself. A revenant was nothing living; it was only a spark of intelligence clinging to a dead body—how, Nijam had never bothered to ask herself. She had always presumed that the application of electricity stimulated the brain into activity for a time. But if that spark of intelligence could somehow transfer itself to a different body entirely—if that spark of intelligence could use a raven as a mouthpiece—then she had been wrong, badly wrong…

Mimi gave a soft gasp. "Not immortal," she said, her claws trembling. "Dead."

"Death need not be the end," said the raven-revenant. "You know that better than anyone."

"Fire," Nijam whispered, cursing the unlucky chance that had brought her here without her flame-thrower. She slapped her dripping pockets and stared wildly around the room. "Matches!" There was a paper of them on a ledge near the door, and she snatched them up and dropped them through the grille beside Mimi. "Set fire to the body, Mimi!"

Mimi made no motion, except to let her claws sink to the floor beside her, as though they had become far too heavy for her. It was at that moment, to Nijam's astonishment, that Schmidt seemed to take charge of the situation.

"Why should she die?" he called out, and then, in a lower voice pitched to carry only as far as the ballerina at the foot of the door, *"Remember what Miss Dark told us!"*

Nijam stared at Schmidt in disbelief. In her estimation Miss Dark said a great number of things, many of them with no bearing on anything at all. Which one of them was she supposed to remember now?

Endowed with human intelligence, the raven must have found a way to free itself from its perch, for it now took wing and glided down to the stones at Mimi's feet.

"Look at you," it cawed. "Do you think you can be a dancer when you can barely even stand? If your knee had not been so weak I might have done something with you, but as it is…your body will never carry you to greatness."

"No," Mimi said, so softly, and so sadly that Nijam barely heard her.

"No," the raven repeated. "You know that there is only one way to become the soloist you have always longed to be. Die now, and you will dance forever in my *Giselle*."

"You'll be *dead,* Mimi," Schmidt called. "It won't be you!"

"It will be *your* name the world worships," said the raven. "It will be *your* Myrtha that lives forever."

"I don't *want* to dance the same part forever," Mimi said, faint but clear. "I'm more than that."

"More than *my* Myrtha?" the raven asked, and there was a note of contemptuous laughter in its voice. "Which of us is the master, and which of us the student? Make a better choice, girl. Your refusal may cost your friends dear."

"No, Mimi!" Nijam cried. "I have my transmitter. I've already—"

Schmidt gripped her hand and signalled her to be silent. Mystified, Nijam obeyed. What were the two of them playing at? What did they remember that she did not?

"I'm offering you art—genius—glory—things which are immortal," the raven said as though Nijam had never interrupted. "What is a life compared to that? Sixty years ago I created my *Giselle,* and it is still being performed. Sixty years and twice sixty hence it will still be performed. You might be a part of it for more than a single night. How many ballerinas can boast that they were trained by the great Perrot himself?

Will *you* be the reason pure French ballet disappears from the world, only because you wished for *more?* Will you put yourself above the great traditions of the past?"

"No," Mimi repeated, soft and obstinate. Perhaps the revenant only heard the softness.

"Tradition?" Schmidt scoffed. "Of course she wants to do new things. That's the point of being alive."

"You killed Demiana Chalabi," Mimi observed, picking at the ribbons of her dancing-shoes. "Did *she* want immortality, too?"

"She *begged* for it."

"And the tenor, M. Larousse?"

"He would only have held us back."

Mimi made a peculiar sound.

"Why do you laugh?" the raven demanded, but to Nijam, it had sounded at least as much like a sob.

"Larousse, holding us back!" Mimi declared in a stronger voice. "Don't make me laugh! *You* are the one who holds us back!"

The raven hunched its head down with a threatening motion, but Mimi was no longer paying attention. Wincing, she worked the shoe from her foot. Beneath, her stockings were stained from burst blisters.

"You aren't Perrot," she went on at last, contemptuously. "I don't know what *you* are, but if the real Perrot had thought like you, then he would never have created *Giselle* at all. He would have been shackled down by the things of the past." She took a shaking breath. "And maybe you are right. Maybe I *do* have to kill myself in order to become perfect. But in that case I think I'll *live,* thanks."

The raven fluttered back to the piano. "I'll kill you!" it

squawked. "I'll find another Myrtha! And every name and memory of Mimi Laine will perish!"

"And I'd be rich and famous if I only kill myself here?" Mimi demanded, taking off her tiger-claws in order to draw her lock-picks from her hair. "Let me tell you what, you feather-duster! Your precious *Giselle* is completely out of date! In Petersburg it would be laughed at!"

"I'll kill you!" the revenant screeched, leaping from the piano. "By God I'll kill you!"

"God take your soul and be damnation to you!" Schmidt bellowed, pounding a fist against the door. Mimi shrieked, ducked, and threw at the swooping raven the first thing that came to hand, which happened to be her shoe.

At the same instant there came from somewhere a flash of unbearable light and a crack like thunder, exactly like an electrical fuse being overloaded. It puzzled Nijam because she had not seen a single sign of electrical wiring anywhere in the room. For a moment they were all blinded; and then Nijam's vision cleared and she saw that the raven was no more than a heap of smoking feathers beside Mimi's shoe on the floor.

Nijam rattled the door, understanding only that they had a moment's respite in which to free themselves. "Quick, Mimi—pass me the lock-picks—!"

Schmidt's hand covered hers. "It's over," he said, very calmly. "See?"

Restraining herself with an effort from doing some screeching of her own, Nijam turned her attention back towards the opening. The shoe—the bird—the mummified body were each laid upon the floor, equally lifeless. Mimi stood once again gripping her tiger claws, ready to defend herself.

For a long, long moment nothing in that place seemed to

draw breath—with the sole exception of Alphonse Schmidt, who seemed not at all concerned.

"Something's burning," Mimi hissed, long after the silence had become unbearable.

Nijam sniffed. Beneath the unmistakable smell of burning feathers another scent was perceptible and becoming stronger by the moment. With it came familiar sounds—first ticking, then groaning.

"Overheated metal," Nijam said, with a fatalistic shrug. She had passed the limits of her understanding approximately fifteen minutes ago and could now only collect data. Perhaps the revenant was taking some new, sinister revenge. Or perhaps someone had found the flame-thrower at the bottom of the cellar steps and, in fiddling with it, had set fire to that great stock of backdrops. Perhaps the Opera was at present burning merrily over their heads, and was about to obliterate them in a mighty downfall.

The thought of death had a bracing effect, because *that* was something she perfectly understood.

"The main door's on fire," she announced, cheerfully. "We're about to die."

"What?" Mimi gasped, and then all of a sudden, with a mighty blow, the main door burst open. It admitted a cloud of stinking black smoke—and a coughing, be-flame-throwered Anton Lupei.

"I found you!" he announced happily. Mimi gave a hiccough of emotion. Nijam, feeling more cheerful still, revised her estimated chances of imminent death sharply downwards.

"What has been going on in here?" Lupei asked, advancing into the room and fetching up quite still once he caught sight of the dead bird and the mummified corpse.

Mimi turned and began—at last—to pick the lock on Nijam's cell door. "I think it's dead," she commented, but she kept sending suspicious looks over her shoulder, anyway.

"Would you like me to make sure?" Lupei asked, raising the overheated nozzle of the flame-thrower.

"No," Nijam and Schmidt cried at once. They would have been too late, because Lupei had already set the mechanism working; but to no effect. A tiny puff of flame emerged from the nozzle and dissipated.

"Out of fuel," Lupei said sadly. "I must have used it all up softening the lock."

At last, the cell door opened. Schmidt gathered up Mimi in a hug. Nijam picked up one of the ballerina's discarded tiger-claws and went down on her knees by the body. It took her a moment's searching to find the sigil: Mimi's first attempt with the claws had just missed it, for the emblem had been marked in blood very high on its chest. Nijam cut three slashes across the mark, and then she felt as though she could really breathe again.

If a revenant's intelligence could move from its host body to a dumb animal, then perhaps the sigils were not as useless as she had thought.

"Mimi, *mein Schnecke*," Schmidt said, holding the ballerina at arm's length. "Are you going to be all right?"

Mimi sniffed. "Of course I will," she said. "I had to let him think I might do as he said, didn't I? If he'd stopped talking and resumed his corpse it would have been over for all of us."

Nijam was not certain whether she believed her. Still, the main thing was that Mimi was alive, and the revenant was done for—but how?

The same question had occurred to Lupei. "If you didn't

set it on fire," he said slowly, "and if you didn't deface its sigil, then how *did* you get the best of it?"

"Ah," Schmidt said happily, pulling his waistcoat on again. "Miss Dark told us that the shades of the dead must always leave quickly for the next world, but that a revenant like this one is able to hide by clinging to its own body. It seemed to me only logical that if the shade left the body for any length of time, natural laws would take their course." He gave a sunny smile. "It worked, didn't it?"

"I've seen something like it before," Mimi said, in a hushed sort of awe. "But that was on holy ground. In a church."

Nijam felt herself turning to gaze down at the sad little heap of feathers upon the floor. Every hair on her head prickled and stood to attention. Again, she found herself far beyond what her data could account for.

She wondered what data Schmidt had, that he could fit this so calmly into his understanding of the world.

Lupei seemed as uncomfortable as Nijam herself. "We should leave this place," he blurted out. "Because of the police, I mean. The managers are on their way down, and they have a pack of gendarmes with them. Come on."

"No," Mimi said. She had her arms wrapped around herself, and looked rather pale, so that Nijam wondered again whether she really had been as much in command of herself as she claimed. "There's something else we ought to do, first. Let's open up that third door."

Chapter XXIV.

"Mon Dieu, it's a revenant!" Vasily cried, recoiling from the mummified corpse on the parqueted floor. "Look, there's a sigil carved into his flesh!"

Our procession—Vasily and myself, together with the gendarmes, M. Dumortier, and the slight gentleman in the mask—had made good time into the cellars, sped on our way when Nijam opened her transmitter to inform us that the revenant was dealt with and all our friends were safe. Needless to say, she had put our minds greatly at ease with this news. Vasily sent me a look of melting relief and promptly became ebulliently histrionic.

The door to the famous studio hung open, scorched and blasted about the lock; and within was only emptiness, echoes, and death.

"Look," I cried, entering into the spirit of the performance. "Here's M. Christophe's wand."

Vasily beheld it quizzically. "Hullo! There's a monogram engraved upon it. M. Dumortier, do you recognise this mark?"

"That's old Perrot's monogram," Dumortier said, rather sulkily, "but—"

Vasily made a sweeping gesture. "My dear monsieur! Are these indeed the last mortal remains of the great Perrot, which were stolen from the family tomb two years ago?"

"These? Certainly not!" Dumortier said, turning red. "What a ridiculous notion!"

Vasily could not be repressed. "Do you really expect us to believe that a *revenant* has been teaching the ballet corps these past two years, and you didn't *know* about it?"

"What do you mean to insinuate?" Dumortier protested. "Am I to be blamed for *everything* that happens at the Opera, only because of some libellous accusations in the newspaper? Inspector, this is persecution! I appeal to your sense of justice!"

The Inspector looked as though he might be about to say something mollifying, but just then, a gendarme who had put his nose into one of the other rooms, let out a sudden shout of alarm.

"Look here!" he cried. "More dead!"

The Inspector rushed to peer into the charnel-house which Mimi described.

I grasped the arm of the masked man to prevent him following. *He* did not need to see what was there. As for me, I knew that they would have discovered precisely what Mimi had found there—but with one very important difference.

"Look here—and here," Vasily proclaimed, as lantern-beams flashed from within that stifling darkness. "More sigils! These, too, were made into revenants!"

"What?" Dumortier asked in a stifled voice, over the Inspector's low whistle of amazement. "*More* revenants? How?"

"How indeed!" the Inspector exclaimed, giving Dumortier a searching look.

"This explains everything," Vasily added, emerging from the

room. "How Mlle Chalabi was able to continue dancing night after night, but never returned home to her family. Does it not, M. Chalabi?"

The man at my side removed his mask, disclosing the sun-warmed skin and reddened eyes of the grieving father.

"Please," he begged. "Let me see her."

Vasily exchanged a glance with the Inspector. "Not now," said the Inspector, "it isn't a pretty sight."

I felt then a twinge of guilt for what we had chosen to do with the bodies, marking that unholy sigil upon them, to provide what was lacking in the way of hard evidence. At least I had insisted upon using a variety of ink that would wash away!

As for Dumortier, he stared at M. Chalabi in speechless horror. I think it was at that moment that he truly felt that he had been trapped.

"You remember M. Dumortier, don't you?" I asked the Egyptian gentleman. "I believe he visited you before you left Paris."

M. Chalabi pointed a shaking finger at the manager. "This man told me not to go to the police, that my daughter had chosen to take up residence with a lover! I knew that it was a black lie, but he threatened me! No, I don't care—my Irina is now safe in Alexandria. Inspector, M. Dumortier promised to denounce one daughter if I sought out the other! Why should he do so unless he was trying to conceal my Demiana's death?"

There was an awful silence. The Inspector pursed his lips, and Dumortier turned pale with mingled terror and fury.

"*You* were threatening to stir up trouble against the Opera," he snarled. "You would have blackened the name of this sacred institution—set back the cause of Art—"

"How long has your daughter been missing, monsieur?" Vasily interrupted, very light and urbane. "Not as long as two years, I think?"

M. Chalabi shook his head. "Oh, monsieur, no—not above two weeks!"

"Then," Vasily said, delivering the *coup de grâce,* "this is wonderful news, gentlemen. It seems that the secret of revenant-making has been re-discovered—and here, in Paris of all cities! Inspector, I congratulate you upon this fortunate discovery! You're about to become the toast of France."

The Inspector seemed fully alive to the possibilities of the situation. "Fortunate indeed!" he mused. "Imagine the Russians or the Americans—or God forbid, the Germans stumbling upon it first! Tell me, M. Dumortier, what did you know of this?"

Dumortier was trembling now. "Nothing, I swear to you."

Vasily shook a speck from his irreproachable cuffs. The effect would have been better had he been wearing fine Mechlin lace; but that had been out of fashion for a century or two, and I must say that he made a fine show of it all the same. "You'd better tell the truth," he said. "*Someone* has been making revenants, and that man has now the most sought-after brain in Europe."

The Inspector, with a gesture, sent his men to surround Dumortier. At that, the old gentleman broke down entirely.

"I didn't kill them," he cried. "I didn't turn them into revenants! I don't know how!" —He tried to back away, but the gendarmes seized him. "I swear to you that I took Perrot's body to Heidelberg—that is all!"

"Aha! A confession!" cried Vasily.

"All right; M. Dumortier, please consider yourself our prisoner," said the Inspector, "under the suspicion of grave-robbing, murder, and creating revenants without a permit."

Without a permit! I shook my head. Naturally it was perfectly all right to create revenants so long as they were put to work for the state!

"But I tell you I haven't *made* any revenants," Dumortier almost screamed. I think the same ideas must have been going through his head, as had occurred to us regarding Schmidt—that if he was suspected of possessing the most valuable secret in Europe, he would never be permitted to see the light of day again.

"There, now, don't be coy with us," said the Inspector, who had got the scent of the glories that were to come his way. "These bodies have clearly been dead for weeks, yet half of Paris will swear to it that they've been performing *Giselle* every night. *Someone* has been making revenants here in the Opera cellar. I wouldn't be surprised if all that business about the tenor was true, also. Take him away, and be sure he doesn't speak to anyone…But is there no sign of the missing woman, Mlle Laine?"

"None whatever," Vasily said with a grimace of sadness. "It *does* look as though she managed to escape, though, doesn't it?"

Glancing from Vasily's bland face, to the motionless revenant and the blasted door, the Inspector gave a philosophical shrug. "As you say—but I shall wait upon you in the morning, Baron, to receive your statement. Let us hope that Mlle Laine will then have reappeared. M. Chalabi, I beg you'll accompany us now."

Away went the Inspector, very pleased with himself and his

prisoner, leaving a pair of his gendarmes to guard the scene of the crime. Vasily offered an arm to me, and the two of us followed them into the cellar and waited in the shadow of the hanging backdrops until the policemen were quite departed.

Then the great canvases stirred, and the rest of our friends—Nijam, Schmidt, Lupei, and Mimi—emerged from the shadows. I folded Mimi into my arms, silently thanking Heaven that she had been restored to us safe and sound.

"Not a bad evening's work!" Vasily said happily. "The revenant dismantled, and Dumortier bound for a cell at the bottom of whatever they're using these days for a Bastille! But who could have guessed that the revenant was man-made, and not natural?"

"*I* thought so," Mimi said at once, with a ferocious scowl. "The *real* Perrot knew better than to live in the dead past. That wasn't his shade; it was something else."

Nijam also scowled, but said nothing. She had only recently accepted the existence of ghosts; I suppose it was a bridge too far to expect her to accept the existence of—*something else.*

Schmidt looked horrified. "That thing was *made?*"

"Yes; in Heidelberg," said Vasily. "Ow! Molly-my-dear, you're standing on my toe!"

I removed my boot with a sigh. Evidently Vasily did *not* understand the significance of that great university city to Nijam and Schmidt. At the name of it they had both gone perfectly still.

"What's the matter?" Lupei asked them. "Your faces have fallen off!"

Neither made any response to that. I cleared my throat.

"How do you feel, Mimi? I suppose you're pretty tired. Shall we take you home?"

Mimi shuddered, no doubt imagining how chill and dark the house would be at this hour. "I'm hungry," she said. "I want my dinner first."

"Let's go to Maxim's!" Vasily declared. "Come on, all of you—we have done a good night's work, and ought to celebrate!"

Chapter XXV.

Since Nijam and Schmidt were still damp from their hasty descent into the cistern, we stopped by the tenement in the Boulevard Haussmann so that Schmidt could find some dry clothes. As for Nijam, Mimi and I were united in insisting that the shabby black dresses she habitually wore were not at all suitable for Maxim's, even had the best of them not presently been lying at the bottom of the Opera cistern. We whisked her into my flat, therefore, and very quickly wrestled her into one of my own white lace frocks. Having done so, Mimi and I stood back to consider our handiwork. It fitted her not too badly after a few stitches to tighten the bodice, for there was somewhat less of Nijam than of me.

"This isn't my style," Nijam said, scowling at the lace.

"What style?" Mimi asked, scornfully. "Would you prefer red velvet?" That silenced all complaint.

The night was clear, if cold, and we were in a companionable mood, so it was quickly decided to walk the short distance to the famous Maxim's Restaurant. Vasily and I led the way, arm-in-arm, while Schmidt and Nijam more silently brought up the rear. That left Mimi in the midst to be squired—or more precisely, to be driven to distraction—by Lupei.

"There's one thing I still can't figure out, Laine," said Lupei.

He paused, no doubt for effect. *"Why* would you risk your neck to appear in such a lousy ballet?"

"Well, of course it's a lousy ballet!" Mimi declared. "But at least I got to play the only *sensible* character in it!"

"Who, the wicked queen? But she's not sensible at all—she had the wrong man danced to death! …Look, I reckon I could fix it, though. All you'd have to do is switch the rôles. Have the Duke die, and the huntsman be saved. Then everyone would get his just deserts."

Mimi snorted. "Can you imagine it? The Duke getting his just deserts, and the huntsman made the hero of the piece? Everyone would write angry letters to the newspapers, and the director would be pilloried as an anarchist."

"That's the problem with the Opera," Lupei said. "It's nothing more than a tool of the state, used to justify the violence inherent in the system. Why serve it at all? Why not burn it down?"

Mimi sent him a look of daggers. "No, thank you! I'd rather get paid."

"And you an artist!" Lupei scoffed. "I'd rather die than debase myself like that for money!"

"I can see to that," Mimi muttered.

Vasily sent me an expressive glance, and I repressed a giggle. I had truly imagined them as bosom friends; but evidently they were much too similar for that.

"You are a brave man and an idealist, Lupei," I told him. "But I'm afraid that we are only a pack of cunning cowards, whose gifts lie in another direction. Call it—plundering the Egyptians, as the Hebrew slaves did, upon departing for the Promised Land."

After that we walked in silence for a while; and I think that

Schmidt must have spent the whole time working himself up to speak. He rubbed at his chest, and at last he cleared his throat.

"What do you think Dumortier meant by saying that he took Perrot's body to Heidelberg?" he asked. "Miss Nijam, do *you* know?"

In the frosty light of the street-lamps, I glanced back at Nijam. Clad in white lace, the tendrils of her hair still a little damp where they escaped the knot at the back of her head, Nijam reminded me a little of Giselle in her mad scene. Unlike Giselle, she seemed reluctant to answer with anything beyond a ferocious scowl. I began to think that she meant to leave the question unanswered, when at last she said:

"Heidelberg is the place where Stefan Schmidt and his brother once studied revenant-making under Caspar Auberlen. Professor Auberlen was the originator of the art, of course. No one understood the process like he did. If Dumortier took Perrot's remains to Heidelberg two years ago, it's barely possible that he may have gone in the weeks between the downfall of the revenants and Auberlen's death. The old man was ailing then; but before he died, he might have found a way to revivify one last corpse. Of course, in those first days of the downfall, no one knew how troublesome the stoppage might be. Plenty of people expected a quick solution to be found. Perhaps, before he died, Auberlen did just that."

There was a silence, before Schmidt said, "Or it's possible that it was another of his students who found the solution, and they are still in possession of it."

"It *had* to be Auberlen," Nijam said softly. "He had three students only. One of them is dead; the second has forgotten, and the third has never spoken."

Three students! I do not think that any of us were in any doubt as to the identity of the third. Not even Alphonse Schmidt, who stopped in his tracks and said, "Miss Nijam, a moment."

Nijam only looked at the pavement at her feet. For a moment no one spoke, and then Vasily, much to my annoyance, said, "Meet us at Maxim's, but don't be too long about it, or we'll think Schmidt has been picked up by the Okhrana."

Then he marched us inexorably on; without even giving me the opportunity to slip a live transmitter into Schmidt's pocket! Alas!

It was not for many years that I *did* hear about that conversation in the shadow of the great neoclassical church of the Madeleine. Nijam looked at her feet until her four companions were out of earshot, all the time reflecting that the hour had come to lay her cards on the table. Whatever the cost, she could conceal the truth from Schmidt no longer.

"It is as you guessed," she said, turning to face him. "I knew you in Heidelberg, Alphonse Schmidt. You and I and your brother Stefan—all of us worked together in the same laboratory."

Once again Schmidt clutched his heart. "Making revenants," he said.

"I'm not proud of it, either."

There was a silence. His hand was splayed on his chest. "The sigils," he said, in a low voice. "I recognised them. I've seen one before."

"Where?"

Schmidt gulped, hard. *"Here."*

Then, to her consternation, he unbuttoned his shirt-front and pulled the collar aside. The triangle of chest he displayed—evidently shaved for the purpose—showed a faint pattern of silvery scars. The shape they traced was horribly familiar to Nijam, save for the long slash that had at some point been scored through them.

Alphonse Schmidt had a revenant's sigil marked upon him.

This, too, was a horror beyond the scope of her comprehension. "But you're *alive*," she heard herself saying, as though from a long distance away. "You're *warm*. Why would anyone carve a sigil into *living* flesh?"

"I hoped you might tell me," he said, buttoning his shirt again. "I've always known that this marked me out for some evil fate. Now I know for certain."

A few brief hours ago she would have told him that a sigil meant nothing. Now—she bit her lip, so that the pain might distract her from the cold, slithering doubt in her guts.

His brother must have done this to him—but *why?*

"Don't be afraid," she said, as much to herself as to him.

"But I have been," Schmidt said, very calmly. "Desperately afraid. You were right about that. I'm sorry."

In silence, he re-tied his cravat. Nijam said nothing. How could she? She needed more data.

Schmidt tucked in the silk ends of the necktie. He did not look her in the eye, but he said, "I suppose that I have always loved you, Padma Nijam. They could take away my memories, but they couldn't take that. I'm sorry for being afraid, and I'm sorry for letting you think that I wouldn't face my fears for you."

Nijam stared at him. She had to moisten her lips before the words would come. "What are you saying, Alphonse

Schmidt?"

"That I can't go on like this," he said, softly. "I want my memories back. Won't you help me find them?"

More than that, neither of them would tell me. But I take it that for Schmidt, too, virtue was found to be insufficient as its own reward.

***

"Wait," Lupei protested, once we were safely out of earshot of the pair. "What's your lover doing with the inventor, Laine?"

Mimi rolled her eyes. "He's not *my* lover, you tallow-brain; he's hers."

"He's pretty free with his embraces," said Lupei critically, no doubt alluding to the way Schmidt had greeted Mimi after the defeat of the revenant. "She doesn't mind?"

"Listen," Mimi said, "you can tease *me* all you like, but if you say a word out of place to my Schmidt, I'll—"

"What's the matter with you, Mimi?" I asked. "Have you lost your touch? Normally at this point in a job you'd be adding Mr Lupei to your string of admirers."

Two explosive snorts echoed across the Place de la Madeleine. *"Him?"* Mimi protested.

"Don't worry," said the anarchist, with a chuckle. "I'm married."

"My condolences to the unfortunate Mrs Lupei," Mimi retorted, and after that we proceeded to the restaurant in perfect amity.

Maxim's was a lush Art Nouveau paradise, all fitted up in darkly gleaming wood and red carpets and creamy plaster, with everywhere the liquid, swooping lines of nature—

chandeliers like bunches of lilies, carved panels like Gothic arches, curved wooden armchairs as comforting as a mother's embrace. The place was full of people and noise and music, and Vasily was in his element. Making the false Order of St George on his breast sparkle in the electric lamplight, he cheerfully brazened his way into the establishment's best table on the edge of the dance-floor.

"I hope Mr Lupei's principles will allow him to indulge in a little aristocratic excess," Vasily said, helping Mimi and myself into our chairs.

Lupei shrugged. "You're paying. Where's the bar?"

"That way, I presume, but show some restraint! I'm not made of money!"

"Call it *plundering the Egyptians*," Lupei said wickedly, as he departed.

A band was playing a waltz, and several couples revolved upon the floor. I had never before visited an establishment where the patrons were encouraged to dance; it was a new and daring fashion, but I thought it a rather pleasant one. I leaned towards Mimi and said, "I hope that you don't mind watching other people dance for a change."

There was a look of defeat in her eyes. "I think this is where I will be doing most of *my* dancing from now on. I'm not good enough for anything more."

"Don't say that!" I protested. "It was sinful how that creature drove you. Surely, with a little more rest—"

"No," she said. "He was right; I was just too stubborn to see it. I have talent, but this body is not enough. It will always hold me down. But you were right, too. Not everything can or should be sold… Maybe it will be enough, just to dance for myself."

I squeezed her hand. "At least you had tonight."

Her face lit up. "Think of it—Me, Mimi Laine from a village no one has heard about, dancing Myrtha before all of Paris! If you had told me a year ago that I should do such a thing, I would have laughed!" She let out a wistful sigh. "There are so many things I learned from him—and from Taglioni."

"Why not teach?" said Vasily unexpectedly. "I believe a position has lately opened up at the Opera—and I'm told the ballet brats have already been going to you for tutoring. I am the sole manager of the Opera right now. I daresay I can arrange it!"

Mimi's mouth fell open in shocked delight. "Could I?" she breathed. "But don't we have other things to do? Important things, like we did tonight?"

For a moment there had been a light in Vasily's eyes that quite surprised me—but that quenched it. "I suppose we do," he said, with a glance in my direction. But as for me, my heart had burst into song.

"I don't know that we must answer that question tonight," said I.

Mimi bit her lip with happiness. Vasily laughed silently and wryly to himself. Lupei returned from the bar with a bottle of champagne and a fistful of glasses.

"Champagne, Lupei?" I asked, with a raised eyebrow.

"Why not? I had it once, in a certain castle in Hungary, but I wasn't paying much attention at the time," he said. "Besides, the bloodsucker is paying."

As Vasily saw to uncorking the bottle. Mimi played with the string of pearls at her neck. "I need to ask you something," she told me in an undertone. "I have to sell my pearls and give the money to God."

"Good heavens, why?"

"Because I promised to do it if He got me out of that cellar alive," she said dolefully, "and after what happened when I threw my shoe at that raven, I think He heard me. Anyway, my question is this: Do I have to give the money to a church, or will He be just as happy if I give it directly to the poor? I suppose God is all right, but I don't trust His priests."

"The poor belong especially to God," I said, trying not to laugh. "I'm certain that He'll accept such a gift."

"Then that's what I'll do," she said, with mournful resolution. "Pour me some champagne, Vasya."

All the same, the more I thought of Mimi's bargain, the more I felt that my advice had been incomplete. "It will be a great sacrifice," I said. "But God is a person, you know, like you and me. He can't be bought with a big sacrifice, once in a lifetime. If we want to be His friends, we must think of Him in small things, every day, and not just when we need something. Oh! Hullo, Nijam!" I added, noticing that she and Schmidt had come up, and were standing behind my chair.

Schmidt sent Nijam a shy smile as he held out a chair. "That's where your data fall short," he told her, as though continuing a conversation they had already been having. "Natural processes can be predicted, but a person can't, always."

Vasily watched me with a faint, rather cynical smile of his own. "I've heard something like this before. You mean that God is not a painting, or a cup of tea. Not a thing to be *had*."

So he remembered that conversation we had once had, that stifling night in Hong Kong! I sent him a smile. "No one worth knowing can be bought like that."

"Yes," said Vasily. "I understand that now." Lupei sent him a rather surprised look, as though he had not expected to hear such a sentiment from that quarter.

Mimi looked horrified. "But then I needn't have promised Him my pearls!"

"Do you really want to explain to Him that you changed your mind?" I laughed, rising from my seat. "Dance with me, Vaska."

He got up quickly and led me onto the floor. I felt suddenly conscious that it was the first time we had been alone since his confession earlier that afternoon; but I took a page from his book, and covered my feelings with humour.

"I warn you—I'll probably step on you."

"Please do, my dear—it would be an honour." He took my hand so gingerly that I knew he was thinking of the same conversation. Then we moved into the dance, which was something of Strauss's, of course. I have not had many opportunities to perfect my waltzing, and I am afraid that at first I *did* step on him.

"You want to keep your post at the Opera, don't you?" I asked him.

"Pshaw!" he said.

"Don't tell me you don't—not when you were offering Mimi a job there." I smiled up at him. "You found something else to live for, didn't you?"

He sighed. "Oh, very well, if I must! After I left Moscow I thought that I was giving up everything, but it seems not. If necessary, I could always run the Paris Opera. There!"

"If *necessary?*" I asked, laughing.

He shook his head; but after a moment went on with an unaccustomed note of solemnity in his voice. "Mimi is right," he said. "There are more important things to do. I've made my great sacrifice, but now I need to do those small daily things. Otherwise I'll be the same creature that took Miss Sharp's blood—no better than that revenant." He looked down at me, and I saw a glimmer of uncertainty in his eyes. "I want to stay with you. I want to do this work with you—if you'll have me."

Around the lump in my throat I said, "Now I know that it's really me you choose. Because you might have chosen differently."

"So might you, I think."

I sighed. "It's true. I used to tell myself that if the family had not been ruined I would never have had to become a thief. I felt guilty, tonight, because I ought to have told Célestin Deleuze precisely what I thought of him, but instead I tricked him into a taste of his own medicine. The truth is, there's nothing in my nature that lends itself to crusading."

Vasily observed me with wide-eyed horror. "What made you think that there was? You're a magnificent deceiver, my dear. Don't waste your talents on crusading."

I couldn't help laughing at that. "Then we are agreed. We remain thieves."

"We remain thieves," he agreed. "Tomorrow I shall buy the Taglioni journal for the fabulous sum of ten thousand francs, and hire Mimi as the ballet mistress, if it pleases her; and then—"

A hand descended upon Vasily's shoulder, cutting off what he had been about to say.

"Baron! Baroness!" It was none other than my old friend, Célestin, who had evidently been dining well, if you take my meaning. "What a delightful surprise to find you here."

"My dear fellow," Vasily said, attempting without success to shrug himself free, "do you mind? I'm trying to have a conversation with *my* wife."

"Pardon! Pardon! Only I was told that the two of you were divorcing. Or was that another of the lady's untruths—like the one earlier, about my good Caillot slandering me?"

One of my fibs, at any rate, had been discovered. Unblushingly, I immediately told another. "I don't know *what* you're talking about. The Baron and I have never been on better terms."

"How can you take him back?" Deleuze demanded, even as Vasily succeeded in removing the truculent grip from his shoulder. "This man cut off your allowance! He installed a prosthetic eye to spy upon you! We both of us caught him making love to another woman!"

There were gasps from the other dancers, who had backed away and now stood eagerly watching the performance. Vasily and I exchanged glances. He hung his head in shame.

"It is true," he said, hollowly. "I cannot deny any of it."

Vasily might be willing to play his part, but I found myself stubbornly disinclined to follow suit. After all, Vasily *liked* managing the Paris Opera! Why should he not continue to do so, if he wished? It would be something to occupy him between jobs.

I drew myself up to my full height. "Yes, it is true," I said. "The Baron has done a great many bad things in the past, but he has now promised to reform himself."

Vasily stared at me; Deleuze gaped. "How can you trust a man like that? Such promises are as easily made as broken!"

I turned fond eyes upon my lover. "They are," I said. "But the Baron has chosen, again and again, to keep his promise— in the small things, as well as the great. So long as he continues to do so, I am willing to take my chances with him."

Célestin Deleuze was rendered speechless. Vasily, hardly less so. Overcome with emotion, he kissed my hand.

"You cannot really mean it!" Deleuze insisted, recovering his voice.

"But I do," I told Vasily. "Every word." I am afraid I paid little attention to whatever Deleuze said from then on. I believe he said a great deal, before flinging up his hands and flouncing away. I went on gazing into my lover's eyes. In my own words I had found an unexpected truth. Whatever his past crimes, Vasily *had* changed for my sake. How many people were capable of doing such a thing? He was not stubborn, as Schmidt had been stubborn. Then, too, he was careful about other people's feelings, as Nijam and Mimi were not. He knew how to enjoy himself without making other people pay for it, as Deleuze himself was incapable of doing.

And no doubt there were nobler natures in the world—idealists like Anton Lupei, who remained inflexibly wedded to what he believed to be right, or hardy pioneers like Mlle Perrot, who sought happiness on no one's terms but her own. But such a lover would not suit *me* at all.

No: on the whole, I could not think of anyone of whom I was fonder, or with whom I might be happier, than my own ridiculous, theatrical, warm-hearted Vasily.

"Are you quite sure?" Vasily asked softly, as the dancing recommenced.

"Absolutely certain," I said, squeezing his hand. "I think that we could all be very happy together in Paris—couldn't we?"

"My dear, I'm not sure I know how to be happy. There is so little dramatic potential in happiness! If you would consent to be my *real* wife, however—"

"Oh, no," I told him. "Not another word! I will *not* be

proposed to in this deplorably flippant manner!"

Vasily's manner instantly became calculating. "Of course not," he said. "How foolish of me to suggest it! Very well: I accept the challenge."

"What is *that* supposed to mean?" I asked, feeling distinctly apprehensive. But he only laughed.

We returned to our table, where Schmidt and Nijam sat beside each other. They gave no sign whatever of any tender understanding—but there! I don't know what else I expected of them. Our dinners had been served, and Vasily sat down, raising his champagne-glass.

"A toast," he declared, "to our Mimi: your very good health!"

"To Mimi!" we repeated, and Schmidt patted her shoulder. Vasily drank off his champagne and made a choking sound.

"What the devil," he began, and then his face went as white as a sheet, and he grasped at something on the table, and held it up to the light.

It was an empty little glass tube, marked with a skull and cross-bones.

Vasily clawed at his throat. "Nijam!" he gasped.

Nijam's face had turned to a stony mask, and for a moment I felt really afraid.

"I warned you," she said, very softly and without a hint of urbanity, "that when I took my revenge it would be far worse than a few little creases ironed into the sheets."

"What have you done? Do I have the plague? Is there a cure? Oh, how my heart beats! How long do I have to live?"

"That depends entirely upon whether you can give Alphonse a decent apology," said Nijam. Oh ho! it was *Alphonse* now! I exchanged a triumphant glance with Mimi.

Vasily gasped again—his breathing had turned into a shallow whoop. "Schmidt, old fellow," he said, "I don't want you as my valet any more."

"Sir? I beg your pardon?" Schmidt replied, thoroughly startled.

"You aren't to call me sir any more," Vasily added in a rush, although I thought his panic had begun to subside. "You're to be your own man, and call me what you like, and make me darn my own socks, and I hope to heaven that you'll intercede with Miss Nijam to spare my life."

Nijam blinked at him; but her astonishment lasted only a moment. "Don't be a baby," she said. "It was only salt-water."

Vasily sank gasping into his chair, and Lupei burst into applause.

"He still means every word of it," I told Schmidt, who was gaping at his erstwhile master as though Maxim's had caved in and fallen upon him. "From now on he'll do his best to treat you as a gentleman."

"Salt-water!" Vasily whispered, regaining a little of his old temerity. "If I'd been a vampire that would have been deadly to me!"

"Yes, I know," Nijam said, breaking into the brightest smile I had ever seen. "How lucky you are, no longer to be one!"

Schmidt reattached his jaw. "In fact," he stammered, "I rather thought you all might like to help—that is, I have a job to put before you."

"Go on," I said, pouring Vasily a new glass of champagne.

"*Someone* made the Perrot revenant," Schmidt went on, "and if by some chance it wasn't my old professor, then we need to find out who, and stop them making any more—or from falling into the hands of a Great Power, now that the secret is out. I hoped you'd all like to come to Heidelberg with Miss

Nijam and me." He looked down at his hands. "I warn you, I don't know how much use I'll be. I've found that I lose my head when the old memories surface."

"Of course we'll come," said Mimi at once, and Vasily raised his glass.

"To Schmidt and his memories!" he declared.

"Will you come with us?" I asked Lupei when the toast was drunk. "You were a tremendous help tonight."

"You are kind, Baroness, but I'm no kind of trickster," said Lupei. While the rest of us talked and laughed, he had been steadily eating. Now he wiped his napkin across his mouth and rose from his chair. "If you'll excuse me, I ought to go home to my wife before she decides to run off with that Polish charmer, Janushek."

Vasily got up to shake his hand. "I'm grateful that you chose not to shoot me," said he.

Lupei sent Nijam an admiring look. "You are in good hands, or I would tell you not to make me regret it." Then he turned to me.

"Baroness," he said, very solemn. "You know, don't you, that if you go to Heidelberg, France will be there too; and where France goes, Russia and Germany will not be far behind?"

I shivered. Lupei had given me one prophecy already which had proven true, and I was disinclined to neglect this one. If the Russians had agents in Paris, they would certainly also have a finger in the goings-on of the offices at the Prefecture of Police on the Quai des Orfèvres. We had little time to waste; at any moment the gun would sound, signalling the start of the headlong race of all the Great Powers to Heidelberg.

And Molly Dark and her crew in the midst of it!

Lupei tipped his hat and walked away, hands in his pockets,

and whistling, so that I do not think he had reached the foyer before a waiter asked him to leave. Vasily sat down, and for a moment complete silence reigned. I looked at the faces about me, seeing them pale and abstracted in contemplation of the truth with which Lupei had so bluntly presented us. Nijam and Schmidt, I saw with a start, had joined hands beneath the table and were holding each other tightly.

"Is anyone having second thoughts?" I asked after a moment.

"No," said Nijam at once. "But we should leave at once—as soon as we can wrap up this Perrot business and get away. The sooner we get to Heidelberg, the better."

"It's my duty," said Schmidt, looking at Mimi, "but no one else's."

Mimi scowled. "Don't be a tallow-head, Schmidt."

That left Vasily and myself. We exchanged looks, and I read the same certainty in his eyes that I felt myself. What had begun as compulsion had become choice, and now we were together until the bitter end.

"Vasily and I have cancelled our divorce," said I. "We are entirely at your service."

Vasily smiled and raised his glass.

"To stealing revenants!" he said.

_S.D.G._

Miss Dark will return in
Dark Secrets

Unhistorical Note

My historical study for this book was limited to re-reading Gaston Leroux's 1910 novel, *The Phantom of the Opera*, and obsessively studying the plans and Google Maps results for the famous Palais Garnier theatre. It is possible that some historical facts have crept in from other sources as well—from Jennifer Homans' magnificent history of ballet, *Apollo's Angels*, for instance, or from John Merriman's utterly fascinating *The Dynamite Club*, to which I am indebted for the anarchist perspective on the Opera as a state institution. But that is all. Comparatively speaking, this book is as devoid of serious history as I could make it.

There really is a cistern beneath the Paris Opera. Gaston Leroux immortalised it as the "lake" across which his Phantom ferries his heroine, Christine, for singing lessons. I was delighted while working on this book to discover a virtual tour of the cistern, which probably allowed me a more accurate description of the place than even Leroux was able to achieve. There is, however, probably no other resource that depicts the nineteenth century Opera in such vivid detail. Even had I not been paying homage to Leroux's story, I would still have relied upon it for a description of the setting.

Jules Perrot, a choreographer of the ballet *Giselle*, did spend many decades as a ballet master around Europe, including at the Paris Opera until his death in 1892. As far as I know his corpse was not stolen for revivification into an undead serial killer. Nor did the historical Perrot have any nieces, so far as I am aware; Mlle Perrot is an invention of my own. In the 1920s, bohemian Paris would see an acknowledged lesbian community centred around figures like Natalie Barney, Gertrude Stein, and the Princesse de Polignac, Winnaretta Singer. I understand that prior to this first sexual revolution, however, same-sex couples might cohabit under the fiction of an inseparable friendship, using veiled allusions to historical or literary figures as a way to find a queer community.

When I began writing this series, I was unaware of the terminology—Side A, Side B, Side Y, or Side X—with which people in the Christian community who experience same-sex attraction or identify as queer designate their theological stances regarding sexuality. All I knew was that many of the queer people among my close friends had chosen to personally accept their sexuality, yet reconcile it with their faith within a framework either of heterosexual marriage or committed singleness—that is, within the positions known as Side B and Side Y. It struck me, too, that I had *never* seen this particular experience represented in fiction. Several years and many frank conversations with friends and sensitivity readers later, I am now better placed to understand the reason for this. Believers in the Side B and Side Y camps, often hailing from theologically orthodox and/or politically conservative communities, often choose to keep their sexuality private, sharing only with a few trusted friends and close family members. On the other hand, those who do choose to come out, and who connect with the secular queer community, may then face a new dilemma: whether, and how, to inform their secular community about their religious convictions, in a context where they may be dismissed as having internalised homophobia.

It is not my intent with this book to say what *I* believe to be right or best, but only to represent, to the best of my ability, what must sometimes be a difficult, painful, and very lonely experience; and to honour the faith, love, and hope of the Christian siblings of mine who have walked this path with so much courage.

From the bottom of my heart, and with this book more than ever, I thank my beta and sensitivity readers. Christina Baehr, Schuyler McConkey, W.R. Gingell, Claire Trella Hill, Irina Le Corre, and Grace Kielstra. I could not have written this book without you. Thank you all—especially Irina, for providing me with so many more Names For Upperclass French Twits than I could ever possibly have used.

Suzannah Rowntree
October, 2024.

About the Author

Suzannah Rowntree lives in a big house in rural Australia with her awesome parents and siblings, drinking fancy tea and writing historical fantasy fiction that blends real-world history with legend, adventure, and a dash of romance.

You can connect with me on:
🌐 https://suzannahrowntree.site

Subscribe to my newsletter:
✉ https://subscribepage.io/srauthor

Also by Suzannah Rowntree

The Miss Sharp's Monsters Series
The Werewolf of Whitechapel
Anarchist on the Orient Express
A Vampire in Bavaria

The Miss Dark's Apparitions Series
Tall & Dark
Dark Clouds
Dark & Stormy
Dark & Dawn
A Stab in the Dark
Dark Secrets

The Watchers of Outremer Series
A Wind from the Wilderness
The Lady of Kingdoms
Children of the Desolate
A Day of Darkness
A Conspiracy of Prophets
The House of Mourning

The Pendragon's Heir Trilogy
The Door to Camelot
The Quest for Carbonek
The Heir of Logres

The Fairy Tale Retold Series
The Rakshasa's Bride

The Prince of Fishes
The Bells of Paradise
Death Be Not Proud
Ten Thousand Thorns
The City Beyond the Glass